DEADLY COLD

DEADLY COLD

DEADLY TERROR IN THE ARCTIC

WILLIAM W. BENNETT

Auctorem House
276 5th Ave, Ste 704-2591
New York, NY 10001
www.auctoremhouse.com
Phone: 1 888-332-7718

Published by Auctorem House: 09/26/2025

ISBN: 978-1-968059-14-9(sc)
ISBN: 978-1-968059-15-6(e)

Library of Congress Control Number: 2025920936

To my children: Jeremy, Jeff, and Serena

Special thanks to my beloved wife, Cathy.

[5]Now He who prepared us for this very purpose is God, who gave to us the Spirit as a pledge. [6]Therefore, being always of good courage, and knowing that while we are at home in the body we are absent from the Lord—[7]for we walk by faith, not by sight—[8]we are of good courage, I say, and prefer rather to be absent from the body and to be at home with the Lord. [9]Therefore we also have as our ambition, whether at home or absent, to be pleasing to Him. [10]For we must all appear before the judgment seat of Christ, so that each one may be recompensed for his deeds in the body, according to what he has done, whether good or bad.

–II Corinthians 5:5-10 NASB

PROLOGUE

Winter of 1742 had been the harshest in the chief's memory. Word of the white men, their rituals, and sacred texts, and forcing their religion on the local tribes reached as far as Eneekaii Han (Husky Channel), the story coming from Unalakleet. Food was plentiful because the annual trek to tuk Njik (Fish Creek) brought back a bumper crop of char. Gwich'in depended on char for one of their main winter food sources. Even as he contemplated the weather, he could smell the fish smoking in the smoke houses.

Fur trade was vigorous between the Russians and the Spaniards, and his tribe had profited from a good year. Caribou were plentiful as well. Why then did he feel this great weight upon his heart, a sense of doom approaching. He knew.

His father, chief before him, died suddenly when a great white bear with two cubs to feed attacked him. The secret to the cave was gone with his father, and he would not journey there on the quest. And the stranger from the land of the sun gods was well, surviving his illness and wounds, and now knew their language. His life was spared because the old chief had drawn the bear from him. He, at least, had seen the cave, and now he told other stories, showing the copper plate often, talking constantly.

It was the story about a mountain range far to the south that rivaled his own land, but where the temperature was moderate, not frigid that rang in his head. This stranger with his odd speech talked of his journey along the coast; north, until he came at last to Eneekaii Han, traveled with the chief to the sacred cave, and on the return journey, nearly lost his life.

And then yesterday two infants had perished in the plunging temperatures of the ice storm. Igloos had not been finished in time to save them. With a sigh the chief turned to the stranger.

"We will journey south to this land of which you speak," he announced solemnly.

Shivering with cold the man's face looked relieved as he heard the chief's words. Nodding in agreement he huddled tighter in his sealskin robes. Today he had eaten his food, signifying that he was whole again. He might be thin, but he was strong. Much of the journey would be harsh until they passed Hoqnah. After that, things would be easier. There were many trinkets to trade with the tribes they met.

Over the next three days activity in the village was unusually busy as the people prepared for the journey. At last, the weather broke as spring finally took hold, a good sign. Nearly seventy small boats set off on the journey, and by the time they reached the Andes half that remained.

During the journey the stories of the man from the land of the sun gods inspired the medicine man of the tribe and between the two of them they began to establish a much more formal religion. In the Andes they would meet the Incas, and the copper plate would be given a place of honor to commemorate their journey. At last, it made its way to the Lost City of Z, and into the hands of Dr. Gregg.

Strange as it may seem, the man from the land of the sun gods could not remember the directions to the cave that held the astounding evidence that his people had been before him, and stranger still that the Gwich'in that traveled to Peru would be swallowed by the tribes there, their language and traditions lost, all except the copper plate.

CHAPTER 1

Bringing both ships in under cover of an early Autumn storm at 2 a.m. in the morning was risky, but worth it. Inside Beardsley's huge warehouse the war rooms were being removed prior to the sale of both ships. Jim stood quietly off to one side and winced as another piece of steel fell to the deck with a clang. Watching the acetylene torches cut away the belly of *Coral* was as difficult as had been the work on *Pearl*. Once sold, the ships must be back to original design, and no one must ever guess what once hid beneath those decks.

His face was set, determined, as it always was, but inside he felt a strange reluctance to say goodbye to these fine vessels. Yet the new ship was far superior and much better for the future of the company. Making the decision had been all business, but now the emotions he felt both confused and frightened him. He'd forgotten that mere things of metal and steel could be more than just another vessel.

"We're watching an old friend slip away," Cecilia mourned, coming to stand beside him, worming her fingers into his hand and feeling him relax slightly as she snuggled into his arm. It was like trying to snuggle up to an oak tree, which told her how tense he was, and how hard he was working at keeping his emotions damped down. She understood. Her own face was tearstained and reddened from weeping over the loss of these two old friends. Jim, she knew, would hold it all inside, compartmentalize it, analyze it, and repress it. But he was getting better, at least with her, when it came to showing emotion.

First his relationship to Christ, his marriage, and then the plan for fatherhood, Jim knew, had changed him in fundamental ways that both frightened and thrilled him. He was more than a soldier now. He was a follower of Christ, a son of the Living God. As a husband and future father his life had changed so dramatically that he wasn't sure he could keep up with it all. However, he set his mind on becoming the best husband he could be, and the best father he could be to whatever children God chose to give him.

Strong emotion frightened Jim, and Cecilia giggled softly at the thought. He looked down at her, wiped away a fresh tear, and raised an eyebrow.

"A giggle?" he objected. "At a time like this? What's that about?"

"You're afraid of deep emotion, my dear. Imagining you afraid of anything is rather amusing. Every adventure we've been on you have taken incredible risks, accepted pain and deprivation, and yet you're afraid of giving in to what you feel. I think the thing you fear most of all, is fear itself," she smiled sadly at him.

"Yes. I suppose I am," he admitted, thinking about her words while keeping his eyes focused on hers. They had softened considerably as he wiped away her tears. Now he folded her into his arms and rested his chin on her head. "I know what I am capable of, and if I let myself go, it might one day be rage that takes over. I fear that most of all. And you're right about me being afraid of fear. My greatest fear is that in a moment of fear I will hesitate, and men and women I love will die," he admitted.

She knew that he was telling the truth. What he feared most was what he could do as a soldier, trained to kill and destroy, and to lead. Her husband hated killing, hated that it was sometimes necessary when carrying out orders, and that a world with sin needed a death sentence. He also took his responsibilities as the leader of these gallant men very seriously. Cecilia had seen him in action, and she knew that his fears were founded on reality. Few men could stand against Jim Shepherd and hope to survive in battle, and not one, she was certain, could lead as he led. It thrilled her that her husband was such a formidable man.

Most men began to lose their physical edge as they neared thirty. Jim was as strong, if not stronger, and as fit, if not fitter, than he had been at twenty. So far, he hadn't slowed. In fact, because of his training and diet he had grown even faster. With the host of weapons available to him, and his skill with those weapons, he was an implacable force against evil in the world. She took courage with those thoughts.

For a few minutes they clung to each other, Cecilia taking strength from her husband's embrace, he, taking strength from hers. He sighed and finally spoke.

"We all agreed. This is by far the best course of action at this time," his voice sounded matter of fact; all emotion tamped down tightly.

"Did saying that make it any easier?" Cecilia asked, taking out a Kleenex and blowing her nose. "Because, if it did, could you say it again and maybe I'll believe it!" she mocked with another giggle.

"It reminds me of the time we sold Dad's tug and fishing boats," Jim said softly.

"Not easier?" Cecilia asked, burrowing into his arms again.

"No," he answered, hugging her tightly. *My human weakness attaches emotional value to things that really have little value.*

Eventually they left, holding hands, climbing out of the hold and then down to the shop floor. Together, holding hands, they walked out through a back door, careful to make sure no one saw them, and traveled to the rental car. Jim drove to Crownhill where they were staying at a local hotel under one of their legal aliases. Crewmembers were spread far and wide, staying under cover, using aliases they would never use again. Once the work was finished, they would slip away back to sea and arrive as scheduled. They were all praying for another storm to cover their movements. This time of year, storms were a regular occurrence, but one never knew.

Jim knew that his ships and company were big news today. The discovery of the City of Z had put them on the map. At the moment they were supposed to be at sea, heading here from America to sell their boats and take possession of the new ship. Once Calvin Beardsley had finished the work of restoring the vessels they would slip away again and appear on the appointed day, ready to give up both ships to the sale agent. Hopefully no one would know they'd made this one clandestine trip to alter their ships back to original design.

After that the new ship would be winched into the warehouse where it was to be painted and have the cabins and other rooms built by Beardsley's company. Designs, plans, drawings, and even examples were publicly displayed for the curious. However, once the publicly displayed conversions were finished others would be embarked upon that no one would witness. When that work began the warehouse would be sealed against intruders.

After a quiet dinner in their room, they sat at the table by the window and played scrabble, going to bed early, as usual. Jim was especially gentle and caring that night and Cecilia responded. Sighing after their intimacy she fell asleep in his arms. It would be a night both would remember with fondness.

Checking out the following morning they returned the rental and took a cab to Plymouth, walked about town for a while, and then made their way to the warehouse. In twos and threes, the crew gathered there, awaiting darkness to slip back into the water for the final voyage of *Bring It Up Coral* and *Pearl*.

Late that afternoon boxes arrived by delivery van with their new uniforms, complete with the newly designed MOS patches and boxes containing the new pins, insignia, service ribbons, medals, and commendations. The latter had been Frank Miller's suggestion, leading to the entire crew working together to design them. It had been, Jim decided, their final act of respect for the two ships they were about to retire. Those ribbons and commendations would serve as a constant reminder of how they began.

A raging Autumn thunderstorm rolled in making slipping away easy, and they moved through the channel undetected except by radar. Once at sea they traveled far enough out to turn about and return, for the following morning they were to arrive in Plymouth to the fanfare of the press, several treasure hunting clubs, and a host of other important persons from museums and universities.

Every man and woman prayed together that God would protect them from detection, and it appeared that their prayers were efficacious. Not one item of news or photo of the two ships appeared in the morning press, much to Jim's relief. Zeke nodded once after reporting to Jim that they had once again remained undetected.

In the morning they entered the English Channel to the hooting of a multitude of horns from smaller craft paying them homage as they passed. Jim stood in the bridge beside Andrea. The two men knew what they were doing was best for the future of the company, but it didn't make it any easier. Andrea often sighed and Jim was silent. What they shared, they shared as men of the sea, knowing how the other was feeling, and it was enough to draw comfort from each other's company. Both watched the approach of the tugs that would nudge them into the docks where they would tie off for the last time. Jim looked at his crew gathered at the railings and began to feel the stirrings of that spirit of adventure. Perhaps it was the new uniforms and decorations that inspired him.

Every crewmember had at least three rows of service ribbons, medals, and commendations above his or her left breast pocket. These were meticulously designed by the crew; argued over, laughed about, and even cried about, but they belonged to the crew of *Bring It Up* alone. That was important.

Saba's Barge Expeditionary Medal was first in the row of those who began with the company. Not everyone wore that one. It was burgundy with four narrow gold stripes, a wider tan stripe in the middle, with a stripe of dark brown and black between the gold strips on either side of the tan.

The Amazonas Region Expeditionary Medal bore the colors of their ships, burgundy and aqua, the stripes of this one horizontal. In the center a wide black stripe contained intricate pictures of cartography tools, with a gold stripe dividing the black from burgundy and blue. Distinctive and unique it represented a journey completed; a mission finished.

Next was the Dolomites Expeditionary Medal, also with horizontal stripes, the burgundy at the top and aqua at the bottom. A green stripe with mountain ranges ran through the center, again set off by narrow gold stripes. Jim liked the simplicity of the ribbon and the way it contrasted with the ribbon before it.

At the end of the first row, for all who had been with the company since the very beginning, was the Rum Cay Expeditionary Medal, burgundy with a black stripe running vertically in the center, and two sets of two narrow gold stripes on either side. It too was very simple.

On the next row at the beginning was the Loihi Volcano Expeditionary Medal, again with the burgundy, black, and aqua stripes running horizontally. Palm trees stood on either side of a cave in the black stripe to commemorate the discovery of the ships in that underwater lava cave. Again, the design was simple and held the colors of the ships.

Next to that was the Mato Grosso Region Expeditionary Medal. This one was aqua with a tan stripe running vertically down the center. On either side the aqua and burgundy of their ships stood separated by thin gold lines. Depending on accomplishments the ribbon clusters varied.

Every crewmember wore the *Bring It Up* Rifle Marksmanship ribbon paired with the *Bring It Up* Pistol Marksmanship ribbon. Aqua ribbons both; the Rifle ribbon had two white stripes running vertically at either side, and a red stripe in the middle, with two narrow white stripes on either side. The pistol ribbon had two red stripes at either side, with narrow white stripes on either side.

Some wore the *Bring It Up* Distinguished Rifle Marksmanship ribbon next, burgundy with three gold lines running vertically spread across the burgundy background. Next to that some also wore the *Bring It Up* Distinguished Pistol Marksmanship ribbon with two gold stripes spread wide apart on the burgundy background. Those who had all four had them clustered in one row.

Other ribbons included the *Bring It Up* Medal of Honor, *Bring It Up* Silver Star, *Bring It Up* Bronze Star, *Bring It Up* Meritorious Cross, *Bring It Up* Purple Heart, *Bring It Up* Legion of Merit Medal,

Bring It Up Distinguished Service Medal, *Bring It Up* Distinguished Achievement Medal, *Bring It Up* Superior Service Medal, *Bring It Up* Meritorious Unit Commendation, *Bring It Up* Distinguished Flying Cross, *Bring It Up* Distinguished Ordinance Decoration, *Bring It Up* SAR Distinguished Service Medal, *Bring It Up* Combat Ready Ribbon, and finally the *Bring It Up* Combat Action Medal.

There were new patches, pins and insignia displayed proudly on the uniform sleeves and collars as well. Sparks, Hammer, and Loony sported the newly designed Aviation and Maritime Electronics Technician patches, all certified and qualified to work on the electronics of the ship and aircraft belonging to the company. Elliptical in shape it had a black border, the sides squared, with a gold band across the top and bottom. At the top the words *Bring It Up SAR* were sewn in black letters, and at the bottom the words *Aviation Electronics Technician*. In the black center was the company logo eagle, the traditional AT symbol used by most military and police forces, the wings, and concentric circles, and in white the letters A and T on either side, and the names of the three aircraft the company now owned printed beneath the green wings.

Sharky and Ives wore a similar patch with the words *Ship's Clerk Sea Venture* across the top stripe and *Bring It Up Oceanic Research • SAR • Salvage* across the bottom. Two golden feather quills crossed in the center with the company eagle logo beneath and two MacBook Pro laptop computers on either side. Each man wore a fancy gold winged shield pin on his collar with the quills and computer beneath and the words *Ship's Clerk Sea Venture* on a ribbon shape across the bottom. On the other side of the collar, they wore the silver pin signifying their rank of Lieutenant Junior Grade.

Cecilia, Pippi, Zeke, News, and Rock 'n Roll each had a shoulder patch with the traditional intelligence symbol in the center, a lightening flash in the center with two concentric circles behind and two silver stars. The patch was circular with a burgundy border and an inside circle around the symbol of aqua, the company colors. Around the patch, between those two lines were the words *Bring It Up • Sea Venture • Search and Rescue (SAR) • Oceanic Research*

Vessel • Intelligence Technician Service • Bring It Up Coral • Bring It Up Pearl. Though the latter two ships would no longer be part of the company they wanted them on the patches, a reminder that they had served upon all three.

On each collar they wore the gold intelligence pin, two concentric circles with two stars and four points in the center. Zeke wore a pair of silver bars on his other collar signifying that he had been promoted to Lieutenant. Pippi also wore the Lieutenant bars on her other collar. Cecilia had been promoted to Lieutenant Junior Grade. Nelson was an ensign and News a PO3, or Petty Officer Third Class. Nelson's pin was white enamel with a gold rope border, the eagle logo, and a single red stripe beneath the eagle. All of them wore the fancy gold winged shield pin with the photo of a satellite, Cray computer, laptop, and magnifying glass in the center. It was a fascinating pin with filigree to set it off, designed with real 24K gold over a black background that made for an interesting contrast.

Jim looked over at Frank Miller waving at a boat that had just hooted at them. Frank wore the Submersible Pilot patch on his shoulder, similar to the ship's clerk patch. In the black center was a picture of the *Sea Bullet,* two dive helmets and skull and crossbones at the bottom. Both FM and Driver had insisted on the skull and crossbones pirate symbol for some reason.

On their collars they wore the Pilot pin, a gold hatch portal with a gold shield set on a black background in the center. On the shield the words *Sea Venture Submersible Pilot* were written, and Frank had *Sea Bullet* on his pin while Driver's had *Steel Crab.* Both had a schematic drawing of their submersibles on the pin with the company eagle logo beneath.

Jack Boswell would be wearing the W2 pin on his collar, three burgundy strips with two blue stripes between, signifying his promotion to Warrant Officer 2. Frank wore a PO1 pin on his collar, white enamel with a gold rope border, the company eagle logo, and three red stripes beneath signifying his rank. Jim had to admit that the uniforms looked resplendent, and the men and women wearing them seeming to exemplify what those uniforms and decorations communicated. Competence, Courage, and Excellence were the words that came to his mind.

Jim decided that the uniforms and insignia set his crew off as unique, and they were unique, every one of them. It was no longer just a military unit coupled with a science team. Somehow, over the past year, they had become a cohesive organization, more like a family. All of them knew each other intimately, got along like brothers and sisters who loved each other and their entire family, and pulled together in each and every endeavor to ensure success. He was more than proud to lead such men and women.

Finally, the tugs approached the two ships and nudged them to the docks where they were tied off. Gangplanks were lowered and one by one the crewmembers made their way off the ship, carrying suitcases and duffle bags neatly packed, saying their final goodbyes to what had been home.

Last to leave the ships, Jim and John walked down their gangplanks. They were both wearing their game faces, keeping the emotions tightly repressed. But both knew in a single glance at each other what thoughts ran through their heads. Once they had placed their bags together off to one side the crews returned, standing in a straight line, and at Dorf's barked command they saluted the two ships.

For a full thirty seconds they held that line, and then Dorf barked another command and they neatly turned about and returned to their bags. To everyone watching, it was obvious that this was a well-trained organization with military precision. Also obvious was the fact that every individual was saying goodbye to something he or she loved. Some were openly weeping, all had misty eyes, and in silence they gathered their bags and moved to the warehouse. Jim, John, and Wade remained with Finn and Ives, each of the latter holding an official valise, to turn over the papers of ownership to the sales agent.

For its own oceanic research, *Pearl*, already purchased for the agreed asking price, was going to the Chinese Navy. A representative of that military organization with several underlings stood off to one side while the papers were signed and witnessed. He seemed anxious to take over the ship for some reason, and Jim and John both thought of the Triad that plagued them. The Chinese Admiral stepped forward and shook hands with the three men, and then the four of them bowed to each other properly.

With pride Jim watched the men walk up the gangplank to take possession of their ship. He knew, without a doubt, that it was spotless and as pristine as the day it first rolled out of the shipyard. How long it stayed that way was up to the new owners. John, in turn, turned over ownership of *Coral* to a UK Search and Rescue company. Proud of his crew, and its accomplishments, Jim sighed once and then squaring his shoulders he followed John and Wade into the warehouse. His thoughts, as he walked behind his two closest male friends, were not melancholy but looking forward.

Beardsley met them outside the doors of his warehouse, waiting for them, and he nodded at the two ships. "They were good ships, lads, and if I'm any judge of a ship's condition, your crew has done you proud in keeping them in perfect condition!" Calvin Beardsley said, shaking hands with the three as they came through the door. "It's tough to say goodbye to old friends," he added unnecessarily.

At that moment Cecilia brought a woman in a neat business suit forward. She wore typically English countryside clothing, in layers, and a heavy winter coat. Her eyes studied the three men shaking hands with Calvin, curious and excited to meet them face-to-face.

"Jim, this is Wanda Powers, the real estate agent who brokered the Hill House deal," Cecilia said. Her voice had only a slight quaver to show the emotion of the morning and Jim was surprised that he was intensely proud of her in that moment. He looked into her eyes and saw her slowly blush. Then he turned his eyes on Wanda, shook her hand gently, and thanked her for brokering the deal for his company.

"Listen up everyone!" Jim said loudly enough to bring silence to his crew. "We're going up to Hill House to get settled in. Your vehicles are over there, and the keys are in them. He pointed to a line of vehicles with the company logo on each door. Pick one, fill it with bodies, and follow us to the house. Once we're settled, we'll change and come back and get to work," he led the way to the cars with Cecilia and Mrs. Powers.

Frank was already at the rear door of the Bentley and had it open. He ran around to the other side and opened the other door and the three of them climbed in the spacious back seat. FM closed the doors and took his seat on the left side of the car, appearing confused as if he had just realized the steering wheel was on the other side. Naturally he knew the difference, but as usual, he was lightening everyone's moods.

"Something's wrong boss," he said with a grin. "Someone put the steering wheel on the wrong side of the car!" he slid behind the wheel.

"This is England, Frank. They have right hand drive here," Cecilia said with a giggle. "Please make sure you drive on the correct side of the road! That would be the left side."

"I always suspected the U.K. had leftist tendencies!" Frank quipped.

One by one the cars left the warehouse, and a long line of vehicles made their way up the hill to Hill House, situated on the furthest point overlooking the ocean on the Rame Peninsula occupied by the town of Torpoint. Jim took the time to study the old mansion as they approached. When Ken Worthington bought it the property and houses were in disrepair, the roofs full of leaks, and the grounds poorly kept. Today it looked vastly improved. Jim decided they would enjoy their stay at Hill House while they worked on the new ship.

The old mansion was surrounded by other homes, all of which Worthington had purchased to turn the property into a summer vacation spot in southeast Cornwall. As they approached the property Jim noted that it was green and lush with sweeping lawns and an amazing view of the Hamoaze tidal estuary. Across the water he could see Devonport and Plymouth. From the house they would be able to see the warehouse where Beardsley now kept their new ship, *Sea Venture.*

Ken insisted that Hill House be fully renovated from the basement up, keeping only the outside walls, which had been carefully repaired. Inside the house was much more practical with modern facilities, though Worthington had kept most of the floor plan, adding bathrooms only where necessary. Jim had seen pictures of the frame going up inside the walls. Because it was framed inside the window wells were deep and pleasant, some with seats built in to enjoy the sun. The walls were now insulated properly, thanks to that inside framing.

The ancient structure was almost square, four stories with three wings built on over the years. One of those wings had been left to crumble into ruin but Ken had seen to it that it had been restored from old pictures to look much as it had in its days of glory. Those who lived in Torpoint were impressed with the number of jobs the renovation created, and the number of staff hired to keep the place up. Good wages were offered, and local people had been hired in the various positions; a move purposely made to cement good relations with their new neighbors.

As the cars pulled into the beautiful, curved drive Jim sighed with pleasure. This would be a haven for a time that everyone needed. Even though it began to drizzle as they pulled under the covered porch his spirits continued to lift. Here they would work on the new ship, bonding with it as they had with the old, and healing would take place. Besides, the new ship offered so much more to everything they did. Each moment the sense of adventure grew, and it was with renewed hope and vigor that Jim emerged from that short ride to their new domicile. Looking at Cecilia he could see that she too was showing signs of renewed hope and rising mood. She offered a tentative smile.

CHAPTER 2

Liveried servants lined the hall just inside the door to greet the new owners. First in line, opening the back door of the Bentley as it pulled up was the butler, Mr. George Tuggle. He was a medium sized man with a pleasant face, twinkling brown eyes, and a very deep voice. The white-gloved hand he extended to Cecilia was friendly and as he helped her to her feet, she decided she was going to like him.

"Hello George and thank you," she said, smiling at him. His answering smile was quite winsome.

"Nice to meet you, mum," he said. "Sir!" he addressed Jim.

"George, so pleased to finally meet you," Jim responded honestly. Before Hill House became an empty shell, George served the old family, Jim knew, and was very pleased to be serving the new owners in the same capacity, though at a much higher wage. Instead of saying goodbye to an old friend, he had seen that old friend repaired and renovated and occupied.

Frank pulled the car away so the next car could release its passengers beneath the cover of the carport. George turned and looked up the steps. He waved at a plump lady standing by the door.

"Mrs. Tuggle will introduce you to the rest of the staff, sir. I'll just greet each car as it comes," George said after shaking hands with Jim.

He watched the tall soldier walk up the steps and decided that

Mr. Shepherd would do all right. Turning to the next car he helped Penelope from the back seat while John and Wade stepped out of their respective doors. Driver was behind the wheel. Having studied the photos George knew each person by name and was surprised that two American brothers had both married British women.

Inside the house the Shepherd's were introduced to the staff. Mrs. Tuggle seemed to be in charge of the maids, of whom there were eight, two for each floor. The cook was a very large woman named Mrs. Jennings. Her hair was silver-gray, her eyes blue, and she had very bad teeth behind a nice smile. Paul Jennings, towering over her, heard her name and hugged her.

"Mom!" he said with a laugh. Paul was a black man and Mrs. Jennings chuckled when he finally let her go, rearranging her hair. The hug had been warm and genuine, a surprise from the handsome young man.

"Behave now, young man, or I'll have at you with a wooden spoon!" she threatened with mock sternness.

PJ put his hands on his bottom and scurried away as if fearful of that punishment, getting a laugh from everyone. By the time the introductions were finished nearly forty minutes were gone. No one seemed to chafe at the time spent meeting everyone on staff or making introductions. Mrs. Powers left shortly afterwards, and people moved to their respective rooms.

Tuggle studied the group as he took them through the house, noting that they listened carefully to him as he gave them the basics, showing them each room. They were attentive as he spoke, never interrupting him, and asking intelligent questions. But there was something else about the group that began to register with him, and at one point he paused in his dialogue and looked hard at the men.

These were not frivolous Americans, given to narcissism and seeking only pleasure and fun. Most of the men had eyes that never stopped moving, taking in everything, and, he guessed, missing very little. Energy seemed to almost crackle from the bodies of most of them and they reminded him of the coiled spring of a steel trap he had seen once.

Thus far they had been more than polite, and they used words like opulence, substantial, lavish, extravagant, and replete. He even heard snippets of poetry from Abercrombie, Keats, and Kipling. Even the beautiful young ladies were reserved in their speech, even cultured. Very quickly he was adjusting his concept of his new charges.

As they climbed from the basement to the ground floor, and then up to the first floor the ladies began to claim bedrooms in pairs. Married couples would occupy the corner suites. Tuggle noted that the oldest were located on the first floor, and the younger couples on the second. No single men claimed a room on the second floor.

All the men claimed rooms on the third floor, again in pairs, and Tuggle noted that no one shoved a door open carelessly or ran and jumped on a bed. Very pleased he finished his tour, with the Shepherds still in tow. As they made their way to the lift (something recently installed next to the main staircase) Jim asked about the schedule for meals and was eventually taken to Mrs. Jennings, who agreed to early breakfast, regular lunches and dinners, and a menu that was surprisingly healthy.

Instead of driving back to Devonport they walked together to the Ferry and buying a month pass climbed aboard for the first of many such trips. Jim made sure everyone knew the schedule and would not be late for the ferry that would bring them back for dinner. Folks on the ferry looked at the Americans, Brits, and Aussies with interest, listening to both strange and familiar accents as they spoke together.

Work on *Sea Venture* began that very day, and for the first months Jim allowed visitors to the warehouse to see what was being done. VIK Sandvik, A/S of Norway built the ship specifically for *Bring It Up*. It was classed as a CAS Salvage, DSV-SAT, Ice Class B, DP-2 vessel and would, when the time came to christen him, fly an American flag. An horrid shade of orange covered the hull, but that was being remedied as *Bring It Up's* colors were applied. The paint was designed for ocean-going vessels and though expensive, well worth the price in Jim's estimation.

Far more advanced than even *Pearl* this vessel offered both a research capability, and the search and rescue and salvage capabilities

Bring It Up needed. He was a strong vessel, with deck strength of $10t/m^2$ or the ability to withstand 32.8 tons per square foot! Fuel tanks held 2800 cubic meters of fuel, or 9,186.24 cubic feet of fuel, enough to keep the ship running for 90 days at sea. On board were freshwater tanks that held 1100 cubic meters of water, or 3,609 cubic feet. His deck was larger, 4,921 square feet of space, or 1500 square meters, depending on which country one was measuring from.

Length over all was 493 feet, or 150.3 meters. His breadth molded was 98.4 feet or 30 meters. He drew 24.6 feet when fully loaded, or a draught of 7.5 meters. There were also two moon pools (pools at the bottom of the ship allowing entrance into the water from the ship itself). One pool was 13.8 feet by 15.75 feet, and the other 23.6 feet square.

Beneath the decks in the engine room were four 12-cylinder GE Diesels with 718 cubic inches per cylinder generating 6,574 Ship Horsepower. Those engines could move the 7,483-ton ship from a stand still to 21 knots, and also tow a fully loaded container ship without difficulty. Two 4000KW diesel oil generators operated below decks, along with two 4000KW hydro generators charging a 72-battery power storage facility with inverter beneath the hydro generators themselves. Also, on board, was a 520KW emergency generator.

Driven by two main azimuth retractable thrusters, each 3500KW made by Rolls Royce, and two-2000KW tunnel thrusters made by GE the ship was powerful enough to break through ice or power through a force-five hurricane. In front was a 1500KW retractable thruster, also made by GE to help maneuver the very stable ship. Mighty indeed, Jim was anxious to get him on the water and see what he could do. All of this would play a key roll in their newest contract.

Sea Venture was going to the Arctic Ocean for research to study the ice flows and oceanic temperature shifts for AOOS (Alaska Ocean Observing System). One other contract was offered, as well as their quest for the sacred cave mentioned on the copper plate. *Bring It Up* needed to get the ship done so they could arrive in Alaska at their base study point no later than June 15.

Even though they faced a deadline no one rushed. Every job needed to be done correctly the first time, and that took time, careful work, and steady discipline. Various people came to watch the work simply because they were curious about the company and its new ship. Others came to see what secrets might be learned. Right then, no one had time to worry about the latter, and since no secrets were to be had no one thought it important. Zeke did record every visitor to the warehouse as a precautionary measure.

Catching the ferry that ran at 1626 that afternoon they traveled across to their new home, walked to the estate, and made their way to their respective rooms to wash up for dinner. Tuttle was pleased to see that the men wore casual dress clothes, including a sport jacket, rather than loose-fitting pants and shirts. Most of the women wore a dress or skirt of modest length and he saw that most of them did not wear heavy makeup or heavy lipstick. Some of them were breathtakingly beautiful, while others drew one's eye because they were lovely in most pleasing ways, especially in spirit and character.

Mrs. Jennings had a kitchen crew of six helpers, again hired locally, and provided a scrumptious evening meal of roast prime rib of beef, mashed potatoes, broccoli, Brussels sprouts, a fruit salad, and a green salad. She certainly couldn't complain about appetites and was pleased and blushing as they sought her out to thank her for an absolutely delicious dinner. Although she didn't know it, every one of them would thank her for every meal, and many would ask for tips on preparing something.

Paul Jennings came into the kitchen and put his arm around her shoulders, looking at the men who had followed. The other helpers in the kitchen looked on with curiosity as the tall athletic PJ smiled his handsome smile.

"Can my mom cook, or what?" he asked. Ready for his antics this time Mrs. Jennings playfully swatted him with a wooden spoon, and he looked positively crestfallen, both hands over the spot she'd swatted. "What did I do?" he asked, rubbing his bottom. His lip curled in a pout as he looked down at her and she almost giggled.

"That's to make sure you behave!" she said sternly, while her blue eyes twinkled at him. "You boys are all very polite, I'll say that for you. Come in later for some peach cobbler if you like," she invited, giving PJ a hug with one arm. As they filed out after thanking her, she sighed with pleasure.

"They're a fine lot, those boys," she said to the helpers.

"Nice of them to hire locally. Jobs was scarce 'til they came along!" one of the ladies said, wiping a stray strand of suds from her arm. "Easy to serve, that's for sure," she added. "Ever so polite and always sayin' thank you. Brought up proper, they were!"

"Frankly, I didn't expect it of Americans or Aussies. So many of them seem so self-centered. This lot is a nice change," another woman commented.

"I suppose it will make waiting on all the nibs during the summer a bit easier," one girl giggled. "Imagine this house full of people on summer holidays! It'll be just like old times, and good business for our town!"

On the following day, as the maids and servants gathered in the kitchen for lunch there were many comments shared. Mrs. Jennings and Mr. and Mrs. Tuttle listened with surprised and pleased nods. It seemed the new owners were very neat.

"Can you imagine? Someone dusted the room before I came in to clean! Beds all made, no clothes laying about, everything spit-spot!" one of the third-floor maids said happily.

"And every loo was clean as a whistle!" another added.

"'Twas the same in every room I did on the second floor!" another maid piped up. "I didn't have to rush to clean and finish all the rooms!"

"Too right!" another said with a sigh. "Not a thing to pick up or put right in the house! All I had to do was Hoover and polish. Every room was already beautifully done. They're a clean lot, this bunch, I'll say that for them!"

"Well girls, we get the afternoon to enjoy ourselves!" Mrs. Tuttle announced with a happy smile. You've all completed your work and the house is immaculate! Just be back in time for tea and to get ready for dinner again, please," she added. "Mrs. Jennings, these sandwiches are so delicious!"

"That giant of a fellow they all call Sturdy called the butcher from his work and sent the meat over. He called the greengrocer and sent the tomatoes, onions, pickles, cheese, and lettuce as well. According to him he wants us to know how much he appreciates our service! Pity he's such a frightening looking man!" Mrs. Jennings said, shaking her head. "A bit off-putting, that, but still a gentleman through and through. Even the bread is fresh!"

"Did you see them after breakfast this morning?" Tuttle asked.

"Oh, my yes!" one of the maids sighed. "Glory! Muscles everywhere!" she giggled.

"Hmm, yes!" Mr. Tuttle said quietly. "Those would be the men who ran ten miles. Fifty-eight minutes it took the slowest one! And everyone looked like he loved both the exercises and running. Formidable men with amazing strength and speed! I wouldn't be surprised if they were military."

"Most of them were," Mrs. Tuttle said, nodding her head, knowing she'd found out something before Tuttle did. "Mrs. Shepherd told me. That's why they keep in top condition. Learning the discipline in the military they've carried it over to their own work. That's one of the reasons they are so successful."

"Rather!" Mr. Tuttle said with a smile. "That last venture of theirs netted the company over a hundred million dollars! Mr. Shepherd claims that their solicitor will double that sum in a short period of time. He paid cash for this place! Bought out the other houses by offering more than they were worth so the whole point belongs to Hill House just like it used to. Captain Shepherd claims they'll make it all back in three years of operating a summer resort. I believe him!"

Each day passed much the same, to the surprise of the maids and servants. Every occupant worked hard to keep his or her room pristine and tidy out of habit, rather than doing the maids a favor, and their work was made easier because of it. Evenings at the house were quite interesting as well. Three nights a week, game tournaments took place, and everyone was invited to join the fun. In fact, in the space of a month the staff became close friends with the Shepherds and their crew, feeling that they were more of a family than anything else. That was a surprise to all of them, and comments were heard in the village about those fine young newcomers.

That too had been part of the plan. Jim needed to know his staff intimately, and you couldn't know business associates intimately. So, he followed Abe's suggestion and involved them in almost everything, including making decisions about the property. After two months had passed Jim noted that people in town were calling him by name and stopping to chat when they could.

Good will was imperative and Cecilia and Pen discovered that the old Parish House was in terrible condition, so terrible that the Vicar and his family, whom everyone loved, were thinking about leaving. Immediately the two women moved the Vicar and his family into one of the newly remodeled houses on the point and hired local contractors to bulldoze the old residence, and to build a brand-new house.

Being intelligent women, they organized a fete to raise money for the project, allowing everyone in the community to contribute and quietly made up the difference of the cost of the project from the *mission* fund of the company. *Bring It Up* was not a company that allowed people to make decisions alone, so everyone voted to save the Vicarage in a unanimous decision, much to Penelope's delight.

Cecilia laughed at her when she admitted that she had been afraid the vote would not be unanimous, since it was a private funding. There were other ministries that were equally important, if not more!

"I rather think this crew would vote unanimously for anything either of us suggested," Cecilia said, hugging Penelope. "Within reason," she added. "I don't suppose they'd allow us to purchase a new wardrobe out of that fund, but anything ministry related is sure to pass."

So cleverly did the women arrange the funds that the community fully believed they had raised most of the funds at the fete and corresponding bake sales and car washes. Giving in the church grew exponentially with the addition of 82 new visitors each Sabbath, and attendance grew as the curious began coming to church to see the new owners of Hill House. Some were even shamed, because a group of strangers were more faithful in attendance. Reverend Allan Candle came to life with the changes.

A weekly Bible study was held at Hill House every Thursday evening, taught by Abe and Sturdy. Jim Warner took a back seat, for he was leaving when *Sea Venture* was finished, retiring a wealthy man to spend quality time with his family. So too were the Wozniac's finally stepping down. They were taking a post as missionaries in Mozambique, before finally retiring to a yacht and traveling the coastal waters of the United States.

It was at the Bible studies that Jim realized how much he would miss his three friends. He had always known that the time would come when crewmembers would leave. Having it happen at the same time they were saying goodbye to an era of their company only added to his sadness. This loss was a good loss, not a final goodbye, but a parting as friends. Yet it left an empty hole in his life, and he began to understand his Savior's passion for ending death. It was much like losing his father had been, he was surprised to note, and he filed that bit away for future reference.

Bring It Up was picking up the mission support for the Wozniacs, and also providing enough funds to help them purchase much needed medicines and medical supplies. Whenever his expertise was needed Jim Warner promised to accept the call and come to their aid. Jim knew that at the end of their first mission they would return here, or at Live Oaks Retreat, and they knew that TRT would come to help whenever necessary. He was also consulting with GE regarding marine engines. Proud of what TRT had accomplished Jim missed his pithy comments during teaching sessions.

An unexpected outcome of the Bible studies was a renewal of faith and commitment on the part of Reverend Candle. He spoke often and for long periods of time with Abe and Sturdy, asking questions that helped them realize that like many in Great Britain, his faith had waned. Part of that was because the Church of England moved away from following Christ and began to follow another path altogether.

But Allen loved his congregation and hid his own doubts behind the façade of oratory and evensong. Not wishing to dash the hopes of those he loved he carried on his duties, never realizing that he was slowly moving closer to an understanding of who his Savior really was. As Abe and Sturdy unfolded the Gospel of John in the Bible study on Thursday nights, he met that Savior face-to-face and realized he had a decision to make. Did he believe? Could he take that leap of faith? And then he realized that it wasn't such a great leap after all, but rather an acceptance of truth based on real evidence.

He found that no matter how hard he tried he could not dismiss the reality of the resurrection of Jesus, nor other evidence of the deity of the eternal Christ. Overwhelming legal historical evidence substantiated the resurrection, and with that realization he came to understand that it was that one truth upon which all of the claims of the Savior were based. His words were proved true by His resurrection. And in the study of His works and words Allen realized that Jesus had authority. Like C.S. Lewis he could not ignore the evidence and gave his life to Christ.

The good Vicar was a changed man. He could neither hold back his enthusiasm for God's Word, nor hide his excitement about his ministry. Many thought it was the new Vicarage, but Jim knew better. Well he remembered his own conversion and how Jesus changed his life. Allen had a new lease on life, and the Spirit had filled him with a fiery passion.

It made Jim think that if his team could change lives like this, they could make the world a better place. But he soon realized that such thinking was arrogant. Only God could change a life. If he were obedient to God, his Master would use him to reach others. But even if he were disobedient God would bring another messenger, for God's plan was not dependent upon man! Feeling very insignificant Jim turned his attention to the study, glad to have this chance to learn more. More than ever, he appreciated the omniscience and omnipotence of his God.

CHAPTER 3

As the third month of their stay in southeast Cornwall opened, they welcomed December's first snow. Beardsley's warehouse was now closed to all visitors and the work in the belly of the ship creating a war room, and the modifications to communication, navigation, and computer equipment went on as planned. In fact, if there were no delays, they would finish the work just before Christmas, ahead of schedule. Proud of the efforts of his crew Jim encouraged and complimented men and women often.

Off to one side of the warehouse stood the three aircraft the company now owned. Each had been repainted in the company colors. Wheels chocked on the PBY Catalina Flying Boat and CH-53D Sea Stallion, and the AH-1W Super Cobra sitting on its skids looked quite dashing with their underbellies painted an aqua blue, the upper fuselage painted a pearl white, and a burgundy stripe on wings or down the center of the fuselage on the choppers. *Bring It Up's* logo eagle was on each aircraft along with the proper registration.

Ostensibly the AH-1W Super Cobra was now a research aircraft, and at the moment it was mounted with a plethora of sensing equipment. However, in twenty minutes or less it could be transformed into a fully functioning attack aircraft with full capabilities. Pairs of men worked in tandem flying the chopper on a regular basis, practicing attack and evasion techniques, shooting at targets when out to sea, honing their skills.

Each pilot and gunner wore a pin on his collar, a stormy background with three lightening strikes to the water. In the center the traditional wings, single lightening bolt, and orbiting circles of military and police were painted in white with the *Bring It Up* Eagle coming in for the kill. Above the eagle were the words *Bring It Up SAR* in gold and in red, along the bottom, the words *Aviation Operations*. Jim liked the pins and what they represented. His teams were very close, just tenths of seconds separating them in timed runs.

When not in use the PBY would be chained down in one of the holds, surrounded by supplies. On deck a crane could lift it up and set it in the water for use when needed. Jim was pleased by the appearance of the classic aircraft and knew that in their newest venture it would prove an important tool. That plane would supply the ship as it worked in the Arctic Ocean, and the teams on land. Aptly chosen it was a workhorse the military had proven over and over.

Jim, John, and Wade had a very difficult assignment in deciding how to approach the three-pronged mission before them. First, there was the contract with the United States Government helping with the Alaska Ocean Observing System. Much of the grant was being funded by oil companies in the hopes that when the system was completed the government would become friendly toward offshore drilling in that arena. AOOS, once in place would provide much needed information about currents, ice flows, and temperature changes in that part of the world.

Their second objective was hunting for the sacred cave mentioned on the copper plate found in the Lost City of Z. Alistair was convinced it was in the Brooks Range, in the higher elevations, close to the very center of the range itself. Satellite images had identified some cave systems in the mountains they could check. But Jim knew the dangers of that part of the world were in sudden weather changes, and fierce predators. The Brooks Range was, for the most part, the domain of Alaska's huge brown bear, the ferocious Grizzly, and wolves.

Admiral Runion and his wing of the newly formed *Omega Force*

Remote Intelligence Division (RID) uncovered rumors of an attack on the Trans Alaska Pipeline. Defending the pipeline was an impossible task, but he believed that Jim's special talents could ferret out the location of the attack force and stop them before any serious damage was done. When he learned that they would be operating in Alaska he tasked *Bring It Up* with the near impossible mission of finding the radical ecological terrorists in that region and putting a stop to their plans.

Another bit of information came from Runion's group. A German from Mexico City was finding apartments and houses in the Chicago area, and also paying two year's rent. Occupied by men from middle eastern countries though only one was on the watch list made them extremely suggestive. TajUdin Odeh was the one on the watch list, with known associations with ISIS, and though the police agencies in Chicago had been informed that he was in the city, no manhunt was under way. Jim shook his head. He had to take care of this other business first. It was shaping up to be a very busy year!

What surprised everyone came in the discovery that the money behind the three groups involved in Alaska traced back to the Zhanzhu Triad, now headed by Yao Li Wu. That meant that they could very well meet up with Xun Hao and whoever was chosen as her partner assassin. The men of *Bring It Up* did not like that connection at all. *Omega Force* became very interested in that organization's movements when assets from espionage resources across the globe were secretly mobilized.

On paper, dividing the labor seemed simple, but these experienced soldiers knew that no mission was ever easy. One planned the mission, and contingencies, but combat was always fluid and changing and one also had to be able to adapt instantly to a new threat or unexpected event. Danger levels would be high for all three groups because they were not operating together but would be separated into three different teams in three different geographical locations with only the pilots providing support when necessary.

Jim was going into the Brooks Range with the team in search of the sacred cave. He had suggested that Bulldog accompany his own team of Omega 1. Terrance Red Claw led Bulldog and because of his experience in the Rocky Mountains of America and his native heritage he would be a good addition. But Jim also needed the team's best sniper, Sid Barrett, and so Firefox, under Bill Dodge would accompany him.

Led by Jim, Omega 1 included Zeke Kline, Frank Miller, and John Smith, a navigator of uncanny skill. Zeke and Smitty would make a good team using Satellite technology and other assets to set each day's course. Frank Miller was a good man to have at your side against any enemy, a calm and dedicated soldier that knew the risks and had reserves to draw upon that rivaled those of Jim Shepherd.

Chief, as everyone called Red Claw, was a formidable soldier in his own right, a full-blooded Blackfoot Indian with a proud heritage of serving his country. His grandfather rode in the cavalry against German tanks in Africa during the Second World War. Family and tribe thrived in the Rockies hunting, trapping, and living off the land. Jim knew that Chief knew mountains.

With him were Gene Hardesty, Neil Meyers, and Mel Pierson. Hayseed was the nickname given to Gene, a six-foot five-inch Pennsylvania farm boy with an easy-going nature. Neil and Mel were a matched pair of marines, an inch apart and five pounds difference between them. Taller of the two Meyers was lighter by five pounds, weighing in at one hundred and eighty pounds of hard-packed marine muscle. MP's build was slightly stronger though the two were evenly matched. Chief had a good team that worked well together, knew each other intimately, and trusted each other implicitly.

A decorated soldier with experience in the mountains of Afghanistan Dodge led Firefox. Barrett, Corrigan, and Colt looked like they'd been cut out of the same Marine mold. Using the Barrett M82A1 SASR sniper rifle Barrett was unmatched by any of the team. He seemed to have a special bond with the rifle, though he claimed his name and the rifle's name being the same was mere coincidence. Colt, on the other hand, scored as high as Jim with a pistol, and the two led the teams in pistol marksmanship. Corrigan made that foursome a deadly group of soldiers.

Dr. Gregg, Gwyneth Gregg, Dr. Van Haaten, Dr. Mirelle, René and Tiffany Millstein, Elizabeth Minor, Stephanie Morris, and Cecilia Shepherd made up the civilian team in the search party. Determined to tackle that difficult mission the civilians were working hard to build physical stamina, and to master the skills of mountaineering that would be necessary for survival. Despite their age, Dr. Gregg and his wife were in the best physical shape of their lives and eager to make the trek.

Knowing he would have his own mother and stepfather to care for added a burden of responsibility to Jim that he welcomed. He liked Alistair and respected the man. Gwyneth's excitement and physical improvement made him happy as well. Seeing her avid attention to detail and enjoyment of the training gave him a sense of accomplishment. She never complained or asked for preferential treatment because her son was in command.

Mato Grosso expedition proved the ability of the civilians in working with his military teams. Morale, he knew, would be high most of the time. But there was that nagging understanding that the Brooks Range was a deadly adversary, offering challenges in weather, nature, and terrain.

John led the expedition to find the ecological terrorist groups working to sabotage the pipeline. Wade Adams, C.G. Franklin, and Vince Hall made up Zulu with John at the head. Raider and Sniper would be joining them. Penelope Shepherd would also be part of John's team.

Led by Calvin Weston, Raider was a perfect team to have in a counter terrorist operation. Donnelly, nicknamed bear, towered over his teammates at six feet six inches, weighing a massive two hundred and sixty pounds, all packed into a powerful muscular frame capable of amazing feats. Donnelly was built like a gymnast and had physical skills that would shame many professional gymnasts of the day. His weight would not be a detriment to the team. Banks, Carr, and Weston were all built similarly, hard and muscular, able to go the distance, skilled in weapons, hand-to-hand combat, and explosives.

Norm Geissler led Sniper. Lee Ainsworth, Lloyd Brookstone,

and Earl Duncan had proved their metal as Team Sniper. Physically they were as different as any team could be. Geissler stood five feet ten inches tall and weighed in at one hundred and seventy-five pounds. Ainsworth was four inches shorter and fifteen pounds lighter, lightening quick on his feet and one of those soldiers that could run ten miles with eighty pounds on his back and then fight for ten hours straight. Brookstone was six feet one inches tall and powerfully built with whipcord strength weighing one hundred and eighty-five pounds. Duncan, an inch shorter, weighed in at two hundred and twelve pounds with broad shoulders and a powerful body. Yet they operated as smoothly as any of the teams, working together with amazing cooperation.

That left Delta, Knife, and Nightfall to the science team on the Arctic Ocean, battling incredible cold, ice, and dangers only the sea could offer. Yet Jim had to admit that those twelve men working together rivaled any platoon anywhere in the world!

Dorf Bernard led Delta. He was an unusual soldier to be chosen for the SEAL team program, and few believed he would qualify. Standing an impressive six feet nine inches in height he weighed in at two hundred and seventy-five pounds, all packed onto a powerful frame that combined strength and speed in incredible balance. His best friend Mark Drumheiser stood only four inches over the five-foot mark with a gymnast's body weighing in at one hundred and eighty-five pounds. In martial arts he was unrivaled, having mastered eleven. Four inches taller, Jack Boswell packed one hundred and sixty-five pounds on his frame, with fast reflexes and the ability to drive anything. Bill Kline was Zeke's identical twin and an expert in munitions.

The Aussie's of Knife fit right in with Delta. Led by Sean Oxton the four former SAS soldiers formed a cohesive unit. Ox was a soldier first, but also a field doctor. Although only five feet nine inches tall he weighed one hundred and ninety pounds, with the body of a gymnast and an inherent quickness that surprised many. Brown was six feet tall and weighed an impressive two hundred and five pounds though he looked twenty pounds lighter. Edwards and Eustus were an inch apart and both weighed in at one eighty, the latter the tallest at five feet eleven inches. When it came to hard fighting, they could be depended upon every step of the way.

Team Nightfall included Tom Izbicki, Steve Coleman, Bernie Finlay, and Richard Kagan; all former SEAL team members that served with Dorf in the past. Izbicki packed one hundred and ninety-six pounds of muscle onto his six-foot two-inch frame, a powerful soldier with the impressive skills of a SEAL.

Coleman, nicknamed Santa, was two inches taller and weighed two twenty-five. Finlay was five feet nine inches tall and weighed one hundred and sixty-five pounds, and though he wasn't as impressive physically as Izzy or Santa he could stand toe-to-toe with them and hold his own. Kagan, nicknamed Fagan because of his comically sinister face was two inches shorter, five pounds lighter.

People often looked at taller, stronger men, with a sense of awe, never realizing that soldiers like Kagan and Finlay were equally deadly. That was one thing the men learned early. It wasn't about size and strength. It was about skill. All of them had mad skills and unbelievable stamina. Jim, John, and Wade knew that the science team on board the ship would be in good hands.

Dr. Copeland, Alice and John Dinsmore, Rachael Hague, Mary Anne Lewis, Dr. Lowe, Dr. Putnam, Lynn Ross, Dr. Rysdale, and Barbara Stafford would make up the Science Team on board the ship and with the crew would venture into the Arctic Ocean and face its perils together.

Dorf would share command with Andrea Orvieto, both experienced at sea. The medical team of Axlerod and Penny would care for any medical needs on board the ship. Leo Axlerod and his wife René were the new additions to take the place of the Wozniacs. Leo was thirty and René 28, adventurers that served four years on the mission field and were newly added to the crew.

Mark Drumheiser and Sean Oxton would second Dorf and Andrea. In the kitchen Abe and JimJim led a crew including Bill Franklin, Bob Hinkle, Paul Jennings, Frank Lafayette, Wendall March, Tom Patterson, and Tom Sturdevant. Zeke Good, Mike Romentowski, and Walt Rule would form the mechanical crew while Sam Hammer and Loony Johnson maintained the electrical department.

Marvin Finn and Tom Ives were the ship's clerks. Richard Nelson and Ned Vintner would hold down the computer center with Bob Neff standing in as Navigator. Jim didn't doubt for a moment the qualifications and dedication of any of his crew and felt a stirring of pride as he thought of all of them working together on this mission to make it a success. He hoped it would be a success.

Sighing he moved away from the railing to check on the ongoing work on his new ship. As he moved through each section, he patted shoulders, bumped shoulders, shook hands, and encouraged, complimented, and helped his crew. Everywhere he and John went spirits lifted and work got done a little faster and with great care.

CHAPTER 4

Outfitting the teams for this mission involved some new challenges and an exciting list of equipment. Of course, the purchase, restoration and modifications of the PBY, and the modifications of the two helicopters made for interesting and creative times. For the past three months the teams had been training for the cold weather they would be facing, studying together the dangers and precautions necessary for survival in such a harsh and unforgiving climate.

Each team met together to decide on outfitting for the mission. Brooks Range team faced the challenges of weather, nature, and terrain and chose wisely. Instead of the usual military side arms the men and women of the Brooks Range team would be appropriately armed with powerful revolvers meant to protect against bears. Revolvers included Colt's Anaconda .44 Magnum with the eight-inch barrel. Ruger's Super Redhawk .44 Magnum with the seven-and-a-half-inch barrel and the Smith and Wesson N Frame Model 29 .44 Magnum with eight-and-a-half-inch barrel were also included.

Rifles included Winchester's Model 94 Big Bore Side Eject .356 Caliber with a twenty-inch barrel. Mark X American Field Series Centerfire Bolt Action 30-06 joined the list. Also present was the 300 Winchester Magnum with adjustable trigger, sights, and twenty-four-inch barrel. For shotguns they would carry the Remington 870 Wingmaster 12-gauge.

Knives were carefully selected and included the Combat Smatchet with ten-inch blade and bevel-ground edge, black Lexan plastic handle with longitudinal grooves and lanyard hole. Popular with the men was Gerber's Bowie knife with a nine-and-a-half-inch blade and the SOG SEAL knife 2000 with a seven-inch blade.

Chief, Corrigan, FM, and Hayseed were expert bowmen and selected compound bow crossbows with steel broadhead arrows for Corrigan and Hayseed, as well as two Carbon compound bows with steel broadhead arrows for Chief and FM.

Arctic and mountain expedition clothing included Wilderdown pants, Canada Goose Snow Mantra Coats, Gorilla Balaclavas, Gripper gloves, Baffin Apex Boots, Down Gloves, fur-lined Aviator Hats, Russell Outdoors APX Gale Jackets and pants, Cabela's waterproof Canadian Coverup Jacket, and insulated snow bib overalls. Bulky as these clothes were, their protection would be appreciated. Those clothes would protect them against the harsh weather they would encounter, and perhaps save their lives if they were caught in a storm.

For tents they selected the Hilleberg SAIVO 3-person tent. In the Brooks Range three-person teams were mandatory. Nobody did anything without two other persons present, including using the latrine! Those precautions were necessary because of the predators that inhabited the region, especially the Grizzly.

Necessities included self-heating full MREs, magnesium (flameless) heaters, first responder first aid kit, 12-hour light sticks, Gerber bear grylls hands free torch lights, solar powered radio, solar generator, and a gas generator.

John's team worked on their list and put together what they needed in outfitting the group for the mission. Because they were patrolling the pipeline their outfitting included four Jeep Rubicons modified for the Alaska terrain, and a converted six-wheeler "deuce-and-a-half" made by REO. Pippi and Donut were assigned to fly the AH-1W fully armed over the pipeline.

All five vehicles were modified and converted by TRT, Wade,

and Goody to run on hydraulic power instead of with an internal combustion engine. Each had an engine, but only to get the vehicles started to build up the hydraulic power until they could run on hydraulic power alone. This made the vehicles virtually silent running and though experimental, the theory was sound and had been used successfully before. It was, as always, the question of power, and TRT and Goody put their heads together and solved that problem. Not only had the five vehicles performed above expectation, but they were also even more powerful than ever before.

Once again Jim sighed as he thought of loosing Jim Warner. How did one replace a man like Jim Warner? Jim didn't have an answer to that. Yet he knew deep down inside that no one was irreplaceable. Life taught him that. God was always in control, and He would bring the right man at the right time, as He had done with the Axlerods. At just the right time they appeared on his radar, a missionary doctor with a heart for God was perfect for his team.

Dr. Penny and Sean Oxton would teach Leo everything he needed to know about military medicine, and he would share things he'd learned recently with them, improving the medical skills and knowledge of the whole team. With that thought Jim began to look forward to meeting Jim Warner's replacement.

Pipeline Team would, of course, carry their usual military weapons, but they also had to outfit clothing for the mission. Their clothing included the same as Jim's team and they chose the same tents and necessities. Along with those things they needed to carry diesel fuel for the deuce-and-a-half and gasoline for the Jeeps as well as Aviation Fuel for the chopper.

Using the deuce-and-a-half to pull a tanker for the chopper, and steel cans for the other fuel in the bed of the six-wheeler solved that problem. John felt that his team was more than prepared, though they were training for a very different mission than Jim's team, and Dorf's team.

The AOOS team took their lead from the other two teams when it came to clothing but chose Arctic 10 Oven tents and sheet metal heaters for when they were away from the ship. Those times would be few and far between, but they were prepared for even the coldest temperatures and most difficult challenges. Much study had gone into the necessary supplies. Being prepared was what it was all about. That and trusting God for the rest was all one could do.

Having analyzed the lists of all three teams and knowing the challenges they faced separately Jim decided they had done everything possible to prepare. Now they had to execute the plan.

At Hill House the daily routine continued right up until the fifteenth of December. On that Saturday work on *Sea Venture* came to a halt mid-morning. Taking advantage of a very bad winter storm the crew loaded all the weapons and explosives into the war room while a blizzard raged outside. Finally, a little after noon, the bulkhead doors slid closed, effectively hiding away the war room in the belly of the ship. A minute inspection declared that the work was now complete.

Getting back to Hill House was an adventure, but the crew managed, deciding to divide into their three groups and see how they worked together. There was a new dynamic developing with the teams that Jim couldn't quite put his finger on but disturbed him none-the-less. However, he had his own team to get back to the house and concentrated on that detail. Despite his efforts, he couldn't shake the feeling that he needed to address the issue.

Once they were back at the house, he still felt uncomfortable. Something significant was happening, something disturbing, but so subtle he could not fathom what it might be. Two days later the matter rose once again, something said, something gestured, he was not sure which, but again that doubt nagged at his inner being. It was Abe who drew him aside that evening with a strong hand on his shoulder.

"Jim, could Sturdy and I have a word with you?" Abe asked softly. Jim looked at the massive cook and nodded. They stepped into an alcove and stood close together.

"You're worried about dividing into three teams, and the others of the crew are picking up on that. Also, training separately has created a separation the crew is not aware of. Each team is striving its best, but they are not striving as a whole cohesive unit! They are missing their friends and they don't know what to do about it," Abe said softly.

It hit Jim then. Abe was right. That was the thing that had been nagging at him. His crew was no longer a cohesive unit, but three separate entities. Emotions raised by this situation frightened Jim, and he felt wholly inadequate and woefully equipped to handle separation anxiety and a division of unity. He looked at Abe.

"I'm not sure I know how to deal with this!" he admitted freely.

"We need a project that everyone can work on together, one that will supersede our upcoming adventure. It needs to be something that will tug at the heart of every crewmember and bring them together in one purpose, reestablishing the bond," Sturdy said with a smile, placing a huge hand on Jim's shoulder. He was pleased that his captain admitted his need of advice, and that he would take advice from one of his men, even a member of the galley team.

"I'm open for suggestions," Jim said with a sigh, realizing the huge man was correct.

"At this time of the year the Devon Shelter is overtaxed, underfunded, and dismal. There are entire families that are homeless staying in the shelter right now. In a shelter, men are separated from women and children, so these families can't even stay together. We have this huge house, this great kitchen, and some funds to help make this Christmas something special for those families. May I suggest that we bring the women, and families with children to Hill House and give them a Christmas to remember?" Abe was smiling as he spoke, knowing that Jim would jump at the chance to help those women and families. He was not disappointed in his Captain.

"So, do you two guys have some sort of extrasensory equipment to find these shelters?" he asked, jokingly. "I love it! We'll get one person from each team to work together finding out exactly what each woman or family needs, and then bring us a report with suggestions. Then we will all find a solution together, making sure it is one that will benefit the family in the long run, and provide everything necessary to get them back on their feet and independent." Jim said. "Thanks guys! You've given me exactly what I needed to bring us back together. Helping these families will stretch us, but in a good way."

"You're right about that! That should do it!" Sturdy said, slapping Jim on the back hard enough to stagger him.

"Hey! Take it easy on your Captain!" Jim said, shrugging his shoulders and grinning at Sturdy.

"Sorry, Shep! I let my enthusiasm carry me away!" Sturdy chuckled.

"That must be some enthusiasm!" Jim replied with a wink and a laugh. "Let's go tell the others!"

Jim rang the bell that would call everyone to the dining room for a conference, including the staff. When they had all gathered, he walked to the head of the table and put his hands on the back of the ornate high-back ladder chair, and everyone grew silent.

"I've been alerted to a distress call for rescue," he said, looking around the room as everyone straightened a little. "Shelter Devon is in trouble, and they need a number of women, and families with children to be rescued from a dismal Christmas season. I propose that we open Hill House North Wing, determine the needs of each individual and family, and decide on a course of action to meet those needs while they are our guests. I also propose that we give them a Christmas they will never forget. Above all, we must instill in them a sense of their own dignity and worth!

"Staff, this is indeed an unexpected and extra burden for you, and we will help in any way we can. When we vote on something the vote must be unanimous, or we don't do it. Please understand that if you want no part of this, you have the right, and the responsibility to vote no. However, if you think we could help these folks, and give them a hand up instead of the usual government hand out, I hope you'll vote yes. I'll give everyone two hours to think it over and ask any questions you might have. After two hours we'll take the vote and see what happens. Abe, Sturdy, and I will be available for questions and discussion.

"If we vote to take on this mission, one person from each of the three teams will be assigned to work together to determine the needs and course of action best suited to meet the needs of each individual or family with children. You will make an assessment and come up with viable suggestions and bring it to all of us. We will then discuss your ideas and suggestions and vote to adopt them or to amend them and everyone will work on the solution together. We do this as a team!" Jim stepped back and looked at the beautiful coo-coo-clock hanging on the wall. "Let's meet back here for the vote in two hours, and then we'll have dinner at the regular time. Team leaders, please stay for a moment."

"Pipeline team! We meet in the billiard's room in ten," John said loudly. His men nodded.

"Would the AOOS team please meet me in the library as soon as Papa and I am finished here," Dorf said, nodding to Andrea.

"Okay. Brooks Range team will gather in the game room upstairs," Jim added.

As the teams moved away Jim explained the plan to his team leaders. They all agreed that this was just what everyone needed to reestablish the bond that had been missing for the past few days. Agreeing to divide the unit into letters would work best, and then the three with the designation "a" would meet and be assigned a case to work. After seven minutes of discussion, they gave each other enthusiastic high-fives and parted. Jim turned to George, who was waiting respectfully by the door.

"Mr. Tuggle, please give each person a designation letter," Jim said. "If we agree to do this, you'll be helping someone find a way to self-dependence!"

"What type of people might we expect, sir?" that was Darla Engle, one of the maids. Jim smiled at her as he thought of an appropriate answer. It came to him quite suddenly.

"Desperate, Darla. Some of them will not trust us at first, others will be angry and frustrated, and all of them will be very needy. But over all they will all be desperate," Darla flushed crimson when Jim used her name, even though he always called her by name. He never forgot a name. She pondered his answer all the way to the kitchen with the rest of the staff. One word kept coming back to echo in her mind and tug at her heart.

"No one should be desperate at Christmas!" Darla said when the door closed behind them all. "That's just horrible!" Everyone in the kitchen nodded their heads in agreement.

"We've got quite a store of baby clothes, diapers, and rubber pants boxed away in the attic," Ruth Tuggle said quietly. "Wouldn't it be nice to hear the happy voices of children over Christmas in the old house?"

"Not to mention the fussing and crying!" Mrs. Landon said with a laugh. "It will liven the old place up a bit, that's for certain!"

"We can teach the women how to cook and serve, how to clean a room and make a bed, and tidy up, get them fit for a job of work when we're done with them!" Mrs. Jennings said with determination. "Once they're trained up, they can keep the North Wing clean and be paid for it. I imagine some of those women never had a mother to teach them such things."

"Struth! They wouldn't be homeless if they had, now, would they?" Martha Finchly said, nodding emphatically. "We'll give them something to feel proud about!"

"I think, at this point, I should ask if anyone is against the idea," Mr. Tuggle said, taking advantage of the short pause between comments.

"Good Lord, no!" Mrs. Tuggle said as if outraged. "Do you think one of them would vote against it?" she asked, waving her hand past the kitchen door.

"Do you think we can decorate for Christmas?" Judy Carlisle asked excitedly.

"I imagine we will!" Cynthia Essex laughed. Just then Jim came into the kitchen.

"I'm sorry to interrupt," he said as they all turned. He was always so polite it set them all at ease as he moved into the room.

"No, sir! Go right ahead," George invited with a smile. He was enjoying this young master of the estate who was always so polite.

"If we decide to do this, I would like to extend an invitation to all of you to include your families in our Christmas celebration. We'll need to decorate, of course, but we can talk about that after dinner. I think it would do every one of those folks from the shelter good to enjoy Christmas with normal families," he added.

"Who says my family is normal?" Mrs. Osborne chuckled! "Do go on young man! I'm quite sure none of us will ever forget this Christmas. Would you mind if we included some of the folks at the church?"

"That's an excellent idea! I'll leave that to you, Mrs. Osborne?" Jim asked.

"My pleasure," she replied, blushing slightly.

"Judging by what I've heard so far, this staff is a perfect addition to our team!" Jim said, leaving them with a wave. They exchanged looks filled with pride as he departed.

At the appointed time Jim cleared his throat and the room grew silent. He looked at everyone for a moment. "Do you want a written vote, or a show of hands?" he asked.

"Show of hands!" Almost every voice spoke up and he smiled. There had been no hesitation in that decision!

"Very well then! Those in favor of opening Hill House for Christmas to the women and families at the shelter, raise your hands." When every hand went into the air enthusiastically, he felt hot tears spring to his eyes, and he looked with incredible pride at his crew and staff. Pulling a handkerchief from his pocket he wiped his eyes and nodded.

"No Captain ever felt such pride in his crew as I do at this moment. Your generosity and courage are an amazing attribute, and you inspire me!" he commended. Turning to Abe he smiled, still struggling with his emotions.

"I'll leave it to you to make the arrangements. Tomorrow we'll decorate and prepare, and the day after we'll have them all moved in. After that we can assess. Santa is going to pay a visit to this house on Christmas Eve, and when those kids and women get up in the morning, they're all going to have presents to open," Jim grinned.

"Now I know how Scrooge felt on Christmas morning!" Fagan

said, rubbing his hands together. Obviously, he had been preparing, for he walked out of the room singing new words to the song from the musical *Oliver*. "I'm reviewing, the situation! All those presents will be valuable, I'm sure!" he sang as he left the room. Cecilia shook her head.

"Perhaps we should chain him to his bed Christmas eve!" she suggested with a chuckle.

"I like that idea!" Barbara and Mary Ann said in unison as everyone laughed.

"Oh, a villain is a villain till the end!" echoed down the hall in response. Everyone roared at Fagan's antics. He was quite good at mimicking the infamous Fagan of the movie musical *Oliver*.

CHAPTER 5

By the end of the following day Hill House had been transformed into a Christmas wonderland! There were fully decorated trees in the game room, the dining hall, the front foyer, and the library, all of them over eight feet tall, and each one delightful to look at. Outside lights had been strung carefully to outline the house in flashing color and spell Noel on the roof. Every hallway was decorated and glistened with Christmas cheer.

Food was purchased in preparation of feeding sixteen single women, six married couples, five single moms, and twenty-six children, a total of fifty-nine extra mouths to feed! Of the twenty-six children nine of them were still in diapers ranging from six months of age to twenty-six months. The other seventeen children ranged in ages from three to nine, and the three-year-old and a five-year-old would need diapers at night. Despite those added responsibilities no one felt indisposed toward any of the new arrivals. Perhaps it was the novelty of it all that made it so much fun, but the staff and crew thoroughly enjoyed that first day.

A very nice tour bus, hired by *Bring It Up*, brought them to Hill House. Abe and Sturdy purchased trunks and suitcases for their belongings, urging them to leave the shopping carts at the shelter. Those two even helped some of the folks pack their things, because they just didn't know how, or couldn't figure out how to fit everything. Abe assured everyone that they would have enough cases and trunks for everything.

When they arrived at the house, men from *Bring It Up* carried suitcases and trunks into the house and into the North Wing, allowing people to pick whichever room suited him or her, or a family. Family units included a sitting room, two, three, or four bedrooms, each with its own bathroom, a small playroom, and a den. The opulence of the accommodations was overwhelming, and many voiced concerns. Jim, John, Wade, Sturdy and Abe were quick to assure them that these rooms were theirs until they were on their feet and able to support themselves. It was no surprise to those worthy men that none of the people believed them. All too often they had been promised permanency, only to have it snatched away. Expecting the distrust didn't make it any easier to accept, but they were able to maintain a positive attitude through prayer and patience.

Wisely, the teams meeting with individuals and families met first with Abe and Sturdy and learned how to do an assessment, how to talk to people in this situation, and more importantly, how to zero in on the real needs. It did no good to miss those. That meant they had to listen to their guests carefully, and to allow them to participate in the process.

None of them would be satisfied with a cursory assessment, but instead chose to do it right, making sure they had as much information to work with as possible. One other thing they all did, thanks to instructions from Abe and Sturdy, was to include the individuals and families in the action plans. Giving them the opportunity to have input increased trust. Trust was critical in this phase.

Often, during this stage, the men and women of *Bring It Up* had to stop the assessment process, and then explain again that they were not like other wealthy philanthropists and offering to solve problems by offering money. What they were offering was a hand up, not a handout. Slowly, as always, trust was established, and the people from the shelter began to soften toward the people of Hill House.

Not at all a surprise to Jim and the crew, the children took to Abe and Sturdy like kittens to fresh milk. What was a surprise was the amount of attention Fagan got from some of the older boys. Once Jim learned he was using them to steal cookies and other treats from the kitchen it all made sense. Mrs. Jennings was aware of what he was doing, and she would often storm into his room while he was surrounded with the boys, chase him around the room with her wooden spoon, and take it all back to the kitchen.

Fingers would sit quietly while all the hullabaloo went on around him, pocket several of the cookies, and when Mrs. Jennings was gone hand them around. Santa would arrive in the room with a pitcher of milk, glasses, and a plate full of cookies and everyone would quickly hide the stolen cookies, because Fagan and Numbers had convinced the children that Steve really was Santa in disguise.

Single mothers were employed in the kitchen and with the cleaning staff in the house and began earning money almost immediately. Jim insisted on this, allowing Mrs. Tuggle to set the wages for the women, and Mr. Tuggle to set the wages for the men. Often, Jim found himself offering a prayer for difficult cases, women who had no idea of a work ethic or how to respond to authority. In each case, as he prayed with a staff member, he asked for patience and love. It was love that won the day. Single women were encouraged to volunteer to help and offered classes. At first only a few came into the kitchen during the lessons, but as others tasted the wonderful confections, cakes, cookies, and other baked goods the class soon grew to capacity.

JimJim bought a local restaurant that had been vacant for more than a year, with the plan to turn it into a tea and sandwich shop that offered special hot drinks all day long, breakfast rolls, and freshly baked cookies, cinnamon rolls, and coffee cakes. In the summer they would have Italian Ice drinks, and various fountain drinks. He hired the fathers of the homeless families to help him renovate, decorate, and run the business.

Two of the men were good with their hands, seasoned and experienced carpenters. Another was a plumber and pipe fitter by trade. One had talent drawing and designing so JimJim set him in charge of designing the inside and outside of the store to attract and bring back customers. Of the other two one was willing to learn any trade that would guarantee him a job, so JimJim sent him to business school half the day and working the other half managing the store. Last of the father's was a man who loved the kitchen and food industry, and JimJim took great pride in training him how to bake the goods and make the delicious sandwiches they would sell. He took great pains to teach the man every trick to producing delicious food, and he encouraged him to think about training others to work with him in the kitchen.

Suddenly the men were earning a weekly wage and had something in which to take great pride. That they had to work for their wages, and to learn to get along despite their differences and backgrounds, was something they accepted with much less difficulty than anticipated. The only real problem JimJim had was helping each man believe in himself. Each one realized that he had been given a very special chance to pull himself out of the hole he was in, rather than having someone else do it for him. Jim watched those men return each day, weary, talking animatedly, walking with their heads held high as they entered the house through a side entrance to greet their wives and children.

It had been Windy that insisted the wives and children meet the men as they returned from a hard day's labor, impressing upon them the importance of letting husband and father know how much he was loved by his family. None of the wives or children objected to the greeting assignment, and in fact, took great joy in welcoming father and husband home. As Jim watched the various greetings, ranging from tender to awkward, he put his arm around his mother's shoulders.

"You always had us meet Dad at the door with you unless he was coming back when we were already in bed. I think I'll be a better Dad because I had you to teach me some of these things," he said with his eyes glistening with unshed tears. "He always cheered up when he saw us!"

It confused him to have these strong emotions. Before his marriage, and perhaps before he came to know the Lord Jesus as his

Savior, he lacked the ability to allow himself to feel such emotions. Now he didn't exactly welcome them, but he accepted them as part of God's changing his heart.

"I'm rather anxious to have some grandchildren!" Gwyneth said, smiling up at him with twinkling eyes full of mischief. "I hope you heard that!" Gwyneth said to Cecilia as she arrived.

Cecilia came up at that moment and snuggled into Jim's other arm. Looking into her eyes Jim surprised a look he had never seen before. He raised an eyebrow as Cecilia turned and to his mother. She looked across at her mother-in-law and smiled. "You'll have to wait at least another eight months," she said softly.

Jim's mouth dropped open, and he looked at her as several different emotions played across his usually taciturn face. She laughed quietly as he finally settled his face into its usual neutral look, though his eyes were softer than she had ever seen them.

"We're pregnant?" he asked, his voice cracking a little as he spoke.

"We are!" Cecilia said. "I just found out this morning," Jim noticed that she looked like she was glowing with health and happiness and tucked that knowledge away.

"I think I just got the best Christmas present ever!" Jim said, hugging Cecilia. He breathed in her scent as he hugged her and felt the wonder of the news he'd just so joyfully received.

"Teach your brother how it's done, dear," Gwyneth said, patting Jim's shoulder with a smile and a wink.

"Teach me what?" John said, joining the group. Penelope was holding his hand and Jim noted quickly that she too had a new look, as if she was almost glowing from within. He knew without realizing it and threw back his head and laughed.

"I want Jim to teach you how to have a baby, so I can have grandchildren!" Gwyneth said, looking at Jim in surprise. He rarely displayed this much emotion. He was still laughing, and John hugged him and began laughing too, turning to his mother.

"Too late, mom!" John said lightly. "We just found out today that we are going to have a baby!"

"You are too!" Cecilia and Penelope hugged, laughing, and crying at the same time.

"Wow!" John said to Jim as they shook hands and bumped shoulders.

"Us!" Jim said, laughing with delight.

"What's all this? Did you two win the lottery or something?" Andrea said, coming in the side door with his wife Rosa. She'd flown in that morning for Christmas.

"Yeah! What's with all the joy?" Wade said, joining the group. As usual, these days, Angela walked beside him, her tiny hand in his, looking more like a child beside her father than a girlfriend beside her beau. Dr. Rysdale caught on immediately. Her lovely eyes grew wide, and she laughed with joy.

"Both of you?" she asked, her face breaking into a huge smile.

"Will somebody tell me what's going on?" Andrea begged.

"You're going to be a great uncle twice over," Jim replied with a huge grin, hugging his uncle.

Dinner that evening at Hill House was a festive affair and the announcement of the blessed events was received with joy. Their guests were getting used to sharing meals with a crew that was more like a family, and with a group of people that were very real about their faith and love. Some of them were still trying to find their place in the midst of it, but that night everything seemed to fall into place. Those who were mothers found Cecilia and Pen more than willing to take advice, and that alone endeared them to those women. Both of them actually wrote down suggestions and asked questions.

After dinner Jim asked the parents of the children to join him in the library, and assigned Abe, Sturdy, and Fagan to look after the mites until their parents were finished. He shared with them the letters that Steve Coleman had received, slipped under his door, by many of the children. Looking at the parents he smiled.

"We want this to be a Christmas the kids never forget, and since they're convinced that Steve really is Santa, we're going to let him play the part. He's agreed and will have some helpful elves to make everything happen just right. However! I'd like all of you to write a letter to Santa, asking him for what you think your kids will enjoy the most. If you don't object, we'll purchase those things, let you wrap and label them, and then Santa will put them under the tree early Christmas morning.

"I know that you are all just getting your feet under you, and you're not ready to purchase the gifts your kids really want, but we've come to love you folks like family, and we'd like to help. This is for the kids, more than anything else. Will you allow us to help in this fashion? We would never do this without your agreement," he added.

"You've been so kind, and you've done so much already!" one of the fathers said quietly. "I'd like my little ones to have a great Christmas, and I'm not too proud to accept help offered that way, Captain. You're a generous man, and you've given us a chance to make good, and get on our own feet with our own hard work. The way things are going, we'll be on our feet in only a few months, thanks to you folks. I'll write that letter," he finished, with tears running down his face.

The others nodded in agreement and Jim sat back. It felt strange to hear such accolades from these men, who had suffered so much. He looked at them and then spoke.

"Thank you. I'm convinced that the Lord put us here at this time and in this place to touch your lives with His love. I don't know what you think of Jesus, or if you even believe in the God of the Bible. I do. If I understand His word correctly, every human being has value that can never be measured in human terms. Jesus died for us. I couldn't put a value on one drop of His blood. Because He shed it for you, that makes you worthy in ways I can't even fathom. Me too.

"In the midst of your trials you've blessed us as much, if not more, than we have blessed you. I'm amazed at your resilience and courage. There's not a one of you I wouldn't welcome as a member of my crew, and I mean that. Don't think we don't notice how hard you work, and the pride you take in your work. We gave you the chance, you proved yourselves worthy. Best of all, I think we're becoming friends, and friends are a precious gift," he nodded as he said the last.

"Aye! You've no shown any condescending attitudes, as some do in these parts. An' yer true to yer word, Cap'n! Friendship may be the only thing I can repay ye! I'll do me best to make it a friendship worthy of the name!" The man who spoke was Welsh; with an accent so thick, Jim had trouble following it. But he took the man's hand with a smile.

"What say we show this town how to celebrate Christmas again!" Jim laughed.

"Aye! I believe we'll do that!" the man answered.

On the following day two farmers with sleighs and horses to pull them arrived at Hill House and the children took turns riding around the grounds and through town while it snowed and blew, turning everything white once more. Children in town were permitted a ride as well, and many took advantage of the fun. Snuggled beneath the thick rugs provided for the rides the children laughed with delight as the snowflakes fell. The sleigh gave Steve Coleman an idea and he arranged with Jim Warner a very special effect for the sake of the children.

Jim Warner, as one of the last services to the team, fabricated sleigh rails and reindeer tracks that would appear in the snow on the one flat portion of roof, with just the sleigh tracks going up the peak of the roof beyond, as though Santa had flown off. His own children and grandchildren joined him that week at Hill House and the grandkids were soon playing with the other children as if they'd been lifelong friends.

Kids from the families of the staff were also about often, and the older girls often offered to care for the infants and little ones to give moms a break. In the midst of it all, Jim watched his crew, once again whole and bonded in spirit, doing what they did best. Working together to accomplish a worthwhile goal, whatever the odds, they knew that working together would ensure success. Countless times he had come upon them huddled in prayer, earnest in their desire to do the very best.

It snowed again the afternoon of Christmas Eve, and despite the new snow, the congregation at the old church crowded in, filling every seat, and some chairs hastily set up to accommodate the crowd.

Sturdy read the Christmas story from the Scriptures, and they sang favorite Christmas hymns and songs together. To many it seemed that a special spirit had settled upon those gathered in the old church, and when they left it was with hearts that were full. Once again, the wonder of the Christmas story had penetrated the hearts of men, women, and children. Jesus, the greatest gift ever given, had come to earth to save mankind!

Jim watched the children look around for Steve Coleman, and not finding him have a moment of doubt. He assured some of them, with a straight face, that Steve had an important job to do that evening and would probably return sometime tomorrow when he was finished. When they asked him what Steve was doing, he put a finger up to the side of his nose and winked.

"I can't say! I don't want a piece of coal in my stocking!" he said.

"He's delivering toys!" several little voices whispered.

"Yes! But if you see him, because he looks very different when he delivers toys, you must not let him know you know it's him!" Jim cautioned with a serious face. "When I see him, I pretend I didn't, so he doesn't put a lump of coal in my stocking!"

At five the following morning a voice echoed through the house, thanks to the work of Zeke, Rock and Roll, and News. It was Steve Coleman's voice saying "Ho! Ho! Ho! Merry Christmas! Happy Birthday, Jesus!" It seemed to come from everywhere, followed by tinkling bells and sounds from the roof as his voice faded away. Sleigh bells and hoof beats also faded away. Though quite theatrical, it had the desired effect!

The children rushed from their beds to the big Christmas tree in the library and stopped in the doorway, their mouths open, as they stared at the presents heaped beneath the tree. Bright wrappings of amazing Christmas patterns greeted their eyes in a heap of neatly stacked presents. Jim came up.

"Who was just on the roof?" he asked, as if perplexed.

"Santa! It was Santa!" a little three-year-old girl whispered, taking his hand. "Did he leave tracks in the snow?" she asked.

"Let's go look!" Jim suggested. And he led the children up the steps to a window where they could see the tracks in the snow.

When they returned to the library everyone was up and the children noticed something about the tree. There were papers, rolled up like a scroll, with red ribbon tied on them, hanging on the tree. One of the older boys looked at one closely.

"Hey! Dad! That's your writing!" he said. His dad came and took the scroll off the tree, unwrapped it, and looked at it as if amazed.

"It's the letter I sent to Santa!" he said.

"You sent him one too?" his son asked with eyes opened wide.

Cecilia stepped up and took over at that point. With a cheery smile and dressed in her soft blue robe, she instructed that the oldest child would pick a present that didn't have her name on it, and take it to that person, who would open it, while finding presents for each person in that family. Then that person would go and get the next presents for the next family. Some of the children groaned, but the anticipation was too much, and they settled in with their families to wait their turn. Everyone enjoyed the excitement and anticipation of the children as the process unfolded.

Every person opened presents with excitement and anticipation, exclaiming appreciation and joy as the treasures were uncovered. It was a scene Jim would hold in his heart for many years, a scene of laughing, tears of joy, cries of surprise, and eyes bright with wonder. This was what Christmas should be like, and he determined in his heart that every Christmas he spent with his children would be like this, with emphasis on Jesus and His wondrous gift.

Breakfast was served quite late that morning, but it was a happy crowd that gathered in the dining room to eat. After the meal the adults cleaned up the library and carried the torn wrappings out to the dumpster in the back, talking about the morning's wonder. No one missed the fact that Jim and John were among those cleaning and carrying trash away.

"You're as strange a Captain as I've ever seen!" one of the fathers spoke to John as they worked together stuffing trash into bags. "You do work most Captain's would order done and leave it to lesser men!"

"Lesser men? Didn't Jesus say that anyone who wanted to be great in His Kingdom must become the servant of all? I don't think of my crew as lesser men, but equals, and I would never ask them to do what I was not willing to do myself." John replied.

"I've seen him get on the floor of the bathrooms on our ship and scrub the corners with a toothbrush!" Sturdy said, joining them. "None of us would do less than our best for either of the Shepherd brothers!" he added. Clapping John on the shoulder he turned about and headed back in out of the snow. John moved his shoulders as if they hurt.

"He nearly dislocated my entire right side with that huge hand of his!" John grinned at the father who was walking beside him. "I love that giant, as I love my own brother, and I know he would easily die for me if it was necessary. That means more than I can ever put into words!"

"He also claims your brother could take him in a hand-to-hand fight! You too!" the man said.

"Sure!" John said with a laugh. He ran ahead and grabbed Sturdy around the waist as if to stop him, and he was dragged several feet while he pretended to be trying to wrestle the man down. Slowly he slid to the floor where he finally let go. He got up and dusted off his hands.

"Showed him!" he said.

"What? Did you say something JR?" Sturdy said, turning around as if puzzled while everyone who saw the whole funny escapade laughed. Scratching his head Sturdy looked quizzically at John.

"I showed you!" John said, waving his finger at Sturdy. John grabbed Sturdy by the front of his shirt. "And don't forget it!"

"Right JR! I won't forget it! What did you show me again?" Sturdy asked.

John threw out both hands and turned around, looking at those watching. "Am I talking to myself here?" he asked.

"Why don't you show me again?" Sturdy said.

John grabbed him from the front around the waist this time and pretended to be struggling to move him. When that didn't work, he grabbed a leg. When that didn't work, he tried to hit Sturdy, while Sturdy held him off with one hand on his forehead. John swung several times and then stopped.

"Let that be a lesson to you!" John said.

"Sure thing, JR!" Sturdy said, slapping John on the back. John pitched forward, and he fell theatrically to the floor. Sturdy looked shocked and quickly grabbed his belt lifting him bodily from the floor up into the air to look at him. "Sorry JR! You okay?" he asked. The kids were laughing so hard they were crying.

Abe came up and put a hand on Sturdy's arm. "Don't treat the captain like that!" he admonished. Sturdy dropped John, who landed on the floor, making a loud thud, and groaning theatrically. The two giants walked away as if they hadn't noticed. Abe continued. "You have to be gentle with the captain's clothing. Picking him up by the belt could have stretched it."

"The belt!" JR groaned from the floor. "You're worried about the belt?" Abe and Sturdy turned around. "What about me?"

"I don't understand the question. Do you understand it?" Abe asked Sturdy, who shook his head and shrugged his shoulders. They turned and walked away.

"He's so far above our understanding," Sturdy said as they moved away, both men grinning as John played his part, continuing to groan as if in great pain, complaining about being left on the floor.

Fagan appeared to help John up. When he'd brushed his Captain off, he turned to go but JR stopped him with a stern voice.

"Fagan!"

"Yes sir!" Fagan replied, turning around.

"My wallet!" John held out his hand. Fagan rubbed it over his sleeve.

"I was just dusting it off, sir!" he said sheepishly, handing it back. Once again, he turned to go.

"Fagan!" JR's voice stopped him. "My watch!"

"Just polishing it up for you, sir!" Fagan answered, returning the watch. After Fagan left everyone noticed that John was no longer wearing shoes. He looked down at his feet and threw up his hands.

"Fagan!" he shouted to the laughter of everyone. It had been masterfully orchestrated, and Jim watched with laughter as his brother marched down the hallway in his stocking feet looking for Fagan. Shaking his head, he turned to find Cecilia laughing behind him.

"How do they think those scenes up?" she asked when she caught her breath.

"I don't know." he answered honestly. "It was fun watching, though!"

Other struggles arose when the guests from the shelter realized that the men and women who had come to their rescue were leaving. Jim took note of the fear he both saw and felt, especially with the single moms in the group. None of them wanted to return to the shelter, and he had no intention of suggesting that. They, however, had no way of knowing that. Individually he met with each family, sharing his goals of keeping them at Hill House until they were sure they could stand on their own two feet out in the world. With the help of Reverend Candle and Abe and Sturdy he finally was able to convince all of them that they were both welcome and loved, and they could stay as long as necessary. Three of the men who had accepted the most help from *Bring It Up*, following through with every bit of advice, especially from JimJim, stepped forward at this point, and Jim recognized the advantage they had in helping the others see the truth. They trusted JimJim, meeting with him previously, and they helped the others come to a place that they believed this wonderful promise.

Later that week Jim met with the three men who had formed a company and were working so hard. JimJim helped them put the company together, and the work they'd done on the restaurant said volumes about their motivation. He tasked them with taking over helping the families and single women at Hill House become self-sufficient, working closely with Reverend Candle. Pointing out that they were eminently qualified for the work he was able to convince them to follow his lead, to help by serving, and to accept failure, giving multiple chances to try again. Abe and Sturdy worked with them, teaching them how to do just that, and when it was time for

Jim to leave, he was aware that the families and women at Hill House were in good hands.

His staff was attached to all of those rescued from the mission and were glad that when Jim and the teams left, they would continue the work of helping those people heal and get on their feet. Many of them thought that several could be hired to help during the summer rush. Knowing they were in good hands Jim sighed as he planned to leave for Alaska. Somehow, helping those people had given everyone a new lease on life, and no one was willing to fail. Lifting his head to the Lord, he breathed a prayer of thanks.

CHAPTER 6

Restructuring the company took a great deal of time and effort for Jim, John and Wade. Instead of two ships they now had one, and though it should have been easier with just one ship and crew there were new developments that added layers of sophistication to the company. That meant a large amount of paperwork and legal hassles, all of which had to be surmounted before they set sail on their maiden voyage.

Finn and Ives stepped forward and proved their worth to the effort in sorting it all out and making sure that everyone understood what needed to be done, how things needed to be worded, and what legal obligations needed to be met by what deadlines. Jim, John, and Wade grew to appreciate the two clerks even more during that time, and for the first time in his work on the crew, Finn felt like he was finally contributing to the mission. Jim was glad to see that he was making friends with some of the men and unbending a bit. Much of that was due to working directly with Ives. Finn and Ives were inseparable these days, and it did Finn good to have a close friend who understood and even appreciated why he was the way he was.

The change in Finn was commented upon and appreciated as he unbent just enough to become one of them, a stalwart companion who pulled his own weight. For the first time he made new friends among the men of the crew, and even unbent a little toward the ladies. Jim decided that Finn was becoming almost human.

Along with all the legal documentation and licensing there were other difficulties the team faced during January. Extreme cold meant serious consequences for the aircraft. Eventually a company in Norway offered a solution and modifications that made all the pilots breathe easier. And then there was the problem of ice forming on the superstructure and deck of the ship and the wings of the airplane. Several vessels experienced severe damage when over a foot of ice formed on the outer structures of the ship, bending, and even springing seams during ice storms, a common occurrence in the Arctic Ocean, even during the warmer weather months.

Dr. Putnam stepped forward, developing a nanobot technology that produced millions of tiny nanobots that adhered to rubber, metal, fiberglass, glass, and plastic on the outer structure of the ship and vibrated, keeping ice from forming on those surfaces. They tested it first on an automobile in an ice chamber. Without the nanobots ice formed quickly and crushed the vehicle. With the nanobots no ice was able to adhere to the surface of vehicle and it remained unscathed. At least it wasn't crushed by the weight of the ice.

There was the problem of paint being vibrated off the material, but Dr. Putnam solved that by making a change in programming so that the nanobots only vibrated on the upper surface. After a successful test lasting seventy-two hours the vehicle showed no signs of damage of any kind. Soon the technology was used on the plane and helicopters with great success as well. The patents alone for this new technology paid for itself in just a few months with government contracts.

It took the men a full month to get the store up and running, and JimJim and the kitchen crew spent much of their time putting it all together. It was an instant success, and according to the Chamber of Commerce, the most attractive storefront in town, with the most interesting and best decorated interior. The two carpenters used their wages to renew their licenses, and they founded a small remodeling agency. Several stores hired them immediately, and they brought the designer into their company to help them succeed. By the end of February all three men had rented a place of their own for their families, and were hard at work, despite the winter weather.

Again, Jim marveled at the creativity and genius of the men and women that served on his crew. February came, and on February 14 *Sea Venture* was ready to be christened. Sir Angus Merril, newest addition to *Omega Force Ground Intelligence Division* arrived in Plymouth and took a cab to the warehouse to christen the ship. Angus was tall, thin, and looked like he might have been a runner in his youth. He introduced himself to the crew.

Press and other interested parties arrived at the appointed time to watch the ceremony. Most of them wore several layers of clothing against the cold. Jim and his crew, ever practical, did not wear dress uniforms for this auspicious event. Instead, they all arrived in work coveralls, waterproof boots, and slickers against the blustery winter weather. In this instance, not looking like a military crew was important to the Shepherds.

Jim read Jeremiah 29:11, and Sturdy led them in a solemn prayer. Then the crew raised their voices in the worship song, *Purify My Heart*, having practiced for days to get it right. There were those in the crowd that frowned on such an open religious exercise, while others respected it. None of the crew cared about the opinion of those watching. They knew the importance of faith, especially a shared faith.

Represented among the crew of 82 were thirty-eight denominations, all professing belief in the Eternal Christ Jesus, Savior of the world. One of the things that Abe and Sturdy brought was a healthy dialogue when it came to doctrinal issues, stressing that the believers remain united, agreeing to disagree on various points without needing to force others to believe exactly as they did. All agreed that all authority belonged to God alone. Many had not changed their views but had changed in their willingness to accept other believers, as long as they agreed on the important issues. A simple statement of faith was drafted and accepted by the entire crew. Lutherans, Baptists, Methodists, Pentecostals, Anglicans, Presbyterians, Independents, and others lived in unity under the banner of Christ because they knew He desired that commitment. This did not mean there were not heated arguments or hurt feelings, distrust and other emotions when one's core beliefs are brought into question. Yet their family perspective and deep love for one another won the day each time those occasions arose.

The local Vicar said the benediction and Sir Angus expertly shattered the bottle of Champagne on the bow of the ship as the brakes were released, allowing the huge cradle carrying it to slide into the water. On board the crew formed a circle, holding hands, and at Jim's nod shouted: *"Bring It Up!" Sea Venture* was successfully launched.

Making the ship fast to the dock the cranes began to load the holds for the expedition while news people and other interested parties took tours of the ship. Some wandered off alone, watched, but never denied access to any place they wandered. Cabins and births were all prepared for the crew, but none had moved their personal belongings in yet, due to the curiosity factor and danger of losing valuable personal items.

The last of the curious was escorted off the ship and the crew gathered their duffle bags, suitcases, and other travel bags and climbed the gangplank, heading for their rooms. Tonight, they would sleep on board the ship, and early the following morning set sail for Alaska and their first port of call, Kotzebue. No watch was posted on the ship. Instead, Calvin Beardsley hired a professional security company to patrol the dock. A Chinese man, who had been on board the ship earlier, saw the guards and decided not to try to approach the ship again. Zeke watched him walk away to his car.

Inside his car the Chinese man made a phone call, which Zeke immediately captured and recorded. The conversation was in Mandarin, so he fed it through his computer system getting an instant translation in English flashing across his center screen, rather than getting Jim or Mark up to translate for him as he listened.

"There are no guards posted on the ship itself, only on the dock. Earlier, on the ship, I was permitted to go anywhere without surveillance. Looking at the manifests it is obvious they are going to the Arctic Circle to fulfill the contract for AOOS. Nothing suggested a military presence, other than the men of the crew. My earlier search turned up nothing suggesting they knew about the Trans Alaska Pipeline plans. In the morning I will fly to Alaska and join Xun Hao there. We will watch them closely and take any appropriate steps necessary. Do you have any other orders for me, Master Wu?" there was a pause at the other end of the line.

"Be wary Jing Ke Yi. I know you are skilled, but Xun is your master, and she claims she cannot defeat the captain, or the man named Mark. Follow her orders. Do not make the same mistake her brother made. Call me if there are any developments in Alaska." Wu clicked off.

"Got him!" Nelson said as Wu hung up. "Guangzhou corporate headquarters for the Zhanzhu family. This must be Yao Li Wu, new CEO of the corporation."

"Interesting protections on the computer systems in the building!" News added, his hands flying over the keyboard. Like Zeke he used more than one keyboard, sometimes simultaneously. "I'm in. Let's see what this corporation is up to!"

Zeke grinned. He, News, and Cecilia sat in the CIC at their own computer stations, surrounded by multiple computer screens, and supported by three Cray super computers giving them incredible power. Zeke knew that no one spotted the three Crays hidden among the banks of servers. There was a fourth Cray on board, in the Science Computer Lab that everyone who would note such things must have seen. His crew of computer experts had the capabilities to do more with computers than ever before, and he loved it. Even the speed at which information flashed across his screen pleased him. Every system was the newest operating system available, and information was more accessible than ever.

"Roger that, News. Love this system!" Zeke replied.

Early the following morning *Sea Venture* moved out into the Channel and got underway. Wrench, Inchworm, and Goody moved through the engine room checking gauges, seals, and making minute adjustments to the four 12-cylinder GE diesel engines powering the ship. Each one generated 6,574-horsepower and presently were synchronized perfectly and running strong. Experts in hearing what an engine was doing as it ran, they detected no problems.

On the bridge Jim stood at the wheel getting a feel for the helm. Unlike his other two vessels this one responded with much more precision and power. Above him the helideck shaded the tinted front windows. Twenty-three meters in diameter it now supported the CH-53D Sea Stallion. In his head Jim did the math and converted the metric system to feet and inches, reminding himself that the deck was a little over seventy-five feet five inches in diameter above him. He liked the shading effect.

"How does he feel?" John asked, coming into the bridge.

"At this speed I believe he could come about in the space of his overall length!" Jim exaggerated, allowing a small smile of satisfaction to appear on his face for a moment. His eyes continued to scan the equipment around the wheel. Between those scanning looks he watched forward, to either side, and in the mirrors reflecting what was aft. There were only a few times he would be here, he knew, and enjoyed the experience.

"With the Rolls Royce azimuth retractable thrusters and the tunnel thrusters GE produced, this guy is quick to respond," Jim added. "You can feel it."

"Smitty, what's your feel for the DP system?" John asked, moving into the navigation part of the bridge. DP stood for Dynamic Positioning and Smitty was responsible for most of the equipment in that area.

"With this equipment I can pinpoint our position with a high degree of accuracy, JR!" Smitty declared with a huge smile. "It took a couple of hours of work to configure in the E6B, but Zeke and News figured out where the problems were and fixed them. The automatic microwave position system didn't like the E6B configuration, according to News, and he had to give it an attitude adjustment," Smitty smiled again. "Computer geeks!" he added as Zeke came through the door.

"And proud of it!" Zeke responded without missing a beat.

"Kongsberg's AS, SDP21 is top of the line, but the idiots configured it with a Dell! I practically had to tutor it to work properly with a Mac front-end system, but it's behaving now," Zeke said, nodding at JR as he passed out of the bridge. Smitty and JR grinned at each other. Neither understood what Zeke had just said, but that was par for the course. JR knew it had something to do with the difference between Macintosh operating systems and lesser operating systems. At least to Zeke they were lesser operating systems. Zeke swore by Mac and would not allow any other computer operating system on the ship!

Jim followed the shipping lane through the Channel and out to the Atlantic with ease, letting the autopilot do most of the work. While the ship moved sedately along at the prescribed speed of twelve-and-a-half-knots, just fifty percent of the maximum revolutions to conserve fuel and limit pollutants, he noted once again the striking colors of the ship.

Sea Venture's hull was aqua blue, and the superstructure pearl white, with the burgundy trim showing on the walkways and railings. Cranes and other steel structures were painted pearl white. Eight enclosed twenty-five-man lifeboats, four on each side, were tucked away beneath walkways and out of the weather. On one side the HSB was also tucked into an open alcove, while opposite the two submersibles shared a birth. *Steel Crab* and *Sea Bullet* both followed the color scheme of the company, but the HSB was camouflaged to disappear on the surface of the water, a mixture of grays, greens, and blues in a digital pattern that made it difficult to pinpoint amidst the waves.

Tucked into one of the holds the AH-1W Super Cobra and PBY, positioned to be raised to the deck and prepared for takeoff in only minutes, meant both were also protected and out of the weather. Jim glanced back over the huge deck area noting that snow was beginning to lie on the surface. England rarely bored one with mundane weather! Men and women on deck moved carefully, because of the slippery conditions, but spirits were high, and Jim saw smiles on every face despite the inclement weather.

Dorf came into the bridge, ducking through the hatch and

standing up carefully. On the bridge there were spots he could easily hit his head. He looked around as he dusted snow off his gloves and clipped them to his utility belt before stepping carefully to stand beside Jim.

"All secure, Shep," he said easily, looking out the front window. Like Jim he liked the shading from the helipad and thought that it would be very nice to have that shade in the southern hemisphere. "This ship rides differently," he added.

Before Jim could reply the hatch opened once more and Wade stepped through. John stepped over and the two exchanged a high-five slap of hands that echoed in the room before Wade moved over to stand beside Dorf. The bridge was large enough to accommodate everyone.

"Wait until you feel how it handles!" Jim said, stepping away from the wheel. Wade's smile widened as he stepped in.

"Commander Adams has the wheel," Jim said, automatically. Every voice in the room repeated the words to show they heard. Ship policy demanded such repetition, and no one thought it odd or not worth following.

"You lettin' a Marine drive?" FM's voice sounded over the headset. "There's a whole passel of traffic out there, Captain!"

"Aargh!" Wade growled. "Let's get some scratches on the paint, some blood on the deck, and see how many ships we can send to a watery grave! There's one!" Wade twisted the wheel, surprised at how quickly the helm responded and the ship turned.

"What ham-fisted lubber just tried to change lanes?" Goody's voice piped up.

Jim grinned as Wade brought the ship back on course with a smoother motion. Some of his crew tended toward the comical, and Wade was one that loved acting. John, going along with the fun grabbed his binoculars and trained them on a pleasure boat some distance from their bow.

"Let's see how that pleasure craft passes through the screws, Commander!" John urged with an evil grin.

"Don't you dare!" Inchworm snapped, as if the two were serious.

"We just plated those screws, and this water is too cold to go down and do it again!"

The bantering went on as the ship moved through the channel. Chuckling at his crew's antics Jim left the bridge for his own inspection of the ship. Stepping out into the blustery winter weather he breathed in a deep breath and sighed with pleasure. It was great to be back at sea again. He might miss the staff at Hill House, but this was his true love.

Of course, a brand-new ship seemed to make everyone work a little harder at keeping it pristine, and Jim certainly found nothing out of place or out of order during his two-hour inspection. He noted the steel steps winding down into the bowels of the ship and knew he and his men would run those steps until they knew each one intimately.

Down in the engine room he could feel the vibrations of the huge diesels like a pulsating source of power, hidden, dangerous, and mighty. Once he opened the hatch into the engine compartment, he found Goody and Inchworm busy over one of the engines. He paused beside them as Wrench joined them, holding up a small o-ring coated in oil. Goody nodded, took the rubber part, and slid it in place, closing the section he'd opened. All three of them looked at a gauge before nodding and turning to Jim.

"Bit of fluid leaking around that port set off a warning. We'll check them all now. This o-ring was defective, cracked here, which allowed it to leak," Goody said, explaining and pointing out the miniscule crack.

"What would cause that?" Jim asked, genuinely curious.

"When you put these on, they should be dipped in oil, like we did. Oil helps set the seal and keep it from drying out. This one was put on dry and if the injector sat for any length of time it would crack like that. That's why we'll check them all and replace them all, just to be on the safe side," Goody explained. "Of course, it could just be a defective ring. You never know. My guess is they were all set dry in the factory. If I find that to be true, I'll write it in a report, and we'll complain about it. Someone was careless, and the company will want to know. GE is very careful about that kind of thing," he finished.

"Let me know, and copy me on the report, please," Jim said, nodding.

Goody sketched a two-fingered salute as Jim turned to leave. His inspection assured him that his mechanics were on top of things, and had already caught a problem, studied it, and solved it. He was surprised at how proud that made him feel. Wrench watched the captain take the steps two at a time as he climbed out of the engine compartment with a smile. He'd learned that Captain Shepherd was a unique leader of men.

"Always a please at the end of a request!" he said, shaking his head. "I swear I'm never leaving this crew until I retire!" Wrench grinned at Goody.

CHAPTER 7

Rivers Noatak, Selawik and Kobuk drain into the Kikiktagruk or Kotzebue Sound near Kotzebue. Kikiktagruk, pronounced *qikiqtagruk* in Inupiat, was a trading and gathering center for the entire area. After all, the rivers that drained into the Kotzebue Sound formed a center for transportation to points inland. In addition to people from interior villages, inhabitants of the Russian Far East came to trade at Kotzebue. Furs, seal-oil, hides, rifles, ammunition, and sealskins were the most popular items traded.

In the Inupiat language the name Qikiqtagruk means "almost an island" which is an apt description of the spit of gravel upon which the town was erected. Located 66° 53' 50" N x 162°35' 8" W Kotzebue lies on a gravel spit at the end of the Baldwin Peninsula. It is approximately 33 miles north of the Arctic Circle on Alaska's western coast. Gateway to Kobuk Valley National Park and other natural attractions of northern Alaska the city serves as a supply point for inland towns and villages.

Sea Venture docked on the 15th of May to resupply, having ordered everything necessary shipped there ahead of time. A tug nudged the ship to the dock behind a cruise ship that dwarfed *Sea Venture*. Jim watched his crew work, making sure the ship was secure, and went to the gangplank already being lowered to the dock to pay for dockage and to pay the captain of the tug for his service.

He was in his full-dress uniform and Jing Ke Yi watched him through narrow eyes. Mark, up on the helideck, gazed through his binoculars and spotted Xun hanging back among some brick buildings. He pressed the talk button on his communication headset and spoke quietly to Jim.

"Xun is here. Jing is at four o'clock," Mark announced.

Jim nodded his head and clicked his button twice to acknowledge the transmission.

After caring for the formalities, with Rock 'n Roll beside him for the documentation Jim turned back to *Sea Venture*. Jing sauntered into his path and stopped, expecting Jim to do the same. Realizing what the Chinese man was trying to do Jim changed directions abruptly and went around the man, making sure Nelson followed suit. But Jing followed, much to Xun's dismay, stopping them at the gangplank.

"You are Captain James Shepherd, are you not?" Jing asked, his dark eyes flashing anger.

Sturdy, Dorf, and Bear approached from behind Jing, and he looked nervously at the huge men and stepped away. Jim immediately motioned for Nelson to go first, and followed, and they went up the gangplank. Grinning at Dorf Jim nodded for them to turn about, and they did, leaving a very frustrated Jing at the bottom.

"Give Xun my regards," Jim said over his shoulder, seeing the narrowing of Jing's eyes. Jing hadn't expected to be known as an associate of Xun. He spun on his heels and left, frustrated that he had not been able to goad the captain into aggression.

On deck Jim assembled the crew. Outside the temperature was a moderate 60°, warm for that time of year, so everyone was wearing their dress uniforms with the coats. Rather than having them stand in lines Jim ordered the crew to make a semi-circle around him. Once everyone was close enough to hear he spoke.

"Xun is in town with her partner Jing. Try to avoid them if possible. You all have three days leave. All meals are your own responsibility. Enjoy the local food and culture. We'll load the supplies in four days, and then depart for our next port of call. This is our chance to visit this town and see its treasures! Enjoy your visit. Discover everything you can. I'll expect a scintillating report when we meet to discuss what we learned," he smiled and waved that they should disembark.

Jim was pleased to see that instead of breaking into their three teams, the crew was back to sticking together. He smiled as Wade took Angela's tiny hand in his and walked down the gangplank. Cecilia wormed under his arm and smiled up at him. Jim smiled down at her.

"Are you ready to enjoy the company of your Captain?" he asked, kissing her nose.

"Is it ever warm here?" she queried, reaching up and grabbing his face and pulling it down for a kiss.

"June and July are the warmest. But it is warm today, for May. The average in May is just a little over 50°. It's ten degrees warmer today! Of course, the record low in May was -22°, so the weather is quite unpredictable. Kotzebue is a lot like a woman!" he grinned as he said the last.

"You're going to pay for that!" Cecilia chided with a smile. They were the last to walk off the plank, leaving the ship unguarded and unmanned. Jing counted them as they came off. People that had something to hide didn't leave a ship unguarded! Since he'd already toured the ship in England he left.

Still, he wasn't satisfied. The crew, except for the scientists, was obviously military. Xun told him about Mark and Jim defeating her, and he found that difficult to believe. Hung Fat and Tiger Fist were formidable martial arts, and he had yet to meet someone, other than Xun, that could defeat him. In a short period of time, she would no longer be his master; he would be the master. Even with that thought he felt his own strength with a deep sense of pride.

Jim noted that the children of Kotzebue flocked to the taller men of his crew, especially Sturdy and Dorf. Wade too got a lot of attention, as did Bear and Santa. His men were gentle with children, very protective, and Jim felt that the children must instinctively realize that. Parents looked on first with hesitation and then amusement as the giants played with the kids.

Sturdy, despite his burnt and scarred face, would lift the children to his shoulders and carry them about, or he and Abe would toss them back and forth while the children squealed with delight. Of course, the clowns of his crew were busy entertaining the children as well. Even JR was having fun.

Jim watched him with an amused smile on his face as his brother rushed at Sturdy, grabbing him about the waist, pretending to try to wrestle him to the ground, while Sturdy continued playing with the children. All the children laughed at this outrageous behavior. Eventually he would step back and wave a finger at Sturdy.

"Let that be a lesson to you!" he would say, and the children would giggle.

Jim and Cecilia sought out the Tribal Council chambers and Jim sat and talked to men of the council for most of that morning. They were proud of their heritage, and Jim, who always did his homework, praised them for the NANA Regional Corporation's successes over the past year. NANA Regional Corporation was one of thirteen Alaska Native Regional Corporations created under the Alaska Native Claims Settlement Act of 1971 (ANCSA) in settlement of Alaska Native land claims.

Jim knew NANA's mission was to improve the quality of life for the Inupiat shareholders by maximizing economic growth, protecting, and enhancing their lands, and promoting healthy communities with decisions, actions, and behaviors inspired by their Inupiat Ilitqusiat values consistent with their core principles. In his opinion, the organization was very good at keeping the best interest of its people in the forefront of every decision.

The NANA region in northwest Alaska encompasses 38,000 square miles, or 98,000 square kilometers, about the size of the state of Indiana. Most of it is north of the Arctic Circle and coterminous with the boundaries of the Northwest Arctic Borough. About 7,300 people living in 11 communities populate the region, with more than

85 percent of the region's residents of Inupiat descent. Before NANA the poverty in those regions was a serious problem.

Until 1971, land ownership issues in Alaska were divisive. Oil was discovered on Alaska's North Slope and naturally, Alaska Natives, including the Inupiat of northwest Alaska, worried about maintaining rights to traditional lands and the ability to protect their subsistence resources. Jim knew that subsistence played a key role in the lives of the Inupiat. In fact, he envied them because they lived off the land, hunting, fishing, and cultivating their food. He also knew that the preservation of subsistence resources is a vital element of the Inupiat culture and values. He was glad that ANCSA helped resolve many of the issues surrounding land rights. The tribal leaders were impressed with his knowledge of their history and efforts.

NANA lands make up one of the largest, unexplored onshore basins in North America. The land is mineral-rich, and NANA works with its partners to develop the resources to the benefit of its shareholders. But through all of that the Inupiat believed that subsistence is the highest and best use of their lands and so regulated all projects so that they were in alignment with that priority.

In 2013 NANA Regional Corporation, Inc. announced a shareholder dividend of $7.72 per share. That meant that approximately $12 million dollars was paid to NANA's more than 13,000 Inupiat shareholders. Millions of dollars were also contributed to scholarships, medical, burial, and disaster assistance, village economic development, language preservation, and other important social, cultural, infrastructure and energy programs for shareholders and Northwest Alaska.

Explaining the purpose of his archaeological search for the sacred cave Jim so impressed the Tribal Council that he received permission and the blessing of that august body in his pursuits. He also met with Board Directors of NANA, receiving the same blessing and permission to explore in Brooks Range. In both cases he left behind men and women impressed with his ambassadorial skills as a negotiator.

In fact, the men and women of the *Sea Venture* crew made a very good impression on the people of Kotzebue. Extremely polite and very curious about everything native, by late afternoon news had spread and doors were opened to them wherever they went. Jim and Cecilia, walking down one of the main streets of Kotzebue saw Wrench and Goody helping a mother with three children who was experiencing car trouble. Curious people watched to see what would transpire.

He and Cecilia wandered over to see what the situation was. Goody looked up as they approached. He had removed his dress jacket and rolled up his sleeves, and he and Wrench were under the hood checking the engine. Goody nodded.

"Hey Shep!" he said by way of greeting.

"What seems to be the problem?" Jim asked.

"Starter is gone, and this lady has a battery so old and tired the poor thing has gasped its last!" Wrench said, looking up. "Inchworm is across the street getting what we need." He added. Indeed, Inchworm was coming out of the store carrying a starter under one arm, and a battery in his other hand by a carrying strap. They looked to be heavy, so Jim moved across the street and took the battery.

"Thanks, Shep." Inchworm grinned.

Jim put the battery on the ground near the front of the Grand Wagoneer and watched as the three men quickly hooked up the new battery. Wrench found a cardboard box somewhere that he had broken down to lay flat, slid it under the vehicle, and from beneath hooked up the new starter. They all stood there for the fifteen minutes it took him to wrestle the heavy piece of equipment in place and hook it up properly.

Goody was examining the belts and he shook his head. "These need to be replaced," he said. Jim, who was holding one of the little boys nodded. Quickly crossing the street Goody purchased a new serpentine belt and another belt, bringing them back to adjust them properly. He also brought back a bottle of Gojo hand-cleaner and some shop rags. When Mike Romentowski slid from beneath the vehicle his face and hands were filthy. He accepted the Gojo with a nod, and cleaned hands and face, glancing in the side mirror of the Jeep Wagoneer often to check his work. Jim waited patiently, knowing that eventually he would hear the story. Wrench put all the dirty rags in the store bag and turned to Jim.

"We're related," Wrench said, nodding at the pretty woman.

"How's that?" Jim asked with a smile.

"Her last name is the same as mine!" Wrench said with a wide grin. "She's a long-lost cousin."

"Her husband is working at the Red Dog Mine, so he wasn't around to fix the car. When we noticed she was looking under the hood with a lost expression we decided to ask if we could help in any way. Once she told us her story we decided to help, since she's his cousin," Inchworm said. He was now holding the third child.

"What do I owe you?" the shy woman asked. It was obvious she was worried about the price of fixing her car.

"Just spending time with these great kids is all the payment we need, ma'am," Jim assured her, handing her the boy he'd been holding.

"But the parts!" she cried, dismayed.

"You'll have to understand that these men live to be knights in shining armor, constantly coming to the rescue of a fair maiden in distress," Cecilia laughed, hugging the woman. "You wouldn't believe how they rescued me!" she added, smiling at Jim.

Goody got behind the wheel, turned the key, and the car started easily. He got out, gathered the old parts and Gojo, and held the door for the woman. She got her kids settled in their car seats and with tears in her eyes drove away.

"Very noble," a bantering voice said from behind Jim. He turned to see Jing standing there.

"Just helping a poor gal stuck with three kids," Jim commented urbanely. He took Cecilia's hand, but Jing stepped in his way.

"I hear you're very good with your hands and feet," Jing said, his eyes shining with the desire to fight. Suddenly Jing threw a kick, and to his surprise Jim avoided it easily. He walked away with Cecilia.

"You should watch it with the captain, buddy," Wrench warned quietly, looking Jing up and down. "Just a friendly warning," he added as he and Goody and Inchworm moved away together.

Frustrated, Jing baited Jim twice more during the afternoon.

Finally, in a rage he leaped out from between two buildings not at Jim, but at Cecilia. Two policemen passing by saw the attack and screeched to a stop, but Jim was already moving. Jing's kick never touched Cecilia, but it did ensure that Jim was now ready to fight. Excited that he had finally engaged the famous Jim Shepherd, Jing launched a full attack while the policemen watched with concern.

At first Captain Shepherd merely blocked his kicks and blows, as if measuring him. Jing had power, and he was fast, one of the fastest Jim had ever faced, but his art limited his ability, and when Jim was satisfied he knew enough, he countered. Suddenly, as he was completing a vicious kick, Jing felt the blow smash him to the ground with a punch so hard it took away his breath. He rolled quickly to his feet, but Jim was already there and a second and third blow landed. Each blow was like being hit by a sledgehammer, and Jing felt his jaw shatter with the last blow. Trying to roll with the punches, to block them, he was helpless, and Jim's final kick sent him flying six feet through the air to thump against a brick wall and slide unconscious to the ground.

Both policemen moved up slowly, and Jim relaxed when he saw them, standing up straight, no longer in his fighting stance. They saw in his eyes something that made both of them wary. What they'd just seen had been fast, so fast the human eye could barely follow the moves. To them, it was obvious that Jing had begun the attack, and done most of the fighting, but Jim had certainly ended it authoritatively.

"What's going on here?" One of them asked softly.

"I'm truly sorry, sir." Jim said, letting go of the aggression. "He tried to hurt my wife. She's pregnant." Jim replied evenly.

"I saw him jump at her," the other policeman agreed. "Then he attacked you. He seemed pretty competent as a fighter."

"Black Tiger Fist and Hung Fat Kung Fu. It's very impressive as a dance form, and for producing power, but as you can see, not much use in a real fight," Jim replied, shaking out his fist and feeling the bits where he'd be bruised. As fast as Jing was, he hadn't been able to hurt Jim. *You've still got it, Marine!* Jim smiled at his thought.

"Do you know why he attacked you?" the lead officer asked, pulling a notebook from his pocket.

"Because he is full of pride and very foolish," a Chinese voice answered from the side. It was Xun. "He is a student of mine. I am training him in the art of Black Tiger Fist and Hung Fat. Today's lesson, I fear, will not dull his desire to defeat you, Mr. Shepherd," Xun said, looking at him with hatred in her eyes.

"Do you want to press charges against him, sir"? the lead officer asked.

"You really can't put someone in jail for being stupid and hope it will do any good," Jim philosophized with a slow smile. Then he looked at Xun. "If he tries to hurt my wife, who is with child, I will kill him." He said in Mandarin. She nodded once.

"You will do what you must do," she replied in the same language, bowing. Jim bowed in return.

When he looked at the policemen, he realized they hadn't followed the words he spoke, but they were still wary and unsure what to do. It saddened him that Jing pushed things to this point, but he'd protected his wife and unborn child from harm. He had no regrets.

"I think we can let it rest, sir," Jim said. "Thanks for stopping. Can my wife and I treat you two to dinner?"

"No need for that, sir," the lead officer said, putting his notebook away. There was something going on behind the scenes here, but he couldn't put his fingers on it and guessed correctly it had to do with some previous conflict between the Chinese woman and Captain Shepherd. He eyed Jing, still unconscious. "Do you think he needs an ambulance? I don't like the sound of his breathing and his face is swollen pretty badly."

"His jaw is shattered. He will need medical attention," Jim replied.

"Right then!" the man said.

"I will take him to the clinic," Xun announced to the police officer. "His foolishness does not need to extend to the use of important resources like an ambulance," she put her hand over her fist in recognition of his authority and bowed her head. To the police officer it was an odd thing to do, but he understood the intent. He nodded.

"Can you come to the station and make a report, sir?" the lead officer asked, turning to Jim. Perhaps this stranger could fill in the blanks he knew were there.

"If you'll give us a lift, we'll be more than happy to do that," Jim replied. He walked away with the two officers and Cecilia, and they went to the station to give their statements. Jim explained why Xun hated him, and why Jing probably attacked him. The policemen had, of course, read of the discovery of the City of Z and the adventures of *Bring It Up*. The presence of these two Chinese operatives concerned them.

"Why are they here in Kotzebue?" Officer Pungowiyi, the lead officer in the car asked. Jim's estimation of the officer proved correct. He'd gone to the very heart of the question. Sighing, he realized that he knew part of the answer, but was not at liberty to share that with these men. All of this passed through his mind without showing on his face.

"I don't really know," Jim mused. "They might be here because they knew we would be here and are out for revenge," he suggested finally.

Later, after his jaw had been set, Jing winced in pain while Xun chastised him verbally for his foolishness. Unable to respond he took the rebuke, but his eyes told her there was trouble ahead. Her brother had been much the same. Jing vowed in his own mind that he would have his vengeance on Jim Shepherd.

In his own mind he went over the fight, remembering feeling powerful and in control when suddenly everything changed. How had an American moved with such grace and power, and how had he defeated Jing's attack? Remembering the power of those blows he winced again, feeling the pain, and channeling it into resolve for revenge. Xun shook her head.

CHAPTER 8

At Cecilia's suggestion, Jim made the trip from Kotzebue to Barrow a slow trip with frequent stops to enjoy whale pods, sea lions, and other natural wonders Alaska offered. His science team went into action recording everything, testing the water temperatures, testing for toxins in the water, and recording whale sounds. Each day was filled with new discoveries, amazing beauty, and excitement.

In the evenings, during the Bible study and prayer sessions they held Jim heard the underlying concern in everyone as they faced their toughest challenge yet. Not only were they facing human enemies, but they were in the most unforgiving climate in the world, a climate without mercy, unpredictable, and deadly. Coupled with that was the danger of natural predators. In the slightly early thaw, there had already been two deaths recorded and attributed to bears. Bears that awoke from hibernation early were notably more aggressive and dangerous. Knowing that his team understood the dangers he also realized they were facing their fears with courage and prayer.

Jim set up the shooting range on the deck so they could get used to firing the weapons they would carry in the cold. Shooting a revolver, especially a .44 Magnum was very different than shooting a pistol. Jim practiced with and without gloves, learning the differences, working until he could place every shot exactly where he wanted it.

He found that shooting without gloves was preferable, but he bowed to the necessity that he might very well not have time to get them off before he needed to take a shot. Therefore, he practiced hard.

Some men were born with a natural affinity to shooting, and Jim was one of them. There were few that could match his skill with pistol and none with a revolver. John and Wade watched Jim place all six shots within the space of a quarter in his target and shook their heads, grinning. Red Claw had them putting the targets where they might be if facing a Grizzly or Polar Bear. Standing upright, on all fours, and running at them the targets all represented real danger, and no one missed the reality of the practice. Chief was teaching at the moment.

"Remember," Chief said seriously, "if the bear gets on you shove your revolver into its mouth and keep firing!"

"How in the world are you supposed to think straight when something like that is happening?" Dr. Wonderland asked, shaking her head.

"You have to stay calm or you're dead," Chief replied simply. "Even if you play dead a bear can still do horrible damage. When God made Grizzly's, He gave 'em a rage you wouldn't believe. And Polar Bears are just plain mean and cunning. You see one, shoot in the air. If it runs, good! If it doesn't, drop it where it stands! With Polar Bears there are no second chances! They're fast killing machines, destructive and bent on one thing: your death. Remember that!"

"Isn't that just a little bloodthirsty?" Tiffany asked, looking sad as she thought of someone shooting one of those beautiful animals. Although she had never faced such a creature in the wild, she couldn't imagine just killing it.

"Survival in battle is always bloodthirsty. If a Polar Bear decides it's going to come after you, your life depends on your accuracy with a rifle. It will kill you or you will kill it. That's the nature of dealing with these bears and with men set on killing, and it will be until God sets things right. Once He establishes His rule then bloodshed will no longer be necessary," Chief said. "I love those bears as much as you do, and I love life. But I love you more than one of those bears, and if one tries to eat you, I'm going to put it down," Tiffany blushed at Chief's words.

"Can't say as I blame the bear!" Santa said, looking at the twins and winking at them. "They sure look delicious!"

Bear moved behind them and rubbed his chin as if pondering. "Hmm! You have a point, Santa!" he said, licking his lips.

Everyone laughed, which was the intended result of the joking. Jim marveled at his men's ability to defuse situations like this without causing rancor among the crew. None of the girls ever took offense at such comments. Gwyneth patted Sturdy's arm.

"If a Polar Bear comes around us, we'll just show him Sturdy, and he'll turn tail and run!" she said with a smile at the giant.

He pulled Winky in front of him. "I'm ready for any bear attack!" he said fiercely. "I have my bait, and when the bear takes the bait, I can run!"

Winky flexed his impressive torso and grimaced. "I'll take care of it Sturdy. Don't worry my little friend. Winky will protect you!" That got more laughter. He said it with a very fake French accent, which made it even funnier to the crew.

Abe moved over to stand near Bear, stroking his chin as if in deep thought, staring at the man. Bear, knowing Abe was up to something funny, swallowed dramatically and took a slow step back. "I don't have a recipe for bear," Abe said, rubbing his chin. He looked at JimJim. "Do you?" JimJim and Abe both stared hard at Bear and he swallowed dramatically to more laughter.

JimJim looked at Bear, standing behind the twins, rubbing his chin, and nodded. "Broiling, I think!" he said.

René and Tiffer were suddenly hugging Bear. René looked accusingly at JimJim. "This is our Teddy Bear! You can't broil him!" she challenged. They looked so comical, their heads just reaching the bottom of his breastbone that everyone laughed again.

They reached Barrow on Monday of the second week of June. There was still snow on the ground in places, but it was melting away. Looking south toward the Brooks Range Jim saw that some of the slopes were visible, but the rest were still covered in white. In the range of his natural sight there were no less than four separate weather patterns, snow, rain, sunshine, and rain mixed with snow! He sighed. His wife was pregnant, and he was taking her into a virtually unexplored mountain range!

Zeke's voice sounded over his COMLINK. "Shep, could you please come to the CIC?" Jim responded in the affirmative and left his office, running up the steps to the CIC. He loved the steps on the new ship and the effort it took to run them.

"Xun and Jing are here. They've been checking our bona fides, making sure we actually have the contracts to do the two studies. I don't think they've tumbled to the pipeline patrol yet," Zeke said.

"Are they using disposable phones?" Jim asked, curious.

"Actually, they're using encrypted satellite phones," Zeke replied casually.

"And you were able to unscramble that code?" Jim asked, impressed.

"It's the Crays, boss!" Zeke said with some pleasure. "We ran a couple of algorithms and hey presto! Unencrypted phone!"

"So, what do we know?" Jim asked, grinning at his computer techs.

"They've dismissed us as a threat to the pipeline plan. Yao Li Wu is a little more suspicious. He doesn't agree that our ship poses no threat and has commanded that Xun and Jing follow your expedition," Zeke replied. "He must think you're going to follow the pipeline. That will help us. They'll follow you and allow John and his group to go virtually unnoticed."

"Why is he so suspicious?" Jim asked, sensing something more. Zeke looked crestfallen.

"Uh, well, he somehow discovered that his firewall had been breached and someone was listening in on both his phone and looking in on his laptop. He disposed of both, and he sent new phones to Xun and Jing. We've already got them. I've got his new computer too because he used the same firewall. I was able to get in undetected this time. Sorry about that," Zeke admitted.

"His techs are having kitten fits!" News said from his computer center. "They couldn't trace the signal and they don't know we're back in this time. His techs told Yao Li that it would take multiple Crays to do that, and there is only one on board our ship. I guess Jing missed the three in the server room." News was practically laughing.

"Does he suspect us?" Jim asked.

"He did. But now he suspects MI6. He's aware that they've taken an interest in his corporation," Zeke replied. "We're still suspect, though, as far as he is concerned, because I'm on the ship," Zeke added.

"How much does he know about you?" Jim inquired curiously.

"He has a full dossier on all of us, including our military records, that no one is supposed to be able to get, but everyone does!" Zeke sounded disgusted.

"Okay. Keep me posted. Do you know if our supplies are here?" he changed the subject.

"They arrived yesterday. When *Sea Venture* goes out, we'll be fully supplied," News reported.

From Barrow they sailed to Prudhoe Bay where the teams would separate for their unique missions. Once again, they moved along the coast enjoying the beauties of Alaska, taking their time but not wasting any. Once in Prudhoe Bay activity on board the ship increased as the sensing equipment ordered for the AOOS contract was loaded on the ship.

Jim went ashore to arrange for the twenty-one horses and eight pack-mules for his team. In the morning the horses would arrive near the ship and his team would load the mules for their journey into the Brooks Range. Knowing there would be gawkers and press surrounding their activities Jim thought about it and decided that was to their benefit.

When he returned to the ship, he stopped by the CIC to make sure everything had been loaded and the fuel tanks topped off. When he saw that all was as it should be, he nodded.

"Good. Let's get everyone in the conference room for our final planning session," Jim nodded.

Once they dropped anchor in the gentle swells the crew was called to the conference room. This room was large enough to hold everyone, filled with two horseshoe-shaped tables with 90 seats, each with its own laptop. No one had to shout to be heard, because a speaker system at each station provided the means for everyone to hear clearly.

Once everyone was in his or her respective seats Jim opened the meeting with a word of prayer. When he was finished, he nodded to Zeke and News, who fired up the computer systems, synchronizing the laptops. Whoever spoke would appear in a small screen at the top right of the computer. Jim was first to speak.

"Yao Li Wu is suspicious," he announced. "He's ordered Xun and Jing to follow our exploration team, which is to our benefit. Because of this, we will leave first, drawing them away, before John and his team unload the vehicles and get moving along the pipeline. They won't see the trucks and guess our plans. Where are we at with the vehicles?" Jim finished. He'd seen the men in the holds busy with the trucks.

"The NANA Regional Corporation logo decals are all in place. Anyone who spots the vehicles will assume we're bona fide. The Jeeps and Deuce-and-a-half are painted white, but we have the vinyl digital camouflage covers if we need them. They are magnetic for the body and fitted for the tops," John replied.

"Alice, is your team ready for the deployment of all that sensing equipment?" Jim asked.

"If we place it properly it will improve hazard forecasts for coastal communities, climatologies and syntheses, and for the first time, satellite systems will be able to determine ice thickness, extent, and trajectory. We'll also be able to keep tabs on acidification of the waters, shoreline and water level changes, and ecosystem conditions. That, of course, will help the integrated datasets and displays for ecosystems, fisheries, and water quality.

"With our sensors in place, and the underwater monitoring system we can track regional ecosystem assessments or syntheses, distributed biological observations, and provide early warnings for hypoxia, harmful algal blooms, and pollution," she was excited as she spoke, and Jim understood. What they could learn over the next ten years from this installed system could change everything. And we will have a copy of everything they learn! He smiled and nodded. For his science team information was always going to be top priority.

"Air support, where do we stand?" he asked.

"Air support is good to go, Shep," Dorf replied. "We'll unload the PBY now but wait until you've been gone a day or so before we bring up the AH-1W. Everyone knows we have it, but it won't hurt to keep it under wraps until later."

"Excellent. Communications?" he asked, looking at Zeke and News.

"News will be on the ship monitoring all three groups and keeping us all in communication. Remember that ship-to-shore transmissions can be heard by anyone, so be careful what you say. Many ears will be listening to our exploration team and the AOOS team. John's group is the only one that will used scrambled transmissions, and only to the ship," Zeke replied. "Our field radios are top of the line and all three teams have redundant back-up systems for communication."

"Brooks Range Team leaves at 0830 tomorrow morning," Jim said after a moment of thought. "Questions?" When none were offered, he nodded again.

"Everyone knows what to do, and we've trained hard. We have a sixty-day window of opportunity here. Let's make the most of it. Mark, will you close us in prayer, please?" Jim asked. He was pleased to see everyone stand and hold hands around the tables for the prayer.

Twenty-one horses and eight pack-mules stood in line, heads down, munching on some alfalfa spread on the ground in front of them. Jim checked the last mule, making sure the load was secure and balanced properly. He headed to the front of the line where Dr. Gregg already sat astride his feisty Appaloosa, patting its eager neck as it pranced, ready to begin. Grinning at his father-in-law Jim stepped into the saddle of his own horse, a beautiful black Friesian. None of them were at home in the saddle yet, but Jim loved riding and it all came back almost immediately. Guiding the horse expertly he took the lead, and standing in the stirrups, waved an arm in the traditional cavalry forward signal.

All that was missing was the loud "Forward Ho!" and Jim smiled as he settled in the saddle and adjusted his stance until he was moving in time with his horse. Cecilia trotted up to ride beside him, her face aglow as she rode. She loved riding horses. Being six-months pregnant didn't seem to concern her.

"I'm glad we're not doing this when I'm eight or nine months pregnant!" she said after a few miles, smiling at him, her face still glowing with excitement. "My hat is off to the pioneer women who did this!" she added. "This saddle is hard enough! Imagine riding on the hard bench seat of a wagon!"

"Is everything okay?" Jim asked, concerned.

"Your son loves riding horseback!" she laughed. Jim grinned, in spite of his worries. Cecilia always seemed to know the mood of her baby boy.

Instead of wearing their usual COMLINK headgear, they would be using walkie-talkies for the journey. Only a few of them had the radios that would reach the ship without anyone hearing the conversations. Jim lifted his unit to his lips and pressed the button.

"How's everyone doing?" he asked.

"Are we there yet?" FM's voice came over the radio.

"I have to go potty!" Stephanie Morris piped up.

"My butt hurts!" Dr. Mirelle said.

Good-natured laughter followed, and then everyone acknowledged that they were still good to go. Jim picked up the pace a little, wanting to cover at least twenty miles their first day out, and since they were on a dirt road leading out of Prudhoe Bay and following a stream at only a slight incline the horses did well.

"Shepherd One, this is *Sea Venture* News. Do you copy?" Jim replied that he copied News five-by-five.

"Roger that. A contingent of two horses and two pack mules left town an hour behind you," News reported.

"Copy News. Thanks," Jim replied. "Over and out."

Every hour Jim dropped back to ride along the line and talk to everyone in his party, making sure they were settling in. At the end of the day, though it would be light all night long, he stopped finally at a spot that looked promising for a camp. In short order the seven tents were up, including the supply tent, all in a neat configuration.

Jim and Cecilia would sleep in one tent, and Alistair and Gwyneth in another. All six girls would share the largest tent. The men would be divided into threes in the other tents. Jim and Cecilia, Alistair and Gwyneth would each have an escort of three of those men if they left their tents to use the facilities or for any other reason. Once camp was set up the perimeter fence was strung, and the generator turned on to energize it for a test. While they slept the fence would repel any bears or other predators. Guards would patrol the camp that night, three at a time, in two-hour shifts.

Once the fence was tested, they shut the generator off and sat down around a small fire. Self-heating MREs were opened and consumed. As usual the men traded parts of their meals. Jim was eating a roast beef dinner and Cecilia was enjoying her personal favorite, a turkey meal. They ate and talked until eight o'clock, when Jim announced curfew.

Their first night everyone was surprised that they slept soundly, despite the light of day that would continue for the next few months. Each unit of guards had nothing to report, traded a few comments, and switched. Jim took his tour of guard duty in the last three hours before waking the camp. He enjoyed taking that last shift, seeing the morning approach in a sky filled with daylight, getting a feel for the weather for that day.

CHAPTER 9

"**I**'ve got Xun and Jing about two miles back," Viper reported as Jim approached him.

"Just the two of them?" Jim asked, surprised.

"Yep," Viper snorted, pointing, and handing Jim his binoculars. Jim focused in on the camp and saw that the two didn't even have a tent pitched. *What will they do in bad weather?* Their two horses and two pack mules were hobbled, not tethered.

"If wolves get wind of those animals, they might spend a few days chasing them!" Jim chuckled.

"My guess is they're not that familiar with the territory," Viper replied. "Up until about an hour ago they were trading off every three hours or so keeping watch, I think. Anyway, as soon as Xun fell asleep Jing crawled back in his sleeping bag.

"He's awake," Jim shared, watching the man pick up his binoculars and train them on the camp.

Getting the camp up and ready to go didn't take long. Chief policed the camp, making sure there was no residue left of their stay, and nodded in appreciation. Everyone had cared for garbage and latrine duty exactly as commanded. In groups of three and four the campers moved to the horses, mounted, and prepared for another day's ride.

Jim felt better in the saddle and settled into a mile-eating pace early on. Smitty was guiding them, following some path that would lead them to the first cave. Chief, bringing up the rear, radioed ahead that Jing and Xun were following. Zeke grunted. It was a problem he knew would need some creative solution and he bent his mind, even as he spoke.

"I don't like it, Shep," he said, riding up beside Jim after a few minutes of thought. "They're assassins and we're out in the open here!"

"News will know if they're ordered to kill any of us, won't he?" Jim asked, his own face creased with worry. Zeke was right. He didn't like having them tailing him so closely. Finally, he lifted his walkie-talkie.

"Chief, can you come up here for a minute, please?" he asked.

Moments later Chief thundered up, his Appaloosa eager to run, reining it in and calming it without difficulty. Jim appreciated the way the man sat in the saddle, completely at home.

"What's up, boss?" he asked laconically.

"Would you please ride ahead and find a trail where we can distance ourselves from those two following?" Jim asked.

"Shouldn't you be calling him Kemosabe?" FM quipped to Chief.

"Does he look like some nuked sushi to you?" Chief responded with a deadpan face. Everyone who heard burst out laughing. "Chemo? Isn't that like some radiation thing? And what the heck is Sabe? Some kind of fish? Sounds like sushi!"

"It was what Tonto called the Lone Ranger," FM said, shaking his head.

"Idiot white man! Tonto was a Comanche. Do I look like a Comanche to you?" Chief shot back.

"I don't know. All the Comanche on TV looked like Italians!" FM replied without missing a beat.

"Will you two stop!" Cecilia burst out, wiping tears from her eyes. Like the others she had been laughing at the antics and statements. "You're making me laugh so hard my stomach hurts!"

"Kick her, kid!" FM said with a grin.

Cecilia pulled her foot out of the stirrup and kicked FM. "Don't try to teach my son bad manners!" she said, sticking her tongue out at FM, who was laughing at her.

Chief nodded at Jim, still grinning widely, and moved off ahead, looking for a trail to lose their shadow. His own smile in place Jim got the rest moving, knowing that Chief would return when he could. Half an hour later he returned, his rifle in his hand as he rode. When he pulled to a halt in front of Jim, he slid it back in the sheath attached to his saddle.

"Saw a bear up ahead. It took off running when it saw me, but it was a Grizzly, so I was cautious," he said when Jim raised an eyebrow. "There's a nice trail up ahead, all rock, we can turn left there. I rode ahead on the other trail for about a mile so they would follow the tracks. At least I hope they'll follow the tracks. I'll have my guys follow me on that trail for a while so they will probably follow it. That's where I saw the Grizzly. I'll bring up the rear and make sure we don't leave any tracks going up. As soon as you're up a way it turns again and follows a canyon, so we'll be hidden."

Chief turned and led them at a gallop to the place where the trail turned left, and waved his team to follow him, making more tracks before returning to follow. Later, after they'd returned to the turn-off, Hayseed led his horse while Chief brushed away any dirt or telltale sign they had passed that way, and when he was satisfied he ran ahead, turned the corner, and found his men waiting.

Soon they rejoined the others and waited quietly to be sure that Xun and Jing took the bait. They did, following the tracks at a walk, seemingly unconcerned, apparently unable to tell that the tracks went both ways in the dirt. Quietly Jim led them on up the trail, and they began to climb now, hidden by a canyon as they moved upwards, following a stream. One worry, for the moment was taken care of, at least for several hours. Jim sighed.

Back at the ship John watched as the Deuce-and-a-half was unloaded. It was the last vehicle and Wrench lowered the huge vehicle to the ground as gently as any chef might lower a freshly baked quiche. John noted that the springs didn't even depress. Shaking his head at the precision of the mechanic running the crane he climbed up and tapped on the glass. Wrench opened the window, slowing the engine.

"What's wrong, Captain?" Wrench asked, surprised to find his boss at the glass.

"That was beautifully done!" John said with a smile. "The springs didn't even bounce!"

"It's this crane, boss!" Wrench said, pleased by the praise. "I've never had one so finely tuned!" he added.

John held up his thumbs as the men below unlatched the hook of the crane. Smiling, Wrench lifted the hook up and parked the crane in the travel position, since he was done unloading all the supplies. Quickly he joined Goody and Inchworm as they checked the vehicles to make sure nothing had been jarred loose during the trip across the oceans. When they were satisfied, they put charged batteries in the vehicles and started them, listening with critical ear to the machinery. Each vehicle was test driven ten miles, hydraulic systems checked to be sure they were working properly, before they were returned, and the tanks topped off for John's team to begin patrolling the pipeline. John appreciated the care given to his equipment.

Pippi was already in the AH-W1, the turbines rotating at full speed as she completed her pre-flight check. Fully armed the helicopter rose from the ground. Earl Duncan was in the gunner's seat, and he read off the gauges as the chopper rose into the air, exchanging information with Penelope. John listened, knowing the drill, making sure the chopper was working properly. His wife and son were going to be up there! Even with everything working properly, a helicopter could still create problems for the pilot. He sighed and looked at the team, waving. The rest of John's team deployed to the vehicles.

Bear hopped into the six-wheeler. Bond and DC climbed into the second Jeep, Matthew behind the wheel. Lord Lee and Rock climbed into the Jeep behind them, with Ainsworth at the wheel. Weston and Geissler climbed into one of the two rear Jeeps. They would be patrolling all roads leading to and from the pipeline.

John and Wade climbed into the front Jeep, John at the wheel, and C.G. and Vince climbed into the second of the rear Jeeps. Vince was at the wheel, and he grinned at C.G. with anticipation. They both knew that most of what they would be doing was simply driving along one of the most beautiful routes in all of Alaska.

They set off with excitement and anticipation, and a few miles outside of town were able to switch to the hydraulics. It was odd, driving along at forty-five miles per hour and hearing only the scrunch of the tires on the gravel road running parallel to the pipeline. John and Wade drove ahead a mile and waited for the others to catch up, making the comment that they didn't hear them until they were just a few yards from their position. Delighted with the discovery they continued the journey, talking to each other about the wildlife they spotted along the way. For the most part it was Caribou, though they all spotted a large Alaskan Brown Bear.

Paul Donnelly, who was nicknamed Bear, received a good bit of teasing. After a particularly funny comment about it possibly being a sister he got on the radio, his voice deadpan and quiet.

"No. All my family are Grizzlies!" he joked. "Besides, my sister's butt is way bigger than that!" He didn't have a sister, but he did get a laugh from everyone. He continued. "When she passes wind all the doors blow out, and that's a feat, because all the doors at the house open inwards!"

"I have a lock on the REO," the impassionate voice of Donut came over the COMLINKS. Everyone laughed at that.

"Don't shoot! I'm done!" Bear said dramatically.

"We shoot the bad guys, not the bad jokers," Pippi chided, just as dispassionately.

"Oh! Okay," Donut said. "By the way, locking onto the REO is impossible with that pipeline right there," he added. "I tried locking onto the engine heat, but the oil pipe is nearly as hot!"

"I wondered about that," John spoke into his COMLINK. "Do your helmets still track individual targets?"

"Roger that," Pippi said. "The targeting systems in the helmets work for the mini, but missiles are going to be a problem."

"Blast!" John said with heat.

"Uh . . . what do you want me to blast boss?" Donut asked, getting another laugh.

Suddenly John slowed the Jeep as a herd of Caribou looked up startled at the appearance of the quiet vehicles. They scattered immediately and John looked over at Wade. They grinned at each other appreciating the beauty of the creatures as they bounded away. Wade pressed his talk button.

"Somebody radio Santa and tell him his reindeer are loose!" he said.

"Those are Caribou," John corrected.

"There were three reindeer over there on the edge of those woods." Wade pointed, and John saw one now, peeking out from inside the foliage.

"Wow! Neat!" he said.

"No! No! No!" Pippi said quickly. "You're practicing to be a dad! You say, 'look at the reindeer.'"

A chorus of whining voices suddenly sounded over the radio. "Are we there yet? I have to go to the bathroom! Daddy, D.C. is singing! Mommy, Rock won't let me play with my gun! It's my turn to drive. I want to drive!" John laughed and shook his head pushing his talk button.

"Children are supposed to be seen and not heard!" he said, repeating a line he'd heard his mother use often.

"Whoever said that never had kids!" C.G. replied.

"Whoever said that had kids like you!" Pippi said with a laugh. "I'm just passing over our first camp site. There are a thousand places a team of terrorists could hide out here," she added. That she had noted almost immediately, and it didn't make their job any easier.

"Roger that," John replied. He didn't think much of their chances either, but he knew that often God stepped in where man was out of his depths. "We knew that patrolling the pipeline was pretty much impossible. Let's hope we get blessed."

"Beginning our aerial sweep now," Pippi said over the radio.

It was half an hour before the AH-W1 passed overhead of the silent vehicles. From combat John learned that figuring out where a helicopter was coming from wasn't always possible. He was pleased when he found himself looking in the correct direction as the chopper showed up above them, and then realized that he knew the search grid patterns and so had anticipated that Pippi would follow them. Shaking his head, he grinned at Wade.

"I was proud of myself because I was looking right at the spot the chopper appeared. Then I remembered I knew the grid pattern!" he said.

"You could've checked the radar unit," Wade said, nodding his head at the unit in his lap. John laughed.

"Didn't think of it," he admitted, shaking his head again. Then his mood changed. "We have to be sharper than this to succeed!" he said, setting his jaw. Wade nodded. It always took a few hours to regain that sharp edge a soldier needed in the field after a few days of R&R.

By the time they reached their first campsite John noted that his men had entered that zone where every sense was on alert, and they were focused on the mission. The AH-W1 was already on the ground and covered with a camouflage net. Since all the camping gear was on the truck Duncan and Pippi had to wait until it arrived. Neither were near the helicopter when the truck pulled up.

"Arriving at camp," John said into his microphone.

"We're about a hundred yards north of camp," Pen replied. "We wanted to get back in the woods a little distance and see if we could hear the vehicles. Coming in now."

"You didn't hear us?" John queried.

"No. Not from our position," Duncan replied.

"Stealth mode!" C.G. said with a grin.

Quickly camp took shape. John's tent was the largest, a three-room Coleman cabin tent big enough to sleep ten people. He and Penelope would share one room, while Wade, Vince, and C.G. would occupy the other room. The rest had two-room tents made by Coleman. Raider had one tent and Sniper had the other. Everyone agreed they wanted to stay close together, and this seemed the best arrangement.

John and Penelope dug the latrine and set up the privacy curtain around it, and then put up the solar heated shower unit. When the tents were in place and everything else completed Sniper strung the electric wire around the perimeter of the camp while Zulu got the generator up and running to power the fence and provide electricity for computers.

Watching his men position themselves for the best vantages for defensive maneuvers John nodded in satisfaction. His men were ready for anything. Anyone stumbling upon their camp would immediately recognize it for a military camp just by the way the men arranged themselves spatially, and the weapons they kept near at all times. But that was their mission and purpose. Even his wife, pregnant though she was, had taken a position that gave her a clear arc of fire.

Penelope looked over at John and noticed him checking out positions. She smiled. "Our child is going to be born thinking about defensive maneuvers and offensive positions for the best deployment of munitions!"

"Good. He or she will appreciate the early training," John said with a wolf-like grin. "Getting him ready early seems like a good idea! This world isn't exactly a safe place," he added.

"Let's get our child out of diapers and through grade school before he or she learns too much military skill," Pen laughed.

"Yeah! You don't want the little kindergarten tike kicking some third-grader's bottom because the third grader is a bully!" Hobbs said lightly.

"They suspend kids for fighting these days," Bear said with a grunt. "They should just let them slug it out and learn. Fighting never solves anything!"

"This from a guy sitting with an M16A2 in his lap!" C.G. said.

"Yeah. Well, I got a job to do. But when the fighting is all over and the bad guys are stopped, have we really solved anything? No! There will be another group of bad guys that need to be put down. No, the fighting ain't gonna end until Jesus comes back and sets things to order!" Bear replied. He bit into his sausage, cheese, and egg burrito.

"Very philosophical!" C.G. replied with a grin. "I agree to a point, but I gotta ask the question we've all been thinking the past few weeks during Bible study: Is what we're doing furthering the Kingdom of God?"

"I think it is," Rock offered after a moment of thought. "We protect the innocent for the right reasons. We're not aggressors or despots. Our service is a necessary one that provides balance. What we're doing here is a good thing. Some very bad people have accepted money to destroy part of this pipeline. That will be very bad for the ecology of the district, dangerous to the animals and plant life God put here, and very dangerous to people. Terrorism of any kind is evidence of great evil in the human condition, and we stand against that. We've all seen the result of unchecked chaos and anarchy! Too many have already been affected by those results."

"But aren't we just as bad, accepting money from a government to stop them?" Lee said, folding his arms and shrugging. It was a valid question, and no one gave him a hard time for asking.

"The Bible is pretty clear about the need for governments to punish those that do evil. Our government, corrupt as it is, still recognizes law and order, up to a point," Norm sat back in his chair and crossed his feet. "That government has asked us to be the arm that provides law enforcement. We just have to be careful that we accept the job with the humility necessary to keep us in line. Any of us are capable of terrible evil, but we know that, so we pray, study, and work out our salvation with fear and trembling, knowing that God created us for good works. That's the measuring stick we use to determine that what we are doing is in keeping with His will and purpose, and therefore furthering His Kingdom."

"Well said, Counselor!" Wade nodded his head once. Norm grinned at him.

The conversation continued, each person adding something of value, and John listened intently. It never ceased to amaze him how deeply some of his men delved the philosophies and ideas floating about the world. Most of them knew their Bibles well, evidence of the many studies led by Abe and Sturdy. What came out in those discussions was the depth of their faith, and the goodness of their hearts.

CHAPTER 10

Xun and Jing came to the end of the tracks and cursed. An entire day was lost finding where their enemies turned off the trail, and another day was lost when they made a wrong turn again. Yet a third day was lost when wolves caused their packhorses to bolt in terror and they had to chase them down before continuing.

Jim's group knew and witnessed none of this, for they had enough problems of their own. It took several days for most of them to get accustomed to the saddles, even though they rode regularly before the trip. Riding a horse in rough terrain is different and riding one all day long takes a toll.

Each day Chief, Dr. Gregg, and Smitty would sit down and converse about the direction they wished to go. Often, because of the terrain, they were forced to go miles out of their way to reach a point on the map. Yet Jim knew none of his team minded the delay. This was amazingly beautiful territory, seemingly untouched by man, full of life. Every single vista they saw produced wonder and awe of God's creation.

It was also a cruel place. Temperatures could drop incredibly fast and one day they passed through rain and snow as they meandered up and down trails, shivering, wet, and miserable. Everyone brought the correct clothing for the trip but riding in the rain and wet snow wasn't pleasant, despite the proper clothing, and Jim thought about the explorers who first came to this land and the hardships they endured.

He kept his rifle clean and ready to use, and often eased his Smith & Wesson N Frame Model 29 .44 Magnum in its shoulder holster. On his right hip he carried his Ontario SP5 Survival Bowie knife. Constantly his eyes roved, seeking possible predators and danger, for now he had not only his wife to guard, but also their baby. Glancing over he saw Cecilia smiling at him.

"I'm quite fine," she said in her clipped BBC accent. "Our baby enjoys riding horseback!" she added, rubbing her stomach.

"At the moment he's probably the only one enjoying this day's ride!" Jim said, watching water drip from the brim of his hat.

"He is!" Cecilia said, tilting her head. "My parents had a girl first, but I'm having a boy! Why is that do you suppose?"

"Shepherd's always have boys first," Gwyneth said, riding up beside Cecilia and smiling at Jim. "Genetics are against having a girl first."

"Ah! I rather think you're both right," Cecilia said. "Judging from some of his kicks and punches he's going to be quite like his father!"

"Aye! He'll be a bonnie lad!" Alistair said from behind.

Ahead Jim saw Red Claw waving. Kicking his horse into a gallop he rode up the incline and reigned in, his Friesian rearing up and pawing the air with a fierce cry. Chief smiled at the man and horse, understanding both. Without speaking he pointed down the trail. Jim looked and saw one of the biggest Grizzly's he'd ever seen standing in the trail looking up at them.

For a few moments the two stared at each other, dark eyes boring into hard green eyes. The bear did not move. On all four paws he looked like he might tower to fourteen feet on his hind legs and his body was powerful and sleek. Jim studied the bear critically.

"He's not afraid of us," Chief said quietly. The growl of the bear at the sound of Chief's voice made the horses dance nervously. Red Claw noticed with appreciation that his Captain calmed his horse easily, sharing his own fearlessness with the huge horse. In answer to that sharing the Friesian reared again, pawing the air and sending out a challenging scream. Feeling his horse's mood Jim let out a rebel yell at the same time and was surprised when Chief joined with one of his own. There was an unexpected exhilaration in that act of challenge.

The bear stood up on its hind legs, turned, and padded off down the trail.

"We'll see that bear again," Chief said softly when the bear disappeared around a corner. As if to answer the bear grunted, its voice echoing up the canyon.

That night the wolves surrounded their camp until a warning shot from Viper sent them running off in the darkness. During the day they spotted the wolves following them. Fortunately, there were no narrow ledges to traverse that day because the horses were nervous and difficult to handle. Each night the riders checked the horse's hooves for rocks, cleaning them carefully before hobbling the horses and tying them securely to the picket line.

Once supper was finished in camp, and the guards in place, Cecilia opened her computer and hooked to the satellite feed to see if any caves were in the immediate area. Caves would be difficult to find in the present temperatures, but she was accessing photos taken two months before, when the heat signature from a cave exit or vent would be obvious.

To everyone's disappointment they were still a few days from the first cave. Again, that night, the wolves padded close to the camp and had to be driven off with a warning shot.

Sea Venture

On *Sea Venture* the first few days of their journey into the Arctic Sea was quite mild. However, the real problem was snow blindness! Alice and John made sure everyone wore sunglasses, even if they were just glancing out one of the windows. Low-grade headaches were a common problem in sickbay for the first few days as those who forgot suffered the consequences.

Sea Venture was equipped to break ice, but so far, they were merely pushing floating ice away from the bow of the ship as they moved through the lane selected for dropping their buoys and other sensing equipment. This was a dual effort because the sensors that needed to be submerged at a specific depth had to be anchored to the bottom with a length of cable and a flotation buoy at the top, with the sensing equipment located beneath the flotation buoy. That meant lengths of cable needed to be cut and then fastened to anchors or buoys.

Most of this was done in the machine shop on the ship where it was warm, but some of the work required being outside in the cold temperatures where waterproof insulated suits were valuable tools. Hands were the hardest hit because they often got wet and coupled with the cold, and working with steel cables, left aches and pains the workers rarely suffered elsewhere.

Dorf and Papa watched over the crew carefully as they supervised all the activities of the day and evenings. Dr. Axlerod and his wife René didn't take long to earn their own nicknames or endear themselves to the crew. Leo became "Dr. Gearhead" to the crew because of his name and his fascination with super cars. René became R&R because of the letter's "R" and "N" on her pin, and the first letter "R" of her name. Both seemed to appreciate the nicknames, recognizing them as terms of endearment from the crew.

René got used to people saying: "It's time for some R&R!" They became good friends with Will and Donna Penny but bonded closest with the Shepherds, who were closer to their own age. Papa, especially, looked out for the new couple during the first months of their duty and was very pleased with the way they settled into the routines of the company.

Though constantly surrounded by men of military bearing, René realized that she had nothing to fear from any of them. She came to look upon them as older and younger brothers, uncles, relatives with whom she was always safe. These men respected her marriage and never flirted with her. On top of that they respected her for her knowledge and understanding of her duties. She commented on that one day to Penny.

"Everyone treats me like I know what I'm doing! That's refreshing!" she commented after Walt Rule left the sickbay. He had an infection in one of his toes and she told him what he needed to do. He'd listened carefully, repeated her instructions, and thanked her.

"That's a special perk of working with this crew," Donna said. "They believe that every individual on the crew is vitally important to the whole operation, and that we are the experts in our field. They respect our knowledge and training, and they understand our value. We're quite safe with these men too. That's helps," she added.

"Why are they so different?" René asked.

"They are the kind of men that make our world a safe place to live. Honor is important. Each one has a personal relationship with the Lord Jesus and takes that very seriously. I've seen them fight as only brothers can fight with one another, and then hug and forgive each other with real repentance and true submission. These are men who believe that the Christian walk is attainable, and they follow Jesus. It makes them very powerful, and very vulnerable," Nurse Penny sighed.

"I hadn't thought of them as vulnerable," René confessed. Her eyes were puzzled as she looked at Donna. The comment gave her pause and her eyes narrowed as she thought about it. Nurse Penny didn't answer immediately. Finally, she spoke.

"Some of the things they have to do are horrible. None of them can take a life without taking serious hurt emotionally and psychologically. Listen carefully. You will never hear one of them talk about the men they've killed, or the men they served with who died. I was with them when they wiped out a band of soldiers so vicious that the world was at risk. Yet they have never spoken of those hours in the jungle when they fought for their lives against incredible odds. One would think they would climb on the rooftops and crow with pride. They don't. I think it has to do with the fact that they hate the killing, and even the necessity of killing.

"Deep down in their soul they know that killing is the worst result of sin. That people like they have faced needed killing was not a question. They did. But every one of those men who took those lives is haunted by the evil of it at a level you and I will never understand. They know the brevity of life and so they are casual when they face death, unafraid, because they have seen it many times and know that one day it will come for them. What they need most is to be doing what they should be doing when it happens.

"I don't know if there is healing for them. David didn't get to build the temple because he had blood on his hands. I've often wondered how he felt about that. Anyway, because they are such honorable men, they will do what is right, even if it means sacrificing their lives. And so, they are vulnerable on many levels," Donna looked at René with compassion.

"I guess I have a lot to learn," René said softly.

"And that, my dear, will take you exactly where you need to go!" Donna smiled. "Never stop learning. Never stop asking questions. Never be satisfied with the status quo!"

"Don't worry. I won't," René said, hugging her friend.

Later that evening she sat at a table with Ox, Santa, and Fagan. They were all entered in the Monopoly marathon and were the four finalists, fighting it out to the final victor. Quite a crowd gathered to watch the fun, tease, and cheer on their favorites. René listened to the men talk and discovered that despite what Donna told her they were generally light-hearted.

Only occasionally did she sense that depth of sorrow and horror she knew lurked beneath the surface. Fagan, of course, was up to his usual antics, putting on his most evil face when he took money from one of them, stroking his chin when it was his turn and humming the tune from *Oliver* that went with his character.

Despite his actions he was a good player and a good looser. Ox put him out of the game when he landed on one of his properties with a hotel on his first throw of doubles, and another property with a hotel on his second throw, also doubles. On his third throw he landed again on one of Ox's properties, lost the rest of his money, and ended up in jail. He retired from the game singing "I think I better think it out again!"

Santa, who owned one entire corner and one side of the board put Ox out of the game a few moves later, and René laughed as she approached his properties. She managed to miss his properties on two throws, and he shook a huge finger at her.

"There will be a lump of coal in your stocking this Christmas, young lady!" he said with a smile.

Stretching her money as far as she could she bought one of the properties that Fagan lost, and one that Ox lost, only to land on two of Santa's properties the next time around and lose it all. She got up from the table and curtsied to Steve, who nodded his head sagely as he counted his money.

"Okay! I'll forego the coal this time!" he said magnanimously.

"My husband would like a Mercedes AMG!" René said with excitement in her voice. Leo suddenly appeared and sat in Santa's lap. He put his head up and looked longing.

"Please Santa? Please! Please! Please!" he begged.

"Do you realize you could put somebody's eye out with that thing?" Steve asked, looking very serious! Everybody burst out laughing at that. "I've heard that if you slam on the brakes in an AMG the passenger's eyes come right out of their sockets, bounce off the windshield, and return backwards!"

"But I won't do that! I promise!" Leo pleaded, folding his hands in supplication.

"I'll see what I can do. It's going to make a mess of your chimney when I bring it down though!" he added. Leo jumped up.

"You all heard that! Santa promised to bring me a Mercedes AMG for Christmas!" he said.

René laughed aloud the following week when something banged against the register in the ceiling of their cabin. It was a silver Mercedes AMG die cast model in 1/32 scale, still in the box, with a ribbon tied around it and a note from Santa warning Leo not to put someone's eyes out. Her husband grumbled about having to unscrew the register cover to get it out.

At breakfast several of the men asked if they could have a ride in his new AMG. Eventually Leo approached Santa.

"I wanted a real one!" he complained, his lip thrust out in a pouting expression. Her husband had a very comical face.

"Oh! You didn't ask for a real one, son. I deal in toys! I though you knew that!" Santa said. "Ho! Ho! Ho!" he laughed.

"Eventually, Santa, you're going to need some shots! I've got a special syringe just for you!" Steve swallowed dramatically and everyone laughed as Leo stood pointing his finger at the huge giant of a man. Steve walked out of the dining room holding his hands on his bottom and wincing with every step.

It was moments like that René knew the crew looked for and appreciated. Everything else was routine and hard work, but occasionally they could all laugh about something, at someone, or at themselves. She stored that memory away and walked with her husband from the dining room. He kept the car on his desk.

CHAPTER 11

Warning shots fired at the wolves each night were only adding to the stress of Jim's team. The animals were getting bolder and bolder. Jim knew it was only a matter of time before they had to do something drastic. But Red Claw came up with a wild plan that actually worked.

Late one night he shot the leader of the pack with a tranquilizer dart, putting the animal down. He positioned himself so that the animal would fall at his feet as he stood up, a looming menace in the shadow of a rock outcropping. The other wolves hesitated as they saw their leader stumble and fall. Confused, because they didn't smell death, they moved back and forth some yards from the silent man. At his feet the leader remained still and unmoving, further confusing them as they nervously padded back and forth.

For twenty minutes he stood without moving, a huge knife in one hand, his pistol in the other. Eventually the pack leader whined, lifted its head, and stood. Unsteady on its feet it looked up at Chief, who stared back at it with teeth bared in a feral grimace. Slowly he showed the wolf the knife and the pistol, and then let them fall back to his side again.

Still groggy from the drug the wolf turned and moved away. After a few yards it regained its full motion and with an angry snarl called the others to follow. As they left, they cast looks over their shoulders at the silent man who remained without moving until they were out of sight. At last Chief sighed, moved his shoulders and neck relieving the strain of that stillness and turned to the camp.

"I think it worked," he said quietly. Walking silently, he headed back in. His team had been posted with good shooting positions. They stood as he passed and followed him in, walking backwards, making sure there was no threat.

The wolves did not return.

"How did you know that would work?" Jim asked the following morning as they sat eating breakfast.

"I didn't. Animals are notional. They could have attacked me, which would have meant several if not all would die. I was hoping it didn't come to that," Chief bit off some bacon, chewed it thoughtfully, and looked out over the wilderness. "I like wolves. For the most part they're clean animals. They may not be pretty, as a breed, but they do serve an important purpose in the balance of things out here," he said, biting off another piece of bacon.

In the middle of the day Chief, who had ridden ahead and was at a high point, looked back and saw a big Grizzly dogging their trail. The animal seemed to know Red Claw was watching it, because it rose on its hind legs, sniffing the air, and moved off to the side out of sight. When Jim caught up, he spoke quietly.

"Got us a big Grizz on our tail," Chief reported. "This one is going to be trouble. I think it's the one we saw a few days ago. It isn't afraid of us, just cautious, and that makes me nervous."

"Thanks," Jim said. He keyed his walkie-talkie. "Listen up. Watch yourselves at the rear guard. There's a big Grizzly following us," Jim said.

"Roger that, Captain," Sid Barrett slid his rifle from its sheath and checked the chamber to make sure he had a round chambered.

"I'm sure glad it stays light all night this time of year!" Sid said later that evening as they set up camp. He was on guard duty, and he could clearly see the huge animal from time to time as it tried various ways to get at the food supply or one of the horses. Its grunts and growls nearly panicked the horses and at one point it stood to its full height where everyone could see how big it was, as if to demonstrate its superiority in size and strength.

Near three in the morning Jim was on duty at one of the points the bear could approach the camp when it appeared in a gap between two rocks no more than twenty feet away. He hauled out his Smith and Wesson and pulled back the hammer as the enraged bear stood up and roared. Aiming for that open mouth as the bear charged forward, now on all fours, Jim pulled the trigger twice and the bear thudded to the ground, two feet from his toes. It was dead.

For a moment he merely stood there, looking at the magnificent animal, sad that he had been forced to terminate its life. The one foot forward had claws fully six inches long, deadly fighting tools in a battle, and its teeth gleamed in the early morning light, large and fierce. He breathed a silent prayer of thanks.

"Uh . . . you okay boss?" Frank asked, coming to stand beside him and look at the carcass.

"I may need to change my underwear," Jim joked quietly.

"Good Lord! Look at the size of that thing! Where were you when you shot it, honey?" Cecilia asked as she came to a stop beside the dead animal. Her hands covered her mouth in horror.

"Right where he's standing, Bright Eyes," FM said softly. "He just hauled that cannon out of his holster, took aim, and fired twice. That bear was coming right fast, missy!" FM breathed quietly. "The first shot blew half its skull off, and I don't know where the second one went but wherever it went it put it down to stay."

"Left shoulder," Jim said quietly, squatting down to look at the bear's teeth. There were bits of cloth stuck in the back teeth. He pulled at them. "Looks like cloth," he surmised.

Frank looked at the left shoulder and saw where the second shot went true, right into the heart of the already dead animal. Shaking his head at the shooting of his Captain he leaned down to look at the cloth.

"I think that's like the cloth we saw back in Prudhoe Bay, at the museum," he said softly. "I hate to think how it got caught in this animal's teeth, boss!" FM shook his head.

"Yes. Somewhere not to far away is a dead or wounded Native Alaskan Nunamiut. We need to find him!" Jim said.

"We lost that bear yesterday afternoon for about an hour," Chief said, squatting down with Jim and FM. "I can probably track him to where the attack took place."

"I'll go with you, if I may," Jim requested. "We'll take your team."

Chief smiled at Jim, shaking his head. "You asked if you could go along with me and my team," he chuckled. "You're the Captain!"

"Yes, but when it comes to tracking a dead bear and finding a wounded man, you're best qualified. So, I'm asking permission to come along and learn, and help," Jim was serious.

"Yeah. You can come along," Chief announced. "Anyone who can hold his ground in the path of a charging bear is welcome in my camp anytime!" he added under his breath. Only FM heard him since both were rising to their feet. FM nodded agreement. He'd seen it and still didn't believe how calmly Jim had aimed and fired.

"Let's go find a wounded or dead Indian, nuked Sushi," Chief added with a grin.

"It's Kemosabe!" FM retorted.

"That's what I said!" Chief snorted. Jim stood up and shook his head, chuckling at his two friends.

Chief was a good teacher, showing all the men how to read bear tracks, even on rocks. There were places where claws had scraped over the surface, leaving telltale marks that his companions might have easily missed. At last, they came to the trail where the bear had turned aside from following them.

"We'll find our man in here," Chief said, nodding toward the canyon trail they were now contemplating. He turned his horse and rode carefully into the narrow canyon, his feet almost touching both sides. Jim had to raise his feet and heard his stirrups scrape a few times as his larger horse followed.

Once the canyon widened, he put his feet back in the stirrups and patted his stallion with affection. The Friesian seemed to like him a lot. Jim decided that if he ever settled down somewhere, he would have a Friesian to ride, perhaps this one. He put those thoughts away as he began once again to study the ground.

They found a very young man deep in the canyon, only because he called out to them when he heard the horses. He had climbed into a fissure in the rocks above them, far enough that the bear could not reach him, but his leg was a bloody mess and badly broken. Jim recognized the courage and effort it had taken that young man to climb up there with that kind of wound, and obviously getting away from an attacking bear. The kind of courage and fortitude that took was worthy of praise.

"I heard you go by yesterday and thought of hailing you," he said weakly as Chief examined the broken leg. "I wish now I had."

"This is bad, Jim," Chief said, patting the young man on the shoulder. "We need to airlift him out to a hospital fast."

"Sea Venture One to *Lightening Bolt*," Jim spoke into his radio, a hand-held unit powerful enough to reach the AH-1W Super Cobra. *Lightening Bolt* was name they'd given the chopper.

"*Lightening Bolt* to Sea Venture One. Go ahead, over," Pen's voice came over the radio sounding tinny and small.

"We have a wounded Native American here with a broken leg. He was attacked by a Grizzly. Here are the GPS coordinates," Jim read off the coordinates from his GPS tracker and said "over."

"Roger. I'm ten minutes away. Over."

They had taken the precaution of attaching two stretcher cages to the skids of the chopper, in case of an emergency evacuation of an injured party. As she turned the chopper hard right, she turned her radio dial to the emergency medical channel. Duncan was impressed by her professionalism and calm.

"Prudhoe Bay Fairbanks Memorial Hospital, this is *Bring It Up Three David Thirty* declaring a medical emergency. We will be airlifting a Native American, with a broken leg who was attacked by a Grizzly. Our ETA to your chopper pad is twenty-eight minutes from mark. Over," her voice was calm as she spoke. A moment later a woman's voice answered.

"Roger that *Three David Thirty*. Winds are north by northeast, gusts to eleven miles per hour at the moment. We will be ready for your emergency. Over."

Just then Donut noticed a flare and pointed it out to Pen. She adjusted a little to her left and discovered they were leading her to a place where she could set down. Pippi and Donut watched from the chopper as the men put the young native in the stretcher. Wrapping him had been the worst, and he'd cried out several times, but they had to keep him warm. Once the cover was down and locked the men stepped back and Chief waved that she could lift off.

Looking at her watch she saw they'd managed to do everything in under two minutes. Pulling the cyclic gently the chopper lifted away and once she was clear of the canyon walls; she pointed the nose to Prudhoe Bay. Inside the plastic bubble, wrapped in insulated cloth, the young native was looking up at her as she flew. What he was thinking she had no way of knowing, but his face was twisted in pain.

Exactly twenty-seven minutes after her call to the hospital Pen set the skids down in the center of the chopper pad and watched as half a dozen medical personnel ducked and ran to the stretcher. She shut down the rotors and climbed down from the cockpit with Donut as they were transferring the young man to a gurney.

A female ER doctor was giving instructions in a quiet competent voice, just loud enough for everyone to hear. She turned as Pen approached.

"It's a good thing you found him when you did," she said.

"I didn't find him. There's an archaeological group out there who killed the bear that attacked this young man. They found traces of cloth and blood in the bear's mouth and backtracked the bear to find him. One of that group is a Native American, a full-blooded Blackfoot, and he was leading the search party," Pen replied. The doctor thought about them going back to find this young man and decided these were the best of people.

"He's in a bad way but I think we can get him stabilized," the doctor said, turning to follow the gurney into the hospital. Pen walked along with Duncan following quietly.

"If you find out who his people are, we'll get them here," Pen said.

"In that?" the doctor raised an eyebrow, pointing at the chopper.

"No. We have a CH53 Sea Stallion we can call upon that's not too far out," Pen replied.

The doctor walked up to the patient and asked him a few questions. Pen noted that she was concerned about the young man's health and spoke quietly. When she was finished, she turned to Pen.

"He's from Sagwon. His folks can drive here. But thank you for the offer, Lieutenant," she said. "Wouldn't your superior's frown on you using the fuel for such a trip?" she asked curiously.

"We're a civilian group on a military contract," Pen replied. "My Captain was the one who suggested I make the offer. He's Captain Shepherd."

"Ah! Captain of the *Sea Venture*! I've heard good things about him. Thank you again, Lieutenant," the doctor said.

"I'll refuel here in Prudhoe Bay and return to my unit then," Pen said, turned around, and headed back to the chopper.

On the way back to the pipeline Pen watched a storm moving in and wondered if she would make it back before it hit. She didn't, but it was perhaps by God's own hand that the storm forced her to circle around the landing zone. Out of the corner of her eye she saw a flash of movement and realized a wall of water was surging down the Sagavanirktok River from melting snows. In the path of that surge of water was a pair of men in an inflatable boat. As she watched they were tossed into the waters. Quickly she keyed her radio.

"John, do you copy. Over," she said tersely. He heard the emotion in her voice.

"Go ahead. Over," he replied.

"Two men were just washed into the river south of your position. There's a flood coming down from melting snow and they got caught in it. If you hurry, you can intercept them. Over," she said. She waited for his reply and didn't breathe until it came.

"On our way, over!" John replied.

He led the way, the Jeeps following as they headed to the riverbanks. Pen placed the chopper above the river where she could watch the progress of the men. Both appeared conscious, grasping at stones along the way. Twice she saw blood in the water. Then John was there with the Jeeps.

"Hook on to the truck and another Jeep!" John yelled at Wade. Both men leaped from the vehicle and hooked cables from the winch on the truck and another jeep to the back of their vehicle. John looked at the men.

"I'm going out into the water!" He yelled, and jumped back in.

Wade jumped in at the same time and the Jeep leaped forward, entered the water, bounced once, settled in, dug in, and despite the force of the water moved in a fairly straight line into the path of the hapless men. The surge was so powerful it began to move the Jeep sideways, and John could only hope it would stay upright as he reached out and grabbed an arm.

Without thinking about the danger to himself, Wade leaped out the door and onto the hood, grabbing the high-lift jack mounted there, and stretching as far as he could he reached the other victim, grabbing the back of his coat, and pulling him up on the hood. Only his quick reflexes and amazing strength made it possible for him to make the grab and pull the man from the freezing water. There was no time. As the Jeep began to lift on one side the two vehicles on shore began to pull it out.

Ten minutes later they were on the shore and loading the two victims onto the stretchers on the helicopter. Once more Pen radioed the hospital and told them what to expect. John stepped back and made a circular motion with his hand to tell her to lift off. She did.

"I'm going to the hospital. You guys keep up the patrol," John said as he and Wade unhooked their Jeep.

"Are you sure it still runs?" Matthew Banks asked.

"We'll let it dry out," John said. He picked up his radio.

Sea Venture Two to *Sea Venture*. Come in, over," he called.

Sea Venture Two, this is *Sea Venture* Three. Go ahead, over," Papa replied.

Please send the CH53D Sea Stallion to this location. Over," he read off the coordinates. "I need transport to the Fairbanks Memorial

Hospital at Prudhoe Bay. We're transporting two injured men to the hospital with the other chopper. Over"

"Roger that. We've been copying your transmissions. Dorf anticipated your need and is already lifting off. ETA one hour and ten minutes, over"

"Thank you, over," John replied, clicking off. He looked at the rest of the men. "Let's get out of this storm so Wade and I can change."

They took refuge in the six-wheeler, under the back cover. It was crowded, but at least they were out of the rain. John and Wade changed into dry uniforms and then ate while they waited for the chopper to pick them up. Outside the storm raged and passed over, leaving the area soaking wet and gleaming in the sunshine.

"Those Jeeps are amazing. With the hydraulics running them, we don't have to worry about airflow," Weston said when the conversation turned to reviewing what they'd just accomplished.

"I had all the power I needed, even when water was half-way up the windshield," John replied.

"It's a windscreen," Weston corrected with a straight face. "Good to know in the future," he added, grinning at John.

"Hobbs, a screen has holes in it. It's a windshield," John argued.

"Does your TV screen have holes in it? I don't think so! Does your computer monitor screen have holes in it? No! It's a windscreen!" Calvin said sternly.

"Okay! It's a windscreen!" John agreed, holding up his hands in surrender.

"We invented English. One would think you Yanks would eventually catch on!" Bond said facetiously.

"Oh, we did! We improved it," C.G. replied. "Then we kicked the British out," he added, cleaning his fingernail with his Mini-Tac knife.

"Yeah! And look where that got you, mate!" Hobbs said with a snort.

"We're in the mess we're in because we're trying to copy you socialists in England!" Vince said with a finger raised.

"Balderdash!" Bear said.

"We have a lot of that in our government too," C.G. quipped. Everyone laughed.

Talk continued regarding the vehicles and how they ran until the sound of the helicopter roused everyone. Wisely they waited until it set down and the rotors stopped turning before coming out of the truck. John and Wade leaped up into the side door and John made the motion to start the engines again. Soon they were in the air.

CHAPTER 12

"**I**ce Storm!" Bob Neff snapped the warning into his COMLINK as the storm formed and hit in the space of seconds! To his relief there were only a few crewmembers on the deck at the time and all made it indoors. It was just as well, because within minutes the doors were frozen shut.

Dr. Dundee, in the computer lab of the science center, initiated his nanobot protocol and watched as the ice fell away from the glass in the porthole just in front of him. He smiled. With his heavy coat on he opened an outside door, finding it opened properly and saw that no ice was forming on the walls or deck.

"It feels good when something works that well, doesn't it?" Alice Dinsmore asked, coming to stand behind him.

"I've never seen anything like this storm before," Mike replied, closing the door and shutting out the freezing tirade.

"Bob says it only took minutes to form," Alice said as she walked beside Dr. Putnam back to the lab. "I think we're going to be stuck here for a while. I'm going to take advantage of that and see what lies beneath the bottom of the ocean floor." He smiled at her as she moved back to the wet lab to prepare the HROVs for descent. For Dr. Dinsmore, thought was action.

Ice storms are not rare in the Arctic Sea, and this one rained ice for three straight days. There were a few areas uncovered by the nanobots and they had over twelve inches of ice covering them. It took crew several hours to chip away the ice. Goody and Wrench went over every inch of the ship and found a few places where paint had been taken off by the ice. Those were repaired, treated against rust, and repainted.

While frozen in place by the ice storm Dr. Dinsmore and her team enjoyed the use of the moon pools, sending down the HROVs without having to enter the harsh environment above decks, dig holes through the ice to deploy the units, and freeze while they watched the information formulate on the computer screens. Instead, they launched the vehicles and sat in the heat of the computer lab, sipping warm drinks and conversing about the various readouts. Most surprising was the difference in salinity at various levels.

"Look at that!" John Dinsmore said suddenly, pointing at one of the screens. "That's the outline of a steamer!" And indeed, it was!

"Then why am I getting heavy deposits of precious metals?" Alice asked her husband, watching another screen. "Gracious! That steamer was carrying a large shipment of gold! It's practically pure for that period of time and there are tons of it on board!"

"Look at that superstructure. It looks like it sank last week, not over a hundred years ago!" Carol Lowe was gazing at the photos. "I'm guessing that the temperature of the water means very low salinity which is why the ship is still in such good condition," she added, almost to herself. "That's fascinating! I've heard of it, but never seen it," she added just as quietly.

"Yes! Look at the hull. See those gaping holes. She hit an iceberg!" John said with awe.

"What are those, on the sea floor off to the right?" Angela asked.

"Skeletons," Alice identified. "They went into the water. At these temperatures anyone would have died in about twelve minutes, or less. Hypothermia sets in at eight minutes."

"Why aren't any of them clothed?" Angela asked. "I don't see a stitch on them!"

John Dinsmore looked at them with a deep sadness in his eyes as the answer came to him almost immediately. His answer, when it came, was even, but his wife recognized the sadness in his eyes, understanding it for what it was. "No. One of the symptoms of hypothermia is a sense of being too hot. They probably stripped their clothing off in the last moments of life. Poor souls," John answered.

"I have goosebumps just thinking about going in that icy water again!" Dr. Iris Copeland said. She shivered. Every one of the crew had jumped in a small hole cut in the ice earlier for training. It was a stern reminder that nature is unrelenting. Remembering the pain and fear almost brought tears to her eyes. That day she had cried, terrified as she underwent the training, even though she knew she was safe.

"We'll document all of this, mark the location, and send in the usual salvage rights contracts. What we won't mention is the gold, or the name of the steamer. Someone may know that gold is down there and when they see we've discovered it may try to take the find away from us!" John nodded his head. "I'll tell Papa."

One nice thing about their new ship was that no one had to go outside to travel anywhere within the ship. Although some of the corridors were colder than others, they were free of ice and the elements from outside the windows. As they ran these steps daily, he was familiar with them in a way he sometimes wished he wasn't. He hustled up to the bridge and found Andrea at the wheel. They weren't going anywhere for a while, that was certain, but he was still at the wheel.

"We found a steamer loaded with gold," John said quietly to Andrea. "Something about this tells me it is trouble," he added.

"Loaded?" Andrea said, tilting his head and narrowing his eyes as he studied Dr. Dinsmore.

"Approximately ten tons of it," John said softly.

"Do you have images of the ship itself?" Andrea asked, taking John by the arm, and leading him back the way he had come. John smiled.

"We do. Three holes in the hull from hitting an iceberg are visible, and she is sitting on her keel on the bottom, upright, with a slight list to starboard. The ship is in surprisingly good condition, considering how long it has been under the water," John said.

"You are thinking we can salvage the entire ship?" Andrea asked.

"I am," John said confidently. Andrea began to rub his hands.

"But you have a feeling about this ship, don't you?" Andrea asked, looking at the doctor closely.

"Yes. I don't know why, but I believe this could be trouble, and if we get the salvage rights, we should do it carefully," Dr. Dinsmore said.

"Ah!" Andrea said sagely. "That much gold can indeed bring great tragedy and trouble," he nodded slowly. "But once we declare salvage rights we are in the open."

"So, let's wait until we are finished with this contract, and hope that no one else discovers it before we do," Dr. Dinsmore said. "It's been down there for a long time undiscovered. We are out of regular shipping lanes. They were also, and I'm wondering why they were so far out in dangerous waters?"

"Yes. The mystery grows now. I will contact Jim and ask what he wants to do. He will probably follow your advice," Andrea opened the door to the computer center and let the crew take him through the discovery, listening to them with a critical ear. For him it was more than an honor to lead such a crew, and especially to have their trust. When they were finished, he pulled out the satellite phone that would give him a secure line to Jim.

"Hello Nephew!" Andrea said when Jim answered.

"Hi Papa! What's going on?" Jim replied, a real smile in his voice. He waited with mounting excitement, knowing Andrea would not call unless a situation arose that required all of command to know the details. Andrea, he knew, understood the trust his nephews had in him to lead, but he always discussed his decisions.

"We are stuck in the ice, and an ice storm raged for three days. It took only minutes to form and covered parts of the ship with over a foot of ice. While we waited out the storm Dr. Dinsmore put down the HROVs and discovered a steamer carrying ten tons of gold on the bottom. She is far out of shipping lanes, even for that time, and in very good condition. She is also carrying nickel and copper in significant amounts. I believe that God caused that storm so we would make this discovery."

"Somebody wants to wait until the contract is finished to announce the find and begin salvage," Jim said flatly after only a moment of thought.

"As usual, Nephew, you have hit the nail on the head!" Andrea said with a smile.

"Do you agree?" Jim asked.

"Yes, I do," Andrea replied simply.

"You're in charge. Do what you think is right. I'll accept your decision," Jim replied. "How is the ship doing in the ice?"

"It is a powerful ship and easily capable of handling whatever nature has given us thus far," Andrea said with pride.

"Good to hear!" Jim replied. "Carry on, Commander! I'm glad someone like you and Dorf are watching over the ship and his crew."

Andrea smiled as the connection went dead. He put the phone back in its case and looked at Dr. Dinsmore with anticipation.

"We shall wait to make the discovery when we are ready to begin salvage then. In the meantime, I need this place marked and watched constantly. I will make the arrangements." Andrea turned and left the lab. As he walked, he pushed his COMLINK.

"Sean, could you please see me in the bridge?" he asked politely.

"On my way, Papa," Ox's voice replied.

On the bridge Ox came into the steerage section and leaned against a bank of instruments, crossing his arms, and looking intently at Andrea.

"We found a steamer, with ten tons of gold, significant amounts of nickel and copper, far off the usual shipping lanes, even for that time. Because we don't want trouble before we're ready we are going to wait to declare the salvage rights and our discovery. It's sitting right below us. I'd like you to be sure no one pokes around before we are ready," Andrea said softly. He watched the young soldier digest the information and waited.

"Easy, mate," Ox said, his Aussie accent strong. "We'll keep a lash on it," he smiled and left, calling for his team to meet him in the conference room.

"They'll be testing that new polar explorer," Neff said with a grin.

"Yes. I suppose so," Andrea grinned. "They can run some tests while they play. This is a perfect time to see what it can do!"

At Fairbanks Memorial Hospital in Prudhoe Bay John walked into the room occupied by the father and son he and Wade rescued earlier. The two had recovered without serious damage to their extremities, always a danger in icy conditions. Both had suffered frostbite on their toes and fingers, but those digits were now fully functional, if a little sore. The two Nunamiut Indians looked up at him with genuine smiles.

"Hey marine!" the father said, holding out a fist and bumping fists with John.

"Hey Army!" John said with a grin. Both had served in the military, and both recognized the tattoos of the armed forces. John looked over at the son who was planning on joining the Navy as soon as he finished college. The young man was fit, though he carried extra weight. He wanted to be a science officer in the Navy and help research the Arctic Sea. Fascinated with John's crew and boat he had hundreds of questions. Today John had a surprise.

"I brought you a present," he said to the young man.

Dr. Carol Lowe and Dr. Angela Rysdale stepped into the room, followed by the Dinsmores. The young man sat up straight in his bed. Today he was wearing pants and a T-shirt and looked ready to go home. He'd brushed his teeth and showered and was glad he had. Carol and Angela were beautiful women! Needing to make a good impression he did his best.

For the next hour he asked questions of the foursome as John and his father looked on amused. He was an inquisitive young man, knowledgeable in marine biology, his major in college, and seemed eager to soak up everything the Marine Biologists before him could divulge. John could tell they were impressed as well, and Alice kept encouraging the young man to transfer to Woods Hole

Oceanographic Institute. She promised to open doors for him, and he seemed amazed at his good fortune.

"You should come on the ship for the duration of our visit here," John said in a lull in the conversation. The young man, whose name was Wolf, opened his eyes wide. An offer such as this had come as a complete surprise, and he grinned as he stared first at his father, and then at the scientists, and finally at John.

"Could I?" his voice was husky with emotion.

"I think it would be good for you to participate in AOOS. It would certainly look good on your resume if you apply to WHOI," John replied. He smiled at the boy with real friendship, knowing that he was going to influence a young life, something he loved. In fact, the whole crew was talking about starting a university on the ocean, if God permitted. Wolf would be a good test case for them.

Suddenly the five around and in the bed were all talking quickly, and John turned back to the father, whose name was Tom. Tom watched for a moment and then looked quizzically at John.

"Why were you so far from your ship?" he asked quietly.

"My team is doing research of a different kind. We're looking for some ecological terrorists who have threatened the pipeline," John answered simply. "If we find them, we will notify the authorities and assist in putting a stop to their plans."

"When I came down the river, I noticed a new trail, one that was traveled by men and machines to the river, probably for water. Wolf and I hid our raft and followed the trail to a camp, hidden in the trees. We heard chainsaws and knew that no cutting is allowed there, so we were very careful. They have surrounded their camp by a log fort, much like those built long ago," Tom said slowly. "They use only deadfall, so their labors are long and hard. If you wish, I will guide you to this place."

"You said you couldn't repay me for saving your life, Tom. Well, you just put me in your debt," John said, taking his hand in a firm handshake.

"Will you really take my son on your ship?" Tom asked, looking over at the group in animated conversation.

"As soon as he is released from the hospital," John said.

"Even with his broken leg and shoulder?" Wolf had a cast on his leg, and his shoulder was in a confining sling affair that kept it still.

"We have very competent physicians on board the ship, and the finest hospital on the ocean. He will be in good hands, and when he returns, he will be whole again," John assured him. Conversation had stopped and the five were looking at John.

"Unfortunately, your son may come home dreaming of driving an Atom, or Mercedes AMG, or some other super car if we let our young Doctor Axlerod treat him," John Dinsmore said with a big smile. "We call him Dr. Gearhead because all he ever talks about are fast cars. He seems to know as much about exotic sports cars as he does about medicine! For all of that, however, he is a very competent doctor, and Will and Donna Penny are also on board! Wolf will be in good hands."

"Dr. Leo Axlerod?" a female doctor entered the room and raised her eyebrows at John Dinsmore. "You have Dr. Leo Axlerod on your ship?" her question was surprised.

"Yes ma'am," Dr. Dinsmore replied.

"You also have Dr. Will Penny on your crew, do you not?" she asked as she moved beside Tom's bed and prepared to take his blood pressure. As she wrapped the sleeve around his arm she continued talking.

"Both of those names are highly respected. And Dr. Axlerod's work on reconditioning after a sports injury is fast becoming the model for pro and college athletes," she squeezed the ball, making Tom wince as the sleeve tightened, listened to her stethoscope, and slowly released the pressure. As she removed the sleeve, she looked at Tom.

"Your blood pressure is good. How's the arm?" Tom's arm was in a cast from just below the elbow, encasing his left hand. He lifted it and wiggled his fingers.

"Everything seems to be working. The swelling is all gone, but you waited for that before putting on the cast, so you already know that. All my fingers work properly and most of the pain has abated. I think I'll recover!" he claimed happily.

"It was a clean break and will heal nicely, I think. You're getting a little old to be breaking bones, Tom," she teased.

"Tell me about it," he said, shaking his head. "It was a water surge, a simple surge of water, but it lifted our raft up just enough for that gust of wind to get under it and dump us in the river. It's running fast this time of year with the snow melting on the lower reaches of the range. I was sure we were both going to die!"

"I saw the chopper that brought in the other young man. What's our military doing along the pipeline?" the doctor asked, looking at John. He smiled, and to her surprise, answered quickly.

"We're on a military contract, but we're civilians. What we're doing is testing some new equipment and while we do it, we're doing a favor for our government. There's been evidence that an ecological terrorist unit has targeted the Trans Alaska Pipeline," John answered honestly.

"Again!" she exclaimed. "So, you're supposed to find them?"

"Not an easy task. Our vehicles on the ground are running on hydraulics, so they're very quiet. We're hoping we can sneak up on them and call in the heavies to clean it all up," John replied.

"I wish you luck!" she said, shaking her head. "Patrolling that pipeline is an impossible task. Everyone says so! We all worry about the possibility of such an attack, and we have since it was built. It is a marvel of engineering and so far, hasn't diversely affected the wildlife in the area."

"Sometimes God steps in and helps us," John said quietly. "It happens more often than you might believe."

For a moment everyone in the room was silent, heads nodding agreement.

"Well, I hope He performs a miracle this time and you do find them," she replied with a smile.

"Are you a believer?" John asked. "I follow Jesus," he added.

"Yes, much to my colleagues disgust," she smiled at him. Our people have known that there is a God, though many of them have yet to meet Him," her eyes were sad at that.

"Please don't tell me your colleagues still hold to the religion of evolution?" Dr. Alice Dinsmore asked.

"Oh yes! I'm Dr. Phyllis Krenshaw, by the way," she introduced herself.

"Perhaps I'll have lunch with you today, and we can pull the rug out from under some of those mental pygmies!" Alice scoffed.

"I'd read you were a believer," Phyllis said, smiling. "The article was not complimentary. Perhaps lunch would be nice. I'd like to see their reactions to your views."

"We're on!" Alice said, grabbing John's hand. "We'll even treat for lunch."

"Why don't we buy lunch for everyone?" John asked. "Invite the whole staff and we can visit with them while they eat during their various shifts. That will give us a chance to build some relationships and share some real truth. What should we provide for sustenance?" John asked Phyllis.

"There's a divine little Chinese place just down the block that caters. If you call now, they may have it ready in time. Their food is absolutely the best and always fresh and almost everyone loves to eat there when they can or have them cater something here. Pharmacology companies use them often," Phyllis laughed. "I'm looking forward to lunch! See you then!"

Good to his word John purchased lunch for the entire staff. Wolf went down to the dining room with the scientists to learn what he could and after visiting with Tom for a bit John left to attend to a few things. Outside, by himself, he bowed his head and thanked God for intervening and helping him find the terrorists, and then asked for wisdom and protection.

Discussions at lunch were lively, professional, and John was proud of his scientists, as they answered questions, asked the right questions, and debated intelligently the case for intelligent design and creation as opposed to blind chance. In his own mind he knew they'd won the debate, but he also knew that hearts darkened by the prince of this world would not easily accept light and truth for what it was. There were always those who allowed the enemy to snatch away any light of truth.

Here too, God showed His awesome love for people, for John later learned that two nurses and three technicians, a young doctor, and one near retirement later accepted Christ as Savior because of the compelling arguments presented that day. That news would come much later, but it would lift his heart immeasurably.

CHAPTER 13

On board *Sea Venture* the last photos revealed yet another mystery regarding the sunken ship. A nautical mile from the skeletal remains, heading back toward the shipping lanes, two lifeboats from the ship sat at the bottom, stern to bow, as if they sank while following each other. In each lifeboat four skeletons could be clearly seen, still seated at the oars, skeletal hands wrapped around the oar handles.

"What do you make of it?" Andrea asked Dorf and Mark, who after returning with the crew from the hospital, were studying the latest photos.

"Ice Storm," Mark said suddenly.

"Ah!" Andrea nodded, having come to the same conclusion.

"The ice covered the boats and crew rowing, and slowly sank the boats. It must have happened fast, like our storm. But why are these men in the boats, so far away from the ship, and what does it mean?" Dorf mused quietly.

"The only way to solve this mystery is to get that ship off the bottom of the ocean, and those two lifeboats," Andrea said softly.

"We should widen our search, see if we can find anything else to help us solve the mystery," Dorf suggested, looking at Andrea, who nodded agreement. "We need all the information we can get. Besides, our new visitor should love watching that," he smiled.

Wolf was indeed amazed at the labs on the ship and was quickly becoming acclimated to the work schedules, mealtimes, and other routines on board the ship. At the moment he was sitting in the lab watching Dr. Putnam test the water samples that had just come up from the ocean depths.

"Dr. Wonderland, this is Dorf," a voice sounded in his ear, and he started. He was still getting used to those communication devices.

"Go ahead, Dorf. What will you bother me with now?" Dr. Alice Dinsmore's voice held the hint of a smile.

"We want to sweep the HROVs in a grid pattern circle covering one nautical mile from the last coordinates you logged," Dorf requested quietly. "Could you please organize that?"

"Oh! A chance to play with my toys! Gladly!" Dr. Dinsmore replied. "Are we still stuck in the ice?" she added.

"Yes. Smitty guesses that a few more days will be needed for the ice to melt enough to allow us to safely move ahead. I think he suggested we wait three days," Dorf replied.

"We'll take water samples and see what's beneath the ocean floor," Dr. Dinsmore said.

"Roger that. Thanks," Dorf replied.

"Dr. Putnam, are you available to help me with the HROV deployment?" Dr. Dinsmore asked next, excited to get started.

"Wolf and I are on the way," Mike replied, winking at Wolf.

Fascinated by the HROVs Wolf lent a hand and did whatever he was told as they deployed the three unmanned submersibles from the largest moon pool. One handed, and hobbling on a crutch, there wasn't much he could do, but he pitched in with excitement and fervor and the crew took note. He watched them sink beneath the clear waters and then slowly followed Dr. Dinsmore and Dr. Putnam to the computer lab. There everyone without duty elsewhere gathered around to watch the screens display what the HROV equipment found.

"Visibility is pretty good at one hundred and sixty fathoms," Dr. John Dinsmore said quietly as the images from the cameras showed the ocean floor. With the lights on the HROVs and the cameras tuned for that depth, they could see almost twenty feet in any direction.

"Look at that!" Carol Lowe pointed to the camera image from HROV-1. The huge skeleton of a whale lay on the bottom. It was upside down and partially buried in the silt. Stretching for nearly a hundred feet the skeleton unfolded before their eyes. Inside the bones various fish swam about, and on the floor of the ocean the usual bottom dwellers moved.

"Usually, whales float for weeks before they begin to sink," John Dinsmore commented quietly. "I imagine this one died and once the sharks cleaned his bones, they sank. You can see scoring on some of the bones from the teeth of the sharks and other fish."

"There's a sleeper shark!" Wolf pointed to the swimming shark. "And look at the coral on the bottom! That's beautiful. I expected it to be mostly mud and rock!"

"You'd be surprised what lives down here," Dr. Dinsmore said, typing in the species she was seeing.

"What is that?" Wolf asked.

"It's a Sculpins fish," she replied.

"No, I mean that trench in the middle of the coral!" Wolf pointed to a screen from HROV-2.

"Trolling!" Alice spat angrily. "Look how they've destroyed an entire swath of sea life!"

"Trolling . . . out here?" Wolf's voice held that incredulity that everyone felt. This was not normal.

"With the ice melting more they are traveling further out. We saw him yesterday. If we see him again, we'll stop him and investigate," Dr. John Dinsmore said emphatically.

Suddenly the proximity warning went off on HROV-3. Alice moved to a keyboard controlling that unit and punched in the codes to identify whatever was out there. She drew in a sharp breath and pressed her COMLINK.

"Papa! There's a Seawolf Class Nuclear Sub below us! Raise them, please, before they damage my HROVs!"

Andrea nodded to Rock 'n Roll as he picked up the radio microphone and dialed to the emergency station for U.S. craft.

"Seawolf class Submarine, this is *Sea Venture*. We have HROVs operating near the bottom. This is a scientific mission, I repeat, scientific mission for the Alaska Ocean Observing System, AOOS. Do you copy?"

"Roger *Sea Venture*, we copy. Will surface behind you. Please prepare to accept a boarding party. Over," the radio operator of the submarine said.

"Copy. We will rig an elevator to bring you up. Over," Richard replied.

Crewmembers were soon busy lowering the platform usually assigned for lifting various crates on board. As the Commander of the submarine opened the outer hatch, he noted that no one was on the stern watching them surface, but that everyone was busy on deck. He studied the ship surrounded by ice.

It was new, and so far, he'd only seen pictures of it on his laptop. To his dismay, when he reported the *Sea Venture* working above his patrol area he'd been ordered to board and search the vessel from stem to stern. He knew the reputation of Captain Shepherd and his crew and certainly didn't understand the orders. But orders were orders, and they'd come from an admiral who had given him strict orders not to reveal his name.

A giant of a man wearing the typical bright orange insulated coveralls for Arctic exploration greeted him as the elevator came level with the deck. Stepping off on a deck surprisingly devoid of ice the Commander shook hands and identified himself. He was not surprised to discover the man to whom he was speaking was none other than Waldorf Bernard, a decorated Navy SEAL and now Lieutenant Commander on board this vessel. Knowing the man's record and accomplishments, he was duly honored.

"Call me Dorf, Commander," Dorf said lightly.

"I've been ordered to search your vessel," Commander Phillips said immediately.

"Not a problem, sir. Always glad to accommodate. Your men are free to search every inch of the ship, and they may open any containers or lockers they desire, or have them opened, if you prefer.

Then you can tell Admiral Hogg what you found," Dorf said, winking at Commander Phillips.

"I did not divulge the name of the officer that ordered the search!" Phillips said defensively. He was deeply concerned because Admiral Hogg could cause serious problems if he discovered it was known he ordered the search.

"No need, sir," Dorf replied without inflection.

"Did you somehow decipher our transmission code and listen in on our COMSAT?" Phillips asked, suspicious.

"No. You can check that too. We know what officers hold us in disregard. If you need clarification on that you may call Duck Ashley. He'll give you the skinny on who wants us shut down," Dorf watched Phillips relax slightly.

"Then there's the matter of your knowing this is a *Seawolf* class submarine. I need to know how you knew that," Phillips commanded.

"Let's go talk to Dr. Alice Dinsmore. Her HROV identified your ship. You'll want to know about this," Dorf laughed.

"We detected no sonar or radar emissions," Phillips said, standing his ground.

"That's because she uses light diffusion and microwave sound transmissions. You have the same technology on board your vessel. If you check, Commander, you bought it from us," Dorf laughed again.

Confused Phillips followed Dorf down to the lab where he was dressed down by a very nice scientist whose reputation was bona fide, and her character known throughout the academic world. Later he discretely checked and discovered that the patent for this technology did indeed belong to *Bring It Up*, and that it was supplied only to U.S., U.K., and Israeli military vessels.

Further, his men searched the vessel thoroughly, were treated to a five-star meal, and spent some time dancing with some very pretty ladies after dinner. As he sat at the table, sighing after the delicious lobster dinner, he looked at Andrea and Dorf.

"Where are the Shepherds?" he asked. "A number of your crew are missing," he was looking around as he spoke, but Dorf and Mark picked up on his suspicions.

"That's no secret, sir," Mark replied with a smile. "They're off on an archaeology expedition in the Brooks Range. They have not found what they were looking for yet, but they have rescued three Native Americans," he added. "Everything we're doing is with permission, sir."

"What are they looking for?" Phillips asked, sitting forward.

"A cave, sir. It is supposed to have some drawings from an Egyptian that sailed over here sometime in 1742," Mark answered.

"Really?" Phillips asked, incredulous.

"We found a copper plate with the information in the Lost City of Z. Dr. Gregg was very excited about it," Dorf responded.

"How did the Egyptians manage to sail across the Atlantic, or the Pacific for that matter?" he pondered, shaking his head.

"The Vikings managed it, and they didn't have vessels that were any more sophisticated than the Egyptian vessels. As far as we know he is the only one of his crew that survived the trip. His ship is hidden in a cave somewhere along the Peruvian coast. The location of that cave is in the cave for which our team is searching. If found, we'll know for certain if the ship did indeed come from Egypt, and also have an idea of the date of that trip!" Dorf added after a pause.

"That's just amazing!" Phillips said. He was interrupted as Angela and Carol came to the table.

"Since Wade isn't here to dance with me, and Carol does not have a partner at the moment, we thought you two would allow us the pleasure of this dance!" Angela invited, taking Phillips by the hand. Carol was no less forward in taking Dorf's hand.

Phillips noted that the giant Waldorf Bernard was light on his feet and a very good dancer, even though he towered over his partner. Phillips, who was just over six feet tall, felt like he towered over the tiny Angela. It was a swing dance, very energetic, and she was a good dancer. It was with a smile of appreciation that the Commander finally bowed to his companion and returned to his table, his face slightly flushed.

Back on the submarine he listened to his men comment on their search of the ship. They sang praises regarding the neatness and pristine condition of the ship, the neatness and arrangement of the quarters, and the storage. Several commented on the Arctic Research Vehicle in the hold, a gigantic AAV (Amphibious Arctic Vehicle) fashioned after a military amphibious attack vehicle, designed and built by *Bring It Up*.

Goody, TRT, and Wade designed the concept and Beardsley built the prototype. After they tested it on the ice other research companies would either borrow, rent, or order another. Jim was quite confident of that. Once he'd seen the drawings and understood the concept of the AAV he'd stood and bowed to his three friends. It was Jim Warner's final hoorah for the company.

Built in three sections the vehicle could traverse the very roughest terrain and float when necessary. The engine, or front vehicle was powered by a Cummins Diesel a 6-liter engine that powered up the hydraulics that once engaged and running at top power produced 4,000-horsepower and could reach speeds on land up to 40 miles per hour and on water up to 36 knots. Once the hydraulics ran at full power the diesel engine could be disengaged completely. Four tracks designed to run better in deep snow were placed in line on each side of the wide vehicle on a set of articulating frames that allowed the tracks to literally pivot ninety degrees up or down.

The cockpit was extremely comfortable and driven by a pilot and co-pilot with steerage and operations on both sides. Visibility was very good because the front of the vehicle was made of a very durable hard clear plastic that could withstand a .50 caliber bullet and contact with the ice at twenty-five miles per hour without breaking. The glass was all one piece, and designed for the best possible strength, much like a bubble front.

The engine and tracks were the heaviest part of the whole vehicle, which weighed in at a surprising 1700 pounds. Behind the engine the second car was a complete arctic laboratory set on pontoon skids, also articulated to pivot, keeping the lab fairly stationary as it moved behind the engine. Solar energy was used to produce electricity, the heaviest part of that car the inverter. Because of the metals necessary for the energy that could not be changed at this time.

The rear car was the cabin for the crew with living quarters for eight. Again, the design of the car was amazing. Insulated against the cold outside the car could maintain an inside temperature of seventy degrees. Every comfort had been considered for the crew. Having looked inside the cars, the men commented most on the comfort provided.

With its amazing hydraulic power system and fuel tank the vehicle could travel nine thousand miles without needing to refuel, and it could stay out on maneuvers and research for sixty days before needing to resupply. With all three cars hooked together the vehicle stretched ninety-eight feet and was eighteen feet wide.

In the morning the ice was breaking up once more. Phillips left with a promise not to divulge the location of the sunken steamer. Alone again the research ship began preparations to continue. Andrea watched from the bridge as the three cars for the AAV were lowered to the ice. Once they were properly attached the rest of the crew climbed back on the ship. On board the *A&P Railroad* (Arctic and Polar Railroad) as the crew named the AAV Team Knife would pilot. Dr. Putnam, Dr. Lowe, and Dr. Copeland would be the scientists assigned to the *A&P* lab.

Black smoke belched from the exhausts running up the side of the engine as the Diesel fired up. Chance and PU were in the cockpit watching the gauges as things powered up. Not until they were sure all was working properly did the command come for them to engage the gears and begin moving on the ice. Chance looked over at his friend.

"Okay, mate, let's not make any blues and we'll reach the back of Bourke!" he cajoled. In his earpiece he heard Dr. Putnam interpreting what he just said.

"What my Aussie companion just intimated was that if we didn't make any mistakes, we could go a long distance," Dr. Putnam said. PU grinned at Chance as they continued to flip switches. Suddenly the engine roared and the vehicle started forward.

"Hydraulic pressure at fifty percent," PU reported to Chance.

"That's a corker of a system!" Chance replied, watching the hydraulic pressure build quickly.

"One hundred percent. Disengage engine, engage hydraulics," he ordered when the gauge reached the green zone.

PU reached up and depressed a toggle switch, and the engine died, and pressed a second switch and the hydraulics kicked in, dropping to eight percent and then building back up immediately to one hundred percent.

The change was palpable. From the roar of the diesel engine to the quiet of the hydraulics was amazing. Power increased quickly and Chance eased the throttles forward until they were moving at a steady fifteen miles per hour over the ice. As he watched the gauges, he noticed that power was still increasing and finally topped off at four thousand horsepower. He looked at his friend and smiled.

"So, let's go fossick through the Arctic!" Chance said with a rebel yell.

"Let's go what?" Iris asked in surprise.

"That's Aussie slang for rummage," Dr. Putnam chuckled.

"Oh! Can't any of you talk plain English?" she complained.

"Quit yer earbashing!" Chance retorted with a chuckle.

"I would, if I knew what that was!" Iris shot back.

"He means that you're nagging," Dr. Putnam said. "Why don't you quit yabbering and concentrate on driving this road train!" he entreated Chance.

"I'll give it a burl!" Chance replied evenly. He grinned at PU and the two continued to watch all the gauges. "What's the ride like back there?" he asked.

"Much like being on a train," Mike replied. "Nice and smooth so far."

"You should be able to engage the electricity and turn up the heat in five, four, three, two, one," PU observed.

"Roger. Engaging power system and turning on the heat," Mike replied.

He reached up above him and opening several plastic covers flipped the switches to the on position. Almost immediately they could feel the heat building inside the cabin and the lights came on all the appliances. Computer stations came to life. Mike reached up and flipped another switch and the skylights opened filling the cabin with sunlight.

"All systems are nominal," Mike said.

"Nominal?" PU quipped. "Let me guess. You were the Dux at your school!" he added.

"Not quite the top of my class. There was a girl who duxed all of her subjects. I only duxed four!" Mike replied.

"You were stonkered by a girl!" Ox snickered.

"Strewth!" Mike replied, looking chagrinned.

"Girls rule and boys drool," Carol said, laughing lightly.

"Quit grinning like a shot fox and get on with your work Sheila!" PU goaded over the COMLINK.

"He just said stop being so smug, girl," Mike said, laughing at her confused expression.

"Guy! Like totally! Talk English!" she gushed.

"Holy dooley! I didn't know you were a valley girl!" Ox said. Carol had mimicked the valley girl accent perfectly.

"What the heck is a valley girl?" PU asked, his eyebrows climbing his forehead as he looked at his copilot.

"Valley chicks, from Southern California, LA basin! You know!" Ox replied, laughing.

"Yeah. A mob of blonde bombshell drongos in skimpy bikinis!" Chance replied.

"Drongos?" Carol asked, one eyebrow raised.

"Stupid person," Ox filled her in.

"They are rather vapid." Iris said.

"You mean you ain't one of 'em?" Lee Roy piped up. "You're blonde!"

"Do you mean you aren't one of them," Iris corrected.

"She ain't one of 'em!" Lee Roy quipped.

"Temperature is now at 70 in the cabin, power is at maximum, everything holding steady," Mike said.

"Roger that, Dr. Dundee. We read green across the board. Our initial test is a success. Let's find some open water and see how we do in the wet."

CHAPTER 14

With the ship free of the ice and moving again Chance took advantage of the broken ice to test the AAV. In the water it performed just as well as it had on land. Power was switched from the tracks to the twin props in the rear of the engine and they glided through the water at a steady fifteen knots. Climbing from the water to the ice proved to be bumpy but manageable with the articulating tracks and the high torque.

Later that day, working in tandem with the crew of the ship, they stayed ahead of the ship long enough to drill a hole in the ice, drop some sensors that stayed just beneath the surface, so they could measure the difference in water temperature at 650 feet and eighteen inches. In the afternoon they broke off, headed back to make sure no one was trolling through the channel they'd carved and stopped some distance from the sunken ship to keep watch.

By morning, however, the channel was frozen over with nearly three inches of ice, and on the following days the ice thickened exponentially, until it was three feet thick. It was proving to be a cold season, and instead of the ice melting at an increased rate, it was thickening as the temperatures dropped.

Three days later they came in contact with an independent Green Peace expedition and stopped to compare notes. With the evidence of the ice thickening at almost record rates in the area they seemed almost morose. It became obvious that they came to add fuel to their dying global warming campaign, only to discover that the problems of the past year were reversing.

When they saw the photos taken of the flourishing coral beds, and large schools of char, salmon, and other edible fish they seemed almost angry. Dr. Putnam didn't give them any chance to ignore the facts. It didn't help that the science crew had such fantastic lab facilities, the ice train that was amphibious, and enough money to do what they wanted as far as research was concerned. It was a rather demoralized group of scientists that left and drove away late that afternoon. On board the crew watched them go with a sense of satisfaction.

"I'd say our Greenies weren't very happy with our findings," Mike said, shutting down the lab and cleaning up for the evening.

"Some scientists have adopted a new religion," Ox replied as he helped store the glass test tubes in their dedicated holders. "They're followers of Figjam," Mike burst out laughing at that comment.

"Figjam?" Iris asked.

"'F' I'm good just ask me," Sean explained sheepishly. "They have such a high opinion of their intelligence and abilities that they cannot be taught, cannot learn, and cannot see the big picture. Michael Crichton dubbed it 'thintelligence' in his *Jurassic Park* series. Of course, he got it from the chaos theory writings. Chaotiticians, to use one of Crichton's words, are correct. Modern science does not offer real answers to the world's problems," he stopped for a moment deep in thought.

"Most men don't know their limitations. We believe that somehow, we are equal to or even more powerful than God," he looked around.

"Yes. We deal with them all the time," Lee Roy said. "And if we're honest, as TRT said in his last Bible Study, we'll realize that within each of us is the same tendency. I want to believe that I am a law unto myself, and that there are no consequences to the decisions I make. Sadly, I'm convinced of my own greatness! So, I always have to be on my guard!"

"And in your humble opinion, Mr. Brown, what is the answer?" Iris asked.

He grinned broadly and spread his strong arms wide. "Wait for God to straighten it out. He's the only One who can!"

"Now that's London to a brick!" Mike said, giving Lee Roy a high five.

"I'm guessing that means absolutely certain?" Iris asked, smiling at the two.

"Yes, miss. That's it exactly," Mike replied with an emphatic nod.

"Like wow! Dude! You're totally awesome!" Carol Lowe imitated the valley girl accent again, and the mannerisms. All the men burst out laughing at that.

"She's a scientist Sheila!" Ox laughed.

"Sounds just like one!" Mike added.

"Narly!" she quipped.

They were scheduled to return to the ship for a celebration dinner Papa had organized. Trooping back to the cabin after they'd secured everything Iris indicated to the engine that they were secured and ready to travel.

Chance and PU depressed their COMLINK talk buttons and snored in unison, pretended to wake up startled. It was PU who spoke.

"Sorry mates! We fell asleep during the philosophy lesson!" he said.

"A pig's arse, you larrikin!" Lee Roy said. "Shut your clacker, drive this road train, and don't come a guster!"

"Don't spit the dummy, ya dag! No worries! We'll get ya jumbucks back to the ship in good order!" PU replied.

"Like, dude! Could you, like, explain, like, what all that meant?" Carol's voice had a whine to it and the men grinned.

"A pig's arse means you don't agree. A larrikin is a bloke who is always enjoying himself, a prankster. A clacker is a butthole and come a guster means have an accident," he looked at Carol with his eyes crinkled in laughter as she pretended not to understand.

"Like really!" she exclaimed.

"Don't spit the dummy means don't get upset. A dag is a nerd. Jumbucks are sheep," Ox finished.

"Guy! You know? It's like living in a foreign country!" Carol whined again.

On that burst of laughter, they settled in to study the ice as the train picked up speed. Forty minutes later they were pulling alongside the ship. Dressed once again in their Wilderdown pants, Canada Goose Snow Mantra Coat, Gorilla Balaclava, Gripper gloves and Baffin Apex Boots they crunched over the frozen snow to the elevator that had been lowered to bring them to the deck. Currently, it was ten below zero and the wind was blowing hard. They were glad for the warmth and protection of their clothing against the inclement weather.

Jim listened to Andrea and Dorf's report that evening on the radio and grinned with pride. John, also listening in, added his praise to the crew for overcoming the ice storm and deploying the equipment that would be so valuable to Alaska and Canada regarding the Arctic Ocean. They were also pleased with the initial test of the *A&P Railroad* AAV. Pictures of the vehicle cruising across the ice were already on-line and they'd seen the photos of it entering and leaving the water, and then skimming over the ice. It was indeed a powerful vehicle and would probably see a lot of use over the next months.

In a way Jim wished he could take a team out on the ice during the months of darkness and put that plan in the back of his mind for further research. Surely, they could find a grant to fund a study of the northern lights and atmospheric conditions, or the effects of static discharge on local weather. He would get his science team working on research for such grants immediately. Carefully he wrote that note down in his notebook, so that he would not forget.

Andrea addressed the crew before dinner, and Dorf led them in saying grace, and the celebration began. Morale was high, Andrea was glad to see, and despite the freezing temperatures and constant danger his crew was amazing. Silently he took his hat off to his nephews for picking this crew, and he felt a surge of pride to be one of the highest-ranking officers among them.

Brooks Range Expedition

Heading deep into Brooks Range Jim followed Chief and Smitty as they plotted their course. Jim was pleased that the expedition often stopped just to admire the amazing beauty of the mountain range, take pictures, and discuss this vast wilderness. Always four men took up positions to guard the expedition from any danger, trading off the duty, vigilant and ready for anything.

It was a cold blustery morning when they stopped by a small stream that glittered with gold. Jim dismounted, removed his gloves, and picked up a particularly large piece, the size of his thumb, feeling the weight surprisingly heavy. He dropped it back in the stream where he'd found it.

Alistair squatted nearby studying another specimen, which he also returned to the stream. He smiled at his stepson and nodded.

"Good quality. There's probably forty or fifty thousand dollars just lying here waiting for someone to pick it up!" he said with a laugh. They stood.

"Aren't you going to pick it up?" Lynn Ross asked, toying with her blonde hair, as she usually did, even though she wore gloves.

"We'll take a few samples and mark this spot on the map. Perhaps we can make a claim. If someone already has, we'll have to give the gold to that person," Dr. Gregg answered. "I'd like to get a good piece that shows the potential of this site," he added, walking down the stream, and then returning to walk further up. At last, he stopped and called to Jim.

"What do you think about that one?" he asked, pointing.

"Wow!" Jim approved, grinning. "That's a good sample!" he waded into the water, his waterproof boots keeping his feet dry and warm, reached down into the stream and lifted a rock the size of his fist. Half of it was gold ore, the other half beautiful quartz. He and Dr. Gregg bagged the sample and marked it.

"Xun and Jing are back on our trail, about six miles behind us," Chief reported, looking through his powerful binoculars. "They look a little worse for wear and they're missing a packhorse," he added. He studied them critically for a few minutes, and then sighed. Having them back there bothered him, but there was little he could do at the moment.

Just then the roar of an angry bear and the shouts of three men echoed from a canyon they'd been about to enter. Jim vaulted into the saddle, drew his rifle, while Chief drew his own. Clattering into the canyon at a slow run, they came upon three men holding off a very angry bear. One of the men was hunched over and obviously in pain, doing his best to help.

Jim drew up, dismounted, rested his rifle on the saddle of his horse and took aim. Chief did the same. Both shots were kill-shots, slicing through the bear's heart at almost the same instant. With a grunt the bear collapsed on the ground and lay still. Sliding his rifle back in its sheath Jim nodded to Chief. He mounted and followed Chief down to the men.

Wounded and winded one of the men sat with his back to the rocks, obviously hurting every time he drew a breath. Jim took one look at his face and pulled the radio from his saddle.

"*Sea Venture,* this is *Sea Venture One,* over," Though his voice was calm those who knew him knew that there was an emergency.

"Go ahead *Sea Venture One.* This is *Sea Venture Four.* Over," Andrea responded almost instantly.

"Dispatch *Sea Stallion* to these coordinates," Jim read the coordinates from his GPS. "We have a wounded man that needs hospitalization. He will be traveling with two friends, and I'll accompany them. Over," Jim finished.

"Roger *Sea Venture One,*" Andrea replied. "Chopper is being prepped for take-off as we speak. Dorf, Mark, and the Axlerod's will take off in ten. Neff will handle communications. Over."

"Roger that. Tell the Axlerod's that victim may have broken ribs and punctured or nearly punctured lung. Over," Jim said.

"Copy. Wilco," Andrea ended the transmission.

"You have a helicopter?" one of the men asked, stepping up beside him. He nodded at the bear. "Thank you."

"Sorry we didn't get here before your friend was injured. Yes, we have a chopper. It will be here in about fifty minutes. Don't move him until the doctors get down here and assess," Jim replied. "I'm Jim Shepherd, Captain of the *Sea Venture*," he offered his hand.

"I am John Pungowiyi. This is my son Noatak, and my other son Lance is the wounded one. We are hunting Caribou," he pointed down the canyon and Jim saw nervous packhorses carrying two sets of Caribou antlers and several packages of meat that was obviously already butchered and wrapped. "We hoped not to have to kill this bear, but he caught us away from our weapons. All we had were our lances. Thank you again," John submitted.

Jim shook hands with Noatak and knelt down in front of Lance. The young man smiled at him; a lopsided smile full of pain. When he spoke, his voice was strong.

"I do not have a punctured lung, but I do have broken ribs and damage to some of my organs," Chief stepped up then with an ampoule of morphine and a saline drip. Together they hooked up the drip and then Chief slapped the boy's arm. Almost instantly he sighed and relaxed as the pain subsided.

"Do not move," Jim cautioned. "You may not feel much pain now, but if you move you could do much harm. It was heroic that you helped your father and brother against the bear, in spite of your wounds. I have met many brave men, and they would be proud to know you as a friend."

The boy smiled and his father patted Jim on the shoulder. "We will sing of his bravery at our village when we return," he said simply.

"I would be honored to hear that song," Jim said, looking up at the father. "He is strong. He will hear the song too," he encouraged.

"We will dress the bear while we wait," the father said. "Can your people guard our animals and meat?"

"We'll take the meat on the helicopter, and they'll keep your animals for when we return. How far is your village?" Jim replied.

"Seven days ride along this trail," John replied. Chief nodded to Jim, letting him know he could follow the trail. He pulled a satellite map from his pack and showed the village to John. John nodded, looking up at the sky. Then he looked down and motioned to his son Noatak to help him. Chief followed along, drawing his huge knife. John looked at him and smiled his thanks.

Most of the expedition stayed downwind of the bear carcass, avoiding the smell as the three men dressed it out. They wore rubber gloves that went to their armpits, and rubber boots over their insulated boots, being careful not to get blood on their clothing. While Chief and John cut the meat, Noatak wrapped it first in cling wrap, and then in butcher paper. He carefully and expertly tied each segment off with brown twine and marked the portion of meat. It was obvious that this was work he did often enough to establish a pattern. He talked easily while he worked.

Once the bearskin had been removed John offered it to Jim who declined. With a smile and a negative shake of his head he put out both hands and spoke.

"I have no way to cure it, and I shot it from a safe distance. You battled it up close. The skin should be yours." He answered. John beamed at him, and Jim knew he'd made the right decision.

"Your village is Gwich'in, is it not?" Chief asked, as they worked together cutting away the meat.

"Yes. We have occupied that village for over 600 years," John replied, grunting with the effort of keeping up with the Blackfoot. "You are Native American, are you not?" John asked.

"Blackfoot," Chief answered. "Terrance Red Claw. My friends call me Chief."

"You have military bearing," John noted.

"I was a Marine," Chief answered. "Now I'm part of the crew of *Sea Venture*."

"Is it a military ship?" John asked.

"No. We are a research, salvage, search and rescue ship," Chief replied with a grin. "We find lost vessels with treasure and recover the treasure when we can. Mostly we do marine research."

"We watched your expedition. They are arranged like a military group, and four of you always break away when you pause to keep watch," John mentioned casually.

"Old habits are hard to break. We've learned that our military training can help keep us alive and safe, so we use it," Chief replied, his razor-sharp knife slicing through a tendon.

"This is good. To keep the things we learn through life, makes us stronger," John nodded. "You did not take gold from the stream, just one rock. Nor do you hunt for food. Why are you here?"

"See that older gentleman over there. That's Dr. Alistair Gregg. We were in the Lost City of Z when he found a copper plate that mentioned a sacred cave in the Brooks Range where a drawing had been made of an Egyptian vessel hidden in a cave. We search for that cave. Our maps show many caves, so we have to check each one carefully. We would like to find that vessel and study it. That is why we search," Chief grunted as he sliced through the meat.

"Some of the old men in my village could help you eliminate some of those caves," John said, pausing a moment. "Would that help?"

"Very much!" Chief declared with a grin. "For many days now, we have searched. Your help will eliminate much time we might waste. Thank you for making the offer. We already have an agreement with your tribal elders that if we find the cave, they will be shuttled there by helicopter to claim it once again," Chief said.

"I have heard of this. We will help you as much as we are able," John replied. He sighed. "I wish I could accompany you."

"Why not?" Chief intimated. "You and your sons would be welcome."

"Truly?" John asked, pausing again to look at Red Claw's face.

"Absolutely," Chief replied. "We are always glad to have help, especially help from someone who knows the land and especially the dangers to avoid. As you can see, we have women with us whom we wish to protect."

CHAPTER 15

Jim, John, and Wade embraced as only brothers can, meeting at the helipad of the hospital. One of the ER nurses paused to look at the three men and smile at them. Her wrinkled face spoke of long years, and her expression of seriousness of long hours in the ER. But that moment she was feeling something she rarely felt, and she paused to address the three handsome men.

"God, in His wonderful providence, has certainly blessed us with your presence in this area," she said, taking Jim and John by the hands. "You have rescued men that may otherwise have died in the wilderness because rescue crews could not reach them in time. I wish you every success in your ventures and will pray for you. Thank you for being here!"

"God often works things out so that the right people are in the right place," Wade replied, smiling down at her. "Your own work proves that. We thank you for being here and doing what you do."

She beamed at them and moved off with the gurney with Lance, his father, and brother following. The three men stood together watching until all three disappeared through the automatic doors.

"Ours knows the location of the terrorist camp," John said softly to Jim.

"Ours is going to tell us which caves on our map are not

possibilities. That will narrow our search some," Jim replied. "Have you been tailed? Jing and Xun are following us," he added.

"No. No one has shadowed us. We ran into two park rangers and a repair crew for the oil line, but we were able to avoid them. So far no one knows we are out there," John answered. "My guys get released from the hospital tomorrow morning, so I'll be taking them out to show us where to look, and then dropping them at their village."

"Don't get dead," Jim grinned, slapping John on the shoulder.

"Jing doesn't seem all that stable. Don't let him get a good line of fire on you," John said seriously.

"Right now, he's six miles behind us, but he'll close that gap a little because of this delay. My team is taking the horses and equipment to the Gwich'in village where these three came from. We'll probably be able to join them tomorrow or the next day. Chief will make our trail very hard to follow once they turn off for the village," Jim replied.

"They could get ahead of you!" Wade cautioned, concern in his voice.

"So far, they've searched for the trail until they found it again. I'll have Chief hang back and watch them. I want to know where they are too," Jim said with a wry grin. "I expect the Gwich'in will help as well. They seem to be a nice people, very willing to help, and very connected to the land."

As Jim predicted, on the following day Lance was released from the hospital, and though very sore and still ill, was able to make the flight back to his village. For the children of the village, it was an exciting morning, watching the huge *Sea Stallion* drop from the sky outside the village.

After speaking with the chief who made the request, Jim gave permission for every child to have a ride in the chopper and Dorf and Mark made sure they saw some wonderful vistas from the sky. He and Mark were also trying to spot Jing and Xun, and they did so on their first pass over the spot Chief suggested. They were looking for the trail, and they had foolishly taken a canyon that led them in the opposite direction. To further confuse them, Dorf flew west for a few miles before circling around and brining the children back.

That night, in the village, the bear was cooked, and a feast was held. As predicted, the song of Lance's courage, and the bravery of his father and brother as they fought the great bear was presented. Although none of the *Sea Venture* crew understood the language, they could follow the song by the expressions on the faces of those listening. Jim ate bear for the first time, and he found that the greasy meat was at least palatable.

Cecilia found the language fascinating, many of the words ending with sounds like *wik, nak, tuk, tak, buk, bak, vik,* and *vak,* all ending with that "k" or even a "kt" sound. She watched the mothers with the babies and sighed with pleasure. Gwich'in were a people that understood and appreciated life far more than most British or Americans. The children, she noted, were happy, busy, and creative. They didn't spend hours in front of a television or iPad, instead, the children used their imaginations and used simple things around them to invent games. Like all children they squabbled and fought, but most problems were solved before they got out of hand. Her own children would be that way, she vowed. Jim was certainly that way. He was never bored.

Much of that came, she knew, from growing up on the sea. As a child he'd gone with his father on the boat when he wasn't in school. Jim, John, and Wade learned from Robert Shepherd to love times of rest and relaxation, games that challenged the mind, and hard work and its rewards. Pondering how parents influence future generations, she prayed for wisdom. Laying her head on Jim's shoulder she took his hand and sighed once more.

After the feast the men gathered together close to the fire and looked at the maps Alistair had. They talked for almost two hours about various caves and what would be found in them. None of the tribe ever thought of using satellite images to find the ancient cave of their people, and they found both the idea and the technology and idea fascinating and exciting.

John Pungowiyi and his son Noatak would accompany the team in their search, as Red Claw promised. It was obvious that his chief and the other men of the tribe held John Pungowiyi in high regard. Chief was convinced that the man would prove worthy.

The expedition stayed in camp the following day to rest, and the helicopter left in the morning to return to the ship. JP, as the men nicknamed him quickly, and Noatak took the Shepherds and Greggs to a beautiful waterfall about three kilometers from the village and they spent most of the day enjoying the beauty of the spot.

John Pungowiyi knew that most mainland Americans didn't know how to enjoy nature. These people, he discovered with a deep sense of relief, were different. They spoke of how the sunlight played across the water and gleamed from the falls, reflecting in a myriad of bright flashes. Pausing often to study a beautiful flower they touched the pedals with gentleness and respect and a deep sense of awe. Some photographed the birds, especially some of the more colorful males, as well as insects. He was very pleased by this as he watched them.

They were careful too. Many hikers that came into the range did not care about things like litter. Not one tiny piece of paper was allowed to fall to the ground that was not picked up and disposed of properly. Nor did they miss the opportunity to drink of the water from the falls. Jim carefully filled all four canteens with the water.

Noatak speared two large trout and his father cooked them for lunch. John took the Shepherds and Greggs off to hunt for berries. They stretched out on the ground near the pool beneath the waterfall and ate the trout and berries, a simple meal but delicious, and talked long into the afternoon. Both the Shepherds and the Greggs were like sponges, learning everything they could about survival in the range, foods that were available, and how to find them. It was near the supper hour when they finally returned to the village.

Jim asked JP to take the whole expedition to the falls in the morning, and John was surprised when they stopped and enjoyed the beauty of that spot until after lunch. It was his first experience with a meal from an MRE package, and he found the food surprisingly good. He and Noatak were both surprised to eat hot food that was not cooked over a fire, but rather, heated in a package.

In the afternoon they came to a meadow filled with wildflowers.

Again, the expedition paused, spending nearly an hour simply looking at the flowers, photographing them, and identifying the birds that stopped by. JP noted again that four of the team remained vigilant, moving so that they were protecting the whole group. Always they faced outwards, watching, and very observant.

Jim was one of them, and he dismounted and squatted in front of his horse, his eyes scanning the area in his arc of protection. John came to squat beside him. Both of them saw it at the same time. A mountain lion stalked across an open space three hundred yards from their position. Watching this new friend JP noted that Jim did not reach for rifle or the cannon he carried on his chest. Instead, he just watched the animal.

"They're amazing animals, aren't they?" Jim asked John softly as they watched the cat pause, look at them, and move on. "I've read that they cover sixty square miles of territory!"

"It has caught the scent of our horses and mules. But the presence of so many people will probably keep it away," John replied.

"Most likely," Jim replied quietly. His eyes took in the fluid motion of the stride, the power of its limbs, and the way it tested the air with its nose, listening with its ears turning about. Secretly he'd always loved lions and tigers and looked forward to the day when he could take his son to the Zoo to see them. Later, when he was older, they would hunt together for food.

"You know, I envy the life you and your son enjoy up here," Jim said quietly. "You can hunt together, and a day does not go by when you do not see the wonder of nature or have to fight together against its fury."

"You live much the same on the sea, do you not?" John asked. He nodded slowly. "The sea is as unforgiving in nature as these mountains. It is good that we have met this way. That our lives have touched, even for a short time, will bear good fruit. I have met few men from the mainland that can teach us things of worth and value," Jim noted the sadness in JP's voice as he stated that fact, and thought, not for the first time, that America had fallen far from its roots in decency and wisdom.

After an hour and a half of enjoying the meadow, they moved on to their first campsite, pitched the tents and put up the perimeter defenses, and settled in for the evening. It was still as bright as it had been all day, but they were used to the constant light, and even welcomed it. Jim wondered again what it was like with constant darkness.

Listening to the discussion that evening with pleasure, Jim paid careful attention to all that was shared. They talked of the waterfall, the meadow, and the amazing vistas they'd enjoyed that day, of the rugged beauty of Brooks Range. Wildlife sightings were recounted, and JP was surprised when they paused to thank God for His amazing creation.

"I have always loved the mountains," Chief said after the prayer. "Often as a teen I traveled far from my own home in the Rockies, just to see something more of the wonder in which I lived. The solitary nature of such ventures gives a man time to think long and hard, and it teaches wisdom.

"What's the point of seeing something amazing if you don't pause long enough to fully enjoy it? People drive by places of beauty and see them in a flash, never able to enjoy the intricacies of nature, the mixing of colors and the amazing abundance of life that goes on around them. Yet these wonders abound, and they live entire lives without ever enjoying them!

"I have stopped to watch a spider build a web, remaining to watch the sun dance on the dewdrops on that same web the next morning. Once I saw a battle between a tarantula and a tarantula wasp. Nature is brutal and savage. But in nature there is purpose in the brutality and savagery. And contrary to popular belief, it is not always survival of the fittest. God's hand is visible, even in the world of insects.

"And so, I know, because I have seen it, that God is not a God who rules from a vast distance, watching rather than taking an active interest. No! God put us in the right place at the right time to save Lance from being killed by the bear. He put John and Wade in place to rescue that father and son. Every moment of our lives His hand is upon us, and we are never out of His sight, or out of His hand!"

"And that lays upon us a solemn responsibility," Alistair continued, picking up the lesson. "We have the capacity to learn, and each one of us has specific areas of interest. Learning everything we can about our world, past, present, and future is of vital importance. In the past we see how God intervened in history. In the present we live in His world. And in the future, He will continue His purpose. In all of that we have a place! That is what always amazes me!"

"Your father speaks wisely," JP said to Jim as Alistair continued to talk about learning. Alistair was a dynamic speaker, and Jim nodded as his stepfather continued his talk. He knew that the words his stepfather spoke would be filled with depth and reverence for God and history.

"It isn't enough just to know about these things. No! I know many who know many things but are foolish men and women. They teach in colleges and universities around the world, and though they are verbose people their words are empty and foolish. None of them would agree with that, by the way. True wisdom comes only from the Lord, and it will always be marked by real humility. True wisdom forces us to humility.

"To many of my learned colleagues I am the fool because I believe in the God of the Bible. They scoff at the myriad evidence that He is. Yet a day will come when they must stand before Him, and then their scoffing will be cut off, and they will tremble in fear. Alas, for many it will be too late. The blundering boneheads will have gone through life thinking they know, only to discover that they were the fools! They should remember the words of Princeton University when it was founded. Cursed be all knowledge that is contrary to the cross of Christ was written in the purpose statement of the college!

"I have personally visited many historical wonders, sites of archaeological significance, but what can compare with this?" he waved his hand around at the beauty surrounding them. "Look at the delicate pedals of this wildflower, its vibrant color, its apparent vulnerability in nature. Yet this flower could break stone! And here it blooms where there are few people to enjoy it. I believe that God looks upon His creation with great joy, and that these flowers are here to praise Him!

"Savor the scents in the air, the magnificent vistas we are seeing, and appreciate that a world is coming that is even more beautiful than this. It is hard to imagine, but I can't wait to see it! And finally, I will be able to learn the things that really matter, to understand this world and that one with a deeper and more lasting knowledge than I have ever known.

"And do you know what I think will be my constant thought?" he looked around at them with a smile of deep appreciation. "I think my constant thought will be that my God is beyond understanding and worthy of all praise and glory!"

"If you find the evidence you seek in this cave, what then?" JP asked in the silence that followed.

"We will know three things," Alistair said softly. "First, we will know that man ranged much farther by sea than historians once thought. Second, we will know the location of where to find this ship. And third, we will have another piece of the puzzle of how ideas spread from one part of the world to another."

"I am hopeful that we will once more know the location of our sacred cave," JP said. And then he laughed.

"Why do you laugh so?" Cecilia asked. Jim noticed that she was moving her hand softly over her extended belly, as though caressing the child that lay within.

"Because I think our stories and memories will change as we look at the cave in the light of our present beliefs," JP said. "The Gwich'in have always considered the importance of our past and have fought to keep our ways intact over the years of change. Russians, Spaniards, and later the English and French have all tried to change those ways."

"Yes. Every culture has sown within it the arrogance that its ways are best," Alistair said with a wry smile. Then his face grew sad. "We have sullied almost everything we have tried to change for the better," he said, shaking his head.

"You are strange, friend Alistair," John chuckled. "I have met many learned men, but you do not have the arrogance they carry like a mantle. I believe you see things much more clearly than they do."

"Thank you, John. I hope so. In my many years of study one thing I have learned that I intend to hold on to with everything ounce of strength. I am at my best when I am a student. There is more to learn than I can ever know!" he said.

"Aren't we all?" FM grunted.

"Hey boss! I think FM is sick!" Zeke scoffed, grinning at Jim. "I think he was being serious!"

"Maybe we should give him some cod liver oil!" Barbara said with a laugh.

"Now I am sick!" FM said with a grimace. "Just thinkin' about drinkin' something that disgusting turns my stomach! Hey! Anyone have any fried tarantulas in their MREs?" Barbara almost gagged at the memory of FM eating one of those in the Motto Grasso region.

"Never mind! He's better," Jim chuckled.

"Hi! I'm Yule Gibbons. This fried tarantula reminds me of smoked hickory nuts!" FM quipped, mimicking the famous natural food guru from the past.

"Stop it, or I'll make you eat an entire bowl of tofu!" Mary Ann said, holding her sides as she laughed.

"I'm sick again boss!" FM said holding his stomach.

"What is tofu?" John asked, laughing with the rest.

"It's sort of a cross between a bowl of snot mixed with some kind of goat vomit!" FM replied.

"You're awful!" Cecilia laughed with a look of horror on her face.

"And I still don't know what tofu is," John laughed.

"Tofu is also called bean curd. It's made from coagulating soymilk and then pressing the curds into squares. Very popular in the east it's a new fad in natural foods," Jim explained, still laughing. The look on John's face was comical.

"I think FM's description sounds quite literal!" John said with some disgust.

"I'd take it over Pemmican any day," Chief grunted.

"I guess we all have disgusting foods in our culture," John grinned.

"When my wife eats smoked char in the winter her breath can peal paint!"

"Don't you eat smoked char?" Cecilia asked, raising an eyebrow.

"Of course, but my breath can always peal paint," John replied with a straight face. His son Noatak nodded and waved a hand in front of his nose.

They slept that night with light hearts.

CHAPTER 16

"**N**unamiut have lived in this region for many hundreds of years." Paneak said quietly. He was the father John and Wade rescued and they were driving along in the Jeep. Paneak was surprised at how quiet the vehicles were running on hydraulics and fascinated by the engineering. His son Mekiana was talking animatedly with Wade about the advantages of hydraulic propulsion, and John was impressed with the boy's knowledge of engineering. He said so to his father.

"Yes. He loves mechanical engineering and has taught me much," Paneak replied with some pride. In a month he will join the Navy so he can go to Wyo-Tech, a school in Wyoming that teaches such things. It has been a dream of his for some time."

"That's a very good school," Wade said, hearing the comment. "It will open many doors for you," he said to Mekiana.

Behind them the convoy moved along the road, the only sound the turning of the tires on the gravel of the road. In the open Jeep Paneak could hear the wind rustling the leaves of the trees and the cries of birds above the sound of the tires. When they came to a steep hill he was amazed at the surge of power as the Jeep leapt up the steep incline. Mekiana noticed as well.

"That's some torque!" he said with appreciation. Wade spent the next half hour explaining how they'd designed the torque converter to provide more foot-pounds of torque to give the vehicles tremendous power over uneven terrain. To Wade's delight Mekiana asked all the right questions about spec changes to drive trains and other power output devices on the vehicle. John listened to it all with a grin, knowing his best friend intimately, and appreciating the ability God had given Wade in engineering.

"Aren't you worried at all that exposing to Mekiana to our world of technology and engineering will take him far from you and your family?" John asked Paneak suddenly.

Paneak smiled and nodded. "We live in this world. If Mekiana goes far away, he will take what he has learned and keep it close to his heart, and his home will ever be in our village and among our people, for there his family dwells. Yet it would be wrong if we tried to hold him back from becoming what he truly desires to become. That, my friend, may seem like an antinomy, but it is the way of life. You are going to have a child soon too. Would you hold him back?"

"No," John said with a smile. "I'd encourage him. That's sort of why I asked," he admitted.

"Mekiana was always able to fix tools and machines. Even as a young boy he could take apart and rebuild the motors of our chainsaws, splitters, and other tools we use. Often, he was able to do it better than those experienced in the work. Such talent is unusual among us, but something to be embraced rather than feared. Fear limits knowledge," Paneak said quietly.

They talked on of this and that as they traveled through the next few days, finally reaching a position about four miles from the terrorist stronghold where Paneak knew they could keep the vehicles well hidden, even from the air. He had never seen any air support, but if any were available, their convoy would not be noticed from above.

It was a perfect place. They drove down into a canyon and beneath a natural outcropping of the cliff face above them large enough to hide even the duce-and-a-half. Toward the rear of the opening was a large enough opening to get them into a dry area. Water dripped from the ceiling of the outcropping, but far enough away from the vehicles to keep them dry.

Paneak watched the men prepare for the night's venture to discover what they faced and looked at his son. Mekiana knew what his father was thinking. The men in the fortress above were not like these men. True, there were bad men in the fortress, men of violence, but they were as children next to these men. The two smiled at one another and nodded.

On a topographical map John noted the exact position of the fortress. Earlier that day Pen took photographs as she flew over the pipeline. Helicopters were used to fly the pipeline on a regular basis, and it had been easy to arrange for their chopper to be used for that day's flight plan. The photos she took pinpointed the location of the fortress and it was now marked on the map, which Paneak was using to show John the best points of penetration.

"We don't know what kind of resources they have," John said to the men once they'd finished preparing their equipment and weapons and gathered around. "Whatever technology they have could detect us, so we'll have to be very careful. Let's be very quiet as we move in close to the fortress. If there are trees around the perimeter, we can get someone up there to look inside. Remember your training and stick to the basics. Slow and steady wins the race!

"Once we know the sentry situation and placement, we'll be able to get some men inside. We can't use darkness this time, so we need to be invisible. Care wins the prize!" he looked at his men and they nodded, already entering that zone of concentration John knew well, the concentration on basic skills that would allow them to move and act as one cohesive unit. He nodded with satisfaction.

"Get something to eat and let's sleep for four hours. We'll leave at 2200 hours." The men grunted, and moved away, pulling out their MRE packs and selecting what they wanted for dinner. An hour later Paneak noticed that Raider left the under cropping to take up positions to watch for enemies.

An hour later they were relieved by Zulu, and an hour later by Sniper. One hour after Sniper took up positions Raider was up again and moving to those guard positions again. Once again, he exchanged a look with his son. At no time had either heard even a pebble disturbed as the men moved.

Later, as the men dressed in the camouflage outfits, and painted their faces, Paneak and Mekiana watched with interest. Once finished the men put on all their gear, and the two onlookers realized it was a great deal of equipment. When they were assembled John went down the line checking packs and vests, bumping shoulders with each of his men as he moved. That was the only sound they heard, the bumping of shoulders, and his hands checking the gear. Both Indians shivered as they looked at the twelve-man team.

Paneak took point with Vince Hall, whose vivid blue eyes seemed brighter against the paint on his face, and they were fierce eyes, looking quickly in every direction as the two moved out ahead of the group. Used to moving through the wilderness quietly Paneak realized that the six-foot two-inch man beside him was even quieter, despite his military garb and boots.

Vince did not hurry. He placed his feet carefully once they were in the woodlands above, near the pipeline. Choosing a good place to cross the open space he moved quickly but silently, startling some Caribou grazing nearby. As they leaped up and ran Vince dropped into the high grass and stopped completely. Not until the last animal was gone and he was convinced no one had eyes on did he move again. Paneak shook his head in wonder.

Once in the woods Vince sprayed something on a tree and turned right. Paneak could see nothing on the bark and whispered his question.

To answer him Vince took off his sunglasses and gave them to the Indian. Once he put them on, he could see the mark clearly, an arrow indicating the turn to the right. He gave the glasses back with a nod.

"It won't stay there. The liquid evaporates within half an hour leaving no residue." Vince whispered.

They moved now very slowly, as if hunting, and Paneak was impressed with the bigger man's ability of stealth. After about an hour of movement they halted, having covered one kilometer. Ten minutes later the team arrived. No one spoke. Instead, they drank from their canteens, sitting quietly or standing silently. Ten minutes later the powerful Clancy Franklin took point with Paneak.

Clancy was built like a gymnast, two inches shorter than his friend Vince, with huge and powerful arms and legs. Again, Paneak was amazed at how slowly and silently the soldier moved. Somehow Clancy seemed even more intent than Vince. He had brown eyes and his head moved slowly, looking down to place his feet, looking up, sweeping from left to right, looking up above in the trees, his constant vigilance a tangible thing.

He did not speak. Vince had whispered a few times. Clancy used hand motions. Once he pointed to the left and Paneak froze. A Grizzly Bear sat clawing honey out of a beehive, the bees buzzing angrily around him. The bear had not smelled them, but Paneak could smell the bear now. Clancy moved on, and the bear never even knew they were near! Hearing the soft triple click ahead Paneak figured that Clancy was somehow signaling the danger of the bear to the men behind.

At the next rendezvous Wade took point. Even taller and heavier than Vince the giant was like a gentle breeze passing through the forest. Like the men before he moved his head the same way, his eyes taking in everything, missing nothing. Even a nut displaced by a scampering squirrel in a nearby tree drew his attention causing him to pause to assess the danger. Nor did Wade proceed immediately. With a small smile he watched the little squirrel dance through the branches.

Paneak was aware that he could hear the tiny claws of the squirrel on the bark of the branches and that his attention level was higher than normal. He knew it was the influence of the watchfulness and care of the men he now hunted with. Again, he smiled. The men planning to harm the pipeline would not succeed.

After the final rendezvous point John took the lead. He would take point leading them to the fortress. Different than the other men he pointed out various birds, a Wolverine, and a Porcupine. At one point he paused and pointed to a deer with two fawns. Both men stood quietly as the three animals daintily stepped through the foliage ahead of them, never aware that they were close to instant death and destruction.

John drew to the very edge of the forest and studied the fortress before him, clicking his communication gear four times to indicate he'd arrived. Paneak listened carefully. No sound from the forest came to him, other than the wind passing through the leaves. A hand landed on his shoulder, and he nearly jumped out of his skin. It was Norm Geissler, followed by Calvin Weston. Both men hunkered down behind the brush, parting it cautiously, looking out at the fortress, unaware of how startled their Indian guide was and not thinking at all of what his thoughts of all this might be. They had a job to do, and the mission was everything at this point.

Geissler made a motion with his right hand, pointing upwards and then at his eyes. Rock nodded once, chose a tree, and carefully and silently climbed into its branches, hidden from view on the side away from the fortress. Again, Paneak listened carefully, but he heard only the creak of the branches receiving the weight of a man, nothing else.

Looking back, he tried to find the team, and located some though they were hard to see, blending so well into the background. He knew they were close but could see only seven of them, including the three he was close to. He shivered again.

On the fortress wall one man could be seen staring out to the west, smoking a cigar, the gray puffs of smoke wreathing his face as they rose. He was at a corner, and he was the only person visible. John made some motions with his hands that Paneak didn't understand, but C.G. responded immediately. He moved farther away and finally Paneak saw him enter the clearing behind the sentry posted on the wall. He was gone a moment and then appeared going over the wall!

A few seconds later a shadow seemed to rise behind the smoker, and he disappeared silently. Absolutely no sound reached Paneak's ears. Four minutes later the body of the sentry rolled over the top of the wall and was lowered down by one leg. Wade sprinted out, caught the body, draped it over his shoulder, and sprinted back to the woods.

The sentry was not dead, but so sound asleep he made no sound as Wade checked the plastic restraint ties that bound his wrists and hands before gagging him and stuffing him under some brush. Paneak relaxed suddenly. These men did not kill unnecessarily. It had worried him. He found John looking at him with understanding. The intense blue eyes of the leader of these amazing men told Paneak he would explain later.

An hour later C.G. appeared at the wall, slipped over the edge, and dropped to the ground softly. He sprinted to the woods and John motioned and suddenly they were all moving back into the safety of the forest. Some distance from the fortress they all came together, stepping silently from the cover of the forest, all except Rock still up in the tree keeping watch.

"SIT REP, Rock!" John said into his COM LINK.

"Nobody's missed the guard, and nobody's up. I saw C.G. pick up the guard's walkie-talkie. If they miss him, they'll probably use that to try to communicate first," Rock replied. "Over."

"Roger that. Keep us posted. Over," John said, releasing the talk button on his headgear.

"C.G., what did you see in there?" John asked, turning to his friend.

"Stupid careless!" C.G. said with derision. "No sentries placed on the ground, only one on the wall, every door unlocked, everyone asleep. Trash everywhere, and they stink to high heavens. Apparently showering is not mandatory. The latrine must be outside the fortress. I didn't see any facilities inside, not even a portapotty!

"I saw a chalkboard outside the main shack. It says they're going to check out the pipeline for placement of explosives at 0900 this morning. Once I saw that I located the explosives shack. There's some nice stuff in there! I also checked one or two weapons lying about. Apparently keeping your weapon clean and operational is not high on their list of things to do. It's the usual AK-47 and M-16 mix, with one or two Uzi's thrown in. Automatic pistols, three or four types!"

"Who are we dealing with?" John asked.

"Mostly French and Canadian passports. The equipment in the

main shack and in the explosive's shack was mostly Chinese. At least two of the sleeping gents in there are American. They tend to be less smelly than the others," C.G. replied. Paneak was amazed that C.G. had seen all this and was undetected. These men were truly ghosts.

"Okay. Get some rest. If they go out to look at where they're going to place the charges we can go inside, and then see what else they might be up to. After that we'll see," John said.

The men immediately broke up, ate something, drained their canteens, and while one man from each unit went to fill them with fresh water from the river, they made a small safe camp up in the trees, using lightweight aluminum frames to create platforms. These were covered with branches and leaves from the trees themselves until Paneak could barely discern their presence.

Into these they climbed, and one man kept guard while the rest rested or slept. Paneak could see Mekiana on a platform not far away, already resting against the bole of the tree, his eyes closed. He too took what rest he could. Morning came, and with it, increased activity in the fortress. Suddenly the walkie-talkie next to John came to life.

"Bonet! Où êtes-vous?" the voice said through static.

"J'ai entendu un bruit dans les bois et est allé à enquêter. J'ai poursuivi par un ours, et maintenant je suis perdu!" John whispered into the unit.

"La rivière est à l'ouest. Allez vers l'ouest jusqu'à ce que vous la trouverez et retour. Tous ensemble, nous allons sortir de la construction du pipeline afin de déterminer où les meilleurs pour porter des armements. Nous trouver, vous idiote!" the voice spat back. John grinned. He translated for the others.

"Our prisoner is named Bonet. I told him I was chased by a bear and lost. He told me the river is to the west, find it, and find them. They're going out to decide the best place to locate the explosives."

"Hope the bloke has a compass," Hobbs said quietly from his platform not far away.

"Not anymore," C.G. commented. "I took all his weapons and equipment away from him."

"I guess he won't find the river!" Hobbs laughed.

As nine o'clock rolled around the men watched the entire fortress empty as the slovenly troops noisily trekked down the trail toward the river and the pipeline. John watched quietly as they went and Paneak noticed that no one moved at all during the entire time the enemy was visible. Only after they were gone did people begin to move. These men were so careful that Paneak knew discovery by the enemy was impossible!

"Nice!" Norm Geissler commented. "They left the front door open."

"Oh! There are two cheap cameras at the front gate. They're the only ones I saw. They're pointing out so we shouldn't go in that way," C.G. said.

"We'll go in over the back wall and make sure we're alone before we search the place," John declared.

The men climbed down, the last ones folding the aluminum platforms and stowing them in packs. Soon they were all inside the compound and John dispersed the teams to search. He and his team took the main shack and there they discovered the full plan, written out, with emails to a Chinese source detailing their operation as well as numbered accounts where large sums had been registered.

"Careless!" John grunted as he copied the hard drives of the two computers onto a backup unit he carried. He searched for the passwords, found them, and wrote them in a small notebook. Zeke and News would be able to crack any that didn't work in seconds anyway. He made his call to the ship and talked to News about what he'd just sent him. News was already studying the information and said he'd get back when he had everything.

"This backup disk is wired into the ship, so that everything I just took off these computers is now in our computer system on the ship. News will put together an information package we can take to the authorities when it's time to round up these hooligans," John explained to Paneak.

"They will resist law enforcement." Paneak said.

"We'll provide backup." John replied without looking at the

Indian. He didn't see the look of satisfaction that crossed the man's face.

Wade was photographing the maps on the walls with the plans for placing the explosives. When he was finished Mekiana stepped up to the map.

"If they blow it here the oil will get into the river and will flow down to the sea, destroying everything as it goes!" he said with some heat.

"Diabolical," Wade replied without inflection.

CHAPTER 17

"**W**e have to move fast," John instructed as they hiked back toward their vehicles. "I want guard, police and forestry department personnel on location tonight when they go to plant those explosives. Catching them with the explosives will be enough to convict them and insure some prison time.

Before nightfall National Guard, Alaskan State Police, and the Forestry Department enforcement personnel were on location. John's INTEL placed them at the three locations where the explosives were to be set. Two of the groups went down without a fight, surprised and frightened by the sudden appearance of National Guardsmen.

The third group was better equipped and trained, holding off the police long enough to actually set the explosives. Watching with concern John and Zulu saw seventeen officers go down. John called in the chopper for air support and in a daring move brought Zulu right into the center of the terrorists, doing serious damage, added to the chopper's deadly fire. Even then John and Wade both took hits from hastily drawn pistols that could have been fatal if not for their protective gear. Grunting in pain both Marines put down the two shooters.

Alone in the middle of armed enemies John and his team didn't hesitate to apply the military solution. Within a few seconds all but the leader, Jenner Danzig lay dead. He stared in disbelief at the carnage around him as the Alaskan State Police officer in charge came into the carnage like a bull in a china shop, his face suffused with color, his walk full of anger.

"Who the hell are you? I wanted these men alive! I did not give the order to take them out! And who was in that chopper?"

Without saying a word John turned to the explosives on the pipeline and pointed. There was less than a minute to go before the bomb blew. That took all the bluff out of the police Captain. Danzig smiled.

"We all die, no?" he sneered.

"No," John replied. "Only your men died tonight, and only because I had to bring my unit in to stop this bomb," John looked at the State Police officer with a stern look and went to the timer on the explosives. Seconds ticked off as he studied it. The officer in charge of the State Police unit, and his men, began to sweat profusely as John studied the explosive, but he did notice that none of John's men seemed concerned. They were calm. Finally, he took a wire cutter from his vest and cut the yellow wire leading from the timer. Danzig's shoulders slumped in defeat as the timer stopped, with just eight seconds left! It just wasn't possible that someone could look at his configuration and figure out how to stop it!

"We weren't expecting the level of resistance," the captain said to John as he turned away from the timer. Sweat poured down his face and he suddenly appreciated the presence of these men and their expertise. For a moment he was sure they were all going to die. John interrupted his thoughts.

"Learn for next time. No one can predict what anyone's going to do, Captain," John said, giving the captain a friendly clap on the shoulder. He had also given the man a chance to regain face. The captain didn't miss that. Squaring his shoulders, he took charge, watching John and his men as he did so, and realized that they weren't glory hounds, weren't going to countermand his orders, or anything else. They melted into the background. He sought them out afterwards.

"I owe you. Seventeen of our people were wounded in that encounter." He said softly so that Danzig couldn't hear. He watched John as the man turned to look at him before answering, and he decided that this was a very dangerous man.

"Don't forget that Danzig didn't run away. He was willing to die right here. Find out why, please," John said equally softly.

Fortunately for them, Danzig did not put together that the soldiers that took his men down were not with the National Guard. In his one phone call he mentioned the National Guard, State Police, and Forestry Department, but no one else. His call was not to an attorney. John knew what would open his mouth and finally Danzig was allowed to use a laptop computer. When he checked his bank accounts his face drained of all color. The money was gone!

Yao Li Wu had intimated that he would not accept failure. Danzig believed it was he who moved the money, never suspecting that *Bring It Up* helped Alaska State Police to confiscate all the funds with the provision that the money would be used to better protect the pipeline. Wu was unaware of this as well. What he meant was that he would soon be sending Xun and Jing to silence Danzig.

Suddenly the three "ecological" organizations became national and international news, ecological terrorists that banded together to destroy the Trans Alaska Pipeline. Detailed plans were leaked to news sources showing the devastation they would have caused had the oil gotten into the river system and flowed to the sea. Organizations previously sworn to protect the ecology of the world were momentarily seen for what they really were. Yao Li Wu saw what he feared most occurring before his eyes. The Zhanzhu Triad was named as the funding organization for this dastardly deed, with proof from the bank accounts, every cent followed to Zhanzhu accounts.

Rather than wait for the leaders of the Triad to decide his fate, Yao stepped off the balcony of his 62nd story office, plunging to his death, literally crashing through an empty bus on the street below. Unable to reach Xun he knew that he would be unable to silence Danzig and the terrorists he hired. John read the news report with a deep sense of sadness.

Knowing that the Zhanzhu Triad would leave no stone uncovered he quickly gave word that his team was to return to the ship, where they were believed to be. He rented a warehouse in which to store the vehicles until his return and flew with Penelope in the AH 1W Super Cobra while the rest of the crew flew in the CH 53 Sea Stallion.

It was, John thought, typical that after a major success they would face a horrendous challenge. Just after arriving on the ship another ice storm formed with record speed and hit the ship. On board the *A&P Railroad* Chance received the news of the impending storm and made a change of direction, skirting the storm so they could study it without actually getting in it.

Once again *Sea Venture* was stopped and covered by ice. Dr. Putnam's bots performed perfectly, keeping the exterior of the ship clear of forming ice. The only surface not protected was the platform they used for moving crates and containers on and off the ship. A full fourteen inches of ice formed on that surface!

That much ice, forming on the surface of the ship, would have caused a great deal of damage, and threatened the ship itself. The sheer weight of the ice was amazing, and as it froze it expanded. Wrench, Inchworm, and Goody planned for that, and used a popular rhino coat on the surface. They sighed when they realized it would have to be recoated.

Another ship was caught in the ice storm. It was the trawler that Dorf believed was searching for that sunken vessel of gold, not trawling for fish. As the ice storm ended their SOS signal came through. The added weight of the ice was threatening to sink their ship, and they were trapped inside, unable to open any hatches or doors. Hearing the edge of fear in the voice on the radio was mute testimony of the predicament.

"Radio the Coast Guard that we can get them off the ship by chopper," John said as he listened to the radio. It will give us a chance to figure out what those idiots are looking for. My guess is our steamer. Rock 'n Roll lifted the radio mic and called the Coast Guard. Their chopper was within forty miles of the trawler. He gave the information to the Coast Guard and received permission to rescue the people on the boat.

"Once you get everyone off see if Chance can mosey over there to take a look before the ship goes down," John added when Rock 'n Roll was finished with the transmission.

"Are you sure it will go down?" Richard asked his commanding officer.

"If we find what I suspect we'll find on board, it probably will sink," John said with a wink.

Delta and Raider went in the chopper with Dorf and Mark at the controls. It took them a little over an hour to break away enough ice to open a hatch and release the men trapped inside. There were six of them and the hours they'd spent trapped inside the ship, listening to the cracking and creaking as the ice hardened about the outer shell of the vessel had demoralized them completely.

The captain of the stranded ship noticed that everyone returned to the chopper, much to his relief, and was surprised that they took the time to store their tools carefully before taking off. As the helicopter rose into the sky he sighed with relief. If the ship sank, he'd been paid enough to purchase another one with the insurance he'd receive. His relief faded when Hobbs sat down in front of him.

"You've destroyed a good part of the coral on the bottom dragging your hooks. That's very careless, and also against the rules," Hobbs said conversationally, fastening his seatbelt. "We took photos of the hooks you were using for evidence."

"Are you going to nark on me?" the captain asked.

"Too late. Dr. Alice Dinsmore has already registered a formal complaint to AOOS and the Conservation Department. We've got detailed pictures of the trench you dug in the coral. Very ugly! No one is going to cut you any slack, so tell me what you were looking for," Hobbs replied.

"It's a fishing trawler! What do you think we were doing?" the captain scoffed. It was the tone of his voice that told Hobbs what he wanted to know.

"Ah! And yet when your ship returned a few days ago you had no catch," he replied evenly.

"That happens sometimes," he replied evasively.

"And yet you deposited a grand sum of money in your bank account!" Hobbs just looked at him and the captain began to think hard.

"I won a bet," he said finally.

"Good on you!" Hobbs said with a smile that never reached his eyes. "Of course, you will report that windfall with the IRS, won't you?" Hobbs added after a moment.

"I don't have to tell you nothin'!" the man snapped.

"I don't have to tell you anything. There's no excuse for poor grammar, old boy," Hobbs smiled at the captain again, making the man swallow.

"You wanna know anything else, talk to my attorney!" the captain said.

"Mr. Donnelly!" Hobbs snapped suddenly.

"Sir!" Bear snapped to attention.

"What happens to a man who is staked to the ice and has water poured on his naked wrinklies?" Hobbs asked.

"As the ice hardens it crushes his gonads, sir," Bear replied. "It's very painful," he added.

"Dorf, put us down on the ice, please," Hobbs said into his COMLINK. Grinning widely Dorf descended to the ice and landed.

"What are you doing?" the captain asked.

"We're going to stake you down on the ice naked," Hobbs informed him calmly.

He stood up. The captain's men tried to defend him, but the battle inside the chopper lasted only seconds. The appearance of several automatic pistols stopped all resistance.

"Now! Unless you want to tell me what you were looking for, and who paid you to look for it, I'm going to stake you to the ice and pour water on your wrinklies until they freeze solid," Hobbs could tell the captain was still looking for a way out.

"Bear!" Hobbs snapped.

Donnelly lifted the captain bodily and headed out onto the ice. D.C. and Bond helped to stake him out and remove his clothing. Naked and shivering the captain watched the first pitcher of water poured over his unmentionables. It took about five minutes for the pain to really hit him, and when it did, he screamed. Another pitcher of water was added, and his mind formed a picture of the ice constricting, doing permanent damage. He broke at that point.

"Okay! I'll talk!" he begged.

"Talk fast. This ice is freezing fast," Hobbs said, squatting beside him. The captain collapsed and spilled the story.

"We're looking for a ship full of gold bullion," he said.

He cried out in pain. "A Dutch firm is paying me to look for it. They're going to send out some equipment but told me to simply trawl where they thought it might have gone down over a hundred years ago. Please!" he pleaded.

"Names, friend," Hobbs said.

The captain gave him the names. Warm water was poured over the forming ice and the man was hauled back on the chopper. Bond silently handed him his clothing and he climbed into it with tears running down his face after drying off. He sat gingerly and stared at Hobbs who did not speak again. Hobbs merely returned the stare.

"I'm going to report you!" the captain finally sputtered. "I'm going to sue you for wrongful imprisonment and terrorist threats!"

"Who will corroborate your story?" Hobbs asked.

"My men!" he snapped.

"What happened on this chopper?" Hobbs asked the first mate. The man would not look at his Captain but looked instead at the floor.

"You rescued us and brought us straight back to the Coast Guard," the man said sullenly. The captain sighed.

"I'll kill you for this," he swore softly. He shivered as Hobbs simply stared back at him, his eyes showing nothing.

"Good luck with that, old boy," Hobbs said after a moment.

Back on the trawler PU and Sean gathered what evidence there was while Lee Roy opened some valves, allowing water to fill about five feet deep in the bottom of the ship. Left that way the ice would crush the hull and take the ship to the bottom.

Back on *Sea Venture* Penelope went to work on the evidence they'd collected. She had a name, a company, a money trail, and new threads to the mystery of the sunken vessel. As the mystery grew around the ship that was so far off course, she sensed there was much more to this story. The people involved in looking for the ship had been sworn enemies a hundred years ago, telling her that their enmity had been nothing more than a cover for something else. Thrilling to the challenge she sighed, tapped her extended stomach, and commented to her unborn child.

"You are going to enter a world of fascination and excitement, little one!" she said softly.

"I take it we have a real mystery unfolding?" John asked as he came to stand behind her. He ran his fingers through her hair and leaned down and kissed the crown of her head gently.

"We do!" she said. "That much gold, that far off course, and the few crew in the lifeboats! I hope our archaeologists finish soon and come back on board. We need their expertise in this!"

"They're about to reach Cave 1," John said, looking at his watch. "We'll keep tabs on them," he added unnecessarily.

Penelope smiled up at her husband and sighed with pleasure. Being a mother had changed her dramatically, and though she still wrestled with the many changes, it no longer threatened or frightened her. She'd been surprised to be frightened to become a mother. Very few things really frightened her anymore. But motherhood had. Now, however, she sensed within herself a new and exciting challenge. She was going to raise a child to face her world!

CHAPTER 18

"**B**ear den!" Chief said as they entered the cave.

"How can you tell?" Jim asked.

"Smell, scat, and general sense that it is empty at the moment. See that scat? That's the winter butt plug, full of grass," Chief pointed to the droppings. John nodded in agreement.

"But the bear could return!" he added, unnecessarily. Four men had already set up a perimeter to guard the entrance.

Exploring the cave took nearly four hours, and though they found evidence of early cave drawings, they found nothing old enough to indicate this cave was the one they were looking for. Alistair took the news with demure, simply crossing off the location with a marker and smiling at the group.

"We know it's not this cave!" He announced. On to the next!" he encouraged.

They camped four miles from the cave that night, discussing the ways the months of darkness affected John's tribe, as opposed to the months of daylight. JP was philosophical. He and his sons often changed their sleeping habits so they could enjoy the Aurora Borealis. Many of the tribe did the same, so that even though they were in darkness almost all the time, at least while awake they had the beauty of the northern lights to enjoy. Still, the depression common during those months of darkness took its toll, especially among the children and women.

On the following day they moved to the second cave to discover it was occupied by a mountain lion with cubs. Not willing to risk any danger Jim ordered smoke grenades lobbed into the cave to drive the animals out. Mother and two cubs left the cave after the first volley. Wisely Jim used two flashbangs to turn her away from the people that dared to threaten her cubs and she led them away sulkily. Chief kept his eye on her and was part of the guard outside the cave.

Once again, they were doomed to disappointment. Even though they did not find what they wanted, Dr. Gregg kept them laughing and enjoying what discoveries they did make, and no one seemed to feel the weight of failing once again. Jim appreciated the ability of others to lighten situations and keep everyone sharp at the same time. He patted Alistair on the shoulder as they walked out last.

"You're a great teacher, Dad," he said with a small smile. Somehow, even though he was used to it now, it still felt awkward to call Alistair Dad. Yet Alistair obviously enjoyed it. He beamed at his stepson.

"Thanks. Coming from you that means a lot!" he commented.

"I really liked what you said about handling the disappointment of not finding what you sought. If you are looking for the wonder of God's creation, and the amazing signs left in any location by both animals and man, you can never be disappointed. You can only be thrilled and inspired. That was good," Jim reiterated, repeating almost verbatim what Alistair said. Gwyneth came up and hugged the two of them around the waist and shoulder.

"My men are very wise," she said with a low laugh.

In an uncharacteristic display of fun Jim put his hand over his heart and drew himself to his full height, putting on a pompous expression. "Yes, we are!" he agreed, lifting his chin. "Behold the mantle of wisdom!"

"Did you need me, dearest?" Cecilia interjected with an infectious smile.

"Behold the cradle of wisdom!" Jim said, lifting his wife into his arms and cradling her against himself.

"Put me down you oaf!" she laughed.

"Oaf! I was just told I was wise, by one who would know!" he said, putting Cecilia down. She looked at his face, saw the blush on his neck and realized how much his moment had cost him. Throwing her arms around him she kissed him passionately.

"I think that's what led to your present condition!" Barbara said with a smirk.

"Yes. Mother told me if I kissed a girl, she would get pregnant!" Jim said with a straight face. That brought a chorus of laughter. FM began to embrace and kiss all the girls, none of whom resisted. Frank was a handsome man. He stood back and shook his head in the positive.

"I'm gonna have a lot of kids!" he declared.

"Keep kissing girls like that and you probably will!" Mary Ann said. "We could try for twins!" Again, the laughter erupted through the camp. And that's when Chief noticed the flash of sun on a riflescope. So did Jim who immediately grabbed Cecilia and carried the two of them to the ground, cushioning her with his own body before rolling her over so his body was between her and the rifle. The wicked ricochet of the bullet and chips of rock echoed in the cave behind where Cecilia's head had just been.

"Scope!" Bill Dodge ordered briskly.

Sid Barrett was already taking a high position. Although not wearing a gilly suit he did have his shade and glare protection on his riflescope. The Barrett M82A1 weighed almost thirty pounds but he didn't mind the extra weight. He adjusted his scope and sights after testing the wind and took a look. Jing and Xun had crept to within a thousand feet of them.

"Don't kill him!" Jim snapped from the ground where he still protected Cecilia.

"Roger that, boss," Scope answered laconically. He was totally relaxed now. "I'm gonna disable his rifle," he added. "It might shake him up some because he's looking down the scope!

The roar of Sid's rifle echoed against the rocks and a startled cry sounded from Jing's position. Sid Barrett was their best sniper, and his shot had indeed disabled Jing's rifle, the bullet smashing the stock and barrel, and spraying Jing's face with debris. Bleeding and furious Jing stood up and threw the rifle.

"He's mine!" Jim said savagely as he stood. "Viper! You keep his girl friend off my back!"

Dodge nodded and the two made their way to Xun and Jing's position. Jing's face was bleeding and bruised but he was in a rage. Xun, wisely, backed away. When Jing went for Jim, Dodge placed himself between Xun and Jim. She looked at him, noting his demeanor and remembering what Jim and Mark had done to her she decided not to test this intense man.

"You tried to shoot my wife," Jim berated quietly. "She is pregnant. Had you succeeded you would have killed the two people I love most in this world. A man who shoots at pregnant women is the lowest of the criminals. You have no honor, and you do not even honor the code of your art. You are like a rabid rat in a sewer, undisciplined and unable to think!"

With a scream of rage Jing launched an attack at Jim only to be smashed to the ground with such force his body slid almost three yards before it came to a rest against some rocks. Jim was in the air, and as Jing's body stopped his knee came down on Jing's solar plexus. Stunned the Chinese assassin felt himself lifted from the ground with a power that was frightening. And then the punishment began.

Jim Shepherd's fists were like sledgehammers, and though Jing's training taught him to accept brutal punishment this was more than he could resist. Bones shattered. A wicked kick ruptured one of his testicles and a roundhouse kick shattered his jaw and cheekbone. Jing flew through the air once again, slid several feet, and lay like a rag doll. Xun's eyes widened as she watched Jim's punishment and saw the extent of the damage.

She looked at Jim and what she saw in his eyes frightened her for the first time in a long time. He stood, relaxed and ready, in the classic fighting stance of the martial artist, but his eyes were full of death. Xun looked away, hated herself, and looked back, and looked away again. At last, she drew in her courage and faced him, eye to eye.

"If I see him again, I will kill him," Jim stated. His voice was level, matter of fact, devoid of emotion. "I'm going to call in a helicopter to airlift him to the nearest hospital. Once he's stable you take him back to China. If I hear he left China, I will hunt him down, and I will kill him. Should I hear that he is working with you when he leaves China, I will kill you too."

"I did not know he was going to shoot," Xun admitted quietly, and this time she looked down, ashamed. "That was his decision. He can no longer work for me or for my company. That is my decision. You will not have to kill him."

The Grizzly came over the rocks with a roar, brushed past Xun, knocking her to the ground, and grabbing the helpless Jing in its jaws the bear dragged him into the rocks where his weak cries ended in horrible crunching sounds. Slowly Xun rose to her feet, her eyes wide. Both of the men from *Bring It Up* had their pistols out.

"I guess you won't have to kill him either," Jim spoke quietly. "Come with us. You are not safe alone."

Xun drew herself up. "I am one with my world! I do not need your protection!" she said proudly.

"Alone in these mountains you will die," Jim said.

"Then I shall die!" she stated sadly.

"You are a fool," he accused, emphasizing the verb and shaking his head. "Die then." Waiting for a moment after that statement he finally nodded to Dodge and the two turned their backs and walked away.

"That bear wasn't afraid of men with guns," Dodge said quietly when they were out of listening range.

"I know. Let's get gone from here. If it follows have Sid take it out. It may stay and feed for a couple of days. I don't know enough about bears to say," he glanced back several times as they trotted away. The attack of the bear had been a terrifying moment and he knew that had he been the target of the bear, he would have died.

"JP does. I'll ask," Dodge agreed as they entered camp.

"Honey, your hands!" Cecilia said, taking Jim's bleeding hands into hers. "Those need looking after!" she led him over to the first aid equipment and began to work on them.

"Did you kill him?" she asked softly.

"No. I was about to call in a chopper to take him to a hospital when a huge Grizzly charged us, took him, and dragged him into the rocks and killed him," Jim was silent for a few minutes while she worked, not even wincing when she scrubbed out the deeper cuts. She saw the tears in his eyes and was surprised. That was new.

Slowly he blinked, let them run down his cheeks and taking her hands in his he bowed his head.

"God, thank you for protecting my beloved wife and child today. And thank you for bringing me to my senses before I killed that man. Vengeance is yours, Lord, and I guess I saw that today in action. I'd like to thank the guardian angel that warned me to look that way just as the sun flashed on Jing's scope. I could almost feel him pushing the two of us out of the way. The thing is, I'm no better than Jing. I deserve death as much as he did. But you love me, despite that. How can one human heart contain all that love?" And then he drew Cecilia into his arms and wept openly, unashamed, hugging her tightly as she returned his fierce embrace and wept with him.

"The reality is, we face death every day. There is no safe place in this world. There is only safety in the Lord," Alistair commented quietly to those watching. Everyone had heard the prayer, and they had stopped because seeing Jim cry was something they'd not witnessed since he'd accepted the Lord.

"I get that, perhaps for the first time ever!" Jim admitted, wiping away the tears and standing up. "I've been trained to go into battle and have always known I could die in battle. But I never really thought about the danger of death that lurks in the heart of our enemy Satan all the time. Car accidents, plane accidents, boating accidents, just plain accidents happen all the time and take lives.

"My child is going to grow up in a very dangerous world. But if I bring him up to know the Lord Jesus, he'll be able to face whatever he has to face. I think we all just got an apt lesson on how God protects us. Safety is an illusion. Danger is reality. And the only person who is never surprised is God. So, I put my trust in Him!" Jim smiled down at Cecilia as she took his hands to work on them some more.

After half an hour of praise and singing they broke camp and headed for the next cave. Just before they left Jim gave a detailed report to John on *Sea Venture*.

"Copy, bro!" John said, shaking his head in amazement. "We've had a plane nosing around us. Don't know who it is. We did pick up a radio signal from your area. Xun reported Jing's death. She was ordered to continue to follow you, but not to interfere. Over."

"I copied that. How goes the research on the ship? Over," Jim responded.

"We're getting through the ice and deploying the sensors and recording equipment in compliance with the grant. We're also learning some things about the ice storms. Our global warming friends are going to have to spin something to fit this! Over," John laughed.

"They will. Over," Jim responded.

"Stay as safe as you can. Don't get dead. Over," John laughed in return.

"Roger that. Over and out," Jim responded.

"Did you get a good look at that Grizzly?" Jim asked Sid as he passed him. Sid nodded, looking down at Jim from his perch on his horse.

"Half his left ear is torn away. I'll recognize him," Sid said.

"Good. If it follows drop it. That bear is not afraid of armed humans," Jim replied.

"They get that way eventually, the bad ones," Chief mused, looking at the two men. "Killing them is the only way," he nodded and leaped onto his horse. Riding to the front he said no more, and Jim followed, mounted his own horse, and they moved away.

Later that day Jim heard the report of Sid's rifle from behind them. He turned his horse and headed back, finding Sid's horse, and then spotting him higher up on an outcropping of rock. Jim climbed up and joined him.

"Eleven o'clock," Sid announced. "I was too late to help Xun. It was her screams that alerted me."

Jim saw the sadness in Sid's eyes and taking his binoculars found the carcass of the bear. Next to it, half buried beneath it, lay the body of Xun, mangled and torn. Her eyes stared at the sky and her entrails were scattered in a wide arc, demonstrating the savagery of the attack. She had thought herself one with her world and had discovered too late that nothing is right in this world, twisted and ruined by sin. Reaching out Jim and Sid clasped hands for a moment.

"Your god was powerless, and now you know that," Jim breathed quietly.

"Will the Zhanzhu Triad blame us?" Sid asked.

"I'll get a chopper to fly over and photograph the evidence," Jim said. "Word will reach them."

From his position Jim pulled out his satellite phone, checked the signal, and dialed the ship. Three hours later the CH53D thundered overhead. Dorf radioed that they had the photographs, and they had picked up both bodies for burial. After seeing that the group was safe the chopper flew on.

Jim did not push them, and they covered only twenty miles that day over the rough terrain. Several times they paused to photograph and study the amazing vistas they were seeing. JP noted that everyone wanted to taste the water from a spring, feel the soft springy turf of a meadow full of wildflowers, and smiled. He felt akin to these people, a rarity among visitors from the mainland.

A storm came in the next day, and instead of moving on they sat in their tents and watched the storm. Several gathered beneath the dining canopy to watch the storm, enjoying the cool water spraying everywhere and the magnificent lightening show in the sky. Jim and Cecilia were among those benneath the canopy, sitting on the camp stools hand in hand, enjoying the lightening and thunder. Comments were shared about the power of nature.

Their clothing was waterproof, and they stayed warm through the entire storm, enjoying nature's display of raw power in the thunder and lightening. After the storm passed, they walked through the meadow to discover how the flowers had fared. As the sun peaked through the clouds, they paused to watch one open up, amazed that it had withstood the wind and rain without harm. Cecilia used her video setting on her phone camera to record the flower opening.

"I was like that," Cecilia echoed when she put her phone away. "After you rescued me, I had closed up to protect myself, and in the light of God's love I slowly opened myself again. I couldn't help it. Needing His love and light I finally opened up fully."

"Did you know you actually glow in the sunlight?" Jim asked, drawing her in for a kiss. "As soon as you became pregnant you took on a very special glow. I've noticed it over and over and it's beautiful on you. Perhaps I shall keep you pregnant to enjoy this special beauty," he teased with a smile.

"We got started late in life. I'm going to have to have our children quickly. Then I'll be fat and frumpy, and you won't think I'm so beautiful anymore," Cecilia predicted with a sigh. Jim was surprised, watching her face, to realize that she actually believed that somehow her beauty could fade.

"I'll love you if you end up weighing four hundred pounds!" Jim promised with a laugh. "But I know you. You'll stay in shape."

"Yes. I'll have to if I'm going to keep up with any of your children!" she agreed, smiling happily.

On the following day they camped within a mile of the third cave. They were on a natural plateau of rock covered by enough dirt to grow wild grasses and wildflowers. Camp that night was a festive occasion with fresh fish for dinner, caught by Noatak and JP, and cooked by those two worthies for their friends. The pond and waterfall at one end of the plateau provided fresh water and plenty of fish for dinner, and the hope that they were finally nearing the end of their trek. Old tales told of a plateau beneath the cave with such a waterfall and pond.

CHAPTER 19

igh above them, at least a thousand feet up a cliff wall, was the opening of a cave. After dinner Jim studied the wall with his binoculars and decided that the climb could be made with free ascent techniques and without the use of ropes. He would of course use ropes for safety and to help others make the climb behind him. His team would use ropes for safety, but he and Frank would make the first ascent without them.

"The object of the quest was for the new chief to find the cave, conquer it, and learn from the messages on the walls," JP shared later that evening. "If this is the cave, I wonder how many new chiefs tried to reach the cave and failed."

"We can determine that by studying the bones we find scattered."

Everyone looked at Alistair as he spoke. To suit his words, he stood up and hiked to the base of the cliff and began to move his feet about through the grass and growth. As others joined, he gave them a grid to work and within an hour they had an assortment of bones. The archaeologists were adept at determining which bones were animal, and which ones were human.

An hour later four piles of bones sat on drop cloths. Alistair knelt next to one at the end closest to the cliff wall. He sorted through the bones and soon had all the femurs in a row.

"I'd say there were at least four humans who died here. This femur is the oldest of the lot, and this one is at least a hundred years old," he pointed to the two and then proceeded to lecture on how to identify indicators of age on bones that lay above the ground. He also taught the difference for buried bones. No one got bored during the hour-long lecture. This was vital information that might prove very useful in the years to come!

"Notice that many of the leg and arm bones are snapped, not gnawed, indicating they broke before the owner perished. Most of these breaks would have been compound fractures. This ribcage suggests that these ribs pierced the heart." He pointed to the ribs in question.

"Cor! It must have been bloody awful to die alone here!" Hobbs breathed. Then he looked up at the ladies. "Excuse my language, please," he apologized.

Jim's men rarely used bad language. JP hadn't heard one word of it during the entire trip, something he'd mentioned to Noatak several times. He looked at Calvin Weston curiously.

"Bad language?" he asked.

"The word 'bloody' is a swear word in the UK," Barbara answered his question.

"Ah!" he said, nodding. "I notice that you do not speak as many tourists do from the mainland," JP said. "And you certainly do not speak like military people!"

"All of us follow Jesus, the Jesus of the Bible, or at least we try to," Jim explained. "Ephesians 4:29 is a verse all of us have memorized. *Let no unwholesome word proceed from your mouth, but only such a word as is good for edification (or building up) according to the need of the moment, that it may give grace to those who hear.* We've also memorized James 3:8-12. *But no one can tame the tongue; it is a restless evil and full of deadly poison. With it we bless our Lord and Father; and with it we curse men, who have been made in the likeness of God; from the same mouth come both blessing and cursing. My brethren, these things ought not to be this way. Does a fountain send out from the same opening both fresh and bitter water? Can a fig tree, my brethren, produce olives, or a vine produce figs? Neither can saltwater produce fresh.*

"Those verses teach us that we should not allow bad words out of our mouths. So, we try very hard to moderate our language, and if we slip up, we apologize. God is the silent witness to every word we speak, and Scripture tells us that we will give an account for every careless word we speak! He's got volumes on me!"

"You!" Frank quipped. "You barely ever talk. He's got a whole library on me!"

"Those of us who are gifted with the ability and desire to talk often are definitely at a disadvantage to those who are stoic, quiet, or analytical," Alistair laughed. "I think, in the long run, we'll discover the curses are the words that God hates the most. We push Him off the throne and curse that which He has made, as though we are able to judge better than He. We are fools at times," he shook his head.

"Few people truly walk the talk," JP said quietly after a pause. "I am blessed to be among such people."

In the morning Jim spent another hour studying the cliff before he and Frank began the ascent. As they stood at the base Jim looked at Frank.

"Remember, a thirty-foot fall is as deadly as one of a hundred feet!" he cautioned.

"Don't get dead!" FM said with a feral grin.

Smiling Jim began the climb, dipping his hands in his chalk pouch and starting up the route he'd planned in his mind. Every fifteen feet he stopped and hammered a piton into a crack in the rock wall, made sure it was wedged tight, attached a carabiner or wire sling and a safety rope. When he could he created a triangle of pitons holding the rope in case one failed.

Once he had the safety rope in place, he slid it through a descender attached to his climbing harness should he fall. FM followed, testing the rope and pitons. Above him he watched Jim swing his body, let go, sail through the air almost nine feet, and catch a ledge. Dangling by one arm he slid a piton in place, hammered it, and after securing the rope to the piton he paused, letting the rope and piton take his weight.

FM knew that the leap had been calculated, but very dangerous. He marveled at Jim's strength and endurance.

"Let's stretch a rope beneath, so others can climb across," Jim suggested, looking down at FM.

"You leave your Spiderman suit in your backpack, boss?" FM grinned.

"Wouldn't it be nice to have those powers!" Jim said with a chuckle. He climbed down the rope a few feet, hammered in another piton, and after attaching a second rope to that he tossed the other end to FM. As usual he hammered in two more pitons, forming that triangle of safety before he moved on.

Four hours later Jim reached up and felt the lip of the cave opening, found a good purchase, and lifted himself, as if doing chin-ups, to peer over the ledge. To his left a magnificent Bald Eagle stared accusingly at this strange apparition that suddenly appeared, and with a harsh cry spread its huge wings and took flight. Baby eagles in the nest voiced their displeasure at mother's disappearance. With a smile Jim lifted himself all the way up and finally stood.

He walked a few feet into the cave, away from the nest, and drove three pitons into the cracks he found there, tying the rope off. FM appeared as he had, lifted himself easily and spun to sit on the ledge. He leaned out and looked down. Jim saw him waving at someone below.

"Too bad we couldn't have rappelled down from the top," FM pointed out, catching his breath.

"No, the overhang is too great for that. But we could rig a sling, and lower folks down, and pull them in," Jim said, leaning out and looking up.

"Hi down there!" Chief yelled, his head suddenly appearing over the edge two hundred feet above.

"Put a weight on the end of a rope, and then send it down. We'll rig up a sling to lower folks and pull them in!" Jim yelled up. He was so excited he forgot he had a walkie-talkie he could use. FM laughed as he handed the device to Jim. Sheepishly Jim repeated his instructions using the radio.

"Push the button and talk. Then you don't have to yell," FM admonished, grinning.

"Shut up," Jim replied, laughing at himself.

One by one the explorers were lowered and pulled into the cave. Cecilia was flushed with excitement when she caught Jim's hand and stepped onto the solid rock of the cave floor. He helped her out of the harness, and it was pulled up for the next traveler.

"That was exciting. The view from up there is exhilarating!" she sighed.

It took all day to get everyone and the equipment in the cave. By then Chief had explored much of it with JP and they were filled with excitement as they returned to the main group.

"This is the sacred cave!" JP said with conviction.

"There aren't any animals down there, but a boatload of bats. I imagine they'll be making their evening flight soon." Chief added. "There's a quartz vein that reaches all the way to the top and provides light in the cave JP is sure is the sacred cave," he added. "It's absolutely beautiful. So is the vein of gold running beside it!"

"In the past chiefs were told that nothing was to be taken from the cave. Each chief is said to have chosen an object to leave in the cave as a token for the Great Spirit," JP paused for a moment. "It is sad to think that many of them did not know the identity of the Great Spirit."

"Tomorrow we shall see," Alistair excitedly stated. "Sometimes ancient people had a very good handle on God."

Just then the bats could be heard coming. Everyone stretched out on the floor and waited patiently as the tiny mammals fluttered overhead and out the entrance. Only a few ended up with guano on their clothing, and it was quickly wiped away. Tents were set up near the entrance and they sat quietly and ate, watching the mother eagle feed her young, she, casting suspicious glances their way constantly.

It was the first night they needed no guards, and everyone climbed into his or her tent gratefully, ready for a night's sleep after the difficult climb. Jim listened to the camp quiet and finally grow silent except for the steady breathing. He held Cecilia against him, enjoying the smell of her hair. It smelled of the flowers she'd adorned her head with earlier, a garland of fresh wildflowers. Where his hand rested on her extended stomach, he felt his child's hand reach out and touch his.

For him it was a very special moment. He let his hand remain and thought of the child, a son he was sure, and moved only after the hand retreated. He patted Cecilia.

"Sleep tight little one!" he said softly.

CHAPTER 20

Jim and Cecilia led devotions that morning and everyone ate breakfast. About the group was a hushed expectancy, a readiness for the task ahead, and to JP and Noatak it was almost tangible. Yet no one hurried about his or her duties that morning. Instead, each person seemed to concentrate on basics, and when it was time to leave, at the appointed hour, camp was tidy, and everything was in place. Every detail could easily have been checked off a list.

Every member of the team carried a pack. JP noted that the soldiers carried packs that must have weighed eighty pounds easily. Women and Dr. Gregg carried lighter packs, but still weighing close to 40 pounds. They would be sleeping deep in the cave later that night, rather than return to the mouth of the cave. Therefore food, sleeping bags, and other equipment needed to travel with them.

Each explorer now wore a hardhat with three powerful lights strapped to the front. The light in the middle pointed down and would show the path ahead. Two other lights, on either side, pointed forward. They were so bright one couldn't look directly into them without experiencing momentary light-blindness. Over their eyes they wore protective glasses and over mouth and nose a dust filter that was light and comfortable.

JP noted that Jim went down the line, checking each person's gear and especially his or her water supply. When he was satisfied that everyone was ready, he went to the front and rejoined Chief, JP, Noatak, and Dr. Gregg. Everyone wore a nylon belt with about ten feet of rope attached to front and back, so that they were all hooked together. This precaution was necessary should anyone fall, or, God forbid, a cave-in occur. Those untouched could follow the ropes to the others for rescue and first aid. JP was ready for this, because he and Chief had been attached this way in their earlier exploration.

Chief led them unerringly into the sacred cave, a hike that took them down a steep trail with a gaping chasm to the right, and solid rock to the left. Those who had been suffering from that nagging headache of high altitude breathed a sigh of relief as they passed below eight thousand feet. A headache at those altitudes was painful and the usual treatments didn't do much to relieve the pain. The sacred cave was at seventy-three hundred feet altitude and opened to the left.

Here the floor was almost level and smooth in places where water had once flowed in a steady motion across the rock. It never ceased to impress Jim how water could wear down something as hard as rock. And yet here they could see how water had carved its way through the rock itself. At one end of the cave was a small spring that flowed out of the rock, fell about two feet into a larger pool, which overflowed into one even larger, finally running off along the edge in a stream that suddenly disappeared through the wall itself. Water had drilled through the solid rock!

The pleasant sound of flowing water filled the cavern and there were expressions of wonder at the light flowing through the quartz. That vein went all the way to the top, and along one side a thick vein of gold flowed outwards. It was quite beautiful. Lights were set in place, and then turned on so photos could be taken.

Light here was ambient, the kind of light one found in studios around the world, powered by batteries. The batteries were charged by solar light. In this instance, they could use the light coming through the quartz to keep the batteries at a full level. Once equipment was in place camp was laid out in a neat fashion close to the water supply.

It was not until all those mundane chores were finished that the scientists approached the two walls covered with painted pictures.

Unerringly, Dr. Gregg went to the earliest drawings. As he studied the pictures, he kept a running dialogue that Mary Ann recorded with a digital recorder. His talk was animated and the only other sound in the cave. Uncovering the stories from many years past he told a unique and stirring history.

"What possessed the earliest explorer to delve this deeply into this particular cave?" Dr. Gregg wondered aloud. "He must have been an intrepid fellow to make the climb, and then explore. This is an excellent place to hide, if indeed he was hiding. Here! Look at these earliest paintings. They're very faint, but you can see this stick figure with the torch following the trail we just followed!

"Yes. I imagine this is the record of the first explorer. He wasn't much of an artist, but I think we can decipher his thoughts. That might be a drawing of a divine being, hovering above the quartz, or it could just be the sun. No! It has eyes! So, he thought this cave was provided by this divine being! Yes! There's the gold vein, and it is connected to the finger of the divine being. Fascinating!" Alistair shook his head as he studied the paintings, often scratching his beard in thought.

JP saw that Heidi Van Haaten was copying the images on the wall, following Dr. Gregg's narrative. Her sketching was amazingly accurate! For a moment Dr. Gregg was silent as he studied the drawing.

"There were no fish in the water. See how he depicts it reflecting the quartz and gold? When he came here the floor must have been covered with water. He shows it flowing out the entrance! That must have been beautiful! It would also increase the light, which was probably what drew him. See how he shows the earlier opening as though it is glowing? Light led him to this cave.

"Here he shows the cave with the bats. You found that yesterday, did you not?" he asked Chief.

"Yes. It's further down the path. Since the bats came out our cave entrance, I guess that the cave ends somewhere down there. It goes deep and it would take climbing equipment to go further than we did." Chief replied. "Is that your assessment?" he looked at JP.

"Yes. We saw no light. The cave itself was quite beautiful. It had stalagmites and stalactites of unusual hue. I think at one time the whole cave might have been under water!" JP said.

"Oh! We have to see that!" Alistair exclaimed with excitement. "However! Back to our story!" he turned back to the wall and studied it again. For several minutes the only sound was the breathing of those standing near, and the water flowing. When he spoke, his voice was almost a surprise.

"He stayed here for seven days. During that time, he ate smoked fish he brought with him and prayed. Note his form kneeling here? It's just possible he was new to the area. See these drawings. This one shows the passage of many months of darkness without the light of day. If this symbol represents night, he thought perhaps a deity of some kind made it dark. Look at this! He believed this creature to be evil!

"Now that is fascinating. The idea that darkness is linked to evil pervades ancient religions. I suppose that is because darkness cannot exist in the presence of light, and light therefore is linked to good. Still, it gives us some insight into the mindset of this man.

"This, I believe, is a map of how he came here. If I'm seeing this correctly, he came from the east, not the west. His roots were probably native to Canada, perhaps the extreme northwest. See this depiction. It shows something akin to an iceberg, but on land. Logically, if he was fleeing flowing ice, he would follow the sun, hoping to find warmer climates. That is my assessment of these drawings and what they teach us."

"Was it ever really warm here?" René Millstein asked.

"At one time the temperature over the entire earth may have been controlled, between sixty-eight and seventy-six-degrees Fahrenheit. If the earth was covered by a canopy of water that would be the case. Many scientists believe that it was.

"Look here!" he pointed to a set of drawings. "He was traveling with a group of people, and he was one of four explorers sent out to find something! Clever! They all traveled west, but two went further south, and one went further north.

"Say! This looks like the southern coast of Alaska! Yes! The fellow who went furthest south is connected to this map. It seems that the whole people moved that way and settled in. But they returned to this cave! See here! Once every five years to begin with, and then the visits stretch out further and further! My guess is this became a sacred place that was visited regularly. Eventually, perhaps only those high in tribal leadership came here.

"Ah! Here is an artist! Look at these paintings! If my calculations are correct this is at least ninety years after the cave was first discovered. Yes! The visits go on every five years for four decades, and then fifty years pass before the next visit. This is a new hand, a skilled hand, and a man of vision.

"Here again is the deity in the sky. But this time he controls the light from his right hand, and the darkness from his left. Our painter was right-handed!"

"How in the world do you know that?" JP asked, startled by the revelation.

"He would have considered light stronger than darkness. Most right-handers are stronger in their right arm, than in the left." Alistair smiled at JP, who nodded. It made sense. "Also, the brush strokes of a left hander are easily discernable from those of a right hander. One becomes used to telling those things after years of practice.

"Now we have this deity creating the world. And here he is creating the animals, fish, and birds. Interesting! Yes! He follows the biblical pattern for the six acts of creation! This, I believe is a depiction of the flood that covered the earth. Now that's interesting! Yes! This is definitely a world-wide phenomenon.

"Here the deity is in this cave drawing the water from the heavens and beneath the earth! See how he creates the quartz to provide light, and as the water fills the earth this cave is protected! The water from the earth comes from our spring over there," Alistair pointed at the spring. "Isn't that interesting? He thought that all water came from here!

"Now this is interesting! He depicts the deity making rules. See this drawing. He has two people bowing down to a great white bear and the deity smiting them with lightening. Here the deity pets the great white bear. Obviously, this man believed that this deity controlled the animals, or at least was never threatened by them.

"This next drawing is a child sitting on his father's lap. His eyes are turned to his father's face, and the father is speaking. This one is perhaps honoring parents. And this drawing is evident. A man kills another, and the deity smites him. No killing of people. No wait! Here's a picture of a battle and the deity does not smite those who kill! Fascinating! Killing in battle is permitted, but not as a personal act.

"Here is a man stealing something from what looks like a pot. Yes! And the deity smites him. Do not steal. See how this man's hand is stretched out toward this other man and his flock. Note that the deity is about to smite him as well. That could very well be the commandment not to covet. Our painter had a very traditional view of morality.

"Now this is interesting. Here are several people bowing down to the deity and he is smiling upon them. I suppose that means to worship him, and him alone. So, they recognized the Great Spirit as God. Here's a drawing of a woman with several children, and she's obviously pregnant. Her husband is off to the left here, hunting. The deity is smiling upon them. Perhaps this means to be fruitful and multiply.

"Here's a drawing of a man giving another food. Look at the clothing he draws. The man with the food to share is wearing brightly colored clothing and good footwear. This man however, the one receiving the food, seems less fortunate. Wouldn't you agree?" he looked at those gathered around.

Heads nodded agreement. And so, they passed very slowly studying the paintings. Suddenly however Alistair drew in his breath in a sharp hiss. The paintings had changed, and others began to see what had startled him.

"These are hieroglyphs! Not only that, they're hieroglyphs from the Archaic Egyptian or Early Dynastic Period of Egypt. They date back to 2600 B.C.! Our Egyptian of 1742 was not the first to visit this cave! See this! This is the name Djedkara Isesi! He's a king of Egypt in the 5th Dynasty of the Old Kingdom period. If memory serves me correctly, he reigned around 2361 B.C.!

"Our Egyptian does not give his name but see these hieroglyphs? They spell out *the writings of the words of god.* Later, here, he names the god, Amun. If I'm reading this correctly, Amun and Sobek led him south around a great continent and then east across a calm sea to a vast continent. He traveled north along the coast and came to the village where the chief seems to have brought him to this cave. The number of months it took him to travel the coast suggests he landed first somewhere in South America!" he paused and studied the next message.

"Aren't hieroglyphs difficult to decipher?" JP asked.

"Oh my, yes!" Alistair agreed, not looking around. "In the 5th century A.D. Horapollo first provided explanations of nearly two hundred glyphs. Only some of those were correct. Then, of course, during the 9th and 10th centuries A.D. Arab historians Dhul-Nun al-Misri and Ibn Wahshiyya added to that. They too were mistaken in much of what they gave us. In the 17th century Athanasius Kitcher added to that. However, all those attempts were all based on the mistaken assumption that the hieroglyphs represented ideas and not sounds of a particular language.

"In 1799 the Rosetta Stone was discovered, a bilingual text in Greek and the Egyptian Hieroglyphic and Demotic scripts. Scholars such as Silvestre de Sacy, Johan David Äkerblad and Thomas Young were able to make real progress with deciphering hieroglyphs. It was Jean-François Champollion who made a complete decipherment of the Hieroglyphic script. He realized that the Coptic language, a descendent of Ancient Egyptian used as a liturgical language in the Coptic Church in Egypt, could be used to help understand the language of the hieroglyphic inscriptions.

"This next message is interesting!" Alistair read the script. "*My ship will, if Sobek grants me journeying mercies, sail back to Egypt to report to my King, Djedkara Isesi, the things I have witnessed. I will take many tokens to show him the truth of my journey. May maat keep the seas calm for my return.*"

"Who or what is maat?" Jim asked.

"Order as opposed to chaos," Alistair responded. "The Egyptians believed that certain gods maintained *maat*, the universal order that was a central principle of Egyptian religion and was itself personified as a goddess. Apep, the force of chaos, constantly threatens to annihilate the order of the universe. Set was an ambivalent member of the divine society that could both fight disorder and foment it. Egyptians believed in hundreds of gods and goddesses," Alistair smiled sadly. "Her Pharaoh's believed that they were imbued with god-like powers, or that the gods themselves resided in them while they ruled. Megalomania is prevalent in the human race.

"Predynastic Egypt originally consisted of small, independent villages, but I'm convinced that the most important predynastic gods were, like other elements of Egyptian culture, present all across the country, not just prevalent in various villages. Satan is always able to counterfeit religion and gods, and if one studies the pantheon of gods of all religions there are elements that are blatantly obvious.

"New gods emerged after the unification of Egypt, when rulers from Upper Egypt made themselves pharaohs of the entire country. These sacred kings and their subordinates assumed the exclusive right to interact with the gods and kingship became the unifying focus of the religion. There are two important deities that made an appearance in the Old Kingdom. One of them is named here. That is Amun. The other is Isis. Isis is a mother goddess and a patroness of kingship. I've seen a relief of Seti I in her lap.

"Of course, there are the traditional gods that make us laugh. Hedj-Wer the baboon god is one of those. Like other false religions, most Egyptian deities represent natural or social phenomena. The gods were generally believed to be immanent in these phenomena – to be present within nature, if you will. Naturally types of phenomena represented included physical places and objects as well as abstract concepts and forces. For instance, Sia personified the abstract notion of perception. Rather than admit that we were made in the image of the one true God, and therefore possessed perception, or that all true perception comes from His mind alone, the Egyptians complicated the issue and muddied it with false doctrine. It is always the way of man to belittle God's true nature and abilities, and to refuse to accept His power to control all things," Alistair smiled at the group. "Humankind does not like admitting that he is limited."

"Now, back to our Gwich'in friends and their record," he said, moving on. Again, he pointed out the salient points of each artist and what was added regarding the history and traditions of Gwich'in. JP and Noatak listened in rapt attention, writing notes as fast as they could.

"Ah! Here we are in 1742, and the visit of our second Egyptian sailor!" Alistair announced. "1742 was an interesting year. Does anyone remember anything from that year in history?"

"Handel's "Messiah" was performed for the first time in Dublin," Cecilia said.

"Well done!" Alistair said.

"Teacher's pet!" FM quipped.

"Ah, Mr. Miller. What do you remember from your history lessons?" Alistair asked with a smile.

"Is there a raise with that promotion?" FM asked with a straight face.

"What promotion?" Alistair asked, momentarily distracted.

"You called me mister," FM teased.

"No, I'm sorry, no raise. Tell us what you remember, please," Alistair chuckled. He was constantly amused by Frank Miller's quips and comments.

"Ben Franklin invented the Franklin stove. It didn't work very well though," FM answered immediately.

"Very impressive," Alistair said, nodding his head. FM stuck his tongue out at Cecilia. "Why didn't it work well?"

"The smoke had to pass through a cold flue set in the floor before it could get into the chimney, which cooled it too much to provide a good draft. One had to keep the stove burning constantly to keep the temperature in the flue high enough to produce a draft," FM answered after a moment of thought.

"I didn't know that," Alistair confessed. "I've learned something interesting today, thanks to you, Frank."

"Didn't the Empress Elisabeth order the expulsion of all Jews from Russia late that year? It was in December, if I remember correctly," Mary Anne posed.

"Yes indeed," Alistair agreed. "That was a sad time for God's people."

"Walpole and his government resigned in February," Mary Ann added in the silence that followed. He became the Earl of Orford, and the Earl of Wilmington took his place. His name was Spencer Compton, and I believe he became the first Earl of Wilmington in 1710. He wasn't the best premier we had, but he was better than Walpole!"

"Mary Ann Lewis goes to the head of the class!" Alistair said with a grin. Mary Ann stuck her tongue out at FM and got a laugh from everyone. Jim smiled at the antics of his crew, enjoying the lesson.

"Nathaniel Green was born in 1742," Bill Dodge piped up. "He was a General in the Revolutionary War. Wasn't that when we kicked the Brits out of our country?" he asked innocently.

"Oh! You're going to pay for that!" Mary Ann said with a laugh.

"William Somerville and Andrew Bradford died in 1742. Somerville was an English poet and Bradford an American publisher," Gene Hardesty said when the laughter died down.

"How the heck does a hayseed like you know about an English poet and American publisher?" Mel Pierson asked.

"My father taught Literature at Penn State University," Hayseed said, his face turning red. "Granddad ran the farm with an uncle."

"A farmer that teaches Literature?" Neil Meyers said incredulously.

"Well done, Mr. Hardesty," Alistair said.

"Now back to our Egyptian. Heavens! This map is almost an exact copy of a map drawn by Thomas Stackhouse for the Lord Bishop of Bath & Wells!" he added, looking closely at the map. "That map was drawn in 1742! Our Explorer's map is a little different, but not much! No wonder our intrepid explorer arrived in Alaska late in the year in 1741!

"And here's a map of part of Peru. Ha! He mentions how the Spanish have destroyed the Inca people. And here he has convinced the chief of this particular village to travel to Peru with him. The entire tribe will make the journey! They waited for the warm weather in 1742 to set off, because the Egyptian was wounded by a bear and nearly froze to death. It seems he lost two of his toes to frostbite, and three fingers, two on his left hand and his index finger on his right hand. Oh my! He can't signal traffic with his left hand, it appears!" It took a moment for that joke to sink in and everyone roared.

"Let me read the directions to the cave where his ship is hidden, if it's still there! *We rowed north from the mouth of the Acari River one and a half days and found a cave to hide our ship and goods. I had only six oarsmen by then, and three crew. Once ashore the oarsmen became very ill, with high fevers, becoming delirious before they succumbed to the disease. Two of my crew also died of the same malady, and I thought I too would perish, but Osiris spared me. My remaining crewmember heard of a gold mine in the jungle, and after recovering before me left with three villagers. None of them returned from the jungle.*

"*I borrowed one of their boats that one man could paddle and set off north to explore this amazing land. A Spanish ship accepted payment of a lapis lazuli bracelet and took me far to the north where we were frozen in the harbor. Eager to know more of this strange and beautiful land I traveled inland but was attacked by a bear. My Gwich'in friend found me and nursed me back to health. He is the chief here and I told him of the mountains in Peru where the weather is warm, and the sun shines every day of the year! We will return together.*

"Do you think he got as far as Marcona?" Alistair asked. Jim looked at his map.

"A day and a half might get him that far with six men to row. It depends on how heavy his ship was, and what the currents are like in that area," Jim mused quietly.

"Marcona's beaches are rocky and there are caves," Alistair defended.

"Yes, but are any of them deep enough and hidden enough not to have been discovered by now?" Cecilia asked.

"Along the coast things change. The cave entrance may be under water now, or blocked by a cave-in," Jim replied.

"We can hope! Our Egyptian's Coptic script is the last entry on the cave wall," Alistair said with a tired voice.

"That coincides with the tradition of this cave being lost. It was the Chief's son who led the tribe south with the Egyptian, not the Chief. He perished that winter," JP added.

"Is anybody else hungry?" Zeke asked, raising his hand.

A chorus of voices answered in the affirmative and the group moved back to the campsite and ate and talked far into the night.

CHAPTER 21

Word went out the following morning that the cave had been rediscovered. Jim Shepherd made the trek up to the mouth of the cave to make the calls, and he arrange for the CH53D *Sea Stallion* to shuttle visitors and the tribal council to view the cave. Jim made a special request to the men on *Sea Venture* to fabricate an elevator platform to bring people from the lip of the cliff to the cave below. Zeke asked Dorf to do a fly-by in the chopper and take photographs so they could design a proper and safe structure.

The eagle didn't like the chopper hovering above the cave, but it was soon gone. Using loose stones Jim and his men built a screen for the nest, so that the Eagle would not see all the people entering and leaving the cave, and the people would not be bothering the nest. Once the wall was in place the eagle seemed satisfied that her brood was safe and stopped her aggressive behavior. The men smiled at each other.

While they waited for the crew to manufacture the crane and elevator that would remain in place for years to come the team explored as much of the cave as possible. They discovered a small cave that held a trove of historical relics left by past visitors. JP and Noatak walked among the artifacts while they were being photographed and commented on their use. Some of the pieces were nearly a thousand years old! Pottery, necklaces, bracelets, weapons, spears, arrows, bows, fishhooks, nets long rotted away, braided rope, stones fashioned for various jobs, stone hammers, and an array of teeth had been carefully placed for observation.

No one thought of moving a single piece, JP noted with pleasure, and watched the scientists move carefully among the artifacts and photograph and sketch them. Once again, he was reminded of the grace and balance these people possessed. He'd watched them each morning and evening as they trained together and understood why.

Some of the braver men climbed down into the cave that had once been underwater. Noatak went with them. Though he was unskilled in repelling and climbing he learned quickly, appreciating the wealth of knowledge these soldiers possessed, and their willingness to teach others. Almost three hundred feet below their original starting position they found another cave.

Inside that cave another vein of gold ran across the ceiling and one wall. Noatak was impressed that the men merely photographed the precious metal but did not take any. It seemed that they were more interested in the beauty than the actual riches. Across the floor of the cave rose quartz crystals lay strewn about. Lance suggested they gather them and pass them out for remembrance to the explorers, a memento of their journey together. Smiling the men gathered all of them, secreting them in pockets and pouches on their vests, and made the arduous climb back to the top.

Viper showed Noatak how to use his legs to help with the climb, moving up the rock wall slowly and carefully, but easing the pain in his shoulders and forearms. At the top they shared the rose quartz and what was left put reverently in the small cave of artifacts. It seemed fitting that they should add to the collection. Jim asked permission to leave a plaque commemorating *Sea Venture's* crew. JP was sure the tribal council would permit this.

Late that afternoon the CH53D returned hauling pieces of the crane and elevator. Once these were stacked in place above, the chopper returned for the crew that would build it, and the rest of the pieces. They worked far into the night and by morning were ready for the chopper to lift the platform and position it over the lip of the cliff.

When everything was in place Goody took the time to inspect the work and finally said that everything was as it should be. Jim, who rose early and climbed up to watch the final assembly nodded in appreciation of the care Goody and his crew took to inspect everything. Wade, Jim was sure, designed the whole contraption. It fit into a fissure at the top, using the tons of weight above that fissure to anchor the bottom of the crane in place. Heavy I-beams spread out in a tripod to brace the crane from bowing under the weight of the elevator and people that would be riding down. To Jim it was obvious the structure was quite sturdy.

In the cave itself a block and tackle pulley system was attached to the ceiling of the cave, so that as the elevator lowered it was pulled automatically into the cave, to land with three feet of the elevator platform inside the cave itself. As it went up the entire structure moved outward again to rise straight up to the crane mechanism.

Using a generator provided by the NANA Regional Corporation, now housed in a heavily insulated metal shed, an electric motor sharing the same space operated the crane. Cables ran in the top and out the bottom of the shed through fabricated slots. Jim was amazed at how clean the top of the cliff looked when the men finally left in the chopper to return to the ship. They would come later to view the caves and the wonder.

Jim and Zeke walked onto the elevator platform, feeling it move a little beneath their feet. On the center post two buttons, one for up, and one for down, rested in a weatherproof electric box. Opening the box Zeke pushed the down button and the elevator sank to the cave floor. It was not a fast trip, but quite safe, and Jim was amazed that there were no sounds of stress signaling danger if too many people climbed aboard the platform. A small sign at the gate indicated the maximum number of passengers, which was an astounding eighteen. Jim stepped off with a smile of pleasure while Zeke closed the electric box.

Three hours later the first of the tribal council arrived from

Kotzebue. Inside the elevator cage they stood at the edges, looking out at the vista below as the elevator went into motion. JP and Noatak were given the honor of escorting the dignitaries to the cave.

Inside the sacred cave the men listened as Dr. Gregg deciphered the drawings and hieroglyphs for them. Three hours later the elders stood facing Jim and his team.

"You have done a great service for our people. We thank you. Honor us now by accepting as a token of our gratitude this necklace, woven by Lance from the bear you killed. Some of the women of our tribe used beads to indicate bravery and goodness of heart. Also, by unanimous vote, we have agreed to adopt you as honorary members of our tribe," he said, handing the necklace to Jim.

"Wow! This is beautifully handcrafted work!" Jim commented, looking at the necklace. "I will wear it with pride, and we are more than honored to be part of your tribe. John Pungowiyi and his sons Noatak and Lance are brave and courageous men and have become good friends. We could never have done this without their help," Jim stated, shaking hands with the elder. He went to each one and shook hands, saying "thank you" to each.

"John Pungowiyi tells me none of you touched the gold here or wanted anything for yourselves. Your request for leaving a plaque is granted. There will be much interest in this cave, and NANA Regional Corporation can be trusted to mine the gold below without interfering with this cave. The gold here will remain untouched, for that is fitting. Also, the sample you took from the stream is high-grade ore, but local tribes control all such mining rights. Your company will be a partner in the mine, and you will be given two percent of the shares and two percent of the gold," the elder said.

"That is incredibly generous! Again, we are deeply honored," Jim replied. Later he would discover that the gold mine produced tons of high-grade ore that would add millions of dollars to his company. That was still in the future, and truth be told, he held no anticipation for wealth.

Over the next few days, crewmembers from the ship visited the caves and spent a night with the explorers. At last, however, the day came for the exploration team to return home. Having already arranged the sale of the horses they left them with John and Noatak and boarded the CH53D *Sea Stallion*.

Once his feet were on the ship Jim felt as if he had come home, and could, for the first time in months, completely relax. He gave the team a day to rest and reacclimatize to the ship and spent that day relaxing in his cabin and in the library reading. His interest had been piqued by some of the conversations and he read through *Christianity and Comparative Religions*, and several works on ancient civilizations, especially related to Egypt. Familiar with Greek mythology and Egyptology he studied the gods' men had created for themselves, feeling a deep sense of shame on behalf of the one true God. Those He had created refused to recognize Him for who He was.

Although they'd taken nothing physical from the cave except rose quartz samples, Jim felt that they had taken the best part in the pictorial records and Alistair's notes. The latter were already being shaped into a new book that Jim was eager to read. It was a slow news week and so major networks and news agencies across the globe traveled to see the cave and then the ship.

Finding the presence of agents of news underfoot was frustrating but the crew behaved properly and put up with the distractions and stupid questions. Two reporters that Zeke found suspect searched the ship from bow to stern, top to bottom, and gunwale to gunwale. What they were looking for they never said.

Zeke, however, planted some tracking devices on the men, devices their own equipment would probably not identify, and he was able to determine that one came from the Zhanzhu Triad, and the other came from the office of Admiral Hogg. Since neither recognized the other, and they did not at any time make contact with each other, Zeke surmised that they didn't know they were both looking for the same thing. Idly he wondered what might happen if Hogg ever connected with the Zhanzhu family. He didn't like it. What if he were already one of theirs?

"Do you know what our Hogg spy was looking for?" Jim asked Duck Ashley later that morning, in the privacy of his office.

"The usual. Military presence, military weapons, uniforms, etc. I listened to his report. Those buttons your men created have paid great dividends. Hogg doesn't like that you have a new ship, and that the old ship he was able to examine showed no signs of any hidden or special chambers for your military gear. His agent was very thorough, but he didn't measure any of the holds, or the container that holds the AH-1W. He reported that your exploration team was the only group absent from the ship. So did the Zhanzhu connection. The Zhanzhu connection was interested in whether some of your crew was missing on military maneuvers. It's a good thing John returned when he did, leaving the cleanup to the local forces," Don paused for a moment.

"I doubt it will take long for the two groups to compare notes and join forces," Jim said in the silence.

"No. I think you might be right about that. There's already a connection between the Zhanzhu family and a former president. If he didn't have his pants down for women, he had them down for the Chinese," Duck replied sarcastically.

"Any Communist he could connect with, I would imagine," Jim added.

"We'll keep our eyes on at this end. Bill, Roger, and Charles are working with Angus on something too. What those four can't ferret out can't be discovered." Duck laughed. They might be retired from their former offices, but those four are an amazing intelligence service! I hear you're paying them as part of your crew! Good move," Don replied.

"I'm going after the steamer with the gold, but I'll do that next year. We'll barely finish our grant work here before the real cold settles in. I'm going to stay up this way through the winter to monitor things. That should settle some anxiety in certain circles," Jim predicted. "Thanks for keeping me in the loop. I'll talk to you soon."

"Goodbye, you pirate!" Duck laughed. "Take me to lunch when you fly this way again," he said and hung up.

It was early in August when *Bring It Up* dropped the final sensor equipment in the Arctic Ocean, completing the grant and giving the people of Northern Alaska a much better warning system for freezing storms and dangerous ocean conditions. Already the icy Arctic Ocean was freezing over, and they left the area to travel to Juneau where the ship would remain safe in the harbor, and they could monitor the equipment to be sure everything was working.

Team Knife remained behind with the *A&P Railroad* along with Dr. John and Alice Dinsmore, Dr. Copeland, Dr. Lowe, Dr. Putnam, and Dr. Rysdale. At the moment everyone was at the lab in Prudhoe Bay, but if anything went wrong the powerful exploration vehicle would be able to take them out to investigate.

Once the ship was berthed Jim allowed his crew the opportunity to tour Alaska's capital, keeping a skeleton crew and one team for security on board, rotating the crew and teams to allow everyone some free time. He also planned for a full staff picnic on a bluff overlooking Juneau to award his crew for going above and beyond the call of duty in their recent endeavors.

Wade and John designed the new ribbon for the Alaska adventure and sent it off to have the ribbons made in time for the picnic. While all of that went on John and Alice Dinsmore reported that the sensors were working, and the science department was compiling a massive amount of data on arctic weather patterns hitherto unknown.

"Our global warming extreme climate shift proponents are going to be ecstatic!" Alice commented dryly. "Mental pigmies!" she added sarcastically. "A picnic in a bit warmer temperature sounds divine about now," she finished. She'd been talking over the radiophone and kept the conversation technical and to the point.

Jim smiled as he put the receiver back on its mount. There were, currently, six science media reporters at the station in Prudhoe Bay monitoring the new AOOS. A great deal of money had been spent not only to design the sensors, but also to position them strategically. His company had come through and he was proud of his new ship and its amazing crew. It was better, having everyone on board one vessel, with room to spare.

Goody stepped into his office hatchway and Jim waved him in. Nelson and Finn looked up as he stepped in and went back to work.

Jim shared his office space with John and Wade, three desks in a large office with chairs in front of each desk. Zeke Good sat down and smiled, sketching a salute at the captain.

"We've sounded the hull and examined every inch of him," Zeke reported. "I've got to say that he can handle the ice very well. Our engines worked great, even in the coldest conditions, though a few of our electric pulleys froze solid and had to be broken loose. There doesn't seem to be any damage to the cables. All systems are at one hundred percent, Captain," he finished.

"What's your opinion of the hydraulic system to power the ship?" Jim asked, steepling his hands and resting his chin on them. Zeke Good had just finished installing a hydraulic system, similar to those in the *Arctic Express* and the vehicles John's force used to power the ship. Parts had arrived in Juneau all summer long, and he and the mechanics had installed the system as soon as they dropped anchor.

"Without sounding like I'm tooting my own horn, that system is genius!" Zeke said with a huge smile. "It works a treat, even in the cold conditions that create thicker fluids."

"What about the systems on board the ARV?" Jim asked. "Did they respond to the cold in the same positive manner?"

"Again, everything worked perfectly. They had enough power to do some amazing things out there on the ice. Designing the structure so that it could withstand extreme movement helped. So did the wider triangular treads for moving through deep snow. It does get deep out there! Lunch Box scared everybody testing it in the toughest areas. Scientists report that the special storage kept everything intact. They didn't lose one beaker!" Zeke exclaimed.

"Excellent. I want to commend you and your crew for keeping everything together so well during the mission," Jim said. "Please tell the men I'm honored to lead such dedicated crewmembers." Zeke grinned, knowing that Jim was serious. For a moment he contemplated his position in this company, and the enjoyment he shared in working for men like Jim and John Shepherd.

"The men will be pleased to hear it, Shep," he approved, getting up. "Thanks."

Dorf and Mark flew the PBY Catalina to Prudhoe Bay to pick up the scientists and Team Knife. Although they didn't encounter any stormy weather, they did experience extreme cold conditions that might have iced the wings. However, the treatment of the wings made whatever ice formed slide off, unable to freeze to the wing itself. Dorf reported the success of the anti-ice coating as he taxied up to the terminal to load his passengers.

Crew pilots loved flying the PBY because it was a piece of history, a fully restored antique, and it handled beautifully in the sky. Passengers, on the other hand, didn't like that there were no windows and that the seats along the fuselage were less than comfortable. Those with tendencies toward airsickness always got sick flying in the PBY and CH53D. Since they knew this ahead of time, they took the appropriate steps and managed the trip without losing whatever they'd eaten last.

Coming into Juneau the pilots could see the entire Gastineau Channel, and both the Mendenhall and Lemon Creek Glaciers perched above the city. It was an incredibly beautiful sight. They brought the plane down and landed in the channel, coasting to a stop next to the floating dock and gangplank leading up to the ship. Goody, Wrench, and Inchworm were there to secure the plane to the crane, while passengers disembarked and climbed up to the main deck. Once everyone was out, the plane was lifted, and left dangling for an hour to drain all the seawater off the pontoons. During that time crews used hoses to wash down the pontoons and underbelly of the plane to remove all saltwater.

Once that was accomplished the plane was pivoted over the hold, lowered to sit in its appointed spot, where Team Raider waited to chain it down. Jim watched the entire procedure from the starboard observation deck and nodded approval. Not only did the ship gleam in the early afternoon sun, it looked pristine, as if it had just been launched, and as the doors of the hold slid closed Jim smiled with appreciation. He depressed the talk button on his COMLINK.

"That was beautifully done! Thanks for putting away the PBY with such care. I couldn't ask for a better crew," he said.

"Thanks, Shep!" several voices responded.

On the following day they gathered in the park overlooking the city and enjoyed an afternoon picnic. People from the local newspaper and news station gathered to watch the crew from *Bring It Up*. Because it was a public park no alcoholic beverages were allowed, and though news gatherers searched diligently they found none, which they found surprising. Most seafaring crews were given to drink, but apparently not this one. Not only that, but the crew seemed intent on enjoying every minute of this picnic. For nearly three hours they played hard, and everyone participated.

Nine slow-pitch softball teams participated in a round-robin single elimination tournament, taking all four of the softball fields in the park. The championship game was played on one field between the two remaining undefeated teams. Bill Dodge was captain of the team that took the trophy and those who watched the fun realized that this crew was tight. There were no arguments, no fights, just a lot of laughing, good-natured teasing, and fun! Competition was taken seriously, but it did not become a cause for anger.

After the softball games, the groups divided into twos and participated in a sack race, a wheelbarrow race, and an egg toss. Chance and PU won the sack race. Abe and Sturdy won the wheelbarrow race easily, outdistancing everyone. Sturdy's long and powerful arms propelled him along and Abe, holding up his 345-pound friend's legs seemed to have boundless energy and stamina. Dr. Lowe and Stephanie Morris won the egg toss.

After this all-American fun-filled afternoon of hijinks the crew gathered around the barbecue pits while the kitchen crew cooked lobster, prawns, and steak shish-k-bob with red potato, green peppers, sweet onion, mushrooms, artichoke hearts, zucchini, sweet peppers, and carrots. It was a very healthy meal with a delicious salad to accompany the main course, and peach, blueberry, and cherry cobbler with a dash of vanilla ice cream for dessert. Appetites were good as the crew gathered around the food, delighted to enjoy the meal together.

After dinner those who could play instruments got them out and for nearly an hour the park was filled with song. Most of the crew would have been amazed to learn that they sounded like a choir, with subtle harmonies, and the usual harmonies evident as they sang together. This was something they did often. Tonight's music was from the late 1950s and early 1960s, favorites from that era sung with enjoyment and passion, followed by about twenty minutes of praise songs from the same period. Many of them had never heard those old favorites, but they enjoyed the praise together, learning the melodies quickly and singing them with fervor.

Abe led them in a Bible Study that lasted for twenty minutes, and then discussion that lasted a good hour longer, before they separated into teams to clean up. One newspaper reporter stayed to the very end and so witnessed that members of the crew not only cleaned their picnic area, but they also policed the entire park, leaving it cleaner than it had been in a long time. Her article in the morning paper praised this unusual group of men and women in glowing terms.

Jim was in his office when the call came in. A travel company lost a cruise ship off the coast of Greece when a boat, supposedly full of drunk Russians on vacation, plowed into its hull at almost seventy knots. All passengers had been evacuated without injury, but two crewmembers perished in the explosion of the high-speed boat once it was imbedded in the hull. The company wanted their ship raised to retrieve the valuables of their clients and to determine the full story of the accident at sea. Unusual as the accident was, Jim was interested to get back to work on the sea.

Three loud whoops of the siren announced that all hands were needed on deck. Jim addressed them, told them about the disaster, and that *Bring It Up* was selected to raise the vessel. It was the usual Lloyds contract. Each of the scientists agreed that they could monitor the AOOS system from the *Sea Venture* labs and agreed to stay with the crew. Jim was pleased. At high tide *Sea Venture* headed out to sea to make the long voyage to Greece.

CHAPTER 22

In a hotel room overlooking the Gastineau Channel two people stood by the windows and watched *Sea Venture* leave port. News of the salvage contract offered, and that the ship was leaving to fulfill that contract, convinced them that the steamer had not been discovered by *Bring It Up*. After all, no one would leave a ship full of gold bullion unguarded. They were not at all pleased that this crew was employed in Greece, for both had a hand in that disaster and feared discovery. Yet that was not their primary concern at the moment.

"She's not where we thought she'd be," that was Viktor Borg, speaking with a heavy German accent. Everything about Viktor was heavy. He stood two inches under six feet and weighed nearly four hundred pounds.

Next to him stood a dark-haired woman of statuesque proportions, standing nearly six feet three inches tall, and with her high heels topping out at six feet six. She was what many men would have called voluptuous, with wide hips and ample breasts. Her face might have been pretty, but the cold stare and compressed lips formed an almost contemptuous sneer she almost always wore. Maganhildi VonSchloss nodded.

"We cannot use our submarine to search because the cursed Americans are going to be under the arctic ice all winter!" she growled.

"We shall have to wait until the ice melts again and try dragging another section. I've plotted where she might have gone down had she been even further north, and also further east. We'll have to wait to see," her mouth turned down at the corners. She hated waiting, especially when so much rested on her efforts.

"At least those meddling *Bring It Up* people are out of our hair here!" Borg snarled with a grunt. "I will make our travel arrangements. Call me in one month if you find anything or not. Someone must have survived! Somewhere there is a faint whisper of where our gold is! I will get everything set up in Greece. Will you use the same men?"

"Ja!" VonSchloss answered, nodding emphatically. "We will continue the search. Our families have searched for more than a hundred years, and I will not fail my father's dying wish! As for *Bring It Up*, tragedies at sea are common. There will be no survivors this time. I will see that the men I use have specific orders."

Zeke, who happened to be monitoring the flight lists of all passengers flying out of Juneau did a cursory search on Borg and VonSchloss for no other reason than he was thorough. As information began pouring in, he sat up straighter. News noticed, glancing over.

"Got something?"

"These two were in Barrow and Prudhoe Bay when we were there. They were also in Kotzebue! Remember that fishing trawler we searched. The check to pay the captain was written by a company owned by this woman!" he pointed at the picture of VonSchloss.

"Yeesh! Scary looking woman!" News commented.

"Yeah! And her fat friend is from a family that tried to steal the mine from which the gold on our vessel came!" Zeke added. "Ho-ho! The plot thickens!" Zeke rubbed his hands together. "You take Blubber Boy and I'll take the Ice Queen!" The names he had just given them would stick for the remainder of their investigation.

A few weeks later Jim wiped sweat from his forehead and wiped his hands on his sweat-stained pants. Cecilia smiled at him, her stomach protruding almost impossibly in front of her as she came close to her due date.

"From the frozen tundra to the sweltering jungle! My, don't

we have interesting adventures? And won't little Robby have an interesting life at sea?" she rubbed her tummy and looked down.

"He doesn't look that little!" Pippi said, coming to stand beside her. "Jimmy doesn't like the heat!" she winced as her child kicked at her side. "Great. I have to pee again!" Pippi waddled off, with Cecilia in tow. John came up to stand beside Jim.

"Looks like JAS is giving my wife a hard time!" he laughed easily.

JAS stood for his initials. John and Penelope decided to name their son James Andrea Shepherd, after his uncle and great uncle. Jim nodded, smiling as he watched the two women waddle along.

"RJ is doing the same to Cecilia." he observed. RJ was going to be christened Robert Jonathan Shepherd, after his grandfather and uncle. JR grinned.

"I can't wait to be a dad!" John said, laughing with delight.

"We won't have to wait long. Our boys will be along in September according to Gearhead!" Jim said, smiling with anticipation.

"How can it be this hot in September!" John groaned, wiping sweat from his own forehead.

"I swear a mosquito big enough to suck Sturdy dry landed on the railing a few minutes ago," Jim nodded. He absent-mindedly rubbed his arm where he'd gotten his usual shots for visiting Guatemala. Every time they passed through the Canal, they thought of Admiral Rook. John looked at the spot where he'd killed the man responsible for the deaths of twenty-six Marines.

"Brings back memories," John said sadly.

"We've got all the scholarships set up for the children of those Marines," Jim claimed, looking at the same spot. "None of the moms have to work thanks to us making them limited partners in the company. Each month they get a check for a little over four thousand dollars. I saw that three of them have remarried too. They married Marines," Jim grinned.

"Once you've had a Marine you can't go back," John said facetiously.

"Once you've had a Marine, it proves your IQ is too low to think of trying anything else!" Santa said, coming to stand beside them.

"Don't you have a deck to swab?" John asked, looking over at his friend.

"Friend, I would never hurt thee, but thou are standing where I am about to swab!" Steve Coleman said with a feral grin. John jumped aside as the mop came around. Coleman put his hand to his face as if in surprise. "I just swabbed that spot you clumsy Marine!"

"Aaargh! Matey! Ye'll swab that deck clean, or I'll have yer guts for garters!" John mimicked the Disney pirate.

"A man who wears garters is probably wearing a girdle and hose. Not really very scary," Santa teased, getting back to work.

Exchanges like that went on all day around Jim, and he appreciated the humor, quick reposts, and camaraderie of the crew. He and John moved away from the deck where Steve was cleaning and walked below to the bridge. Andrea was at the wheel, waiting for the signal to proceed to the next and final lock where they would be lowered to sea level and released into the Caribbean.

Customs officials inspected the ship, and the documents of the crew so there would be no waiting once they were released to continue their journey. Their uncle turned to smile at his two nephews.

"How are my little mamas?" he asked. It was what he now called Cecilia and Penelope.

"Heading for the head, last time we saw them," Jim said.

"I swear; Pen has to pee every eight minutes!" John added.

"I wouldn't if your brat wouldn't shove his foot against my bladder, so it ends up being the size of a pea!" Pen complained, coming into the bridge.

"How come whenever he's doing something you don't like he's my brat, and every time he's doing something you like he's your baby boy?" John asked, throwing up his hands.

"It just stands to reason. Any good comes from her side of the family, and any mischief comes from yours," Cecilia answered, giggling as she pushed her way under Jim's arm.

"Oh! That explains it, I guess!" John said facetiously. "Thanks."

"But Miss Chief is not related to me!" he quipped suddenly. Miss Chief was Rachael Hague, one of the lab technicians on the ship.

Jim laughed at his brother's quip and the two nodded to each other with smiles.

"Nonsense!" Pippi said, lifting her chin. "Your mother adopted her!"

"Ya gotta be quick to keep up with this one!" John said, hugging his wife and laughing.

"A quick-thinking Marine? I think not!" Tom Izbicki said as he entered the bridge.

"How could you? You're Navy!" John quipped.

"How could I what?" Tom asked, and then caught himself.

"Think?" John asked with a grin. Tom grinned back. The two touched fists and Tom went about his business.

A week later *Sea Venture* and the *Bring It Up* crew rescued a container ship in the middle of a force four hurricane, towing it to Miami before setting off once more for Greece. After they dropped the floundering giant off at the shipyard for repairs Jim invited his crew into the conference room to assess how the crew and ship handled the storm.

"This is a lot more stable platform to work from," FM said, opening the conversation. "Out on deck it didn't roll or pitch as much as the *Coral*."

"Getting the Bollard Pull working was easier too," Wrench offered.

"We certainly had more towing power," John added. "Those hydraulics produce a lot of torque, and the new props gave us the perfect balance of power and thrust."

"Having the tunnel thrusters was a bonus, Shep," Bear commented. "Coupled with the retractable thrusters we were able to keep the ship steady, pointed in the right direction, and adjust easily to the force of the storm. I think that helped create that sturdy platform FM was talking about."

"Our training paid off when that one big wave hit us," Dorf determined. "Working on the larger platform creates a spatial phase in which to operate that is very different. I think we've finally got the hang of it. No one on the crew missed a step or made a mistake."

"Uh, did anyone understand what he just said?" FM quipped. "I didn't quite follow that special face operation stuff."

"Spatial phase," Zeke spelled the words, "refers to the actual space in which we organize and work. It's bigger than that of the *Coral* so we have to take more steps to get some things done," Zeke explained to FM.

"Yeah! But whose face was special?" FM said with his eyes crossed.

"Why yours! Of course!" Dorf replied. "I especially appreciated the expression on your face when that wave dropped us a few feet and you straddled the cable," Everyone roared with laughter.

"That hurt!" FM said in a squeaky voice.

"I missed that! Is it on film?" Lee Roy asked.

"I wondered how the difference in size would affect our rescue. Practicing for the rescue seems to have covered all the necessary bases. I didn't see anyone having difficulty and you all worked together like a team. Well done," Jim commended.

"Are you saying that the ship is bigger?" FM asked, looking confused. His eyes traveled around, and his face wore a comical confused look.

"He's not going to get this concept anytime soon, is he?" Loony asked, patting FM on the back. "Take it easy, mate. You'll blow a mental gasket! I'm sure that by the time you retire some of it will sink in."

"Did we sink? How come nobody told me we sank?" FM complained, looking around as everyone laughed again.

"How did the laboratories and medical facilities handle the rough water?" Jim asked, looking at the medical team and scientists, trying to stay on course. He couldn't keep the grin off his face, though. FM winked at him.

"One or two things were moved a bit, but the labs remained unscathed, and nothing got broken," John Dinsmore said.

"I'm going to have to do something with the instruments in the surgery drawer. They made an awful racket in the bigger waves," Dr. Axlerod said.

"I can make a container for that drawer, with foam cutouts for each instrument, and a top layer of foam to keep everything in place," Inchworm offered.

"That would be awesome!" Leo replied, grateful.

"Anything else?" Jim asked.

"One of the bilge pumps failed, but Wrench and Inchworm were able to repair it in less than fifteen minutes. The water level down there rose a mere two inches in that particular chamber. Impellers fail on those things all the time. We keep a good supply of them for that very purpose, and it didn't take long to fix," Goody reported.

"What made it fail?" Jim asked; his pen poised to take notes. Goody noted his eagerness to actually record what happened and nodded approval.

"The impeller had a defect on one of the blades. It caused the thing to snap when pressure was applied. It happened in the factory because those are all new. I checked the impeller we replaced and the new one doesn't have that defect," Wrench said.

"We had a few electrical shorts," Hammer reported. "One of the deck boxes took a hit from something in a wave that washed over the deck and came open. Loony fixed that. The other short was in the kitchen. Motion caused two wires to touch. Whatever bonehead wired that unit stripped too much of the wire off, and rather than clip it short, left the exposed section hanging out there."

"Do you know what hit the box on deck?" Jim asked Loony as he wrote.

"Flipper," Loony responded. "I saw several dolphins fly across the deck. One or two of them hit things with their tails. They were having a lot of fun, or at least it sounded like fun," he smiled.

"How much damage?" Jim asked.

"Not much. I took the cover off once we were out of the storm, took it down to the machine shop and pounded it back in shape. After that I replaced the rubber seal and remounted it. No water leaked into the box after that," Loony replied.

"Could we put a cage around it?" Wade looked around the room with his question.

"Already done," Inchworm said. "All the deck boxes now have a protective cage around them."

"Well done!" Jim stated. "Thanks for taking the initiative," he looked around the conference table. "Anything else?" Noting the concentration on the crew he waited, knowing someone would think of something in just a moment. It was his wife who surprised him.

"Your son thought he was on a roller coaster ride through the entire storm!" Cecilia said crossly. "My ribs are bruised from his wild kicking!"

"Yeah!" Penelope said to John. "Yours too! You'd think the tike would get seasick in his first storm, but no! He has to be just like his dad!"

"Actually, both of them got very sick the first time their dad took them out in his fishing boat," Gwyneth confessed. "Of course, it was freezing cold, and the sea was choppy. And they were both too small to reach over the side of the boat. Jim kept climbing up to vomit over the side and I was sure he was going to end up in the ocean!"

"Wait!" FM said, shaking his head. "He was small?"

"He's still small," Sturdy said, patting FM's head. "So are you."

"Just because you're eleven feet tall doesn't mean I'm small!" FM said.

Angela Rysdale, the smallest of the women, climbed up in Sturdy's lap and pretended to fall asleep. Sturdy was obviously uncomfortable with her on his lap, and everyone grinned as she snuggled into him.

"You're supposed to wrap your arms protectively around her," Heidi instructed, her eyes dancing with laughter.

Angela opened her eyes and looked up at him, batting her eyelashes and Sturdy flushed bright red. The entire conference room erupted in laughter. FM opened his arms to invite Angela into his embrace and she screamed and ran back to her seat. Jim smiled at the interchange. His crew had earned their moment of lightheartedness.

When the laughter settled down, they continued the debriefing until Jim was satisfied. They would spend the evening at anchor and leave in the morning for Greece. Holding his wife's hand, he left the conference room last, having congratulated everyone on a job well done. She didn't mind waiting. Her husband was an expert at keeping his crew on the crest of the wave of perfection, and they needed the encouragement.

CHAPTER 23

Robert Jonathan Shepherd was born early Sunday morning, September 20. Cecilia was in labor for only twenty-eight minutes. She was able to walk to sickbay with Jim at her side after her water broke and the Axlerods, Wil and Donna Penny, and Ox were there to greet her. RJ was twenty-one inches long and weighed eight pounds, four ounces.

Later that morning, as Jim held his infant son, his heart nearly burst from his chest with pride. Cecilia watched him with that special smile she reserved for when she was making a memory. Cameras flashed and digital video rolled as the happy couple welcomed family and friends to sickbay where Cecilia rested. Leo told her she would probably be able to return to her own room the following day. The delivery had been quite short, and he was proud of her.

James Andrea Shepherd was born the following Tuesday, September 22, at the stroke of midnight. Penelope was in labor for nearly four hours. James was nineteen inches long and weighed nine pounds two ounces. RJ was born in the Alboran Sea just off the coast of Spain, and JAS was born in the Mediterranean, just off the coast of Sardegna, or Sardinia.

Everything changed for Jim and John as their sons came into the world. Both men had been coached as fathers and they took their duties seriously. The boys were changed more often by their dads, than by mom, though some thought that might change as time passed. It took both of them a day or so to adjust to the fact that these tiny infants were not as breakable as they appeared.

Both staterooms had a nursery attached, the foresight of Penelope and Cecilia that would eventually become a bedroom for the boys. If they had daughter's alterations would have to be made. Meanwhile, both women were healing nicely and recovering quickly. Dr. Axlerod was pleased that both women seemed to be healing so quickly, and Dr. Penny felt that both were handling the post partum depression nicely. They were talking to Gwyneth and Alice and getting lots of help with the babies. That was important. Plus, both women had done some work since they were on their feet, another good sign. The crew, everyone realized, was like a very big family and that was its crowning feature.

When the ship arrived in Greece the first thing on the agenda was visiting with Admiral Runion and his two roommates, Bill, and Roger. Admiral Runion and his two friends Bill and Roger chose their location wisely. The three men lived in Piraiévs, or Piraeus in English. Their house was a villa, overlooking the ocean, built at the edge of a steep drop of more than two hundred feet to the rocky beach below. A two-story structure it boasted a balcony on the upper floor with a magnificent view, built onto the south side of the house over the main entrance.

Inside was a modest kitchen and eating area, a living room on the north side of the house, and office space for the three men in a large room that had once been three separate rooms. A half bath on the ground floor attached to a laundry room made up the floor plan.

Upstairs were four bedrooms, two bathrooms, and a storage room for luggage. Using their meager funds and savings the men had, over the last ten years of their working careers, overseen the modifications of the house, and now lived in a very beautiful part of a country torn by financial ruin. Thankfully, all three spoke fluent Greek, and they had, in the short time they'd lived there, built up a legitimate business.

Purchasing antiques and present-day Greek furniture they sold it on the Internet, and they were on their way to turning their little business into a six-figure income! Jim wasn't surprised. Nor was he surprised to note that they had very good taste in the pieces they purchased. Most of their sales were in the United States and United Kingdom.

He sat with Cecilia, RJ, John, Penelope, and JAS on the balcony overlooking a peaceful ocean view, the island of Aíyina visible in the distance. The air was cool and crisp, a beautiful October afternoon, and the seven friends drank tea from tiny Greek teacups and ate cucumber sandwiches.

"I'm afraid you're going to have to sail back to America when you've finished this job," Charles said, pouring tea for Penelope. Pen put a lump of sugar in the tea and stirred it with a tiny spoon. "We've uncovered a terrorist cell in Chicago. Whatever they're planning seems to be focused on the Federal Reserve Bank of Chicago."

"What INTEL do you have?" Jim inquired.

"I've sent it all on to Zeke. Here's the main outline of what we know so far. Our source is in Turkey, deep under cover. He's been able to ferret out some very heinous plots against the U.S. in the past," Roger said, handing over the papers. His brown eyes studied Jim Shepherd as he took the papers. Jim, he thought, was up to the challenge.

Jim took a full twenty minutes to read them. John, who had the next set, also read through the pages. Cecilia and Pen were able to read both reports with their husbands, as the children were sleeping. When they were finished, they handed the packets back. Jim was not surprised to see Roger throw them on the small fire that burned in a fire pit between them all.

"ISIS in Chicago," John said with a sigh.

"Do we have eyes on in the city?" Jim asked.

"No. We passed this information on in the usual manner. Duck took it to Homeland Security, and it got suppressed shortly afterwards. Since we have a Naval presence in the city Duck is using local NCIS personnel to try to get some kind of INTEL. He has to do it very carefully, because the President has put him on notice that he is being watched." Charles said. "I hate politics!"

"What's your assessment?" Jim asked, knowing there was more.

"If this goes down, the President will use it to fan the flames of hatred for America!" Charles said with heat. "See! We're evil, and people hate us, and for good reason!" he mimicked the voice of the President fairly well. "Washington will spin it, the right people will rattle their sabers, and the perpetrators will be treated like heroes. I'm sorry for the anger in my voice, but this roasts my balls! Sorry, ladies!" he added.

"I think we can avert any of that," John said, smiling at the anger in Charles against the current political climate in America.

"Tell us!" Roger said, eager to hear.

"We find these clowns, uncover their operation, stir up their neighbors and the local police department, and take them down before they can do anything!" John said. "That's worked in the past. The perpetrators get deported, and no carnage gets done. Our present administration can't use it for its agenda."

"Yes, that has worked. However, you'll have to be very careful. Our President knows people in Chicago, and it will be difficult not to run into his friends. Most of them are corrupt, few are dangerous, but some could be a serious detriment to your plan," Bill said quietly. Bill was the former Naval commanding officer at the base in Chicago, and he knew the city well. He also knew the politics. If anyone could help them there, it would be him.

"The threat of those catfish changing the ecosystem of the waterways should merit a research grant," Cecilia said, shifting RJ a little as he stirred. "They are a keystone species and folks along the great lakes are worried," she added. "The red-eared slider is a good example of what a keystone species can do in our local waterways. That turtle has spread throughout the country and become a true nuisance."

"She's good!" Roger said with a grin. "May I hold that little tyke?" he asked. Cecilia smiled at the older gentleman and handed RJ into his arms. An old hand with babies Roger sat back and admired the infant in his arms.

"Well! We have something to occupy our time until we're ready to go back to Alaska and raise that steamer," Jim asserted with a grin. "I'm going to get our scientists started on that grant idea, but I'd like you three to look into this mysterious steamer and why she was so far off course. I sent you the details earlier. There are other players involved too. You have it all."

"Yes. That is a puzzle, isn't it?" Charles commented. "We've been doing some research, but I don't think we've uncovered anything you haven't been able to uncover yet. However, we will talk to our old friends, and see if anyone remembers the details being spoken of.

"You don't have any friends who actually remember what happened that year, do you?" John asked facetiously.

"Why don't you go for a long run off a short pier!" Charles laughed.

"Someone's father might have spoken of the mystery. The Navy is a tight group. We'll nose around," Bill said, grinning. "After all, you are paying us a nice salary to be your clandestine Secret Service, not to mention the amazing information center you paid for. No one even knows what we're doing here because of our link to that satellite system and your ship!"

The rest of the afternoon was spent talking of the Alaska adventure and they ate dinner that evening in a small Greek restaurant the three men frequented, enjoying local dishes served with delight to new guests. The babies were a hit in the restaurant, and Jim and John were surprised at how many people were allowed to hold the babies. Both of their wives proved to be great ambassadors.

Because the four parents spoke fluent Greek, and were obviously from America and the UK, the patrons of the restaurant welcomed them even more enthusiastically. Most tourists spoke only English, and it was nice to meet people who not only respected the language, but also knew how to speak it, and asked the right questions. All four learned new slang terms, some local phrases they probably wouldn't encounter elsewhere in Greece, brushing up on local customs.

Back on the ship Wade and Andrea had the crew ready for the

job at hand, and they moved the ship into the Cyclades, Kikládhes in Greek, a group of islands off the southern tip of Greece. The cruise ship sank near Páros. When they dropped anchor over the wreck, they could see Páros to the east just three kilometers distance. Numerous islands surrounded them, most notable Antipáros to the south. As the high-speed boat rounded one of those small islands it failed to note the presence of the huge cruise ship heading for the harbor. Reports said that the driver had been turned looking back behind the boat and taking a picture of the island he had just passed. Other witnesses couldn't remember seeing a driver.

Páros Island is a beautiful spot with a rich history. Its greatest length from N.E. to S.W. is 21 km or 13 mi, and its greatest width 16 km or 10 mi. Of a round, plump-pear shape, the island is formed by a single mountain that rises 2,375 ft, sloping evenly down on all sides to a maritime plain, which is broadest on the north-east and south-west sides. Marble composes most of the island, though gneiss and mica-schist are found in a few places.

Historical research indicated that the people of the island were prosperous. Sometime between the fifteenth and eighteenth Olympiad a colony of Ionians from Athens settled on the island. The poet Archilochus, a native of Páros, is said to have taken part in one of those Olympiads.

Shortly before the Greco-Persian War (490 BC), Páros seemed to have been a dependency of Naxos, an island to the east just 5 miles distance. However, in the Greco-Persian War they sided with the Persians and sent a trireme to Marathon to support them. That, of course, led to retaliation by Miltiades, leading the Athenian fleet, and demanding a fine of 100 talents. The town, however, offered a vigorous resistance, and the Athenians were obliged to sail away after a siege of 26 days, during which they wasted the island. At a temple of Demeter Thesmophoros in Páros Miltiades received a fatal wound and died, according to the account of Herodotus. The Archaeologist Ross was able to identify the site of the temple on a low hill beyond the boundary of the town by means of an inscription he found buried there. Such is often the result of events those living them think historic. More often than not they end up buried and forgotten.

In the second Greco-Persian War (480-479 BC) Páros sided with Xerxes I of Persia. For their support of the Persians, the Athenian war leader Themistocles exacted a heavy fine later punishing the islanders. Further historical research indicated that under the Delian League, the Athenian-dominated naval confederacy (477-404 BC), Páros paid the highest tribute of the island members. The tribute is said to have been 30 talents annually, according to the estimate of Olympiodorus (429 BC). The implication was that Páros was one of the wealthiest islands in the Aegean.

In 1537 Ottoman Turks conquered Páros and remained in control of the island until the Greek War of Independence (1821-1829). During the Russo-Turkish War (1768-1774) Count Alexey Orlov, Russian Archipelago, housed his squadron in Naoussa Bay from 1770-1775. Under the Treaty of Constantinople (1832), Páros became part of the newly independent Kingdom of Greece. For the first time in over six hundred years Parians were ruled by fellow Greeks. It is said that at this time, Páros became the home of a heroine of the nationalist movement, Manto Mavrogenous, who both financed and fought in the war for independence. Her house near the Ekatontapiliani church is a historical monument.

Jim stopped ruminating on the islands suddenly and listened carefully to the voices coming in from *Steel Crab*. It was FM's voice he was listening to at the moment.

"The boat that rammed the cruise ship came free as it sank. You're not going to believe what I'm seeing here!" FM reported. Jim moved over to a monitor to see what FM was seeing. Most of the fiberglass of the front end disintegrated in the collision, but beneath the fiberglass was a reinforced steel frame, not part of the boat's original design, but added to give it ramming power. "It kinda looks like this was deliberate!" FM added.

"FM, would you please get us a photo of the registration on this craft?" Jim made the request on the COMLINK. "Also, all communication from here on out will be by COMLINK, if you please," Jim added.

"Roger that boss," FM said. "Driver is moving us around to take a photo of the registration."

Jim watched as the picture formed and knew that Zeke was already adding the photos to his computer system. As expected, the registration was written in Russian, but Zeke was quickly able to translate it. News and Cecilia were working hard on identifying the owner of the craft.

"The cruise ship is owned by an Italian company," Cecilia said over the COMLINK. "Financially the company is strong, and this is the first such loss for them in over twenty years. Several of her passengers were apparently wealthy and had precious family heirlooms in the ship's vault. To limit the lawsuits, they want to bring up the ship and offer the lost jewelry to the owners. They've actually drawn up a contract to ensure that those receiving their valuables will not sue the company. Seventeen crew and thirty-four passengers went into the water, but so far, no deaths other than the two crewmembers have been announced. The body of the operator of the boat was never found."

"Thank you, honey. However, that may change once we bring the cruise ship to the surface and tow her into dry dock," he added. "Wade, what do you think about repairing that hole and bringing her up?" Jim asked.

"Why didn't the automatic system work to seal off that section of the ship?" Wade asked. "That's a fairly new boat and should have had an emergency breach system."

"I've been thinking the same thing myself," Jim admitted. "Goody, do you know if they had to check those systems on a regular basis during emergency training?"

"Yeah, Shep. Every time they had a drill those systems were supposed to be checked," Goody answered from the engine room.

"I have the company records, Shep," Zeke spoke up from the CIC. "The system was checked twenty-eight days ago, and everything worked. I smell a mystery!"

"Okay. I trust your nose, and my men. We bring that boat up and I want Wade to lead a team with Goody, Hammer, Loony and Wrench to investigate that entire system. We need to know where it failed, and why it failed," Jim ordered.

"Hey boss!" FM's voice cut in. "Get Wade and Loony to take a gander at what we're recording at the moment."

Jim turned to look into the monitor, knowing that Wade and Loony were looking at the same picture. His heart sank.

"That's a remote-control device," Wade and Loony said, almost on top of each other.

"So now we know this was deliberate," Jim said softly. "Crew listen up. As of this moment we are on yellow alert. *Steel Crab*, that water is too deep for normal diving, but someone may try to collect the evidence before we bring everything up. Can we bring the Highspeed boat up?"

"Roger that, boss," FM said. "We'll rig the boat to be winched up."

"Good. Make sure that the submersible is on the deck and secured before we try to bring that boat up. It may be rigged to blow," Jim replied.

"How come I have to do that?" Goody's voice came over the COMLINK.

"What are you talking about, Goody?" Jim asked, not catching on at first.

"You ordered me to make sure that the submersible is on the deck and secured before we try to bring the boat up, and then you told me it might be rigged to blow!" Goody replied.

"I said good, not Goody," Jim laughed with everyone else. "And I meant that the highspeed boat might be rigged to blow," he added. "Seeing that you are Navy I have to remember to explain things more simply, seaman Good."

"I am on the sea, and I am good! Now I'm a superhero! Seaman! Like Superman!" Goody chuckled. Jim listened to the laughter in his headset with a smile.

"It's the navy, Shep!" John quipped. "They're not selective like the Marines!"

The bantering went on and Jim smiled as the men worked around him. He knew from the bantering that the crew was in a good place mentally and thanked God once again for a crew like this to lead. It would be dangerous if the boat was rigged to blow, their ship might easily get tossed about in the aftermath. Everyone accepted that risk.

Jim pitched in to help clean the submersible before it was locked into place. Again, the camaraderie around the work kept everyone smiling or laughing. When everything was ready, he climbed back to the CIC and ordered all hands to be prepared if the boat was rigged to blow. It wasn't, and everyone breathed out a sigh of relief, as the wreckage was finally lifted to the deck and placed on a cradle and lashed into place.

"Let's find out as much as we can from the evidence, okay love," Jim said, bending down and kissing Cecilia on the neck. He loved the way she blushed when he kissed her neck and looked down lovingly at his sleeping son. "How is RJ doing?" he asked as he stood up straight.

"He's sleeping at the moment," Cecilia said, rubbing her hand over the mound in her lap that was her precious first child.

"JAS is sleeping too," Pippi said from her seat in the CIC. Jim looked and saw that she too was rubbing JAS as he slept upon her lap. It was a particularly motherly gesture and it stirred within him an appreciation for God's plan for the family. Both women got to their feet and made their way down to the deck, depositing their sons in the playpen to continue sleeping.

"The craft was purchased by a company run by Viktor Borg," Zeke said as Jim turned to leave.

"Borg! Isn't he part of the Russian Black-Market crowd?" Jim asked, surprised.

"One and the same. The cruise ship shouldn't have sunk. I think the boat was meant to strike one particular cabin. The remote control on the boat, the reinforcement to be sure it could batter its way through the hull tell us that." Zeke said, his fingers flying over two keyboards at once. "I've pulled up the satellite photos and studied them. There was a yacht close by and the highspeed boat stopped at the boat momentarily before building speed and aiming for the cruise ship," Zeke looked at Jim.

"Owned by Borg?" Jim asked.

"No!" Was the surprising answer. "The yacht belongs to Maganhildi VonSchloss."

"Maganhildi? Battle Maiden!" Jim snorted. "The plot thickens. Next, we'll have Natasha and Boris walking through the doors with a cannon ball bomb and lit fuse!" he shook his head. "Is it possible they are connected?"

"Not on the surface. Both are connected through a Dutch company that once owned the steamer we found under the Arctic ice. Wikffels is the name of the company and Martin Marius Wikffels is the CEO. His great grandmother was named Wilhelmina."

"Wasn't there a VonSchloss involved in trying to claim ownership of the mine about a year or two before *Wilhelmina's Song* sank?" Jim asked, turning back and coming back beside Zeke.

"Full marks, Shep! Yes, VonSchloss falsified some claim forms to show that he was the true owner of the mine. The claims were shown to be falsified in the battle that ensued in court back then. VonSchloss actually worked for Wilhelmina Wikffels, who summarily dismissed him, and then hired him a year later as CEO of an electric company she managed to take in a hostile takeover.

"Isn't it odd how past sins come to light in the work that we do?" Jim asked, his eyes focused, and his forehead knitted in concentration as he considered the information Zeke had just imparted. Shaking his head, he sighed. "God was clear. Your sins will find you out!" he stated. "What or who is on that cruise ship that they don't want anyone to know about? And what will they do to stop us from bringing it up?"

"Good questions. Should we be preparing for a second highspeed boat attack? It wouldn't work with us, because our hull is reinforced, but it might scratch the paint," Zeke replied. "Besides, if they use a remote-control unit on the boat again, I can jam the signal, take over the device, and stop it," Zeke grinned.

"If I was doing it, I'd rig the boat with enough explosives to put this ship on the bottom of the ocean," Jim said quietly. "I wouldn't use a remote control, but a computer driven program to take the boat right to us. I might also consider an attack from the air with missiles. A couple of missiles aimed properly would not only put us on the bottom; but it would kill most of us!"

The two men looked at each other with drawn faces. Jim pressed his COMLINK.

"Condition red. I want the AH-1W armed and ready to fly. Chief, you're on notice. If we have a high-speed boat heading for our ship you and I go up to take it out. Wade, make sure we are ready to send out sunbursts against a missile attack from the air."

A chorus of voices came through the headset and Jim nodded once, satisfied that he'd done everything possible to avert a disaster.

"They took out the cruise ship after dark," Zeke said, looking at the clock.

"Alright. Eyes on every boat around us within a mile radius! If a high-speed boat stops at one of those yachts it is targeted, and the Cobra goes up. When the Cobra disables the engines, it won't reach its target, but it could be blown from the yacht. When and if that happens, I want a team on a rigid raider ready to take the yacht. I want answers," Jim commanded.

"I'll take the yacht," John offered, coming in as Jim was talking. Jim nodded.

"Roger that. Zulu and Bulldog have the Yacht. That means Sniper has the sunburst defense system," he pushed his COMLINK and gave the orders, alerting the team of the impending danger.

At dinner that evening Stephanie Morris shivered when she walked into the dining room. "Wow! You can cut the atmosphere in here with a knife!" she proposed.

"They're ready for action," Dr. Ross whispered. "I hope none of them get hurt tonight."

Jim and Chief ate together, ate fast, and when they were finished, they headed down into the war room, and after getting ready up to the helipad. Instead of the CH-53D Sea Stallion the AH-1W sat on the pad. Climbing into their respective seats Jim fired up the engine after doing a complete preflight check and listened to make sure everything was working properly, checking his gauges before pulling back on the stick and lifting off the platform.

"*Lightening Bolt* is in the air," he announced.

"Copy *Lightening Bolt*. You are clear to begin patrol," Smitty replied.

For nearly an hour Jim circled within a nautical mile of the ship, watching the water traffic below. He was aware of the appearance of the high-speed boat at about the same time Zeke gave warning.

CHAPTER 24

"**S**hep, I have a highspeed boat leaving Páros harbor with one driver on board, gaining speed fast on a heading of 157.2°," Zeke's voice charged.

"How in the heck do you know there's only one person on board?" Chief asked before Jim could acknowledge.

"I've tapped into the video security system at the harbor. The operator and two other men carried several heavy packages to the boat before it left," Zeke replied.

"Roger that, Zeke. I have eyes on. J.R., are you out there?" Jim asked.

"A hundred yards off the starboard bow of the target yacht. It's the same yacht that was out there when the cruise ship got hit," John's voice replied evenly.

"*Lightening Bolt* will hit the boat from behind if the driver is no longer on board after the stop at the yacht. Depending on speed achieved after leaving the yacht we should be able to bring it to a stop halfway between. They'll consider it safe to blow it from there if they're going to blow it. Don't get dead," he said to his brother.

"Shep! I have a Kamov Ka-50 taking off from the island!" Zeke warned tersely.

"Roger that Zeke. If I remember correctly the Kamov has a ceiling height of half the distance of *Lightening Bolt.* Going dark and going up," Jim's voice was calm. He'd seen the blip on his radar. Using new equipment to jam any radar trying to track him Jim began to climb fast and hard. Chief kept his eye on the attack helicopter and prepared for an aerial combat situation.

"He's already trying to lock on us, Shep," Chief's voice said from behind. Jim maneuvered above and behind the Kamov and dove out of the sky. "Now he's targeting the ship!" Chief snarled. Two missiles left the AH-1W and Jim was already shredding the engine and rotor of the helicopter with the mini gun in front. But the Kamov had fired two missiles as well. From the ship Jim saw the Sunburst Flares designed to attract heat-seeking missiles deployed in time and the missiles both went off hundreds of yards from the ship. *My wife and son are on that ship!* Jim's face was granite as he guided the helicopter.

Already moving to intercept the highspeed boat Jim grimly moved into place, and Chief spoke from behind.

"The vessel is unmanned," Chief said calmly. Jim heard the calmness in his voice and acknowledge in the same manner.

Again, the mini gun spun, and bullets tore through the engine compartment. Black smoke erupted from the engine compartment and the boat slowed and almost stopped. Even as it did an explosion ripped through the night. Beneath him Jim watched the high-speed boat disintegrate, shrapnel flying everywhere and after the bright light of the explosion there was only a burning ring of fire on the surface of the water. Banking hard he headed for the ship.

"*Lightening Bolt,* do you copy?" John's voice sounded in Jim's ear.

"Roger Zulu. Sit rep," Jim replied.

"We have control of the Yacht. Suggest you get back to the ship."

"On my way," Jim replied, heading for the ship. Expertly he landed and watched as the crane lifted the helicopter down into the hold and hanger where it would be refitted. Twenty minutes after landing the helicopter was refitted for research and in the hold. Jim watched the skids settle and helped chain them down in the hold before heading topside to change into his uniform and receive the officials he knew would be coming. He had one nagging thought as he showered and dressed, and when he was ready, he made his way to the CIC.

"Is there any way Borg, VonSchloss, or Wikfells knows we found *Wilhelmina's Song?*" he asked as he stepped into the air-conditioned comfort of the center.

"No," Zeke said emphatically. "They're actually trolling in a different area, still looking for the vessel."

"So whatever sins were committed in the mutiny on that ship, and what's happening today, are about to be brought out into the open," Jim replied. "Your sins will find you out! It appears we're dealing with some very bad people here. Let's get all the INTELL we can on all three."

"The Greek officials are approaching the ship," Smitty said, watching the radar.

"Where is John and his team that took the yacht?" Jim asked.

"Still on the yacht," Zeke looked up. He nodded once and grinned. "They're waiting until the officials leave before bringing the prisoners on board. We don't need that complication!" Zeke added.

Jim walked out to the deck and watched the official police yacht pull along side. A very polite request to board was given and Jim granted permission, watching as the gangplank was lowered to receive their guests. Dorf and Mark appeared on either side of him, and he nodded to them. Both were in their dress uniforms.

"What's the drill, Shep?" Dorf asked quietly.

"We give them a guided tour and let them see the AH-1W," Jim replied quietly. "The engines will still be warm so if they ask, we were doing some work mapping the ocean floor. Zeke has the maps if they ask. The explosion surprised us, and the attack on our ship by the other helicopter. We returned when we knew it was safe."

As the men from the yacht climbed the ramp Jim looked at them and decided that their posture suggested aggression more than anything else. His jaw stiffened when the officer in charge stopped.

"You will explain why there was an aerial battle over my ocean, and why a boat and helicopter now rest upon the bottom!" the officer demanded emphatically. He pointed a finger at Jim as he spoke.

Jim folded his arms over his chest and stared at the man. Dorf and Mark, taking their cue from Jim, did the same. In situations like this Jim knew that silence would achieve much more than speech. A space of about three minutes went by when the official finally exploded.

"If you do not cooperate with me and my government there will be dire consequences. I will seize this ship and arrest your entire crew!" the man sputtered.

Jim's fist lashed out and the man went down hard. Even as the other policemen reached for their weapons, they heard the unmistakable sound of weapons being taken off safety. Looking around they realized that they were surrounded by a dozen men, all armed with shotguns. The slides clacked loudly as shells were jacked into the chamber. The official on the deck was trying the stem the flow of blood from his broken nose with a handkerchief.

"Get up!" Jim ordered.

"You do not order me!" the man sputtered, and then yelped as Jim lifted him from the deck, holding him so that his feet dangled.

"I am Captain of this vessel. We are in international waters. If you speak disrespectfully to me again, I will throw you overboard. Do you understand?" Jim had spoken in Greek, his nose nearly touching the broken nose of the official, his eyes boring into that official's eyes. The man remembered the power of that single blow, and realizing he weighed well over two hundred and fifty pounds he was awed by Jim's strength, and more. The fierceness of those eyes told him much and he wisely remained quiet. Jim put him down without further comment to him personally.

"Dorf, please take this officious little potentate down to sick bay, and have Dr. Axelrod stop the bleeding, but not fix the nose. If he spouts any more of his officious orders throw him overboard." The giant saluted his Captain, grabbing the official by his jacket half dragging him down to sickbay. Watching carefully the policemen noticed that the shotguns did not waver or lower. A lieutenant cleared his throat.

"My superior perhaps overstepped his bounds," he said in Greek. "Do you really need an armed response to officials?"

"Did you or any of your men order the attack on my ship?" Jim snapped, glaring at the man. "That Kamov Ka-50 is a military helicopter, and it fired two missiles at my ship! Until I know who was responsible, and why I was attacked, I will meet aggression with aggression! I have two infants on board this ship, and women! How dare you attack my vessel!"

"Sir, we did not attack your vessel!" the Lieutenant sputtered.

"Did you, or did you not see the sunbursts released from this vessel to intercept the missiles?" Jim's voice was ice.

"We do not know why the helicopter attacked your ship," the lieutenant said defensively. "Yes, we did see the sunbursts. Surely that was a military response!"

"Because of the nature of the work we do we are prepared to repel boarders and pirates that attack this ship. The attack on *Sea Venture*, which is here by contract to raise a cruise ship that was purposely attacked, was unprovoked. Surely you saw the high-speed boat that exploded in the water several hundred yards from my ship?" Jim made it a question. "And yet you come on my ship and show me aggression! How dare you!" Jim snapped with real anger in his voice. "I was attacked! My ship is now prepared to deal with all aggression with a proper response. Your government is officially on notice of this posture!"

The lieutenant sighed and his shoulders slumped. Holding out his hands he appealed to Jim.

"All that you say is true. But there are questions that need to be answered. Why were you attacked, and why by a military helicopter? Why did a boat explode on the water? Who flew the helicopter that was seen landing on this boat? Surely you can see that we need to know these things!" the lieutenant did not see any softening of Jim's eyes or stance and sighed once more.

"You are here on my vessel, asking questions that we cannot answer. I don't know who was behind the attack, or why it was perpetrated," Jim replied, the steel still in his voice. "As to who flew the helicopter, I did. It is a research helicopter, and we were testing equipment designed to map the ocean floor. We did not land until both the helicopter and the highspeed boat were neutralized. From the air I saw the two missiles fired by the Kamov Ka-50, fired at the ship upon which my wife and infant son reside!"

"Witnesses have come forward and reported that this is accurate," the lieutenant said, trying to defuse the situation.

"Then why did you come on my vessel with such aggression?" Jim snapped. "My reputation and the reputation of this crew is known throughout the world! Had you simply come asking questions and gathering information you would have been treated differently, shown respect and cooperation. I see you as an aggressor and until you are escorted from this vessel you will be treated as a threat to my crew!"

"We are not a threat to you or your crew!" the lieutenant said adamantly.

"Did your commanding officer threaten to seize my vessel and arrest my crew?" Jim asked dangerously.

"You struck him!" the lieutenant said, spreading his hands again as if that explained everything.

"Only after he threatened to seize my ship illegally, and arrest my crew, also illegally!" Jim said quietly. "I show respect to officials who show respect to the law."

"Yes! Alright! My superior overstepped his bounds, I agree. Surely, we can settle this without violence!" the lieutenant pleaded.

"You will unhand me! I am an official of the Police! I will have you arrested for this!" the leading official was struggling as Dorf dragged him back. Jim moved and the official found himself flying over the railing. He landed awkwardly in the water, stunning himself, and doing further damage to his face and nose, and rose to the surface screaming in rage. Jim pointed to the gangplank.

"Get off my ship," he demanded softly, his voice full of threat. "If anyone attempts to board my ship again tonight, they will be met with a military response," he stood facing the lieutenant and the man shrugged his shoulders and nodded to his men to head back down the gangplank. Jim watched them board the boat, hauling the screaming official out of the water before they left. Inwardly he sighed.

"He'll be back," Jim said quietly as the gangplank was slowly raised into place. "We'll take them from the water."

"Geeze, boss!" Mark said with a grin. "I guess you don't like it when your crew is threatened by an armed attack! Who would have thought!" he added, laughing. Then his face turned serious. "That was close!" he said. "I'm glad we had those sunbursts ready!"

"Once he fired those missiles, I had no trouble blowing him out of the sky," Jim admitted, remembering his moment of fear when he saw the missiles leave the attack helicopter. "Let's get ready to receive our prisoners, and then the return of our hot-tempered official!"

John arrived a few minutes later, the rigid raider appearing almost silently out of the dark. He had three prisoners secured by restraint ties sitting in the center of the boat. MP and Hayseed were pointing guns at the three, telling Jim that whoever these three were the men of Bulldog took them seriously. He watched as the men were herded off the raider and up the gangplank, appreciating the professionalism of his crew.

"Mercs, boss," C.G. said as he prodded one of them forward.

"Was Maganhildi VonSchloss on the boat?" Jim asked, watching as the mercenary reacted to that name.

"No," John answered. "Two of these idiots died trying to take us after we'd taken the boat."

"And the boat?" Jim asked, watching the men carefully to gage their reaction to the death of their comrades.

"We opened the drain chocks and watched it fill up with water and sink," John replied easily. "That should put a dent in VonSchloss's bank roll," he added with a feral grin. "I removed all the remote gear and electronics before scuttling the boat," John pointed to Wade who was carrying a backpack full of equipment in one hand, with another strapped to his back.

"Right. We have an official who will be returning with a warrant to search our vessel. We're going to take them from the water when they come along side. Put these boneheads in the brig and let's get ready to rumble with the local authorities," Jim grinned at his brother and headed into the CIC to check on his wife and son, and then made his way down to the war room to get ready.

Team Zulu and Bulldog came shortly afterwards, already in their battle gear, and took the time to break down their weapons, check all their loads, and reassemble them properly. Jim took pride in watching them as he went through his own preparations. His men were the best soldiers in the world, trained to ride the crest of the wave of perfection, and they did the basic chores of being a good soldier with the same care and attention they did everything else.

"Okay men!" Jim began as the activity drew to a close. "We're working in our 12-Teams. Delta, Zulu, and Firefox have the deck. JR has command of 12-Team-1. Repel all attempts to board this ship with extreme prejudice!

"Omega 1, Knife, and Raider are with me in 12-Team-2. We take the boat from the stern. I have command.

"Sniper, Bulldog, and Nightfall are 12-Team-3. Tom, you have command," Jim watched Chief and Counselor as he said this and both men nodded without any sign of disappointment or irritation. All three men held the same rank, and any of them could have command. Jim had chosen Tom Izbicki of Nightfall and that was good enough for them. He smiled at both to show them he understood their loyalty to the team. Chief sketched a one-fingered salute and Counselor just nodded. Someone had to have command, and this time it was Izzy.

"12-Team-3 takes the boat from the bow. We are using non-lethals for this attack. Anybody takes a hit that gets past our protective gear goes to sickbay with his partner as escort. We all know the drill and know how to do this. Let's not get dead!" Jim grimaced as he said the last.

There was, he knew, a very good chance that any of his men could be seriously wounded. The officials would use live ammunition, and they should be trained men, which meant they would aim for center mass. His men were protected against live ammunition unless the enemy was using armor piercing rounds. He hoped fervently that none would be used.

"Mark. Please lead us in prayer," Jim commanded. Mark nodded, bowed his head and gave thought to his words.

"Lord, help us to keep from letting our anger flare up and responding with unnecessary force. But help us to know when force is absolutely necessary. Please give us wisdom to know the difference. Amen."

Jim heard several men say "amen" at the end of the prayer and nodded his thanks. "12-Team-1 on deck. The rest of you follow me to the moon pools. 12-Team-3, you have the aft pool," Jim headed out the door of the ready room and up a flight of stairs, across a corridor, and down a flight of steps to the forward moon pool. His men stood at ease around the pool, waiting for the signal from John that the enemy boat was in position before inserting their 5-minute breathers and hitting the water.

While they waited, they put on fins and talked about the mission, who would climb up first of the buddies they always paired up with, and how they would spread out, always watching their arcs of fire to protect one another. Jim listened to the men as they made those decisions and nodded his approval. John's call came half an hour later. Without another word the men put the breathers in their mouths, clamped teeth on the rubber guards, and stepped into the water.

CHAPTER 25

Colonel Marcus Panagos was not used to rebuttal and furious that his authority had been questioned. He'd returned to the island, woken a judge, and received a search warrant for the ship. The judge had not asked, and he did not share that the boat was in international water, making the warrant useless. As his boat came to rest, just off the side of *Sea Venture* several searchlights switched on from the deck above, lighting up his vessel and causing men to cast long confusing shadows. At the head of the gangplank, which was in the up position, Captain John Shepherd appeared in full battle gear. Squinting his eyes Colonel Panagos looked up in surprise. Everyone was looking up and John pointed his M16A2 in the air and fired off a three-round blast.

While all eyes were above Jim and his team, and Izzy and his team slipped onto the vessel. Colonel Panagos' face drained of color as the cold barrel of gun pressed against the side of his neck. Sliding his eyes to his left he saw Captain James Shepherd, also in full battle gear, holding the gun pressed against his neck. When he looked around, he saw his men slowly lowering their weapons and looked around to find that twenty-four men had crept upon his boat and taken it without a shot being fired.

"Order your men to stand down and drop all their weapons,"

Jim said in perfect Greek. Panagos swallowed and gave the order. Several of his men raised eyebrows, but they were looking down the barrels of lethal weapons, held by rock-steady hands.

"Lieutenant Weston! Have your team frisk each man, remove all weapons, and gather them in a bag. These men may retrieve their weapons when they leave, not before!" Jim commanded in Greek.

"Yes sir!" Calvin replied in English. His men were thorough, and all twelve men Panagos had with him were soon relieved of their weapons. Only two had been foolish enough to try to hide a weapon. Weston had been quick to put them on the deck in a painful submission hold when he found a weapon. Experienced fighters, the policemen had been surprised, angry, and then wisely frightened at the speed and precision used to subdue them. They now stood sullenly in a group with their fellow officers, shifting their feet, not daring to look at their colonel.

"Lower the gangplank, please," Jim said into his COMLINK.

"Roger that, Shep," John's voice replied.

"Lieutenant Oxton!" Jim said loudly.

"Sir!" Sean said, snapping off a salute.

"When we are off this boat, move it a safe distance, drop the anchor, and I'll send a boat to pick you up," Jim replied.

"Sir!" Sean said, snapping off another salute. Grinning at him Jim turned back to Colonel Panagos.

"The last time you were on my ship I physically threw you overboard. Speak disrespectfully to me or any of my men and I promise you will never forget the lesson!" One look into those stormy green eyes and Colonel Panagos knew this man spoke the truth. Swallowing hard, remembering the sheer strength and unnerving speed of the man, he nodded silently.

On deck Jim waited, holding the men at gunpoint, until the gangplank was raised again. He nodded at John, pointed to his eyes, his gun, and to the prisoners. John nodded, understanding and his team surrounded them, guns up and pointed, steady in the hands of men who knew how to use them.

"Chance, will you and PU please go fetch Ox?" Jim asked politely.

"On our way Shep," Chance assented, heading back to the rigid raider with his partner.

Jim led the rest of the men down into the war room, removed, stripped down, oiled and treated all of his weapons, and hung his clothing up to dry. Changing into his Captain's dress uniform he looked around the room and saw that most of the men were finished and were finishing changing into their dress uniforms. Nodding at them as he caught their eyes he waited until the last was ready and led them back up to the deck. On the way he outlined his plan and saw with some amusement that his men were both surprised and quite willing to participate. Sean, Chance, and PU were heading down. On deck Jim merely nodded to John and he broke off, his men lowering their weapons and following.

"While my men change will you accompany me to our dining room?" Jim asked politely. Colonel Panagos noted that only four men now stood with the captain. Bulldog had been given the task of escorting the visitors. There were no weapons visible on any of the men.

"I have enough men here to take you and your men, Captain. You are foolish and arrogant," Panagos said, drawing himself up. "Arrest these men!" he ordered.

Something that felt like a sledgehammer smashed into his face, crushing his nose and rendering him unconscious. Twelve against five should have been superior odds, but the five were men of *Omega Force*, and they moved through the dozen police officers like a force five hurricane. Forty seconds later, thirteen men lay unconscious on the deck. Jim had taken four of them down with fierce joy, knowing that this lesson needed to be given.

"Medical team, you are needed on deck," Jim said into his COMLINK.

Making sure there was no blood on his hands and that his knuckles weren't bleeding Jim stood back and crossed his arms. JR, Dorf, and Mark arrived on the deck and looked at the carnage as Dr. Axlerod and Penny moved among the unconscious. One or two of the men were showing signs of recovering by the time they were finished. Leo and Will stood up and approached Jim, both taking note of his stance and the stormy look in his eyes.

"There may be five or six mild concussions, but nothing serious," Leo said, looking back at the men. "The older man will need to have his nose repaired. Did you happen to get the license plate of the semi that hit him?"

"Shepherd 1," Chief said with a deadpan expression on his face. "It was a personal plate," he added. "Mack Truck doing about ninety miles per hour!"

Jim chuckled at that and began to relax. "Would you please take him down to sickbay, fix him up so he at least isn't feeling too much pain, and bring him to the dining room?" Jim asked politely.

"We'll do that, Shep," Will said, patting him on the shoulder. He turned and asked Neil and Mel to bring a stretcher. The two men smiled and moved off to collect the stretcher and carry the Colonel down to sickbay. More men wandered out on deck and finally the twelve policemen were sitting up and tenderly feeling sore spots. Jim finally addressed them.

"I planned to offer you a fine meal in our dining room, and then treat you with respect. You chose to attack me on my ship in international waters. For that offense you will be bound to the railing and forced to wait until I release you," he informed them.

None of the policemen offered resistance as they were handcuffed to the railing with their own cuffs. Their keys were removed, and they were left alone. No one was set to guard them. What they thought of their treatment they kept to themselves. That, at least, was wise.

Dinner was finished when Colonel Panagos was escorted into the dining room. When he saw Captain Shepherd and his brother rising to meet him, he drew himself up. As they approached, he spoke, though obviously with some discomfort. In his mind he was still in charge, unaware that his posturing meant little or nothing to the Shepherd brothers.

"You attacked a policeman on official business with a warrant to search your ship!" he said.

John grabbed the Colonel's nose, bringing a yelp of pain, and then removed his hand as the Colonel grabbed for it and slapped the back of his head, nearly sending the man to his knees.

"Hey puffy face! You just don't learn, do you?" he asked mockingly. "We are in international waters, and on this ship one man, and one man alone is in charge. At the time you were attacked you ordered your men to arrest our Captain and he responded appropriately!" John grabbed his nose again, smiling as tears of pain leaked out of the man's swollen and good eye. "Pay attention!" Since he'd spoken in Greek the Colonel understood every word and his neck turned beat red as his anger mounted. That this man had no respect for him enraged him even further.

"I am a government official!" he sputtered.

"You're a petulant, petty, potentate!" John replied, tweaking his nose again. This time the Colonel took a swipe at John and found himself in a painful submission hold, his face screwed up in pain, making the pain of his nasal area even worse. "Open your mouth again and I will break your fingers!" John whispered tersely. "Do you understand?" The Colonel swallowed and nodded.

"Do you believe this guy?" John asked Jim as he stood up, hauling the Colonel to his feet. As he still had the Colonel's hand in a submission hold the Colonel wisely kept his mouth closed.

"I'm going to let you sit in on our interview of the men who attacked my vessel with a helicopter and a boat wired to explode upon impact with my vessel. I will allow you a copy of the recorded interview. When that is done, I will release your men that I hold prisoner on deck, and you may search this vessel. After completing your search, you will leave my boat and if you ever return while I am in international waters, I will have you caned and thrown overboard!" Jim had taken the front of the man's uniform as he spoke, drawing him close to his face. He shoved him back, not waiting for a reply, and turned to lead the way to the brig.

Sea Venture had six cells and an interrogation room. Jim led the Colonel into the interrogation room, pointed to a seat, and the man sat. The appearance of Sturdy, hauling the first prisoner to the room, was a shock to the Colonel. Without glancing at the Colonel

Sturdy put the man in the chair and snapped the cuffs closed over his wrists, then bent down and fastened the shackles to his ankles. Nodding once at the man he stood to his full height.

"You tell the captain the truth!" he said forcefully, and then nodding to Jim he left the room.

Zeke Kline came into the room with a thick file folder, placed it in front of Jim, and put his laptop on the table, taking the seat next to his Captain. He barely glanced at Panagos. Jim opened the file, studied its contents for a few minutes, and then looked up at the man sweating in the seat across the table.

"Albert Donovan, aka Robert Duval and Bert Vallan. You are a mercenary currently employed by Maganhildi VonSchloss. She paid you a substantial sum of money to attack the MSC Greek Cruise Ship *Aurea* by means of a high-speed boat, remotely controlled, and rigged to explode once it buried its reinforced hull in a ship full of passengers. The exact sum she paid was two million euros." As Jim finished speaking Driver appeared with the remote-control device and photographs of the high-speed boat. These were placed on the table in front of the accused who was now sweating profusely. One by one Jim passed the photos to Panagos.

"I ain't saying nothin' until I talk to an attorney!" the man spat with a strong Cockney accent.

"Albert, you were born in Leads, not within the sounds of the bells of St. Mary's, so drop the phony accent. I have your entire criminal record in front of me. You are on a ship in international waters so normal procedures do not apply here. Should I decide you are guilty, you will be tried by a military court and sentenced to death by hanging. If I grow weary of asking questions, I shall hang you, make sure your men watch, and resume my investigation. Do you wish to cooperate?" Jim delivered the entire speech without inflection, his eyes boring into those of Albert Donovan, his face devoid of expression.

"You got a Greek official here! He ain't gonna let you carry out any sentence!" Albert scoffed nervously.

"I have personally attacked this Greek official and made him aware of how things stand here!" Jim said softly. He turned to Panagos. "Colonel Panagos, do you understand fully how things stand here in international waters?"

Panagos swallowed nervously at the sudden hardening of Jim's eyes and nodded silently. Jim turned back to Donovan. Donovan just didn't believe that Jim would carry out his threat, especially in this day and age, and decided his wisest course was to remain silent.

"Do you, or do you not wish to cooperate?" Jim asked quietly. Donovan swore at Jim and told him to do something biologically impossible in the most disrespectful terms at his command.

"Very well. Your Court Martial begins in fifteen minutes," Jim gathered the papers and stood up. He left, signaling to Panagos to follow him, and as Zeke put away his laptop, he looked at Donovan with distaste. Donovan cleared his throat and spoke, as Zeke knew he would.

"All this posturing doesn't scare me!" Donovan said. "Who does that bloke think he is?"

"That is Captain James Shepherd, and you will be the fourth man he has condemned to death. You'll swing today, whether you believe it will happen or not."

"Bull shit!" the man spat derisively.

At that moment Abe arrived carrying his Bible. He sat down across from the prisoner.

"What are you here for?" Donovan asked.

"I'm here to offer you last rites, or spiritual encouragement of any kind. You are about to be condemned to death. It is customary to offer this service." Abe said sadly.

"Well, you blokes know how to pile it on!" Donovan said, laughing shakily. He looked at Abe. "You a priest?"

"No. I'm a chaplain." Abe replied. That sobered Donovan.

"Get lost!" He muttered. Abe shrugged his shoulders and followed Zeke out.

Panagos was escorted to his men, and he watched horrified as a rope was rigged for a hanging. He had no way of knowing that Jim was talking to the doctors to be sure that once Donovan was unconscious, they could get him down in time to avoid any serious side effects of being strangled. The men rigging the rope looked like they'd done this before and knew exactly what to do.

Fifteen minutes later Donovan and his three fellow prisoners were escorted to the deck. Without fanfare of any kind Donovan was led to the rope where the noose was placed around his neck and tightened, and he watched pale and shaking as a rope was tied to his ankles, and then passed through a ring on the deck.

"Carry out your duty!" Jim ordered. Abe and Sturdy jerked Donovan off his feet, tightening the noose cruelly, while Winky and Frenchy pulled the line around his feet tight and tied it securely to a cleat mounted on the deck for that purpose. Everyone watched in horror as the rope jerked several times and then went still after about ninety seconds.

"Escort the prisoners below. I will interview the next one in ten minutes," Jim ordered. The men saluted.

"What about Donovan?" One of the prisoners spat.

"His worries are over, Mate!" Chance said, dragging the prisoner away. "Don't worry. He'll still be up here when we bring you up for the same!"

No sooner had the men been ushered below decks than the body was taken down and the two doctors brought Donovan around. Colonel Panagos watched dispassionately as the man choked and wept. On one hand he respected the leverage Jim had just gained with the other prisoners, but on the other he was appalled at the total lack of respect for the rights of the prisoner who had just been hung. He was surprised when Jim approached and spoke to him respectfully.

"I'm going to interview the second in command. Will you accompany me?" Jim asked politely, coming to stand in front of the Colonel. Nodding stiffly the Colonel followed Jim down to the interrogation room.

The scene was repeated. Sturdy brought the prisoner in and shackled him properly, told him to answer the captain truthfully, and left. Zeke arrived with the folder and his computer. Jim read the information in the folder without speaking and looked at the prisoner.

"John Tannis, aka Johnny Tanner, Tank Johnson, and John Walace. You are a mercenary currently employed by Maganhildi VonSchloss. She paid your superior a substantial sum of two million euros to attack the MSC Greek Cruise Ship *Aurea* by means of a high-speed boat, remotely controlled, and rigged to explode once it buried its reinforced hull in a ship full of passengers," as Jim finished speaking Driver appeared with the remote-control device and photographs of the high-speed boat. These were placed on the table in front of the accused who was now sweating profusely. One by one Jim passed the photos to Panagos, as he had before, watching the prisoner carefully.

"I have your entire criminal record in front of me. You are on a ship in international waters so normal procedures do not apply here. Should I decide you are guilty, you will be tried by a military court and sentenced to death by hanging. If I grow weary of asking questions, I shall hang you, make sure your men watch, and resume my investigation. Do you wish to cooperate?"

"Too bloody right I wish to cooperate!" Tannis replied. "Yeah. VonSchloss hired us to do the Greek Cruise Ship and to do your ship. We even had two guys up in a Kamov Ka-50 with missiles to take out your ship and keep you from blowing the high-speed boat. But then that chopper dropped out of the sky and obliterated our chopper and crew and turned the boat into Swiss cheese. Donovan ordered us to blow it. He hadn't figured on you having an AH-1W Super Cobra," Tannis sat back, still sweating.

"It wasn't personal!" he added. "We were just doing a job."

Jim was out of his seat, across the table, and pulling Tannis painfully to meet him. Their noses almost touching Jim snapped at him.

"My wife and son are on this ship! We have women on this ship. This is a research ship first and foremost, and a search and rescue and salvage ship second. I don't care if it was personal or not! When you attacked my ship, you made it personal!" Jim shoved him back in his chair and only the chain on the handcuffs going through the ring on the table kept him from going over backwards.

"Look! We didn't know it was you! Donovan was planning to kill VonSchloss for sending us after you if we escaped!" Tannis said.

"Hang him!" Jim snapped.

"Wait! Wait! I can tell you everything! I can tell you why we took out the Greek Cruise Ship, what's on it that nobody wants discovered, and who really wanted that information kept secret!" Tannis sputtered.

"Martin Wikfells wanted the information kept secret!" Jim said. "We know it all!"

Tannis became white as all the blood drained from his face. "Struth! You do know it all!" he breathed.

Just then Donovan was shoved into the room, his neck raw where the rope had burned the skin. Tannis looked at him in amazement.

"Tell them!" Donovan croaked hoarsely, wincing from the pain of talking. "Tell them everything!"

"They already know!" Tannis said.

"You I'm bloody going to kill!" Donovan said to Jim, pointing an angry finger.

"I'll give you the chance when you've recovered from your injuries," Jim replied evenly. "Now sit down. I want to hear the whole story." Donovan sat.

"In the vault of that particular ship is a safe deposit box full of rare blue diamonds," Tannis said. The man who was transporting those diamonds was traveling on board that ship secretly. His name does not appear on the guest list. We were supposed to make sure that he never reached his destination alive, so we buried the bow of our high-speed boat in the cabin where he was sleeping.

"What we didn't know was that he'd suspected someone might be trying to kill him, and he took steps to be sure that if the hull was breached or someone blew up his cabin, the whole ship would sink. None of the emergency hatches closed properly and the ship went down. Nor did we know that the company would ask you blokes to come and raise that ship.

"When VonSchloss discovered you were over the sunken cruise ship she ordered your boat destroyed. She figured with you out of the way some other company would recover the ship and we could attack them and steal the diamonds and other stuff in the vault. We've got sixty men cooling their heels on the island, waiting for the go orders to take out the ship recovering the loot," Tannis paused.

"They're staying at three hotels, divided up in pairs," Zeke said in the quiet. Hitting the command Zeke printed out the records and News came into the interrogation room a few minutes later with the records. Jim handed them to Colonel Panagos.

"You can hold them for seventy-two hours. Before that time is over British forces will take custody of them. Most of them are wanted by the UK. VonSchloss and Borg are mine. You'll get a lot of recognition for this, and I'd appreciate it if you would keep us out of the picture. The less people who know we helped capture this group of mercenaries operating within your borders the better," Jim said.

"I intend to arrest you, Captain Shepherd, despite this gesture. You struck me! You mocked my authority!" Colonel Panagos said, glaring at Jim through his one good eye.

"You may do that. Just understand that if you do, you will discover that maritime law protects ship's captains from bureaucrats like yourself, and when it is all over you will suffer public humiliation. Furthermore, I will then bring a lawsuit against you that will force you into retirement, or worse, have you demoted and removed from the force. My suggestion is that you confer with a judge or attorney before you act against me Colonel Panagos. In the meantime, I offer you my ship to search, as your warrant suggests, and after that I will ferry you to your ship," Jim stood up and motioned for the door.

Panagos walked out ahead of Jim, and then waited for him to lead the way out of the bowels of the ship. His men were released, given their keys, and allowed free reign to search the ship. Knowing that if he found the weapons they had, he could indeed impound the ship and arrest its crew, Panagos instructed his men to search for illegal military weapons.

Two hours later he screamed at his men that they had not searched hard enough. None had found any illegal weapons or military hardware. Furthermore, the AH-1W Super Cobra proved to be equipped for research, not military purposes. No gunpowder residue had been discovered in the chambers or barrels of the 20-mm. three-barreled M197 mounted on the front. Too much time had passed to even ascertain if the engines were warm from the helicopter being flown.

Panagos stormed off the ship, accepting the ride to his ship in the rigid raider. Once on board however, when he'd had time to think, he went to his lieutenant.

"You did not look in the water below the moon pools, did you?" he asked.

"We did check to be sure nothing was attached. I thought of that as well, and even sent a man down into the water to look around. He saw nothing," his lieutenant replied.

"Then they dropped them into the water and let them sink to the bottom. Later they will go down and pick them up. Tomorrow afternoon we will pay them a surprise visit and search the ship again. You will see! We will find those weapons!" Panagos declared.

CHAPTER 26

After checking with the judge, from whom he requested yet another search warrant, Panagos retired to his office frustrated. The judge had confirmed what Captain Shepherd said. Maritime law gave the captain of a ship, in international waters, absolute control. Worse, the British arrived early in the morning to collect the mercenary prisoners, so that no news services could flash his picture across the nation. His pride crushed, Panagos swore that he would find a reason to arrest Captain Shepherd later that afternoon.

He'd had a good story ready for the press, a story that explained his battered and swollen face and would make him seem a true hero. As the day wore on his story became even more far fetched. His men avoided him, and it was not until he called for the ride to the boat at the docks that he spoke to his lieutenant. His lieutenant cautioned him to be courteous and ask permission to board the boat.

Panagos stood on the bow of the police cruiser and asked permission to come aboard and to talk to Captain James Shepherd personally. He was pleased to see the gangplank lowered quickly. As his men prepared to follow him, he gave strict orders. This time they would not be caught off guard!

As he stepped onto the deck, his armed men brandishing their automatic weapons menacingly, television cameras and news cameras turned his way. Dismayed he saw a bevy of reporters and others. It was too late. Drawing himself up he approached James Shepherd.

"I have a warrant to search this boat for illegal military weapons and hardware!" he announced loudly. Panagos noted that none of the crew had reacted to the guns of his policemen. Instead, they were gathered around wreckage at the stern of the ship. Pursing his lips, he watched Jim read the warrant.

"Last night, or early this morning, you went down and pulled something from the bottom of the ocean, did you not?" Panagos almost whispered.

"Oh yes! We certainly did!" Jim replied with a smile. "Shall I show you? These news people have been taking shots of what we brought to the surface."

"Search the ship!" Panagos commanded his men and followed Jim.

On the stern of the ship lay the ruins of the Kamov Ka-50. He saw with horror that four unfired missiles were in place. Inside the cockpit of the helicopter a detailed drawing of *Sea Venture* lay upon the seat while photographers snapped away, capturing the markings of where to place the missiles. The Colonel knew for a fact that six missiles had recently been stolen from his own military headquarters. When his eyes returned to them, he saw the markings that identified them, and his heart sank.

"Here are four of the stolen missiles you reported earlier this week, Colonel," one of the newsmen stated, holding his microphone to his lips as he spoke. "Very careless of you, and they were used against a friendly ship!" he added. Before the Colonel could speak Jim stepped forward.

"You do the Colonel an injustice," he said. "It was through his untiring investigation into this theft that the mercenary group was brought to justice. Fearing that they might have friends in the area that would attempt to free them, he called the British to gather them early this morning, so that no attention would be drawn to him or to his men. His actions were quite admirable. Why, I've heard stories that he faced the leader himself, which is why he is injured, as you can obviously see."

"Is this true, Colonel?" the reporter asked, thrusting out his microphone.

"Policemen often are injured doing their duty," Panagos said stiffly. "I have no desire to talk about it."

Three hours later his men returned. Just the look on their faces told Panagos everything. He sighed deeply and looked at James Shepherd, who was standing with him at the moment, a little apart from everyone else.

"I am not your friend, Captain Shepherd," he said stiffly.

"Nor am I yours. Now get your men off my ship," Jim demanded, just as quietly.

Panagos spun away and waved for his men to follow him. Unfortunately, the news crews were winding down and wanted to know why he had searched *Sea Venture* for military weapons. Not having a good answer didn't set well with the Colonel and it was a thoroughly deflated man who left to return to his office. His day became progressively worse.

An official complaint had been filed by *Bring It Up*. It was accompanied by a letter that spelled out in no uncertain terms that if the Colonel persisted in his vendetta against Captain James Shepherd a lawsuit would be filed. Since the letterhead came from an international firm that had a reputation for winning such cases the mayor was justly concerned. Colonel Panagos was placed on two weeks suspension without pay to ensure that he had no chance to pursue his own personal vendetta. Fuming the Colonel left his office and went home. His mind churned with idea after idea to even the score against James Shepherd.

Early the next morning the NEWT suits and submersibles went down to begin the temporary repairs on the cruise ship hull that would allow them to bring it to the surface. Zeke kept a constant watch on the boats around them while Windy and Looney flew low over the surface in the PBY, obviously taking photographs of everything on the surface.

It was mid-morning when Team Sniper burst into the room occupied by Maganhildi VonSchloss and her four bodyguards. Four single shots from silenced MP5's sounded as one, much like a sneeze, and her guards were on the floor groaning in pain. The bullets had torn through parts of their shooting arm shoulder leaving them quite helpless. Despite the wounds they were turned over and trussed with their hands painfully fastened behind their backs with restraint ties. The entire time Maganhildi stared into the eyes of Sniper's leader, Norm Geissler. Wisely she remained still with her hands where he could see them.

When Earl Duncan moved to restrain her, she went into action, expecting to catch the young man by surprise. The two blows that landed silenced her and put her on the floor, disoriented, momentarily unable to breathe or make a sound! She was trussed like her men and then gagged when she began to scream after her breath returned. The gag reeked of something and made her gag and vomit. Coughing and weeping in fear and panic she felt the gag removed and spit out wads of horrid tasting bile. Duncan pulled her head back by the hair.

"Make another sound and the gag goes back in and stays!" he snarled.

Borg fared no better. As he boarded his private jet Firefox popped up from among the seats, put down his bodyguards and took him into captivity. An hour later he was shoved roughly into a cell across from Maganhildi VonSchloss. Both of them were wearing bright yellow coveralls made of a thin but sturdy material. Their cells were located in the bowels of *Sea Venture*.

Later, their wounds tended, the eight bodyguards were also placed in the other four cells, two to a cell, also wearing the yellow suits. All eight of them crawled onto the bunks and without talking, were soon sound asleep. Without saying a word, the other two prisoners sat down and with nothing else to do soon napped. Whatever was happening, they both felt that this was no more than a gesture to frighten and disorient them.

Outside and beneath the surface work was moving along swiftly. It took two eight-hour shifts for the NEWTs and submersibles to patch the hole and begin pumping air into the hull of the ship, blowing water out. Slowly the ship began to rise, the crane on deck keeping it upright and steadying it against the currents until it finally burst from the depths as if eager to reach the air above once again. Water gushed away and down the sides of the ship as it settled, listed, and then remained steady on the surface.

Four hours later all the water had been pumped out of the ship and *Sea Venture* began preparations to tow it to shore. While that work went on a full investigation was made inside the ship. Cecilia and Penelope led the investigation making sure that all evidence was carefully collected, and photographic records of each discovery made.

Wikfells agent had indeed disabled the safety hatches, allowing the ship to sink when the hull was penetrated. His final words were written on a sheet of Stationary from the ship, and carefully sealed inside two diving bags. In it he penned a full confession, naming VonSchloss, Borg, and Wikfells as co-conspirators. He also left the key to the strongbox in the vault where the diamonds could be found. In his letter he said there was other evidence in the strongbox, detailing how he obtained the evidence and what it meant.

In the vault they used the key to open the strongbox and found the contents undamaged. The other evidence was stunning. Pen Shepherd looked at Cecilia as they finished reading the pages. Both women were now deeply concerned and nodded to one another. This was serious.

"These go in our vault," Pen declared emphatically. "Wikfells will take some serious scrutiny on our part," she added. Cecilia nodded.

"He's going to come unglued when we bring up that ship full of gold," she said. "I'll ask my aunt in Scotland Yard to give us a full dossier on Marten Wikfells."

"Good oh!" Pen nodded. "I'll get Sir Edward cracking on finding everything that can be found. This is a world-threatening crisis!"

"Interesting how sins, past and present, seem to work together to expose the sinners, like the captain said!" Bob Neff added. "What do we do with the blue diamonds? These are very rare, and very valuable!"

"We'll turn them over to MI6," Cecilia offered after a moment of thought. "They have the facilities to track where these diamonds came from, which will give us another lead on Wikfells."

"Yes!" Pen agreed. "They should be able to tell where these stones came from. My guess is they weren't properly registered with the industry. And that must be very difficult! Finding that answer will tell us much."

John very carefully locked the evidence away in the ship's vault, hidden in the war room. There was another vault that could be searched, but this one remained hidden for obvious reasons. It contained the emergency funds, gold, silver, certificates, bearer bonds, and various currencies. Now it contained evidence against another master criminal with a master plan to dominate the earth. When the vault was closed, he turned and faced his brother and uncle.

"I have a sense that this is going to get very ugly before we sort it all out," he said, rubbing his hands as if in anticipation. "At least our lives will never be dull!" he added with a laugh.

"Enthusiast!" Andrea chuckled.

"Just remember that people with a lot of money can create a lot of trouble," Jim warned quietly. "I feel the same way. This is going to get very ugly before we sort it all out. In the meantime, I'd like to know if Wikfells is going to try to claim the strongbox in the vault."

"He'll be very disappointed when he discovers that it's empty!" John gloated.

"It's not empty. It has a copy of the letter his agent wrote just before he died!"

Jim and John both looked at each other and laughed.

"Won't that enrage him?" Andrea said, rubbing his hands and chuckling. "I've heard that his temper is legendary!"

"Yes. He does have serious rage issues," Jim replied. "It appears that a venereal disease is slowly driving him mad. Strange that such diseases often have long-reaching side affects."

"Fitting," John said softly. "God is not mocked! But then I suppose that I am as guilty as he!" Looking at his brother John smiled crookedly. "I try very hard to get it right only to realize that the whole reason Jesus came was because I never could!"

"Well, we have two criminals we need to decide what to do with," Jim replied. "Perhaps we can persuade them to give their hearts to the Lord!"

"Wouldn't that be cool?" John replied, and Andrea nodded. But his face was sad.

"They are full of pride. I do not think they will see the truth," he said. "People like them believe that they are gods."

"Hey Shep, do you copy?" FM's voice suddenly sounded in Jim's ear. Jim pressed his COMLINK.

"What's up FM?"

"We're ready to tow this derelict into shore," FM said.

"Roger that. Andrea is on his way up to the bridge. John and I will be up momentarily," Jim replied.

As soon as Jim and John stepped out onto the deck FM's voice sounded.

"Alright, the bosses are up and out with us, so let's pretend we're competent and busy!" he said, winking at Looney. Taking his cue from FM Looney was suddenly enveloped in sparks and backpedaling wildly, as if seriously injured.

"Ouch!" he said loudly. Jim and John both laughed as Inchworm appeared, swinging from the boom of the crane mast and waving at Looney.

"Make it stop! Make it stop!" he cried, and Looney dived back and stopped the sparks. The boom came to a halt.

"Oh yes! Competent and busy!" John laughed as Inchworm dropped from the boom with a huge grin on his face. It had stopped where they tied it down, and he proceeded to lock it in place. René Milstein passed close to Looney, and he leaned out and touched her, a surge of electricity passing from him into her. She jumped aside with a little scream and rubbed where he'd touched her.

"Oh! So sorry!" Looney said.

"Not yet, you're not!" René said, pointing her finger at him. "I get ahead, I don't get even! It's on now!"

"Shocking behavior!" Hammer commented, coming to stand beside Looney. "Imagine, being threatened by such a pretty little girl!"

"It's not about stature or muscles!" René shot back. It's all about intelligence!"

"She must be talking about you," Looney said to Hammer solemnly. "Nobody's ever accused me of being intelligent."

"I was referring to both of you lumps of muscle!" she retorted, turning up her nose. "Just you wait!"

Lynn Ross sidled up to the pair and pointed at them, singing a favorite song from *My Fair Lady*. "Just you wait Looney and Hammer, just you wait!" she sang as she danced around them, mimicking the Cockney accent perfectly. "She'll be dishing out your payment on a plate!" Jim once again marveled at the creativity of this young woman and smiled at her antics.

"Hey, that was good. It rhymed and everything!" Hammer said to Looney. Looney at that moment caused a huge spray of sparks around the two of them. When it was over Looney looked at his arm with his eyes wide.

"What happened?" Hammer asked, looking at the arm.

"I'm burnt to a crisp. Look, I'm black!" Looney wailed.

"We'd better get you to sick bay!" Hammer said, and the two took off singing Harry Nilsson's coconut lyrics. They were arm in arm and kept tripping each other. René, Tiffer, and Little Miss Sunshine watched them go shaking their heads.

"Those boys have soaked up a lot of voltage!" Tiffer giggled. Jim and John were still laughing when they reached the stern where FM had the bollard pull hooked up and ready to go. He had his face set to show no emotion as they arrived. As they got to him, he spoke into his COMLINK.

"Great job everyone! I'm sure they're convinced we're all competent and busy!" he turned to the two men with a straight face.

John had tears running down his face and Jim was chuckling, his green eyes dancing with humor. FM looked at them and frowned.

"Does our hard work and extreme competence amuse you?" he asked, one eyebrow raised. At that moment a seagull passed overhead and splattered FM's work coveralls from his right shoulder to his waist. John went to his hands and knees laughing and Jim let out a loud guffaw. FM's shoulders slumped and he shook his head sadly. Spreading his arms and raising them he continued to shake his head.

"I get no respect!" he said tragically.

"Argh, matey!" Jim mimicked the Disney pirate accent. "Ye'll be eatin' fish-guts and mealy worms fer yer supper if ye don't drag that scuttled vessel into port properly, ye will!" Jim turned to face the crew gathered around to watch the fun. "The floggings will continue until morale improves!" he roared.

"You heard the captain! Get to work ye scurvy cockaroachers!" John yelled. Just then Nurse Penny appeared, waving a huge display needle she'd found somewhere, fully six feet long. Her face was screwed up comically and she was walking the shuffling walk of the comical Egor of *Young Frankenstein*. In her nurse's outfit, with her face screwed up comically, she was a sight. Jim and John had huge grins on their faces as they waited for what was coming next. That the crew had planned this was evident, but when had they found the time?

"Bend over, master!" she said to Jim, waving the needle. "Obviously you need another shot!" In a very uncharacteristic gesture Jim grabbed his bottom and danced away from Nurse Penny while she shuffled after him.

"What in heaven's name is happening on the stern of this ship?" Andrea's voice came over the COMLINK. "Someone find those wayward nephews of mine and get me orders to tow this ship to the island!"

"Roger that, Papa! Let's get underway," Jim said, putting his hands down and looking up at the bridge. He couldn't see Andrea looking down, but he grinned as he turned and put an arm around Nurse Penny's shoulders.

"That was perfect timing. Did Looney put you up to this?" he asked.

"He and Hammer thought we needed a few more moments of comic relief before we faced the dragons on the Island!" she replied.

"If you see them before I do, thank them for me!" Jim said with a genuine laugh.

After he left for the bridge Donna watched him go as some of the girls gathered around her. She shook her head.

"Marriage has been good for that man!" she said softly. "And being a father has helped too." Then she laughed and hefted her needle.

"He rarely takes part in the fun," Elizabeth Minor said with a smile.

"But he always appreciates it," FM added as he stepped into their circle.

"Will there be trouble when we bring this ship in?" Rachael asked.

"Some. We have two prisoners they're going to want, and Wikfells is sure to try to make a grab for that strong box," FM said lightly.

"And will we give up our prisoners?" Donna Penny asked.

"They perpetrated a military attack on this vessel. That endangered the lives of our women and children, not to mention our own!" FM said quietly. "The fate of those two will be decided by a military tribunal at sea," he added. She noted the grim look in his eyes and patted his hard-muscled arm gently.

"Justice will prevail," she prophesied softly. He nodded and smiled at her, and she thought again how changeable these men were. One moment they could be all laughter and joy and the next death stalking.

CHAPTER 27

Thronged with people the docks to which they towed the cruise ship presented a problem. Jim looked at the throng and turned toward the cruise ship following and sighed. Pressing his COMLINK he spoke.

"This is *Bring It Up One*," he identified, getting everyone's immediate attention. "No one leaves the ship, please. Only those granted permission will be allowed up the gangplank. I want Team Raider armed with shotguns and nonlethal ammunition at the bottom of the gangplank. Team Sniper, I want you at the top armed with shotguns with lethal ammunition. Please get going men. No one sets foot on my ship without my permission. Please don't accept any warrants while you're down there either, gentlemen."

He listened as the men keyed their COMLINKS and acknowledged his transmission. Dorf was at the wheel of the cruise ship, and he too acknowledged the transmission. Once the ship was docked and tied off, he would exit on the seaside and be shuttled back in the Rigid Raider.

"Driver, would you please grab Mark and Bulldog to go get Dorf. I expect an attempt to detain him. Chief, please suit up and go fully armed. I want my Lieutenant Commander back on this boat."

"Roger that, Shep," Chief said as he grabbed his men and they raced for the war room. Mark followed Driver to get the Rigid Raider in the water and ready. FM was already at the crane ready to lower the craft into the water. With a nod of satisfaction Jim turned his attention back to the wharf full of people. With expertise from long hours of practice Andrea guided the ship in, and the bollard pull was released at the last possible moment, allowing the cruise ship to float to the dock and be tied off.

Jim watched as the Rigid Raider circled around to the outside of the cruise ship, and saw Dorf begin to make his way down. Dorf wasn't going to make it. A bevy of people had swarmed onto the boat. Grabbing his binoculars, he watched as Dorf was suddenly cut off by four men in uniform.

"Take them down," Jim commanded. "Bulldog is on its way up to you. Don't kill anyone if you can avoid it, please!" Jim added.

Dorf hadn't hesitated. Before the military men could get their weapons up, he was upon them. At six feet nine inches tall, with all the training as a SEAL and Omega Force, the battle was quickly over. Studying the men Jim noted that three of them were unconscious, while the fourth was holding his groin with his forehead to the deck. Leaping over a railing Dorf dropped to the next level, and leaped again, missing several soldiers trying to cut off his escape. Seconds later Bulldog arrived.

The soldiers who rounded the deck after Dorf stopped dead in their tracks upon meeting an armed military response. Chief kept his men backing toward the steps with the advantage. They had their guns up. One of the soldiers raised his rifle but he never got to fire at Dorf's huge form. Chief's weapon fired first, hitting the man solidly in his shin guard on his left leg, sending him screaming in pain to the deck. The shin guard had stopped the bullet, but he would be in agonizing pain for a few seconds. Everything changed in an instant. Bulldog hit the deck as Dorf leaped the railing, and the soldiers now firing hit nothing. But Bulldog wasn't finished. Their fire was deadly. All four soldiers went down, and none stirred. Jim sighed in frustration.

Bulldog moved carefully, hopping into the Rigid Raider one at a time, keeping their arc of fire clear and Jack sped away, the twin outboard motors lifting the boat clear of the water and hurtling it toward *Sea Venture*. Andrea was moving the boat so that those on board the cruise ship had no target as the Rigid Raider was hoisted on board.

"Twelve Teams! Gear up now!" Jim ordered tersely. He sprinted toward the war room and soon all thirty-six men were fully armed and wearing their protective gear. Jim went down the line, checking vests and packs, and then nodding at the men, he led them back topside. A hundred yards from the docks *Sea Venture* held its position and there was a collective gasp from those present when the twelve teams rushed to the deck and took positions.

From the helipad the CH53 rose gracefully, and from the rear deck the AH-1W Super Cobra sprang into the air, turning so that it shot past the docks. Pen was at the controls, and she brought the ship around to face the docks. Those on the docks were aware that the Super Cobra was fully armed.

"Clear the docks and get someone here with half a brain or I will clear the docks!" Jim's voice boomed over the water. "This is the second time my crew has been attacked with military force, and I am responding in kind. You have ten seconds!"

"Pen. Let's help them decide to clear the docks, honey," John commanded. The mini gun at the front of the chopper began to spin and Pen peppered the rock wall just below where people stood with bullets. The response was instantaneous. People screamed in terror, turned, and fled.

"I've got a chopper taking off from the island airport," News spoke.

"If it is military or police put it on the ground but try not to kill the crew." That was John's voice speaking. Pen raced toward the airport, noted that the chopper was military and smiled as the CH53D appeared to the right. Faced by both choppers the pilot of the military chopper stopped.

"Military helicopter. Put that thing on the ground or I will. I have superior fire power and you know it!" Pen admonished in her clipped BBC accent. She spoke in Greek so they would understand. Because the pilot hesitated, she pushed the stick forward and turning her head targeted the rear rotor, tearing holes in the blades and causing the helicopter to begin to lose control. It lost altitude fast and landed hard, but the men were spared. When they looked up both helicopters were gone. It was at that point that the governor of the island prevailed.

An hour later a party appeared apprehensively at the docks with a white flag. Jim had taken full advantage of that time to get his men out of their battle gear and strip down the AH-1W. He left the mini gun alone this time, not bothering to have it cleaned. He studied the group on the dock.

"Colonel Panagos is with the mayor," Jim said quietly. "Take us in close enough to use the gangplank, please."

Andrea guided the ship in. There were only five people, including the mayor, and three of them were obviously high-ranking police officers or military men.

"As soon as all five are on board head back out into the harbor, please," Jim said over his shoulder as he stepped out onto the walkway.

"Permission to come aboard," the mayor shouted.

"Permission granted," Jim assented. The gangplank extended toward the dock and those on the dock saw Team Raider armed with shotguns. Further up they saw Knife with shotguns. "No one sets foot on my gangplank that is carrying weapons," Jim's voice could be clearly heard by all.

Colonel Panagos snatched at his pistol and doubled over with a sharp cry as a beanbag shot hit him squarely in the groin. Calvin Weston put the barrel of his shotgun against the Colonel.

"Put your weapons on the ground now," he ordered in Greek. Glaring in pain the Colonel dropped his pistol. Weston relieved him of the gun tucked into the back of his belt. The other officials were quick to drop their weapons and allowed themselves to be searched. They were herded onto the gangplank and moved to the ship, fearful now as those guns pointed at them never wavered for a moment. The five men could feel the ship moving even as they were marched onto the deck.

Jim didn't hesitate. He arrived at the gate where they stepped on board his ship and grabbing Colonel Panagos he hurled the man onto the deck. Panagos rolled to come up fighting only to realize that Jim was already there. The fist that lashed out felt like a sledgehammer connecting with his shoulder and he fell back with a cry.

"I'll see him in the interview room in the brig after I've finished talking to the others," Jim said to Weston, who nodded, jerked his head, and watched his men haul a protesting Panagos to his feet and drag him limping and moaning toward the inner parts of the ship. Jim spun and faced the mayor and other officials.

"You mounted an armed military operation against members of my crew. At this moment we are on a footing of war," Jim growled.

"Sir! Please!" the mayor sputtered. "That was all Colonel Panagos. These men will tell you that he spearheaded the response. I believe his plan was to capture one of your men and force your crew to turn you over to the authorities on the island."

"And you allowed it!" Jim snapped. "As soon as you are off my boat we are leaving. The moment I am in international waters I will respond to any attempt to stop my ship or board it as an act of war and respond appropriately. Anyone who attempts such an act will die."

"What of the prisoners you hold?" one of the military men spoke up.

"They will be tried by a military tribunal and sentenced accordingly," Jim replied.

"That is not satisfactory," the man said. His face drained of color as Jim came within inches of his nose.

"They mounted an armed military attack on my ship, threatening the lives of the women and children aboard this vessel, as well as the lives of my men. One of those women is my wife, and one of those children is my son! When you allowed an armed military attack on my crew you also endangered the women and children on this ship, and my men. Do you deny it?"

"Let's stop for a moment, shall we?" Jim guessed that this man was the top military commander on the island. He'd remained calm and interested but showed no fear. Jim wondered why. "Colonel Panagos did not inform me of his plans to capture one of your men and force your crew to turn you over to authorities on the island. We had no knowledge of that plan. If we had, I assure you we would have put a stop to it.

"Captain, your reputation is such that for us to pursue this further would cause an international stir that we can ill afford. As of this moment Panagos is stripped of all rank. He may choose to retire, and collect his pension, or go to prison. He will not be permitted to command troops again. I assure you of that!

"Furthermore, if you would allow one of us to sit on that military tribunal at which the two criminals are tried, I think that would satisfy everyone involved," the officer spread his hands. "I for one do not wish to see men killed needlessly, and an attack on you or your ship would guarantee that many would perish. I sense that you feel much the same."

"My name is James Shepherd, and I am one of the captains aboard this vessel," Jim held out his hand.

"Major General Markos Kladas. My brother Peter speaks highly of you."

In a heartbeat it all clicked together for Jim. Markos had contacted his brother and his brother had told him what he needed to know. He smiled. "You would be more than welcome to sit upon the military tribunal that tries the criminals," Jim said with a warm smile.

"Perhaps you would allow me to escort my foolish Colonel from your ship without further injury to his person?" Kladas asked.

"If you'll follow me," Jim said.

"You will all wait here," Kladas said. "Mayor, perhaps you should join us."

Jim led the two men down to the brig where Panagos sat on a chair holding a bag of ice to his groin. By this time the pain was growing. Leo waited nearby with a shot for the pain.

"Colonel Panagos," the Major General said softly. "You have embarrassed us today by a foolish act of pride and personal revenge.

It cost the lives of four soldiers who foolishly followed your orders. For that you are stripped of all rank. Today you are a civilian. You have a choice. Take your pension and stay out of trouble or go to prison. If it were up to me, it would simply be prison."

"I told you these men had military weapons on their ship!" Panagos groaned. "I told you!" he repeated, as if this vindicated him.

"Yes. I know. I've seen them. I've also assessed that the men on this crew are far better at using them than any of our forces," Kladas continued to smile and stare at Panagos, and it was the latter who flushed bright red and looked away. Jim watched the interchange with interest, and he decided that Kladas was a man to brook no foolishness. "What is your choice?"

"You are serious?" Panagos asked, stunned.

"Deadly serious," Major General Kladas said softly. "Pension or prison?"

"The military is my life!" Panagos said with heat.

"Was your life! You are stripped of all rank and no longer a part of our military forces," Kladas looked at his watch. "You have ten seconds."

"Pension!" Panagos snarled.

"Good. Take off all your insignia and give me your uniform jacket," Kladas demanded. While Colonel Panagos removed the insignia from his collar and epaulets Kladas tore off the patches that had marked his position on the coat. He also removed the medals. The latter he handed to Panagos.

"Give him the shot," Jim said softly to Leo.

"Sir, I have something for the pain. Would you like it?" Leo asked, stepping forward. Panagos nodded, suddenly broken, and fifteen minutes later was escorted off the ship, limping with each step and moaning softly.

"I will join you when you contact me for the tribunal," Kladas said, last to leave and shaking Jim's hand. "I'm sorry for the actions of my men."

"Because you have honored me today, I will ask my crew to award the families of each of those dead soldiers one hundred thousand pounds sterling," Jim replied.

"It is you who have honored me!" Major General Kladas said with tears in his eyes. "Our economy being what it is, we could not help them much! Thank you."

"They were good men, following orders. Their families should not be punished for that," Jim said, and realized that his eyes were suddenly swimming with unshed tears. Kladas looked away, not embarrassed, but glad to see the tears. Jim had frightened him more than any man he had ever faced. His brother had been correct.

Wiping away the tears Jim smiled at Kladas. "Killing is such a foolish waste," he said softly.

Drawing himself up Major General Marcos Kladas saluted Jim Shepherd. The captain snapped to attention and returned the salute. In the eyes of the military, it meant much to both men to receive that salute. With a lighter heart Kladas walked off the gangplank, no longer manned by armed personnel, and made his way to his car. He paused a moment to think about arrogance and pride, and what it cost. And he knew, beyond a shadow of doubt, that the men of *Bring It Up* would win any confrontation with his forces. He smiled then.

In the conference room, later that morning, Jim addressed his men. He was not surprised when Chief spoke up, after Jim mentioned the sum he'd like to award the families of the dead soldiers.

"Why don't we take the profit from this job and put it in a college fund for the kids?" Chief asked.

"Excellent idea!" John Dinsmore said, slapping the table in front of him. "How much profit did we pull down on this job?" he added, looking at Sharky.

"The net take from the ten percent fees from the various insurance companies total a little over one point four million dollars U.S." Sharky replied immediately. "We should net a little more. *Bring It UP* shaved a little off the operating costs and the cost of fuel.

"All in favor of using the money this way, please respond by saying 'aye.'" Jim suggested, listening with a smile as a chorus of "aye's" echoed through the room.

"Those opposed signify with the same sign." Jim said, when quiet reigned. Not one voice objected.

"I can honestly say that I am deeply honored to Captain such a crew," Jim said, feeling his eyes fill with unshed tears and wiping them away automatically. John stood up, his hand over his heart.

"Naturally, with such stirring leadership, this crew has surpassed expectations!" he said grandiosely.

"Somebody put a bun on that hot dog!" Bill Dodge grinned as John sat down. Jim nodded at his brother. The comedy relief had come at just the right moment, as usual. "Everybody knows it's the presence of the Marines that makes this outfit what it is!" he added. Every Marine responded with a resounding "ooh rah!" FM shook his head as the noise died down.

"I told you it was a mistake to invite the Marine's, boss!" he said to Jim with a straight face.

"All you military types!" Alice said with a deep sigh. "Always thinking with the hair on your chest! It is the presence of these great academic minds that raises this group from a mere standard of grunting men flexing their muscles to highbrow sophistication and great success! You will note that not one of us needs to express ourselves with a loud 'ooh rah!'"

"Hooh yeah!" her husband shouted. The room burst out laughing as Alice turned her head to gaze at him.

Alice glared at her husband as the group laughed. FM, who shaved the hair on his chest and back regularly, opened his shirt and looked down at his six-pack abs.

"What hair?" he asked with a vacant look. Alice did not miss a beat.

"Poor man. Without any hair on his chest, he is incapable of producing an original thought. Perhaps that's why he grunts less than his companions." A roar of laughter followed that and several of the men grunted. Stephanie Morris stepped into FM's lap and ran her hands over his smooth and rippled chest.

With her other arm around his neck, she put her face next to his and looked out at everyone. "At least he's warm and feels good to snuggle up to on a cold night!" she said demurely, turning and kissing his cheek lightly. FM turned red. "And he blushes like a country maiden!" she added, turning his head, and kissing his lips.

FM stood up suddenly, putting Stephanie down lightly, and ducked his head. "Sorry boss! I gotta go find the coldest water on this ship and stand in it for the next three or four hours!"

"I understand completely, Mr. Miller!" Jim said, nodding his head. My marriage hasn't changed that very much," he added, looking at Cecilia and taking her hand. She smiled at him.

"Be quiet, dear! Mr. Miller, please sit down until this meeting is over and then you can take your cold shower," Cecilia said commandingly. FM sat down quickly, and Stephanie returned to her seat.

"That is how you conduct a business meeting, dear," Cecilia said, sitting back and smiling at him. The roar of laughter that followed was an opportunity for him to lean in and kiss her. When the noise died down, he spoke.

"Yes Ma'am, Captain sir! . . . uh! . . . I mean Captain's wife, ma'am!" he stammered, saluting her.

"He's come a long way, our captain has!" Donna said to her husband as they stood with the others in preparation for the closing prayer. Will nodded looking down at her.

"That he has!" he replied.

Sturdy led them in the closing prayer, and Jim was proud to see the entire crew surrounding the huge table, all holding hands, heads bowed, as they prayed together. When the prayer was finished, he lifted his head, raised his fist and spoke in a loud voice, filled with pride.

"*Nulli Secundus!*" he declared.

"*Semper Paratus!*" Echoed in the room. Second to none, always prepared! That was the new motto of the company.

"*Bring It Up!*" Followed as all of them shouted together.

CHAPTER 28

Maganhildi VonSchloss and Viktor Borg were both surprised to be escorted onto a Naval Destroyer belonging to the Royal Navy of the United Kingdom. During their stay in the brig on board *Sea Venture* they had been treated well, though given no opportunity to escape or any freedoms they might have been offered in an American prison. The only thing that had been done was to hang a curtain between the two cells in the corridor outside the cells giving them privacy to use the stainless-steel toilet in each cell. Neither could reach the curtain and once it was in place, they had been unable to see each other, though they could clearly hear each other.

VonSchloss was furious over the degrading situation and meant to complain vigorously. Both recognized the military tribunal before which they stood, once on the British ship. The only face they recognized was that of Markos Kladas, Major General on the island where the cruise ship had gone down. The other men all appeared to be military as well. Zeke watched the pair with a critical eye, thinking of them as Blubber Boy and the Ice Queen. The arrogance had not slipped once during their imprisonment.

Admiral John Dooley, as a special favor to Sir Edward Marsh, was presiding over this military tribunal, and once he'd heard the charges and seen the evidence, he was more than happy to cooperate. As the pair sat down at the table allotted to them, he cleared his throat, dropped his gavel, and stood up, facing the British flag.

Everyone followed suit and the pledge was spoken with solemnity. Admiral Dooley sat down, and everyone else followed suit. Pulling the small microphone stand a little closer to him he spoke.

"I am Admiral John Rawlings Dooley of Her Majesty's Royal Navy. Seated for this tribunal are Major General Markos Kladas, Admiral Don Ashley of the United States Navy and Director of the Naval Criminal Investigation Service of that worthy entity, Admiral L. Charles Runion, retired of the United States Navy, and Commander Sir Angus Merril, formerly with the British Secret Service. Standing to accuse you is Captain James Shepherd of *Sea Venture*. The charges against you are conspiracy against both the Crown and the United States, murder in the first degree, terrorism, and espionage. Have the accused been made aware of these facts?"

"Sir!" A senior officer stood behind the accused. "Both have been given the opportunity to have legal representation and both declined, stating that this court has no jurisdiction over individuals of the sovereign nations of Deutschland and Russia. They deny any guilt in these matters and refuse legal counsel," the officer saluted properly and sat down. Jim hid a smile at the smirk that appeared on the accused faces.

"Ms. VonSchloss and Mr. Borg, we are in international waters, and your crimes were military in nature, and therefore fall under the jurisdiction of this tribunal. You are not being tried as criminals, but as terrorists, and though the situation is unusual, it is not outside the law of either of our countries. Now! Will you, or will you not accept legal counsel?"

VonSchloss laughed at the Admiral and told him to do something foul, and Borg just shook his head and waved off the offer.

"Very well. Let the record show the disregard for military law that both the accused have demonstrated," the Admiral stated, his face showing no emotion of any kind. "Mr. Shepherd, I believe you have done the lion's share of the work of gathering intelligence about this pair. Proceed with the evidence."

Jim stood up and walking to the tribunal produced five bound booklets over an inch in thickness. He turned to face the military troops seated to one side and proceeded to unveil the history of Viktor Borg and Maganhildi VonSchloss. His summarization of the case was carefully presented, with the evidence produced regarding each charge. When he was finished, he stood quietly.

"Very well, Captain. Thank you for that fine presentation," Admiral Dooley maintained. "You may be seated." Turning to the two accused he looked at them for a moment. His face was stern, and he thought hard before speaking. Both were still arrogant and proud, and he knew that would change in mere moments.

"Ms. VonSchloss and Mr. Borg. You may present a defense of these charges, but I warn you, any grandstanding, or vituperation, will be all I need to determine that you have no respect for the authority of this court. I will then silence you and carry on without your defense. Do you understand me?"

Viktor was about to speak but VonSchloss raised two fingers in a crude gesture to the Admiral and stated that this charade was at an end, demanding to be turned over to her own government. Borg looked at her with a considering frown but decided to say nothing. Neither believed that anything could be done to them.

"Very well. If you speak again, you will be gagged," Admiral Dooley warned, again keeping his face schooled to show no emotion. At the mention of a gag VonSchloss blanched and closed her mouth. Admiral Dooley turned to his colleagues.

"Let's adjourn to discuss the sentence," he said simply.

They were gone for about an hour, and Jim sat quietly. A crewmember brought Borg and VonSchloss a plastic bottle of water each. Both sipped at the bottle, trying very hard not to show nervousness of any kind. Jim could see that they did not believe that this court could actually do anything in the way of punishment. He smiled every time VonSchloss, or Borg looked at him, a smile that made both very nervous.

When the tribunal came in again the military men rose respectfully. None missed the fact that the two accused remained seated. When they were seated the other men and women in the courtroom sat back down.

"In the matter of the Crown versus Borg and VonSchloss, this tribunal has reached a verdict of guilty upon all charges. Both are sentenced to life in solitary confinement in a British Military prison. You may remove the accused and prepare them for transport," John Dooley dropped his gavel, knowing that they did not believe he could do what he just stated. The prisoners were in for a nasty surprise.

Sir Edward provided a military transport team to bring the prisoners to the United Kingdom, and it was not until the two were on the transport and preparing to take off from an aircraft carrier that they realized the threats were all real. As *Bring It Up* experts suspected, they began to talk. They knew nothing of the terrorist plots in Chicago, but both opened many doors to discovery on *Wilhelmina's Song*.

On *Sea Venture* Jim entered the CIC just after breakfast. His crew looked up as he came in, and everything in the room suddenly paused. They were waiting instructions, knowing that the next assignment would once again thrust them into danger. He looked from face to face and nodded.

"I need three identities for every member of *Omega Force*. No one in Chicago will ever know we were there. I'm going to call a general meeting of the team at 1100 to discuss changing our appearances. While we're TDY in Chicago this ship is going to do some research and make its way to Alaska again. We're going to stay out of shipping lanes and away from prying eyes until the team is back on board, so we won't be going through the canal to the Pacific. Dr. Gregg is going to lead an expedition to find that Egyptian ship and then we go north to Alaska!

"Various members of the team will fly back and rejoin the crew when we land for supplies. Other than those times we will all be on site in Chicago taking down this terrorist cell. Zeke, I'll need you to make sure we have communications with the ship at all times via secure satellite phones.

"In the meantime, let's figure out the most likely targets of our terrorists. If past attacks are any help, the more spectacular the more likely. But we can't be diverted by those targets alone. These men are in place, highly trained and motivated, and we don't have much time to work. So, we'll work smart as well as fast. Any questions?"

"NCIS is on the investigation in Chicago, Shep," Zeke said. "A Commander Coster is in charge of the team there. He's a good man. Since we're not there Sir Edward will be his contact, and he will pass any information on to News, and News, in turn, will get it to you immediately.

"Also, it's safe to communicate by computer or satellite phone. Both are encrypted with our own encryption code, and I doubt very much there is anyone who can crack it, since it changes hourly. Everyone on the team has memorized the sequence for the codes so we should be good to go."

"Thanks Zeke," Jim smiled, remembering the frustration of memorizing the code sequence for that encryption. Almost every team member, including himself, had seen the brilliance of the code, but hated memorizing that sequence. "I'll see you in the conference room at 1100 hours," Jim smiled again and then bent down to kiss Cecilia before he left. His eyes glanced over at his son RJ and nephew JAS in a playpen, a new addition to the CIC. If the motion of the ocean bothered either one, it certainly wasn't obvious.

He stopped in at the Bridge to talk to Andrea who had the helm at the moment. After that he went down to his office, sat down at his desk after nodding to John and Wade, and worked through his stack of paperwork for the morning.

Sea Venture was headed back to Plymouth to restock. The teams would leave from London and Parris to make their way to the United States by air. It would be easier to hide everyone that way. Jim caught John grinning at him, looked over at Wade, who was also obviously excited. He grinned back, nodding, understanding the emotion. They were going on a mission again, going dark, something they loved because it exercised every skill they'd trained so hard to perfect. This was the very first time since saving Ira and Lord White that they were able to go dark.

To be honest, it was fun! One created a character and then played the roll to perfection. Being invisible wasn't difficult if one knew how to choose a proper character and how to act when in public. His men were all skilled in the art. They had hidden in plain sight on five different continents and never been discovered.

At a quarter to eleven Jim signed the last report and filed everything properly, getting up to lay it on Ives' desk. Tom merely nodded; his hands busy at his computer keyboard. John and Wade were dividing their stacks of reports and paperwork between Finn and Ives. For perhaps the first time in Jim's memory, Finn did not stand and salute, but merely sketched a wave as he continued with what he was working on. The man was definitely unbending, and it was long overdue.

In the conference room just those from *Omega Force* gathered at one end of the table. Delta, Zulu, Firefox, Omega 1, Knife, Raider, Sniper, Bulldog, and Nightfall were all present and accounted for. Nine teams of four men, the very best there were in Jim's estimation, was a formidable force. Thirty-six men that could operate as one cohesive unit, ready for action, made Jim proud as he looked them over. Every one of these men was loyal and committed.

"Let's get started. Zeke, what do you have for us?" Jim asked.

"Each of you has been given three new identities, all the background history, and documents you need. We should assume that our terrorist friends have intelligence watching airport and train lists, maybe even those coming in by boat. We are traveling to the cities of origin using our first ID, and then making our way to Chicago from there. Use Passport ID number five to travel to your city of origin."

Jim's *Omega Force* all had six passports with six legal aliases. These were changed once used, so that they always maintained six identities under which to travel. Now, each member had three more passports specific to this Chicago adventure.

"Our communication gear will work great. News, Cecilia, and Pen will be monitoring everyone from here and getting information as needed to you. Use your laptops for any encrypted data. It takes a little more memory, but these new Mac Book Pros are able to handle it all with ease. Don't use the wrong password! If you do, your hard drive will self-destruct!

"Everyone is chipped, so we'll know where you are at all times. If you need help you know how to get the message out. We'll guide the nearest members to you from here. Any questions?" Zeke looked around the table.

"All right men!" Jim said when no one spoke. "This is a go mission. As of now we are going dark. Let's find these terrorists before they hit us!" he stood and the men stood with him, saluting him. Returning the salute, he turned and made his way down the corridor and up to his cabin to say goodbye to Cecilia and R.J.

Jim had an easy trip. He flew from London to Washington, D.C. and the following day flew into Chicago, first class, wearing a very expensive suit and his favorite Carhart riding coat, freshly cleaned and pressed. A wide-brimmed Stetson hat sat on his head and his cowboy boots were shined to perfection. He was Donald Graham, a very wealthy man. The body suit he wore made him look fifty pounds heavier, though it added only ten pounds of actual weight. He wore a mask that padded his facial features, and unless someone touched it, it could not be identified as a mask. From the airport Don Graham took a taxi to the address of the house in the Gold Coast district of Chicago on Bellevue Avenue. It was an historic brownstone building, three stories high with a basement.

At the moment the house stood empty after the remodeling and finish carpentry, as if all memory of past lives lived in the house had been erased to make room for new memories. As agreed, the real estate agent was there to meet him with keys and the deed for the house. She was thorough in showing him every room from the rooftop deck and garden down into the once dimly lit dank basement. Pictures of the house before remodeling began told him that. Now it was a delightful room, sealed against leaks from the foundation walls, sectioned off into a wine cellar, a hobby room, and a laundry room. In one corner the elevator waited to take them back up to the ground floor.

After locking the house Jim walked to the Drake Hotel where he had reserved a suite. Once the hotel staff learned that his credit line on that particular credit card was fifty thousand dollars, he became a person of note, and every effort was made to make him comfortable. Shaking his head at the incongruity of such thinking he saw the last person out the door and sighed at the silence that settled on the rooms.

His coat had a winter lining, and he was glad of the extra protection against the Chicago icy winds and cold temperatures. It was only October, but it felt like winter was trying to squeeze into fall, especially with the wind. Not far from the hotel he found the interior decorators he'd made an appointment with and got right to business.

Once he produced a cashier's check for a hundred thousand dollars the decorators promised to turn the historic building into a showpiece. Jim nodded, very pleased and smiled.

"I have a ceiling of two hundred and fifty thousand for the decorating. My expectations are that you will indeed make it a showpiece. Let me know when you need the second draft of one hundred and fifty thousand and I'll bring the check by personally. May I visit the house at any time during renovations?"

"Of course, Mr. Graham. It is your house!" the decorator said, raising his eyebrows a little.

"The last renovator wouldn't allow me in the house until it was complete," Jim explained. "That one cost me nearly a million dollars. Of course, that house was four times the size of this one. I'm at the Drake meanwhile. Tomorrow I'll purchase all the artwork for the walls, having it all sent here. Thanks," he stood and shook hands knowing that what he'd revealed about past experience and his present occupation would have them all salivating to do their very best.

Meanwhile, Wade walked onto the campus of Lakeview High School, watching students stare curiously as he passed through their hallways. His T-shirt identified him as one of the coaches, but it was stretched tight over his frame, the muscles beneath hinting at his great strength and agility. Smiling at them as he made eye contact, he made his way to the gymnasium and staff offices. Wade liked kids, liked working with them, and was looking forward to this particular part of his assignment. The head coach bounded up from his desk, looking up at Wade with a huge smile.

Coach Norris was still in great shape, although he was nearing fifty years of age, had energy to spare, and shook Wade's hand with enthusiasm. He was happy to have such a well-known and respected coach from Pennsylvania on his staff.

"Frank Moody! I am so glad to welcome you to our staff!" he said. "Let me show you your office and introduce you to the other staff." Norris made a name for himself at the school, and Wade was interested in getting to know him. Having spent hours with the real Frank Moody, he was also excited to begin coaching.

During the course of the day Coach Moody met the entire coaching staff and was delighted. Every one of the men and women were in good physical condition and obviously loved the kids. Although they varied in age, one thing stood out. Dedication to the kids and the part they played in helping these children rise to future challenges was strong.

Coach Norris grilled him extensively and seemed very pleased by his new team's defensive coach. He'd asked the question how Moody had trained so many winners and was secretly pleased by the answer.

"Winners are not what I am after. I train champions, on and off the field," Frank answered easily. Wade loved this part and had thought long and hard about his answers. "Winning is a byproduct of being a champion, heart, mind, and body."

Knowing he was going to play this roll, Wade spent many hours studying Frank Moody's defensive style, talking with the man, and many more hours on the computer studying other coaches, training routines, and everything else he had to know. His greatest challenge was working with kids from the city, and he was determined to spend the next few months changing lives if he could.

Lee Ainsworth as Kendall Tanner and his trainer, Mark Drumheiser as Liam Cleary arrived at Victory Martial Arts on West 18th Street in Chicago just as the doors were being opened. Only one staff person was present at the time, and he took one look at the compact Tanner and pursed his lips in a silent whistle. This was a championship contender!

At five and a half feet in height Tanner weighed in at a solid one hundred and sixty pounds. His trainer was even shorter, though more of a gymnast in build. Both men looked serious, and he watched them both jump rope for twenty minutes and then leave to run five miles before they returned to work in one of the rings.

Lee was among the quickest Jim and Mark trained, and he mastered four martial arts under Mark's program, learning the disciplines and demonstrating his skills with panache. When asked who should represent the London dojo, Mark immediately recommended Lee, because that particular dojo specialized in three of the martial arts Lee mastered. On the flight to Chicago the two men had agreed that winning was the goal.

Matthew Banks as Reid Bigland arrived at the central offices of Alfa Romero in a suit designed by Ermenegildo Zegna, a pair of shoes designed by Sutor Mantellassi, silk shirt and Sette tie, his clothing costing more than five thousand dollars. With his black hair and dark eyes, lean six-foot frame, Italian jewelry and watch he was the quintessential successful businessman from Rome. Speaking Italian like a native of Rome, French, Spanish, Deutsch, and English made him perfect for the job.

At his side he carried a small attaché case containing his iPad, keyboard, appointment calendar, legal pad and pen. As he walked through the revolving doors of the office building, he noted the dark sedan that had followed his taxi from the airport. Someone was watching the airport and taking an interest in new arrivals. The passenger in the dark Ford sedan was crossing the street now and following him into the building.

He listened as Reid introduced himself, taking note of the suit, shoes, shirt and tie, jewelry, and taking a few discrete photos. Mr. Bigland was expected and treated with some deference as he was taken to a bank of elevators. After satisfying himself that Reid Bigland was indeed who he appeared to be the man left. Most of his jobs ended this way, determining that the new arrivals at the airport were who they claimed to be. He wasn't even sure who had hired him for the job, but the pay was good. Whatever the interest of his employer he did his job, curiosity at bay for the moment.

CHAPTER 29

enry Scope drove into Chicago from Plymouth, Indiana in his Honda Civic. The car was eighteen years old, still in great condition, and everything worked. The Indiana license plate on the car was from Marshall County and registered to Henry Scope of Plymouth, Indiana. Following the memorized directions, he drove into the city, parked in a parking structure near city hall, gathered his camera and recording equipment and set off to begin his report.

Sid Barrett, as Henry Scope, purchased all his clothing in Plymouth, Indiana at various stores, and now wore a pair of black Rustler jeans, a white collared shirt, open at the collar, Dr. Scholls tennis shoes, white socks, a gray sport coat off the rack, and a winter coat, open at the front, from Burlington Coat Factory. As he approached, he took note of the century-old, neoclassical Cook County and City Hall building. Holabird & Rochethe, an architectural firm, designed the 11-story structure in the classical revival style, finishing the work in 1911. Striding purposefully past the Picasso sculpture in Daily Plaza he glanced once at the unusual art piece as though familiar and moved on.

As Kastya Panko, Dorf was chauffeured from the airport to the Advocate Center downtown with four other Olympic hopefuls. None of them had met before this, having been handpicked for the team, but they were all excited for the opportunity. Kastya was already an accepted friend, speaking the language like a native, and also speaking English clearly, he had become their interpreter immediately. Karoff was the tallest among them, towering four inches over the seven-foot mark. Shevchenko was the shortest, an inch under six-feet, but a speedster with mad ball-handling skills. Vovk was the point guard, a trim six feet three inches tall with a keen mind and a deep love for the game. Kozak was the other forward, three inches shorter than Dorf with a basketball style that reminded Dorf of Michael Jordan. All five of them were in top physical condition. Karoff was the slowest of them, and Dorf, or Kastya, was the best leaper among them.

None of them had any delusions about their skills. The Bulls were far superior in skill, playing far more often and practicing long hours. They were here to learn from some of the best and prepare for the Olympic games. Dorf was pleased with how well they'd bonded and knew that he would enjoy playing the game with these men. For them, making the Olympic team meant a better life for their families, and an opportunity to travel none of them would have experienced any other way. The real Kastya was actually training at another facility in Brazil, a service provided by *Bring it Up*. Dorf often wondered what his teammates would think when they finally met him.

Driver arrived in Chicago, traveling first class from Miami to the windy city, and walked through O'Hare concourse without hurrying. As Ed Barnes he didn't have to hurry. Wearing a typical American business suit and overcoat, Stetson hat, and cowboy boots he strode easily along the shops and eating establishments, following the first few passengers toward the luggage area. Twice he stopped, once to pick up a newspaper and again to get a cup of Starbucks coffee to carry with him. He picked up his tail immediately and smiled.

After picking up his suitcase he grabbed a cab and traveled to the Radisson Blu. Checking in was simple and he was soon in his spacious room with a view of downtown Chicago. Changing into a bathing suit and T-shirt, and sliding his feet into sandals, he made his way down to the pool and spent the next hour swimming laps, before returning to his room and ordering room service. The man following him asked where guests came from, and the clerk told him various cities his guests had come from. The last had come from Florida, made his reservations over a month past, and worked for a company that sold boats and yachts. Just to be sure the man called the company to discover that Mr. Barnes was looking for boats for the company, taking advantage of the lower winter prices. Barnes was legitimate and he returned to his office to make his report, and then went back to the airport.

Frank Miller arrived at the airport as Commander James Mitchell, aware immediately that someone took great interest in his movements. He began immediately showing pictures of Jane Wickham to every vendor along the corridor, asking if anyone had seen the girl two months ago. At one point the man watching him was right beside him as he made his inquiry, and he turned to the man, looking him over carefully.

"Have you seen this girl? You seem very interested in me!" Frank challenged, his BBC accent perfect.

"Who are you?" the man asked, pulling a business card from his wallet. "I'm a private investigator, hired by a company to check out anyone of a military bearing who arrives at the airport. All of our men are here at the airport doing just that. Someone from the county office hired my company several weeks ago and paid for our services in advance."

Frank looked at the card. "Mr. Jankowski, I'm Commander James Mitchell of Scotland Yard," Frank showed the man his credentials and the man studied them carefully. "I'm here as a favor to this girl's father to help him look for her. Your business sounds like something else, but thanks for letting me know. Professional courtesy deserves the same, eh what?"

Mr. Jankowski nodded and handed the photo back. "I've never seen her, but if she disappeared in this city, you're looking for a needle in a haystack," nodding curtly, he walked away.

Jankowski did not wait long. He made a few calls, verified Commander Mitchell's credentials and reported to his company office. Whatever he was doing didn't make sense, but he was being paid his usual hourly fee plus mileage and parking. It didn't have to make sense. He wandered back to the concourse he'd been asked to observe for that day, looking for other military persons of interest.

That day he checked out Lloyd Brookstone, posing as Paul Davis, a graduate student from Eaton, verified by the Museum of Natural History and Chicago University, both places the man visited almost immediately. He missed Lee Roy Brown, entering as Michael Matthews. Lee Roy made himself look like the academic he was supposed to be, and Jankowski watched him oversee the removal of his animals from the cargo hold, losing interest immediately.

David Carr, arriving as Max Carter caught his interest and he spent two days following the man only to discover he was in Chicago to purchase a specific shotgun at an auction. Again, he made his report to the office, never questioning what he was doing.

No one noticed Steve Coleman coming into Chicago in his company truck as Jim Jacobs of Jacobs Tool and Die. It was a lifted Ford F-350 4x4 with diesel engine, crew cab, long bed, and a handy electric hoist in the bed for lifting heavy equipment into the cargo area.

Sam Colt drew interest, but only long enough to determine his purpose in finding a company to fabricate a new barrel for his kit to build a black-powder army Colt 45 from the late 1800 era. The agent that followed him reported back to the company and returned to the airport for another day of watching a concourse. There were enough of them, he knew, to follow any men who looked obviously military, but he was beginning to wonder about the assignment.

At Union Station an agent watched R.C., as Martin Forry, looking around as though awed by his surroundings. With his black plain suit, black hat, beard without a mustache and shoes he was obviously another of the Amish that visited the city from time to time. He looked strong, but most of the young men who grew up on a farm looked that way. He certainly didn't look military, and the agent dismissed him. R.C. smiled to himself as he passed the man who had so carefully studied him for a moment.

Viper, as Adrian Rogers, strode down the concourse in an exact duplicate of the real Adrian Rogers' dress blues. The agent who picked him up tailed his taxi to a hotel, and then another taxi to an up-and-coming security firm where he learned that Gunny Sergeant Adrian Rogers was training the men. Obviously, this was a military man, but he was here for a legitimate reason. He reported to his company and returned to the airport.

BBC's Top Gear television group arrived, and the agents watched them all move together toward baggage, talking animatedly amongst themselves. No one thought to do more than a cursory check. Bear carried several cameras that had not been checked into baggage for obvious reasons. He looked at home under the burden and joked with the other grips, also carrying various items of importance.

Donut, as Jimmy Miles flew in from Baton Rouge looking like a clothing model, wearing very expensive designer clothing. One of the agents took note of his muscular frame and followed him to the hotel, and then to the studio where they would be filming for JClair fashions. After reporting to his superiors, he returned to the airport, feeling that whatever they were looking for was like looking for a certain spot on a Dalmatian full of spots!

Chance, as Marlin Polk arrived wearing a black suit, pastel green shirt, and a dark green on matching pastel green tie. An agent followed him to his hotel, checked the name under which he registered, and then followed him to a restaurant and finally to the Museum of Science and Industry. After checking, he ascertained that Polk was on legitimate business, and reported to his office.

PU, as Dr. Peter Locke of Blue Water Oceanography, with goatee and a wig to cover his shaved head arrived to be greeted by Dr. Diana Hastings at baggage. As he waited for his luggage, he talked quietly to Dr. Hastings about the problem and the agent walked back up to the concourse, reporting that Dr. Peter Locke was a real oceanographer. His conversation had proved that beyond the shadow of a doubt.

Fingers grinned as the agent who looked him up and down dismissed him as nonmilitary. He'd taken careful pains to dress in western attire, and with his round glasses perched on his nose and his foppish walk he looked anything but a military man. Ned Colson, investigative reporter for Time Magazine had arrived.

C.G. left the Navy base early that morning as Jim Nordstrom. He was dressed in civilian clothing that could not hide his obvious military physique. An agent followed him to his hotel and checked his name and identification. This one might bear watching. He followed him to Chicago University and listened outside the door as he inquired about using his GI bill to attend classes at the University. After careful checking he discerned that Nordstrom had just mustered out of the Marines to pursue a college degree. He called it in, and Nordstrom went on the list as a possibility.

Counselor, as Dr. Maxwell Truman of her majesty's service arrived at the concourse wearing a long wig and full mustache and beard. There was gray in the hair of the wig, mustache, and beard and he walked with a stoop. Not one of the agents thought he looked military.

Vince arrived at O'Hare dressed like he was from Los Angeles. His heavy winter coat looked odd, and he'd grown his hair longer and a soul-patch beneath his lower lip. In a collared T-shirt with the Handel's logo above his heart, he looked the part. The agent that checked up on him after he'd checked into his hotel nodded. Reporting another dead end to his company he returned.

Hayseed, as Reggie Camp, drove into Chicago in a beat-up pickup truck he loved. He'd purchased the truck in Nappanee for six hundred dollars, spent another six hundred getting it running correctly and headed for Chicago. He certainly looked like an Indiana farmer, with his baseball cap sporting a John Deere logo, his corduroy coat, jeans, and worn boots. He'd owned a similar truck in his youth on the farm in Pennsylvania and was enjoying the fond memories.

Tom drove into Chicago from Arcadia, Wisconsin in a pearl white BMW 550i, checked into The Peninsula Hotel, taking a suite of rooms. No agents had been assigned to cover the five most expensive hotels in Chicago for obvious reasons. Tom grinned as he settled into his role.

Fagan Cord drove to Chicago in a dilapidated Toyota Corolla he'd purchased in Kalamazoo for nine hundred dollars. The car ran well but the air conditioner did not work. As it was winter Fagan didn't think he'd need it. He was anxious to try out for his part in the play, establishing his bona fide cover. There were no agents to watch for such an arrival, so he went unnoticed. If he actually got the part, no one would doubt his cover. Excited to make his best effort he thought he had a chance.

Bill Kline, as Dr. James Forsythe of Forsythe Nautical Electronics in Annapolis arrived at the airport and made his way down to the Hertz counter where he rented a hybrid Ford. His carry-on bag held everything he needed and the agent that followed him was able to get his name and address as he filled out the rental agreement. After checking he went back to the concourse. Dr. Forsythe had been in good physical shape, but he did not appear to be military.

Zeke Kline as Dr. Mario Evans arrived looking very much like the nerd he was proud to represent. He had a laptop, iPad, iPhone, and though dressed in a very nice suit he looked like what he was, a computer geek. No one even glanced twice at him. Zeke had died his hair ginger and wore glasses that looked much thicker than they actually were.

Myers and Pierson arrived at the dunes unnoticed by those looking for military men. They were soon tearing around the Dunes in their Bowlers, having a blast. Because they were daring no one doubted for a moment that these two men were experienced rally drivers. Both were determined to learn the skills necessary to make a good showing in the Dune races. Neither minded the tremendous fun and wild rides they experienced as they challenged each other.

Ox got off the plane, paused to check through every pocket, his gray hair and goatee, half glasses, and general air of being somewhere else hiding his powerful figure behind a perfect disguise. One of the flight attendants appeared at the door with his overcoat. She was calling his name.

"Dr. Force! Dr. Force! You forgot your coat." He turned to her and smiled, taking it absentmindedly and when he searched the pockets, he found his baggage claim and sighed with relief. The flight attendant shook her pretty head and smiled at the doctor. No one followed him to baggage.

Chief arrived unnoted in the flatbed truck with the fossilized bones. Everyone who came into contact with the fussy paleontologist decided he was a royal pain, though they hid it well. Enjoying being obnoxious Chief played his part perfectly.

J.R. flew into Chicago in his own private plane, landing at Midway where he paid for storage before meeting an Enterprise agent at the gate. In his rented car he checked into Hotel Chicago as John Voss and spent the afternoon getting ready to meet with city officials about protecting the shoreline of Lake Michigan.

From the records at Midway the agent assigned to that airport was able to report to his company that John Voss, consultant, had arrived as arranged. J.R. was wearing a mask, and he looked like John Voss, though he was an inch taller than the man.

Smitty, as John Jones arrived at O'Hare and the agents watching passed him by. He'd intended that consequence, with his Hispanic looks wearing a thick mustache and dressed in well-worn clothes, carrying several maps under his arm.

Hobbs arrived in a C130 cargo carrier full of his latest additions to his store. He was able to slip past all the agents by having a truck meet his plane, and then driving off with the truck to his store. Everyone was in place. The mission was now a go mission.

In an apartment building on Catalpa Street on the Near North Side of Chicago four men met to go over the reports from the agencies they'd hired. The apartment was sparsely furnished, two of the bedrooms empty, folding chairs in the living room, and a plastic folding table in the dining room around which they sat.

"What is the status of *Bring It Up* and its crew?" one of them asked, after reading through the reports.

"*Sea Venture* is currently at sea doing research, fulfilling two grants by two different governments. The ship is far out to sea and our man agrees that the entire crew was on board when it left the harbor in England. It has not come near the U.S." the man making the report put aside the report he'd just read.

"Our man at the base reports there is no increase in preparations. The informant in City Hall and in the County offices both report that efforts to squash the story of a terrorist cell working in this city have been successful," another man reported.

"We go ahead as planned," the leader said quietly when he'd finished reading all the reports. Early February is the coldest time of year here. Our attack will work best if we have a heavy snowstorm." He smiled slightly. "Let us move forward."

Chapter 30

Hundreds of people visit museums every day. Planning to meet at the Museum of Natural History had been a stroke of genius. *Bring It Up* provided a nice donation to the museum in exchange for the use of one of its many conference rooms, large enough to seat thirty-six men. Jim arranged to meet his men on different days at different hours, being careful to stay away from any set pattern.

"So how many do you think are in this little cell?" Ox asked once everyone had reported on their entry to the city and the consequent observations.

"Usually, the leaders are three or four, and they each have a small cell of three of four people to carry out their dirty work," Zeke said.

"That's about what I figure. How do we focus in on our three or four?" Bear asked.

Jim listened as his men talked, not at all upset in not leading the discussion. He worked with professionals, appreciated their expertise, and knew that by the end of their meeting they would have a good handle on where things stood. He kept his pen poised to take notes. Although he could type the notes on his iPad, he preferred using a pen, and then transferring the notes, organizing them, helping him memorize them.

"The FBI keeps a running record of known terrorists that enter the city and keeps them under surveillance," John said.

"Here's the interesting thing," Zeke acknowledged, manipulating his keyboard as he spoke. "According to their records, there are eight. The last time we saw a pattern like this the terrorists were divided into four leaders, with one overall in in charge, and the other four to recruit two or three men or women each. When their mission was complete, they killed the other members of the unit recruited and left enough evidence to convict all of them. No one looked for the eight after that. This has been done twice. If this is their MO, they will do the same thing again," Zeke finished.

"What is our current INTEL?" Jim asked, looking at Zeke.

"Four of them are students at four different colleges and universities. My guess is that is where they will recruit. I'm watching the usual channels and others to see if they are advertising. The other four have jobs, but they all meet once a week to play dominoes. Meetings are held at four different apartments, all located close to an elevated train platform or hospital. Conversations are innocuous but the FBI can't hear when the trains are passing, and the sirens are blaring. Tapes are sent to a lab to edit out the ambient sounds and the lab takes days."

"How long does it take you to edit out ambient sound?" FM asked with a grin. "You're dying to tell us how clever you are!" he added as Zeke drew in a breath.

"With our Crays and a program News wrote we can do it in twenty minutes or less. Now! May I continue?" Zeke looked at FM until the latter nodded, after both shared a grin.

"All four attend the same mosque for religious observations of daily prayer. During those times they talk to many different people, not just to each other. These guys are pros!" Zeke concluded.

"Code word is Crazy Eight. I want eyes and ears on these guys," Jim said after a moment of thought. "Who is bankrolling this? Do we know who's paying for the apartments and tuition, room and board, etc.?"

"Remember the Germans who were manipulating terrorist's way back when?" Zeke asked, as if musing. "I finally got a lead on the mysterious man behind it all. This is a great grandson of a very bad German, carrying on his family business of subterfuge and terrorism. He's located in Mexico City, and he launders money for his friends in Iran, Iraq, and Palestine as well as providing a pipeline to get terrorists into America. His name is Francisco Eichmann, but he goes under Francisco Turisio.

"He's certainly on the watch list of every three-letter agency we have, and he knows it. Unfortunately, none of them have been able to penetrate his security or get enough dirt on him to bring him in. The Mexican government wouldn't allow us to take him either. It appears he has friends in high places, spreads around seed money to key politicians and makes sure they don't have any desire to look for greener pastures," Zeke looked at his computer screen for a moment.

"His money is coming from the middle east?" Jim asked.

"And from Russia and China," Zeke added, putting the information up on the computer. Everyone looked at the information with bleak faces.

"Is Turisio in contact with any of the crazy eight?" Wade asked in the silence that followed.

"With one. I'm guessing this is our leader," Zeke put the photo and name up on the computer. "So far he has controlled any money sent to Chicago." Zeke added. "Eichmann is the only contact with the Russian Mafia boss and our Chinese group."

"Why hasn't somebody from our three letter agencies taken this clown out?" Dorf asked.

"According to my research, they've tried three times. All three times their agent was killed. Eichmann owns somebody on the president's team, somebody high enough to actually identify those agents," Zeke said. Although Jim heard the words, spoken without emotion, he knew that Zeke was deeply disturbed by this information. They all were.

"How soon before you know who that is?" Jim asked.

"News and Bright Eyes are following the money. Pippi is helping. Between those three it won't be long. I'd say we'll have a name before the end of the week," Zeke replied. "Our INTEL team in Greece is working on it as well. Duck wants this one."

"How did you guys uncover all of this in so short a time?" John raised his hands as if in supplication, looking at Zeke. Zeke grinned.

"Elementary, my dear Watson," he said facetiously. "When I

heard that the information about known terrorists got squashed here in cheery old Chi town, I uncovered who squashed it, who ordered him to squash it, and so on. With the help of Bright Eyes, Pippi, and News I was able to learn a great deal. All eight of these terrorists have visited one very important political figure. After seeing that, it was easy," Zeke buffed his fingernails on his shirt and looked smug.

"You had to ask, had to give him a chance to crow!" Bill Kline shook his head, waving an admonitory finger at John.

"His ability is a reflection of the amazing leadership under which he operates," John hinted, buffing his own nails and looking smug. There was a roar of laughter. Jim spoke when the laughter died out.

"Okay. Let's get to work. Driver, you and FM have a young lady to find. My wife says don't bother coming back without her," Jim smiled as he said the last.

"Too right!" Jack said somberly. "She's been gone long enough to be in a very bad place! If she can be found, we'll find her!"

"If these guys track like last time, they'll have something planned and ready to go by February. Let's put them on ice before they get it done," Jim said, stacking his papers. He looked up suddenly. "No pun intended," he added to a burst of laughter.

"Is this bloody city always this cold?" D.C. asked. "Putting them on ice should be easy. Between the cab and this building my body temperature dropped several degrees, and when I took a whizz, I swear I was pissing snow!" Jim smiled as the others burst out laughing at D.C.'s words, but Mark put the icing on the cake with his next comment.

"Chicago can be deadly during the winter months. But we've been in deadly cold before. Our enemies, however, are facing an even deadlier cold than a Chicago winter!" Mark said softly. "They're facing the deadly cold resolve of Omega Force."

"Well said, Mark. Send us off with a word of prayer, please," Jim said with a grim smile.

After Mark closed the meeting in prayer the men separated, leaving the Museum and traveling through the vast corridors to join other visitors from various places in the building. Although they spent another two hours or more in the Museum building itself, visiting the various displays, no one watching any of them would have suspected they knew each other. There were no nods, eye contact, or other signs. All of them were merely strangers going through the museum.

Leaving separately, they returned to the places where they were staying and prepared to enter phase two of their mission. Each man had a plan of action, and Jim knew that his men were experts, and would adapt to any changes that happened along the way. He smiled as he put on his next disguise.

Jack, as Frederick Wickham, dressed in his British clothes after adding gray streaks to his hair and a fully gray mustache with dark ends, bristly and thick beneath his nose completed the changes to his face. A pair of half glasses perched on his nose was perfect. With his weathered face and bluff features, he looked like a British farmer. His calloused and strong hands only added to the picture. Taking up his walking stick he walked jauntily out of the hotel to meet Commander Mitchell and the chauffeured Lincoln he'd rented.

Together they traveled to the police station at the precinct where Jayne disappeared from her college campus. That afternoon they would talk to several detectives, and every security person they could reach at the college campus, and that night they reviewed hours of security camera footage, some offered willingly, some lifted quietly, and some hacked by Zeke. Both men intended to discover what happened to this lovely young woman from the UK.

It was the latter that finally gave them their first clue. A traffic camera showed Jayne, bound and gagged in the back of a Range Rover. Jane was a buxom girl with pretty features, huge green eyes, and strawberry blonde hair. Her dark eyebrows were distinctive in the photo and Jack caught the face in just a moment of film, ordering Zeke to go back. Having memorized her features picking her out in that photo had been instant.

"She looks terrified!" Zeke commented softly as they stared at the enhanced photo. "Is that another girl further in?" he asked suddenly, his fingers flying over his keyboard and bringing into focus another girl, from the same campus, also listed as missing. Bridget Grogan came into clear focus, also looking terrified.

Again, Zeke manipulated the keyboard and found a camera that showed the driver and a passenger in the front seat, and someone in the back seat, turned backwards, holding what looked like a stun gun. The driver was average in size, rather handsome, but the passenger was a huge man with massive muscles.

"We might need Abe on this one!" FM said softly. "That's a big fella!"

A ding on the computer told Zeke that the license number of the vehicle had been traced. He looked at the address with pursed lips and raised eyebrows.

"This is a wrinkle," he said slowly. Printing out the information he handed the sheets to FM and Driver. Both men read the information before looking up at Zeke.

"The guy driving looks like an aid. This politician is dirty, but he's got connections. What does he want with two British girls?" FM asked. He looked up at Zeke who was typing furiously.

"What are you doing now?" he asked.

"I'm asking Sir Edward to give you temporary diplomatic status, and to alert the Embassy that you will probably be arrested before too long," Zeke said.

"What about me?" Driver asked plaintively. "I get arrested they'll revoke my travel visa and send me home!"

"I think that would be more trouble than they want with the United Kingdom," Zeke said when he finished typing. "We have evidence of the girls bound and gagged in the Senator's personal vehicle, and when I've got identification on these three fellows, we'll probably have employees of his organization. That gives us bargaining power."

"I'm not giving this perp a pass because he's a senator!" Driver snarled angrily. "We're pretty sure what he wanted them for, and what he's going to do with them. God knows what he's done to force them to do his bidding!"

"I wasn't thinking about the senator!" Zeke said, holding up both hands.

"Now I know why the FBI wasn't called into this case," FM said slowly, nodding.

"I think after all the questions yesterday you two can expect a visit from somebody seeking to dissuade you from continuing your investigation. It will probably be some criminal heavy," Zeke said.

"We take the beating," Driver said quickly, looking over at FM. "It will give us even more leverage."

"Great!" FM said, throwing up his arms. "Throw us to the lions!" he was grinning. "You, they'll probably beat. They might hold back on me if I have diplomatic clearance," his face clouded suddenly. "Be careful," he cautioned.

"Force them to come to you. Stay in your room until they come to you. Where are you going to stay, Mr. Wickham?" Zeke asked, looking at Driver with his eyebrows raised.

"I'm renting a room at a motel just off campus," he said. "I rented it yesterday before heading over to the museum. I'll arrive around eleven tomorrow morning. If you hear the pounding begin, call the cops and send them over. I'd like to see their reactions."

"Done," Zeke said, looking back at his computer. "I'll see you guys later."

At the moment the three of them were in a popular coffee shop, sitting away from everyone else, just three men having a conversation like many others. As they left Zeke watched to make sure no one was taking an interest in them. Satisfied he packed up his computer equipment and headed for his own hotel.

In the morning FM was in his uniform when he answered the door to the men who were going to talk him out of looking for Jayne Wickham. He was not surprised to welcome dignitaries from the state government.

"Good morning, Commander. I'm Lee Kowalski from the office of judicial review, this is Lieutenant Brandon Jones of the State Police, and this is Robert Malone from the office of the Secretary of State." FM studied each man, ignoring the credentials offered, looking into their eyes. He grunted non-committedly and turned to usher them into his suite. Eyes narrowed at his response and scrutiny.

"I have to be at the Embassy office in an hour, gentlemen. Please be brief. Since I'm not going down for breakfast, may I order something for you as well?" he picked up the phone. They asked for coffee, and he made the order.

"Sir, we understand you are looking into the disappearance of Jayne Wickham. Word reached us that you were inquiring at the campus and the precinct office that handled the initial investigation. Frankly, having someone of your reputation from Scotland Yard looking into the case does not reflect well on our state's ability to conduct a criminal investigation," Kowalski began.

"Balderdash, young man!" FM said in his haughtiest upper crust accent. "Two months have passed since the girl disappeared and the FBI was not called in. That is what reflects poorly on your state's ability to conduct a criminal kidnapping investigation. Miss Wickham was taken by force from her campus, bound and gagged. I intend to find her and rescue her!"

"We don't know that for certain," Lieutenant Jones began but FM cut him off.

"Then you're incompetent!" he stated, staring belligerently at the officer. "I have photographic evidence of her abduction on the night she disappeared," he produced the prints taken from the traffic camera. It was quite obvious that Jayne Wickham was bound, gagged, and terrified.

"The second captive is Miss Bridget Grogan, also of the United Kingdom. I've been in contact with her mother, who was quite concerned that she hadn't heard from her daughter for some time. She is making an official complaint and report this morning.

"I don't know how you do things here, but in my country, if a young woman is abducted, we do not stop until we have the culprit in hand. I assure you, gentlemen, that I have the license plate of the vehicle in question, the address of the owner, and the identification of the driver and his two male passengers. If you're trying to protect a corrupt senator, I assure you that any argument you might make will fall upon deaf ears." A knock sounded at the door and Commander Mitchell rose, answered the door, signed for the items on the tray and tipped the waiter. It was Fagan who was photographing the three in the room.

"We were unaware that this involved a member of our own government," Robert Malone said stiffly.

"Don't insult my intelligence!" FM roared. "You're here because he asked you to dissuade me from pursuing this matter. In my estimation you represent a corrupt government, and this interview is over. Now get out of my room so I can enjoy my breakfast and get to the Embassy."

"Perhaps we've handled this badly," Kowalski said, rising and looking at the other two. FM focused on the policeman. Jones looked like he was ready to punch FM.

"If you wish to try, Mr. Jones, go right ahead. I don't have much respect for crooked policemen," FM's voice was low and steady. "Shall we see if Scotland Yard's training is up to par?"

"Now, we'll be having none of that!" Robert Malone said with authority, and just that quickly Jones backed down. FM had guessed that Malone was the force behind the three.

"If I discover that you knew anything about this case, Mr. Malone, you and I will be having a very private and very straightforward one-on-one meeting. Now get out!" FM was obviously serious, and Malone slowly stood.

"You're not in the United Kingdom, sir. I'd advise caution," he warned. Suddenly he backed away from FM two steps. Embarrassed and still unsettled he spun on his heel and motioned for the other men to follow him. The look he'd seen in those eyes had unnerved him it had been so intense.

"Sanctimonious do-gooder!" he sputtered after the door closed behind him. He looked at Jones. "Tell your man in the parking garage to kick his sanctimonious ass!" he thought a moment and then grabbed Jones arm. "No! Just a little warning! Rough him up, but not enough to send him to a hospital," Jones made the call.

"What about the father?" Kowalski asked.

"He'll get the message," Malone said quietly. He smiled.

Having the police arrive in a timely manner saved Jack from too serious of a beating. Not fighting back had taken every bit of concentration he had, but he'd pulled it off, accepting the pain and discomfort, thankful that none of his bones had been broken.

FM, in the parking garage, vomited on the policeman who roughed him up. He'd eaten quickly with that in mind, knowing that a hard punch to the stomach would bring everything up. It had almost made him laugh when he covered the front of the man's shirt and suit coat, and most of his pants. The beating stopped at that point and the man moved away, cursing, pulling off his coat and shirt.

Two police officers stepped to either side of Tyrone Cranik and he blinked in surprise.

"You just attacked a diplomat from the United Kingdom. Get on the ground now!" one of them commanded, motioning with his gun. Cranik got down, glaring back at Commander Mitchell. He said nothing. At the moment he had no ID to identify him as a fellow police officer. Malone would arrange for him to be set free, and he no longer cared if he had to leave the force. He watched another officer approach the Commander.

"Sir! How badly are you injured?" the man asked respectfully. Still hunched over FM shook his head and waved a hand.

"Had worse from men who would eat that police officer for lunch!" he scoffed.

"Police officer?" the officer facing him looked over at Cranik.

"A man named Robert Malone will arrange for his release," Commander Mitchell said, straightening up. "It appears you have some bad apples in the barrel. It happens," he pulled a handkerchief from his pocket and wiped his mouth. "I'm late for an appointment at the embassy. May I go?"

"Yes sir. Could I take your statement there?" the officer asked.

"It would be more convenient," FM replied.

"Thank you, sir. I'll do that. Are you sure this man is a police officer?"

"I'm sure. See you at the embassy," FM said, getting into his rented car.

"Why don't you have a diplomatic car and driver?" the officer asked.

"I will after I get to the embassy," FM said with a grin. "How did you know I was a diplomat?"

"Your office called and said you might be in some danger. They described you and I have a photo," the officer saluted, and FM backed out of his parking spot.

"How bad is Driver?" FM asked, once he was out of the parking garage.

"He'll meet you at the embassy. Neither of you are badly injured, but he took a few more hits than you did," News reported from the ship. "Give us some details. How bad was it?"

"Shep hits a lot harder than whoever that was!" FM said with some feeling.

"His name is Cranik, and he works for the State Police," Pippi said. "Malone is on some very nasty payrolls. Watch your back. I've sent the information on to our embassy through the proper channels. These men are obviously used to getting their own way."

"Thanks Lieutenant Longstocking," FM said with a grin.

"Your accent isn't bad. Keep it all up to the front of the mouth, just behind your teeth, and you'll be fine," Pippi said with a smile.

"Ah yes! The upper crust British!" FM said with his accent perfect.

"Go find those girls," Cecilia demanded.

"Or you'll answer to the captain's wives!" Pippi added.

"Yeesh! I'm going! I'm going!" FM retorted.

At the embassy he checked in and a sergeant from the unit serving at the embassy returned his rental car. Driver was nursing a split lip and swollen nose and eye, but other than that seemed to be coping. FM and Driver shared a look for a moment and one of the senior officers shuddered.

"I can almost pity the blokes who did this, gentlemen!" he said blandly. "Almost. Here's the information that came through marked for you. Can you rescue these girls?" his voice was still bland, but his eyes held the question.

"We will find and rescue them," Driver said quietly. It was the way he said it that made the older man nod. The question was no longer in his eyes.

"What can we do to help?" he requested, his eyes now gleaming with anticipation.

"Are these blokes SAS?" FM asked, looking at the men in uniform.

"No. But I can have an SAS unit here in minutes," the ambassador said, coming into the room. "I've taken the liberty of asking them to step over. They should be arriving in about five minutes. Sir Edward said you might need them."

"The senator will have moved them to his most private property. News, Pippi, Bright Eyes! Do we have an address?" FM responded.

"1301 Bison Lane, Hoffman Estates. It is currently being used as private retreat," Cecilia responded.

"The house we suspect is in Hoffman Estates on Bison Lane," FM reported to the ambassador.

"I'm working on a plan now," Jim's voice sounded in FM and Driver's ear. "They won't expect us to move in daylight," he added.

"Bit Public that!" the ambassador said with a frown. "High brow area, lots of feathers to ruffle! I'll have to be at my diplomatic best!" he smiled then. "Serves these cocky Yanks right, what?"

"Hold everything team!" Cecilia's voice came over the communication gear.

"What is it?" Jim asked quickly.

"Our senator just made a call to our terrorist cell leader! He's asking TajUdin to attack the British Embassy!" News responded.

"Who's TajUdin?" Jim asked.

"Oh! We just got a hit on our head terrorist. His name is TajUdin Odeh. He's an Afghani by birth and very high up in ISIS," Cecilia said. "This is a very bad man. He's an industrial engineer and a chemist."

"Great!" Jim and FM said at the same time. Then both of them responded. "Jinx!" Everyone chuckled at the interchange.

"Hey Shep! The Cavalry just arrived!" FM said.

"Good morning, gents!" the sergeant in charge of the SAS group said, coming to a sharp stop and saluting the ambassador.

"No need for that here," the ambassador cajoled, nodding his acceptance. "These Yanks need a bit of help," he added, waving a hand at Driver and FM.

"Frank Miller, as I live and breathe!" one of the men said, looking at Frank with a big grin.

"Adley O'Malley, judging by the general air of having visited one too many pubs!" Frank grinned, rising and bumping shoulders and fists with the British soldier.

"This Yank pulled my wrinklies out of the fire a while back. I guess I'll finally get to hoist one with the famous SEAL from the U.S. of A!" Adley grinned at Frank and the two shared another fist bump. It was obvious they respected each other.

"My good friend and mate, Jack Boswell," Frank waved at Driver, who stood and came to shake hands with all the men.

"So, what have we got?" the sergeant asked, after introducing himself as John Winchester.

"Two ladies from the U.K., kidnapped by a U.S. Senator, and held captive at his private retreat," Frank said easily.

"INTEL?" Winchester asked quickly. "And how do you know the Senator kidnapped them?"

"We managed to get a clear picture of both women bound and gagged in the rear of an SUV from a traffic camera. Our people were studying all the cameras operating the night they disappeared. Bit careless, that! Our Senator apparently believes he owns enough crooked cops to use his own vehicles," Driver responded.

"How did you get a clear photo from a traffic camera?" Adley asked.

"We have some Crays and a kick-ass enhancement program," FM replied.

"On the plasma screen," the Ambassador said. A satellite image of the house came up, showing a huge undeveloped area of dirt and trees behind the house on Bison Lane, between it and houses on Brentwood Drive.

Sergeant Winchester looked at the picture once and then looked at FM.

"Do we have a plan?" he inquired.

"Drop half the men off in the gap on Brentwood, dressed as construction workers. The other half go in an air-conditioning service truck. Coordinate your hit and pull the truck into the driveway and hit the house hard and fast," Jim said to FM through his communication gear.

FM nodded and suggested the plan. Sergeant Winchester nodded quickly. He named off five of his men as construction workers, suggesting that Driver lead that group.

"Why me?" Driver asked with a grin.

"Construction workers fight with each other sometimes," Winchester said with a grin.

"Makes sense," Driver said with an easy nod. He moved off with the five men. "Is there a thrift store near here?" Driver asked suddenly.

"Right down the block. Why?" the ambassador asked.

"We'll look better in worn clothes. Jim, can you get us some construction tools and belts?"

"They'll be there in half an hour," Jim said.

"Who's Jim?" Winchester asked, looking around.

Driver tapped his ear, pulled out the almost invisible wireless device that allowed him to contact the others on the team. Winchester whistled and nodded.

"Would that be Jim Shepherd?" he asked.

"The one and only," Driver replied, heading into a room where they would take measurements, and someone would purchase the clothing for them. One of the secretaries rose from her desk with a measuring tape and followed them.

"FM. Our friend from NCIS has a heating and air-conditioning truck and outfits. He needs sizes and he'll send the truck to you, as though that company is coming to fix your unit," Jim instructed.

FM relayed the information and as soon as all were measured, the men sat down to study the plan, and discuss contingencies. Two hours later two crew-cab pick-ups left the parking garage with three construction workers in each cab. The bed of the trucks had plywood and 2x4 studs, along with some typical equipment, quickly borrowed from NCIS. The heating and air-conditioning truck left fifteen minutes later with the other six men crammed into the back and Winchester and Frank in front.

Although the men in the trucks laughed and joked along the way, that did not mean they didn't know the dangers of what they were about to do. Frank and Jack both talked about the SAS men on their team, men these soldiers knew and respected, cementing a strong working relationship. It helped that O'Malley knew Frank and his reputation. By the time they arrived at their destinations they were a cohesive team.

CHAPTER 31

Both pick-ups pulled off into the dirt beside Brentwood Drive, and the men got out. Driver unrolled a map and studied it with Adley, as though they were looking for something. Moments later he pulled a device for checking for gas leaks from the back of the pickup and the six men set off, following Driver. Two carried shovels, a third pushed a wheelbarrow, and one had a post-hole digger. No one looked twice at the group of men about their business. It was, after all, broad daylight! Driver knew that most thieves worked in broad daylight for that very reason. Few people actually looked closely at other people, especially working people.

When they were in position behind the trees lining the backyard of 1301 Bison Lane, Driver let FM know they were in place.

"Roger that, Driver. We're pulling into the driveway in ten seconds. Cause a distraction in the back yard now, please."

Driver pushed through the trees with the device and stopped in the middle of the yard. Two thugs that looked like someone put a sport jacket on a bulldozer came out of the back door in a hurry. Looking up Driver just nodded at them, causing his device to beep several times.

"Got it!" he said, and another man came through the trees, holding the map rolled up.

"Not the right place," Adley said in his best Southern accent.

When he was within striking distance, he thrust the rolled map into the solar plexus of the largest of the two men, while Driver rotated the device and brought it up sharply between the legs of the other. Following their initial attack, the two soldiers took down the thugs quickly with two more blows each.

More men poured out of the house and the other four soldiers arrived with drawn weapons to stop them in their tracks. The front door shattered inwards as FM and Winchester came through, weapons drawn. Inside the house the fighting was intense, but no one dared use his gun. FM pulled the gas line from the stove as soon as he got into the kitchen, yanked the stove away from the wall, and pulled the hose loose.

"You blaze the whole house goes up!" he said loudly enough to be heard all the way outside. After that the men fought with fists and knives and the thugs were soon dispatched. Three were wounded, though not seriously, and two were dead. The Senator was not in the house.

They found the girls in the basement, in a root cellar, bound and gagged, and quite dirty from rolling around in the dirt and trying to get free. FM stepped into the room first, and he searched with his eyes. Jayne nodded with her chin toward a door in the back of the cellar. FM opened the door quickly and a guard looked down at him from trying to open the cellar door. He'd been shoving it up against the chains locking it down and yelling for help, and Frank's appearance startled him.

As he reached for his gun Frank leaned in, grabbed both his feet, and yanked them out from beneath him, dragging him down the steps painfully. The gun fell free and Frank dragged the man all the way into the room. Winchester picked up the weapon, made sure the safety was on, and pocketed it quietly, shoving the door closed. He was grinning, knowing that Frank Miller was about to have some fun with this idiot thug.

When the man leaped to his feet Frank hit him, a hard blow to the windpipe, and when the man raised both hands to his throat

Frank's foot connected between the man's legs, dropping him to the ground with horrible gurgling sounds.

"You kill him, mate?" Winchester asked, one eyebrow raised.

"He's still making noise, isn't he? He'll live," Frank stated, pulling plastic restraint ties from his belt and securing the prisoner. When he was sure they were tight enough, he knelt down and released Jayne and Bridget. Once they were free, they wept openly, rubbing sore wrists, and finally clinging to one another.

"Jayne," FM's voice was gentle and soft. "Did these men touch you? Did they harm you physically?" FM asked quietly and gently. She and Bridget began to cry harder, their knuckles white as they gripped each other's clothing.

Sitting back on his heels FM watched them, his eyes sad. Winchester stood beside him, saying nothing. Finally, FM looked up at him and stood.

"Let's get them to a hospital," he said simply.

"The FBI will be at the front door in two minutes," Jim's voice alerted FM.

"Lifting the girls gently the two men carried them up and quickly out of the house. Putting them down on the front porch the men climbed into the truck and backed out of the drive.

The others were already sprinting back to their trucks. The FBI, sirens wailing, arrived a minute later to find the two girls still weeping on the front porch. Once one of the agents entered the house, and smelled the gas, he raced around the side of the building to turn off the gas valve. Once that was done, they went through the house opening the windows.

As the trucks sped away the men from the British Embassy removed their gloves. FM and Driver made sure none of them had been cut or bled during the takedown and sat back with satisfaction. The FBI would find no DNA evidence of their presence, and no fingerprints.

"They won't protect the girls in the hospital, mate," Winchester said to FM as they drove away from the scene. "And when they're ready, they'll transport them to the embassy. Those skirts are sitting ducks for being silenced as witnesses."

"NCIS will provide security at the hospital, and they won't be going to the embassy. Two other girls from NCIS will go to the embassy. It's up to you blokes to keep that embassy safe. You need bomb-sniffing dogs along the street, lock-down security, and a chopper standing by with backup when the attack, if one is launched, happens.

"Personally, I think this TajUdin Odeh would love nothing better than to add the Embassy to his plan. I'll be working on the outside, so if you see me in some other guise, you don't know me. Okay?" Frank looked seriously at Winchester.

"What name or names will you be using?" Winchester asked.

"Donovan O'Rourke, a deck machinist from the *Derry Sue*, down on my luck and stranded in Chicago because of a misunderstanding with the captain of that fine vessel. I'll also be Timur Koskov, of the Ocёpt or Ossetra Caviar suppliers," FM looked at Winchester, his eyes showing nothing.

"Thanks for the trust, mate," Winchester said quietly. "No one will hear it from any of us," FM nodded once.

FM and Driver left the embassy together, in the back of the air-conditioning truck that had been borrowed from NCIS. Later that day they took up their second identities and headed out into the icy Chicago weather.

Jack was visiting various manufacturers and dealers of boats as Ed Barnes while FM was lazing about as Donovan O'Rourke. Jack was glad he was wearing a mask disguise to hide his black eye and bruises, but he couldn't hide the cut on his lip, so he invented a story about a bad night at a bar. No one questioned him beyond the telling of that story. He didn't look like a brawler, so he made the story believable. He was in the wrong place at the wrong time.

At the Advocate Center downtown Dorf was having the time of his life. He was playing one of his favorite games, if not on a fully professional level, with enough strength and power to make a difference. Because of his leaping ability and strength, he was pulling down rebounds, even blocking a few shots, but most of all feeding the other players with rifle passes that were so accurately timed none of his other players had to break stride.

Although the Bulls won every game by a twenty-point margin, they did not take these Olympic hopefuls lightly. Karoff was a force to be reckoned with, strong and agile, and tall enough to be a real contender. Kozak was a small forward with great agility and a deadly shot. And Vovk was able to knock down three-point shots when the opportunity arose, seemingly with ease, while Shevchenko managed to steal the ball four times from one of the best ball handlers in the game.

None of the Ukrainians lost their tempers during the games, and Dorf knew that like him, each was awed by the talent of the men against whom they played. Dorf was glad to see the men bonding well with the Bulls players. He was quite sure that no one was paying much attention to him now that he'd been practicing for a couple of days. It was time to slip into his second character as John Hammond.

They met again at the museum, in one of the conference rooms far from the public eye, gathering around the table with their laptops and notes after a week of reconnaissance. Jim watched them come in, one at a time, taking note at how well they fit into the characters that had been chosen for them to play. This particular meeting had been scheduled around Fagan's schedule, since he'd scored the part in the theatrical musical.

It was also odd to see Wade with black hair and blue eyes. As Thomas Perry he looked the part, dressed today in casual slacks and an expensive shirt, no tie, looking like an aviation engineer. He nodded at Jim as he slid into his seat and flashed a grin at John. The three had been close through their entire lives.

Zeke cleared his throat, and everyone opened his laptop and quickly the images from Zeke's computer flashed on the screens. First up was a report from Ira regarding TajUdin Odeh and his connections to ISIS. As usual the Mossad report was concise and as complete as possible. Each man read quickly. INTEL of this nature was vital to their mission, and the men studied the details, committing them to memory.

"Scope has seen TajUdin Odeh twice at the city and county building," Zeke said in the silence.

"Who's he been seeing?" John asked quickly, looking at Scope.

"I can't get past the counter, so I'm not sure, but Zeke managed to tap into the security system. He's visited four offices."

"I don't like what I'm thinking," Zeke began. "I picked up some talk at TajUdin's last meeting about electric grids, and two of the offices he visited hold plans for the grids in Chicago and the entire area. It is my opinion that part of their plot involves taking out the electricity for the entire northern and central part of America," he looked around the table. "I also heard them talk about dropping a tower and taking a Federal Reserve Bank."

"Holy Mary, mother of God!" Wade breathed. "Thousands would die!"

"They are saying that this winter is going to have some of the coldest temperatures in history," Neil said quietly. "Darn global warming!" he added facetiously, getting a laugh.

"To the elderly and children, it will be a deadly cold," John added.

"Why take out the entire grid?" Jim asked.

"Once the entire grid is out, they have only the backup systems to worry about in their plot to break into the Federal Reserve Bank," Rock suggested. "Think about it. If they can take out the electric grid and rob the bank, they can hurt the economy of the mid-west and north for years to come."

"Good thing we're going to nick those plans, what?" Counselor grinned.

"Can they carry it out with the cells in place?" Jim asked.

"If I were doing this, I'd plant the explosives to take out the grid early, and then hook it up to a detonator I could trigger from a cell phone. I wouldn't blow the grid until I was set up to enter the bank and drop the tower," FM suggested after a moment of thought. "They could do it with the people in place if they did it that way."

"There's a lot of gold in the reserve. How are they going to move that? With the electric grid down getting out of dodge isn't going to be easy! Air or water is their only other avenue!"

"They're going to take it through the coal tunnels to the docks, and then take it out on a ship," Zeke said, bringing up a map of the coal tunnels beneath the city. "In the old days they shipped coal to buildings through these tunnels. There's an Iranian container ship in the harbor. It arrived yesterday and is scheduled to leave tomorrow. I believe the vehicles to move the gold are on that ship. They could easily unload the vehicles and hide them in the tunnels.

"Interesting note. The ship is due back the twelfth of February, and to depart at high tide on the fifteenth," Zeke looked around the table once more. "I think we have a date for the attack."

"Why that particular date? And when is high tide?" John asked.

"I think I know the answer to your first question," Zeke replied. "Our research shows that on February 14th in 1979 Adolph Dubs, the U.S. ambassador to Afghanistan, was kidnapped in Kabul by Muslim extremists. He was killed in a shootout between his abductors and police. One of the abductors was Faizullah Odeh. Faizullah was TajUdin's father."

"They weren't all Afghani police, were they?" Jim asked.

"No. There were four American soldiers training the police force. The quick response was due to their influence. Faizullah was captured and died of his wounds two days later. The Afghani police questioned him extensively shortly after they brought him in, which is why most believe he died. I can't tell from the reports. High tide is at 0325 on the fifteenth," Zeke answered after a sobering pause.

"Okay. Now we have a motive. We have a target date and what we believe are the targets. Eyes and ears are on our major players, but I want the rest of those cells identified," Jim said curtly. "Let's get the INTEL we need to wrap this up! The takedown to rescue the girls was well done, men! Everyone thinks they are at the hospital, but they were transferred almost immediately, and our MI6 friends were able to provide two very similar women. With makeup they'll be identical."

"Will the embassy get hit?" FM asked.

" TajUdin Odeh will not risk his secret cells in such an attack. I believe he will contract it out to another group. He's been in contact with our German friend in Mexico," Zeke responded, not looking up from his computer screen. "There are other terrorists willing to come into our country and attack the embassy. Our senator is footing the bill to get them here, and he's paying for their hotel rooms. I've got five rooms rented in five different motels, mostly low rent, for nine terrorists. They're flying in tomorrow and will be studying the embassy for three days before planning the attack. The senator has city maps and architectural drawings to help them, including security schedules and electronic surveillance placements."

"I never thought Chicago a particularly safe place to be," Bear said quietly.

"I take it we will have eyes and ears on our terrorists?" Jim asked with a smile.

"They are in place. However, they will not be activated until our suspicious friends have a chance to sweep the room for electronic devices. Every mirror has been removed from the wall and replaced with one-way glass, and we have cameras behind the mirrors and sensitive microphones to pick up any conversation in the room. The same is true in the bathrooms. Once they sweep the rooms, we'll turn everything on. If they meet somewhere other than the rooms, we'll have to adjust," Zeke replied.

"How much did all that cost?" John asked quickly.

"So far I've spent about forty-two thousand dollars on surveillance on everyone," Zeke replied.

"Money well spent!" Jim declared quietly into the silence that followed. "I approve," he added.

"We'll retrieve almost all of our equipment and have it to use next time. I'm using some from previous work as well." Zeke said, looking around the room.

"Donut, you and Miss MacInnes will be investigating this new terrorist threat coming in to attack the embassy," Zeke added after a moment of thought.

"Bring her to the next meeting so we can introduce ourselves," Jim added to that. "What are your thoughts about her?"

"She's deceptive, mates," Earl replied slowly. "This dish looks soft and sweet, and she's built like Bright Eyes. But behind that innocent exterior is a steel-trap mind and determination. Pippi set her straight about us, so she trusts me. We're both making a bundle modeling!" A photograph of her appeared on the laptops around the table and there were whistles and appreciative looks. Katrina MacInnes was a beauty.

"I think I'm in love!" Rock said with a grin. "Can you introduce me?" he begged Duncan.

CHAPTER 33

Jim looked at himself in the mirror one last time. His new home was finished and perfect, and he was entertaining dignitaries tonight. Senator Henao and John DeFronzo would be attending the party. DeFronzo was a drug boss in Chicago, and Henao was the senator who kidnapped girls from the United Kingdom and had ties to terrorists.

Charading as Don Graham, wealthy philanthropist with interests in a Chicago office he had given specific directions to the agency handling the invitations and party details. The list of guests alone was impressive in Chicago circles, and the only name that surprised anyone was DeFronzo. Several of the political guests had direct connections to DeFronzo, though many tended to overlook that fact. DeFronzo spread money, especially for campaigns, to protect his interests.

A wily reporter from a local news station asked Mr. Graham why he'd invited DeFronzo. Jim's answer was classic.

"I don't know Mr. DeFronzo personally. He has contributed to many of the city, county, and state political campaigns, especially those of dignitaries who will be attending my event. Is there something about Mr. DeFronzo I should know?"

"Are you aware that he is the head of one of the largest drug rings in the state?" the reporter asked boldly.

"I'm quite sure if that were true, he would be in prison," Jim replied innocently. "The agency I hired to put this gala event together was given specific instructions regarding anyone with a felony conviction. As far as I know, no one on my list has been convicted of a felony. So again, I ask if there is something I should know about Mr. DeFronzo?"

"You really don't believe he runs a huge drug ring?" the reporter asked.

"I am quite confident our law enforcement agencies would have him in prison if that were true," Jim repeated innocently. He could be very convincing when he needed to be, and at the moment his acting convinced the reporter, who retired disappointed, thinking Don Graham might know how to make money, but he didn't know people. *Those politicians will eat him alive!*

To Jim's delight the news story aired before the party. John called him after the news story aired.

"Great job of acting, Jim!" John said enthusiastically. "DeFronzo is sure to be at your party!"

"Were we able to get the buttons on Henao's coat?" he asked his brother.

"Zeke tells me that he has a new tiepin too. One of his aids went shopping and bought a new tie for the occasion and the salesman offered a choice of tiepins. All of them are transceivers, so it didn't matter which one he picked. Nothing has been activated yet in case the senator is suspicious and has his clothing swept for bugs."

"Good work. Tell Zeke and his team I said so," Jim requested.

"I'll do that. Be careful! Have you found a hostess yet?" John asked.

"Karen Lawson from NCIS has the job," Jim said.

"Wow! She's a looker!" John laughed. "What does Cecilia think about that?"

"She was the one who suggested Karen," Jim laughed. "Karen is married to a Navy Commander. He's a former SEAL buddy. He and three other former SEALs are serving with the catering team."

"Devious!" John laughed.

"Very," Jim agreed. "Be careful on your end," he added.

"Always," John replied. "See ya!"

Karen Lawson was indeed an incredibly beautiful woman. Although approaching forty, she was still stunningly beautiful, poised, and an excellent investigator for NCIS. Her beauty had often caused criminals to underestimate her abilities. Her husband Paul was nearing forty-four, still hale and hearty and in great shape. At the moment he was involved in weapons training, but tonight he would be a simple waiter. His three companions were similar in age and Jim had no doubts they would never be suspected as anything but waiters. Like his team, they had learned how to convincingly act out their parts.

For tonight's gala event Karen died her hair blonde after having it cut, and she was wearing blue contact lenses. Her eyes were normally green, and they reminded him of Cecilia's eyes. He missed Cecilia and RJ and thought with a smile of the contact he'd had earlier with the two of them via computer. Skype was an amazing tool!

Karen was wearing a formal dress that accented her figure and shapely legs perfectly. Jim thought that most of the men would be impressed by this beautiful woman, wondering who she was. Tonight, she was Diana Masters, a professional hostess with the catering company. Jim had practiced calling her Diana until he thought of her as Diana Masters. He didn't want to make any mistakes.

Guests began to arrive, and he left his bedroom and wandered down to shake hands and greet people. With the gray in his hair, his neatly trimmed mustache and goatee, and eyes colored blue by contact lenses, he didn't look at all like Jim shepherd. Although it would cause pain later, he had slightly stooped shoulders and walked with a deliberate limp. Keeping his shoulders stooped would hurt by the end of the evening, but he was used to such charades.

He wanted people to see him as naïve, idealistic, and easily manipulated. DeFronzo would help with that. Listening, rather than talking, Jim learned much as the evening began. As he suspected, DeFronzo arrived a little late, and didn't introduce himself immediately, choosing instead to study those around him. Once he was satisfied, he came forward.

"Mr. Graham! I am delighted to meet you," he said, shaking hands vigorously. Jim had strong hands, but he did not squeeze hard, like DeFronzo did. "Did you really believe what you said in the news about me?" he asked, studying Jim intently.

"Oh, come now!" Jim laughed. "None of these people would risk their political careers by taking money from anyone that could put them at risk!" he countered. "I get people starting rumors about me all the time. If you have a lot of money people just don't believe that you worked hard for it! I imagine the same is true for you."

Jim watched DeFronzo relax in stages, and he noted that several other people had considering looks on their faces. To them he was obviously ripe for the picking! DeFronzo nodded.

"How did you make your money?" he asked. Jim knew that DeFronzo would already have checked out his bona fides.

"Precious metals, mining, gold shares, and a few other lucky investments in the companies that supply goods to those industries," Jim answered, his eyes wandering over his guests as though he'd told this story many times. Bringing his eyes back he looked into DeFronzo eyes. "My portfolio grows exponentially pretty much on its own now."

"So I've heard! Well! I've got to greet a few friends. Nice to meet you, Mr. Graham," he said.

"Please, call me Don," Jim replied easily.

"Don, then!" DeFronzo said with a warm smile.

Senator Henao reminded Jim of thugs he'd met in Guatemala. The man was obviously from somewhere in that area of the world, though it was said he grew up on the streets of Chicago. Of only average height Senator Henao kept himself in good physical condition and obviously took great pains to dress and look the part. His hair was neatly arranged and cared for, his clothing of the finest, and he exuded confidence with a cultured voice and easy manner.

"Mr. Graham!" he said, shaking hands.

"Please, call me Don. Mr. Graham is my grandfather!" Jim replied with what he knew looked like a genuine smile. "You're Senator Henao. I heard a rumor about you, sir. I hope it's not true!"

"What rumor is that?" Henao asked suspiciously.

"Something about kidnapped girls from a local college, girls from the UK," Jim replied evenly.

"I can assure you, sir, that no charges will be brought against me," Henao said with confidence. "Someone knew my house would be empty and used it. That's all. And if some of my people were involved, they will be prosecuted to the full extent of the law," He promised.

"I'm glad to hear that!" Jim said, almost gushing. "I was hoping to participate in your next campaign. In the Senate you hear of all manner of projects that I could fund, I'm sure."

"Oh! I do indeed. Perhaps we can have lunch sometime soon and discuss some of that. Once this rumored kidnapping business is sorted out, I'll be able to give you my full attention," Henao implied pleasantly. Jim suspected the man was practically rubbing his hands in anticipation of how much money he could con out of Don Graham.

"I'd like that, sir. It would be an honor," Jim replied as if truly impressed that a Senator would invite him out to lunch.

"Give this story four or five days and it will all go away," Senator Henao promised. "Trust me," he entreated.

Jim nodded as if he did indeed trust the Senator and smiled inwardly at the greed he saw in the man's eyes. The fact that Henao was confident that in that period of time his problem would be solved told him much about the trust he put in the terrorists, and the hold he had over law enforcement. Politics could be sickening at times.

During the party Karen Lawson moved through the crowd putting everyone at ease, and in some cases, putting tracking devices where they might not be discovered. Jim watched her work, though seeming not to pay much attention, and thought she was very proficient. He knew what she was doing and had difficulty spotting her work! Shortly after the party began Earl Duncan and Katrina MacInnes appeared.

Jim had to admit that Earl looked like a professional model. The clothing he was wearing had to cost in the thousands. Katrina drew every eye, not only because she was a very beautiful woman, but also because she had a voluptuous figure that every woman would consider enhanced, and every man hope it was all natural. In her case, he knew, it was all natural. She certainly moved with the poise of a model.

"Hey Katrina!" he greeted as if they were old friends. She responded in kind, taking his hand and kissing his cheek gently. Shaking hands vigorously with Earl he almost laughed as Earl shook out his hand as though the handshake had been too vigorous. Earl was a strong man, but in these clothes, he managed to look no more than well built, as many models. Both men caught the considering looks Senator Henao gave Katrina, especially when he heard her British accent. She gave off the impression that her head was empty of thought and all she lived for was to look beautiful and be pampered.

Kendall Tanner and Liam Cleary appeared, creating a stir, and Jim noted that once Kendall appeared Earl followed him around everywhere he went. The effect was simple. Everyone thought he was gay, though he did nothing to overtly announce that fact.

CHAPTER 34

Frank Moody was hired as the defensive coach at Lakeview High School and was thoroughly enjoying his job. Each day he mapped out a five-mile run for the 55 boys on his team and on the following morning he took them on the run. Two of the coaches ran with the team with him and were amazed that he got the heavier boys to run every day. Wade was aware that the boys were in awe of his physical prowess and took full advantage of that, encouraging each runner to make that extra effort, to push himself. Centers, guards, and tackles shed pounds of fat and replaced some of those with carefully worked muscle.

The fact that the coach ran with the best runners out front, and then caught up with the slower runners on his second five-mile trip wasn't lost on the coaches, and they began to follow his example, giving that extra effort for the boys. It wasn't long before Lakeview High School had young men in the best shape of their lives, a strong, fast, determined team. As boys do, each player reveled in his newfound strength and speed, showing it in many ways.

One of the ways they showed it was to begin running together for the first four miles in a cadence that each runner could match. In a line of five across and ten deep they ran, with the slower runners in front setting the pace, the coaches running along the line encouraging the boys. During the last mile the faster runners moved up, each one encouraging the bigger heavier runners as they moved through the ranks, finally breaking away to sprint the last half mile.

TajUdin Odeh sat in his sleek Mercedes Benz and watched the three coaches and fifty-five boys tramp past the electrical relay station in which he was about to plant his explosives. They ran well together and seemed a cohesive unit. When he first saw them, he thought they might be military because of the formation of the runners, but he soon saw they were just young boys, a sports team.

One of the coaches had obviously been military and when he completed his task, he checked out Frank Moody at Lakeview High School. Satisfied that Frank Moody was no threat to his work he moved on to his next target, never aware that he had been both photographed and noticed by the wily coach in disguise. Later that day Sparks, as Mike Sutter, union contractor for the city of Indianapolis, toured the same facility. He was the only one who spotted the explosives.

TajUdin Odeh was a smart operator. He'd carefully hidden the explosives in dummy pressure valve meters strategically placed. Odeh even matched the highest pressure he'd seen in the lines confident that no one in a cursory examination would spot the dummies. Because Bill carefully studied the schematics for the station before his inspection, he immediately spotted the dummy meters and recognized them for what they were. Knowing that Odeh or someone from his organization would be watching he gave no indication that he'd seen anything out of the ordinary and talked knowledgably with the union worker giving the tour. Later that day Paul Fezik did a cursory check on Mike Sutter and was satisfied that the man was legitimately on the site and the explosives had not been tampered with.

Now that he knew what to look for Mike Sutter toured every single relay station, identifying the dummy meters with explosives in five of them. It took a little longer to find the explosives in the two major production facilities the team identified as probable targets. Whoever Odeh was working with was a first-class explosives expert, and that bothered Sparks. He began looking and soon found the man he knew must be working with Odeh. Lojos So from the North Pyungan Province was wanted in several countries. That he was in Chicago worried Bill.

Zeke was quick to get his team involved in finding Lojos So. With the use of the Crays on the ship and the search programs his team had written it wasn't long before they had multiple hits, putting So at each of the places where explosives were placed, and finding his residence. Finding So broke the case wide open and within two days they had the entire organization working within Chicago under Odeh.

Meanwhile Katrina and Donut were keeping a sharp eye on the new group of terrorists in town planning an attack on the embassy. This was no ordinary group of men. All of them were trained soldiers and the tactics they were planning to use had worked at several British Embassies elsewhere in the world.

As Donovan O'Rourke, acting quite drunk, Frank got into a fight with Winchester in a bar near the Embassy to warn him of the tactics the terrorists were planning to use. The fight certainly seemed very real to those watching, as both men exchanged drunken blows. Neither did much damage to the other, and when the fight was over, they left, singing and laughing as though they were best friends. Near the lake they spoke in low tones and Winchester thanked his friend before leaving to return to the Embassy. He made a call and Sir Edward responded, routing a military unit through Chicago for a few days of rest and relaxation. Twenty seasoned SAS soldiers crowded into the Embassy soon after they landed to be briefed.

FM, Driver, and Donut and Katrina were ushered into that ready room shortly after the twenty SAS soldiers arrived. Lee and Mark arrived a few minutes later, as Kendall Tanner and Liam Cleary. Matthew Banks, under the guise of David Webb of Liverpool came in just after those two. Winchester looked at the men from *Bring It Up* and decided they would fit right in. He introduced them all to the two decoy women and got to work planning a counterattack that would guarantee the capture of most of this enemy force alive. An hour later the units left the room to take up their positions.

Farid Ghafoor was sure his plan was carefully laid out, and that the chances of success were high. He'd been successful against other British Embassies with this plan, and even extracted prisoners before. Those had been rescue attempts. This was a simple killing. He would take his men in, kill the two women and as many of the hated British as possible, and escape. Approaching the Embassy, he grinned at his second in command. As usual, the two men standing guard outside were vigilant, which meant they would probably spot the remote-control toy truck carrying the plastique explosives and dive inside for cover. If they were not killed by the initial blast, he knew they would be disoriented enough to be easily eliminated by the first men inside the door. His eyes did not pick out the bomb curtain hanging just inside the front entrance.

When the guards spotted the toy truck with the explosives they dashed inside. Just inside, behind the bomb curtain, two mangled bodies sprawled on the floor, still slightly cold from the morgue freezer. The bomb went off and the two guards removed the bomb curtain while the dust and smoke still billowed and moved further back and out of sight. Protocol for a bomb going off in front of the Embassy was for Embassy personnel to retreat to the interior.

Ghafoor watched the first contingent of terrorists rush into the building, and he followed with the second. As before, no resistance was offered. Two men in tattered, bloodied uniforms obviously dead lay just inside the door and he ignored them after only a cursory glance. Now cautious the men moved deeper into the embassy building, following the plans, keeping away from main corridors that would be heavily guarded.

A back stairway led up three flights of steps to where the two women were being held. His men crept up the steps, guns ready, but so far luck had kept them undiscovered. Ghafoor had taken care of the electricity in the building at the same time the blast tore the doorway apart. None of the security cameras would be up and running, and no lights showed, indicating that he'd also taken out the emergency lighting. There was enough ambient light from the windows to see without night goggles.

All of his men were in the hallway, making their way carefully to the door that would lead them to their first murder victims. Farid began to wonder when they encountered no guards. At the door he paused and nodded, indicating his men should enter. The room was empty. It was at that point that Winchester and his men made their counterattack. Some had come up the steps Ghafoor and the terrorists used, and others came from the other end of the hall. Laser sight dots appeared on foreheads and chests out of the darkness from either end of the hallway.

"One of you so much as twitches the wrong way, mate, and he gets dropped," Winchester said in the sudden silence. A three-shot blast, deafening in that enclosed space, signaled the end of the life of one of the terrorists. All three shots filled the space of a quarter. Ghafoor swallowed nervously and his men looked at him for leadership. Slowly he shook his head and carefully lowered his weapon to the floor. The men saw that he rested it on his foot, and quickly did the same, standing up and raising their hands.

But the gas was already doing its work and one by one they collapsed in ungainly heaps, like rag dolls suddenly released by a child. Ghafoor's last thought was that he had been betrayed. Once everyone was down the SAS troops, wearing masks to protect them from the gas, moved in, stripping each prisoner and binding them with plastic restraint ties. Minutes later the hallway was empty, and the prisoners carried unceremoniously into a bomb shelter in the basement.

Through a secret door in that shelter, they were carried down a long tunnel to another building, an abandoned warehouse, through that building into another basement room, this one designed to be soundproof. Cells lined the outer walls of the large room, and in the center were devices the prisoners could study once they regained consciousness, devices that would fill them with terror. Some of them were old, seen only in museums these days. They were in place for psychological reasons, but they were also viable.

Not long after the bomb attack police poured into the embassy building by invitation. As the men began to conduct the investigation Lieutenant Brandon Jones nodded to Tyrone Cranik who wandered away and followed the same route the terrorists followed up to the third floor. Just outside the door he sought he heard female voices. Pulling out his Sig he checked to be sure the silencer was properly attached, reared back, and kicked the door inward.

The women were already running for the bathroom, and he shot them both in the back twice. Something exploded against his wrist and his gun clattered to the floor and he looked to his left enraged. Commander James Mitchell was retracting his expandable spring baton. Cranik watched him put it away, holding his wrist, working out his hand. The thing had hurt, and he wondered if his wrist was broken. His eyes opened in surprise as the two women moaned softly and sat up.

"Bullet proof vests, old chap," Mitchell said quietly. "We have you on camera kicking in the door and shooting these two lovely ladies. They're not really the targets you were looking for, but decoys who volunteered for the job. You're under arrest for attempted murder," FM smiled at Cranik.

Cranik didn't wait. He lunged at FM, dragging at his knife, his movements hampered by the pain in his wrist. Maybe he was a little slow in bringing it up, or maybe the damn Brit was a little faster than he thought, but his wrist was grasped, and his arm bent back until he felt the bone snap and heard the knife fall to the floor just before he bellowed in pain. The fist that crashed into his face had all the power of a pile driver and everything went black.

FM shook out his hand and smiled at the two women. "That was rewarding," he said. "Ah! Here comes the cavalry!" Lieutenant Brandon Jones stepped into the room, looked down at Cranik, at the knife and gun on the floor, and at the man he knew as Commander James Mitchell. He was in the act of reaching for his sidearm when a cultured British voice spoke from behind.

"What's all this, then?" Winchester asked. Jones looked over his shoulder and saw that the man was holding his MP5-SD steadily in his hand. "Were you planning to shoot one of our decorated soldiers? That just won't do, old chap! Not sporting, what? Let's lose the weapons and have a go at it like civilized men, shall we?"

Winchester was grinning as he nodded to Jones to move forward. "Take this man's weapons, will you corporal?" he ordered, and his corporal moved into the room. Jones stood quietly as he was carefully patted down, and all his weapons removed.

Winchester moved into the room and looked at Jones. "Think you can take the Commander? Have at it!" he invited.

Jones didn't wait. Furious that his plans had been thwarted he stepped into FM to punish him. FM's counter punches took away his breath, stood him up straight, and then the man seemed to flow around him, and Jones was tossed to the floor. Rolling away from FM he came to his feet quickly, and his wind rushed back as he gulped down a lungful of air.

"You're not very good, mate," Winchester said, shaking his head. "Best to quit while you're still standing, what?"

"Shut up, you limey bastard!" Jones snapped. "When I'm done with the old man, I'll show you just how good I am!" he snarled.

Thinking he'd figured out FM's style of fighting he crouched and moved in again. Jones served in the Army, and he was a savvy fighter. Today it did him no good. Even when he recognized the style of a Marine, he was completely unprepared for the strength and violence of FM's attack. Later, when he regained consciousness, he wondered where the British Commander had learned to fight like that. It was far too late for him.

His call to Cranik with instructions to follow the path of the terrorists and kill the two women had been traced and recorded. Cranik had fired two shots at both women, shooting them in the back, and was recorded on camera. His own response was also on camera. Worse, Robert Malone's instructions to him had also been recorded.

Just after making that call Malone turned from his stove where he'd made the call and found Commander James Mitchell standing in the center of his kitchen. Beside him Fred Wickham stood, holding an H&K Mark 23 in a steady hand.

"I'll take that phone," Commander Mitchell said, holding out his hand.

"Throw it on the floor and I'll put a bullet through your left kneecap!" Wickham said softly.

Thinking better of it, Malone handed the phone over.

"There's a police-detail outside, gentlemen," Malone said. "I've already alerted them."

"They're a little preoccupied at the moment, Mr. Malone," Commander Mitchell said softly. Mr. Wickham and I handcuffed them to a police vehicle, then put that vehicle in gear. Together they are enough to keep it from dragging them all away, but just barely. Until we release them, they are going to have very sore wrists. Look for yourself."

Malone looked out his living room window and saw all six officers struggling to hold the car in place. All of their utility belts and weapons were piled on the lawn. How these two men had accomplished this was beyond him, but Malone merely turned back.

"So, what now?" he asked warily.

"I promised that you and I would have a very private talk if I discovered you were involved in this crime. Let's go into your study and have that talk, shall we?" Commander Mitchell extended his arm, toward the study.

"You will get nothing out of me. You cannot come on American soil, kidnap an American citizen, and interrogate him without an attorney present and American law enforcement!" Malone snapped as he moved toward the study. "Even if you torture me the information you get will not be admissible in a court of law!"

"Interrogate? Torture?" Commander Mitchell chuckled. Just then the doorbell rang. Commander Mitchell went to open the door. Two men stood there, looking back at the policemen fighting with their patrol car.

"Come in!" FM said, enjoying the moment.

"Those men are losing the battle with the car!" The taller of the two said.

"Did you bring the contingent of FBI agents I asked for?" Commander Mitchell inquired politely.

"They will be here in thirty seconds." The man replied.

"Let's put the car in park and allow your men to hold those officers. You may wish to question them later." Mitchell went out and put the car in park and watched the men stagger to the bumper and then sit down, rubbing very sore wrists. He returned to the house as the FBI agents pulled into the driveway in four unmarked SUVs. FM smiled at them as the FBI agent came out and instructed his men to hold those officers for questioning. He identified himself to the officers and noted the look of sudden fear that came into their eyes.

Inside the house Malone stood silent. Wickham slapped him on the back.

"Buck up, old bean. It's time to face the music," Malone didn't feel the prick of the needle, but he felt the burn of the drug as it coursed through his body. Wickham put his gun away as Malone began to smile, suddenly feeling very good. The sudden change in emotion didn't register with him.

"This is Agent Patrick Blackwell, a high-ranking agent from Washington, D.C. With him is Deputy District Attorney Michael Putnam, also of Washington, D.C." Commander Mitchell was making the introductions.

"This is Mr. Malone from the office of the Secretary of the State of Illinois. Mr. Malone resides here in Chicago where he serves that office in an interesting capacity. Mr. Malone, why don't you tell us just how clever you are?" Commander Mitchell smiled at Malone, pulling out the chair behind his own desk, and then joining the other men sitting facing him.

Malone, no longer able to stop himself, told them everything. At the end of two hours, he wound down, the drug slowly losing its grip, and leaning back in his chair he fell asleep. The four men sitting in the room looked at one another without speaking. Blackwell felt like he'd been bulldozed as he realized the scope of corruption in the Illinois government. Deputy District Attorney Putnam was staring at his digital recorder, having hit the button to stop the recording.

"Why did he tell us everything like that?" Blackwell finally asked, looking at the two British men.

"My friend Mr. Wickham took care of that. It was his daughter that was kidnapped. I'm quite sure that when we're gone Mr. Malone will feel much more powerful and deny everything he told us," Commander Mitchell answered easily.

"He did open his safe before you gentlemen arrived," Driver lied, nodding toward the safe door that was slightly ajar. "I think you'll find everything you need in there to convict this animal. See to it that you do right by my daughter. She was repeatedly raped and terrorized by this senator Malone talked so much about. If you gentlemen can't do something about that, I will."

It was the way Wickham said it that told Blackwell he meant business. He understood. His own daughters came to his mind, and he finally smiled at the man.

"Terrorist threats are against the law in this country, Mr. Wickham. However, since I have daughters myself, I will pretend I didn't hear any of that last conversation. Is that acceptable to you, Mr. Putnam?" Putnam nodded vigorously in the affirmative. "You two should probably disappear before too many questions get asked," Blackwell said, standing and offering a hand to shake. He liked the respect and appreciation he saw in both sets of eyes.

"Thanks, sir," Mr. Wickham said simply, shaking hands.

"Well done. We'll leave you to it then, what?" Commander Mitchell said with a grin and wink. As soon as he spoke, he and Wickham left the house. Both sketched a wave at the disgruntled policemen as they entered the Embassy car and drove away. Later that day the real Mitchell and Wickham boarded a British Airways jet and flew to London, taking Wickham's daughter, Jane, and Bridgett Grogan with them. The girls, of course, looked very different and were traveling under assumed names.

CHAPTER 35

As February approached a massive cold front moved in from the north and buried the city under three feet of snow in one snowfall. Taking advantage of the storm Jim and his team, moved on the bomb targets at the electric relay stations and power stations, using snowmobiles to approach the targets, and snowshoes to move across the soft heavy snow.

Instead of disarming the bombs, they simply traded out the command chips that would take the cell phone signal and relay it to the detonator. These were replaced with exact duplicates, designed to accept the signal, but rather than relaying it to the detonator, an alarm would go off in the offices of Homeland Security. It would be up to them to trace the signal to the bombs, disarm them, and start the manhunt for the terrorists responsible.

Transferring fingerprints to the inside of the casings was child's play to Jim's team, and he knew that Homeland Security would soon trace the culprits. No one would ever know that *Bring It Up* was responsible. Sir Edward and Duck Ashley would take care of most of the information fed to the local authorities and make sure that the right people got involved.

TajUdin Odeh would know that his signal had been received by the chip in the bomb controls, but not why it didn't work. He would,

Jim hoped, blame Lajos So for the failure. Counting on the fact that Lajos would check his work after the storm Jim smiled as he thought of the North Korean guaranteeing his work was still viable to Odeh.

Both men would be hunted down and arrested. The plot would be unveiled and all the players publically condemned. After that, if any of them escaped, Jim's team would be tasked with hunting them down and eliminating them. That was the whole problem with the world today. Too often good people were punished, and evil men praised. Men and women existed who knew the real dangers and were always ready to respond when necessary. Jim Shepherd and every man and woman who was part of *Omega Force* were such people.

When the electricity failed to go out, the plan to rob the gold deposit would fail as well. When none of the explosives went off as planned, there would be moments of chaos and doubt. Jim planned to take full advantage of that. Odeh, he knew, was capable of having a contingency plan, and mounting a full military attack on the Federal Reserve Bank. Duck Ashley had a unit of Marines standing by, with a credible cover story for their presence in the bank at that time.

Blustery winds and icy weather settled on Chicago as if Winter was attempting to strangle the city. Jim and his team were grateful for their Arctic gear, and on the night of the actual attack the temperature dropped to twenty-one below zero with a wind-chill factor of minus sixty degrees. Had the electricity gone out that night hundreds of people would have perished in the cold.

In the early hours of the morning police responded to an anonymous tip, finding four college students naked and shivering from exposure on the front steps of the tower they meant to destroy. At different locations within the building there were eight other college students, all in the same condition, though none as dire as those that had been trussed up outside. They were held for twenty-four hours, and then exposed to Odeh's plans for them to take the blame for the terrorist attacks on the relay stations and plants, the tower, and the theft of the gold.

Furious when the electricity did not go out as planned, TajUdin Odeh led his team of nine against the guards in the Reserve Bank.

Unaware of the presence of a Marine Force Recon Company his attack met with devastating losses. Seven of the nine were killed during the first volley of shots, and Odeh and his lieutenant were seriously wounded and taken prisoner.

Homeland Security discovered the explosive devices at the relay stations and electric plants, and by morning had names to go with the fingerprints they found. So was arrested later that morning as he attempted to flee the city by boat. News agencies quickly responded to the unfolding events and by that evening the news had gone global.

ISIS had attempted to kill thousands and threaten the financial foundations of the Federal Reserve. Homeland Security acted quickly and decisively, and the public officials that were part of the plot were identified and exposed to public humiliation. Even in Mexico Francisco Turisio was forced to disappear for a time when his name was mentioned, and his connection to his German heritage.

Furious he attempted to discover who was behind this monumental failure. At every turn he hit a dead end. Thirty-six men from *Omega Force* flew to seventy-two different cities around the globe, and eventually, under yet another alias, made their way to the Bahamas, where they returned to *Sea Venture* undetected. In Chicago NCIS and Homeland Security, the FBI and local authorities were applauded for thwarting a major terrorist attack on a major U.S. City. All Francisco could discover was that his terrorists had been careless, leaving fingerprints to identify them as the culprits. He did not believe their statements that this was impossible. It had happened. The evidence was clear.

In Washington D.C. the President screamed in impotent rage as many of his former partners and friends were drummed out of office. Counting on support from the corrupt officials of his home state he felt suddenly alone and vulnerable. Later he made a call, and agents checked *Sea Venture* only to report that the entire crew was on board and working.

Admiral Ashley toured Gitmo, and later, on vacation in the Bahamas, met with the Shepherds on their private island retreat. Quite natural that he should meet with his wealthy friends only the most suspicious minds thought this might be a summit meeting between coconspirators.

"I really must congratulate you on being invisible," Duck said quietly to Jim and John in their inner sanctuary far beneath the house. Diving to the vault, and entering it had been exciting, and now they sat in an impenetrable clean room, surrounded by beautiful art, listening to soft music of the masters, sipping from wine glasses. "Your team is amazing at changing appearance. I've looked at footage from dozens of airports, train, and bus stations, and even passenger loading zones for ships and seen not one recognizable face. How in the world does a man as big as Dorf hide himself?"

Smiling, John handed three photos of Dorf. In one he was a huge fat man, lumbering along in a business suit, obviously tailored and expensive, looking at least sixty, balding and tired from traveling. In another he was a black man with full lips and an afro that made him look seven feet tall. In the third he looked like a tall tourist, slightly stooped at the shoulders, with blonde hair and vivid blue eyes. His nose was long and obviously often broken, and his chin jutted far beyond the usual. Each team member was an expert at disguise, as Duck knew. He nodded with appreciation as he looked at the pictures.

"Masterfully done!" Duck approved, handing the photos back. He was not surprised to see Jim feed them into a shredder.

"What of Francisco Turisio in Mexico?" John asked, sipping from his wine glass after he spoke.

"He's good at hiding. It won't be long before he surfaces again, probably with a new face and identity. It seems he's hiding in Costa Rico, where there are some very talented plastic surgeons. Once he surfaces, he will have to access his accounts, and we have most of those, thanks to Zeke and News. That will tell us his new identity and give us a look at his face."

"What will you do when that happens?" John asked.

"Probably ask you fellows to pick him up for us," Duck chuckled. "I don't want him killed! He's too valuable."

"Yes. If we capture him, we'll have a good look at one of the many ways terrorists are entering our country," Jim pointed out.

"Yes. Just one of many! Some days I hate my job!" Duck said sadly.

"We have to be steadfast, or we will lose everything," John extoled quietly.

"Semper Fi!" Duck said. "Now! Tell me about your next venture!" he grinned at the two of them and listened for the next hour as they detailed how they would raise Wilhelmina's Song and what they would do with the gold.

Later that day he sat on the dock while the Shepherds swam with their children. Though still in diapers the two lads seemed to love the water and were able to go under the surface without fear. They all pretended not to see the yacht anchored nearby, obviously occupied by men trying to hear what they were talking about. The men in the yacht had nothing to report that night after Duck left. All talk that could be recorded had been quite innocent.

Early the next morning the Shepherd's rejoined *Sea Venture* and set course for the Panama Canal, where they would pass into the Pacific and make their way up to Alaska once more. Reasons for the trip were obvious. The equipment they'd distributed needed to be checked and the scientists wanted to study conditions and collaborate with AOOS. Once more the crew of *Bring It Up* slipped into anonymity, nothing more than an interesting crew.

In the conference room the Team gave a report to everyone. Respectfully, those who had not participated in the Chicago investigation listened as the story unfolded. When *Omega Force* completed its report, they science crew shared what they had learned. It did not escape those worthy crewmember's attention that the soldiers seemed more interested in what they were learning about the ocean, than listening to their own escapades. All of them focused on the photos supplied, studying them with attention paid to every detail. Alice asked FM later that evening about the difference.

"What we did didn't change much, and didn't really affect our world, other than to remove one group of very bad people. Another group will fill their shoes in very short order," FM smiled at her, waving a hand as if to dismiss all the work they had done to stop TajUdin Odeh's plot. "What you did will bring about change, protecting the ocean in the future, and creating new avenues of discovery. That's the work that really matters! We learn about God's amazing creation, understand our world a little better, and everyone benefits."

"You surprise me, young man," Alice said quietly, patting his arm affectionately. FM grinned as he moved away.

"I lead astonishing men and women," Jim said, coming to stand beside the Dinsmores. "That humbles me," he touched Alice on the shoulder, and momentarily grasped John's arm. "You did a wonderful job while we were away. Thanks," he nodded and moved away after FM. Alice stood looking after him and took John's hand.

"When I first heard of this opportunity, I gave it a year or two at the most," she smiled at her husband. "We are never leaving this company!" He nodded in agreement.